The WITCH HUNTER

VIRGINIA BOECKER

LITTLE, BROWN AND COMPANY

New York Boston

Copyright © 2015 by Virginia Boecker
Map art © 2015 by Dave E. Phillips
Stigma design based on art by Tricia Buchanan-Benson
Stigma design © Virginia Boecker

Little, Brown and Company

Hachette Book Group
1290 Avenue of the Americas, New York, NY 10104
Visit us at lb-teens.com

Little, Brown and Company is a division of Hachette Book Group, Inc.
The Little, Brown name and logo are trademarks of Hachette Book Group, Inc.

The publisher is not responsible for websites (or their content) that are not owned by the publisher.

First Edition: June 2015

Library of Congress Cataloging-in-Publication Data

Boecker, Virginia.
The witch hunter / Virginia Boecker.—First edition.
pages cm
Summary: "Set in an alternative 16th-century England, Elizabeth Grey is the only girl in the king's elite group of witch hunters. When she's framed for being a witch herself, Elizabeth finds freedom at the hands of the world's most wanted wizard and her loyalties are tested"—Provided by publisher.
ISBN 978-0-316-32700-8 (hardcover)—ISBN 978-0-316-32718-3 (ebook)—
ISBN 978-0-316-32714-5 (library edition ebook) [1. Magic—Fiction. 2. Witches—Fiction. 3. Wizards—Fiction. 4. Loyalty—Fiction. 5. Love—Fiction. 6. Great Britain—History—16th century—Fiction.] I. Title.
PZ7.B6357175Wit 2015
[Fic]—dc23
2014013251

10 9 8 7 6 5 4 3 2

RRD-C

Printed in the United States of America

For Scott
and
For England

Fleet Prison

Westcheap Road

The Shambles

The Square
at Tyburn

Goose Alley

Pheasant Court

Cow Lane

The World's
End Pub

Ravenscourt
Palace

Severn River

Upminster

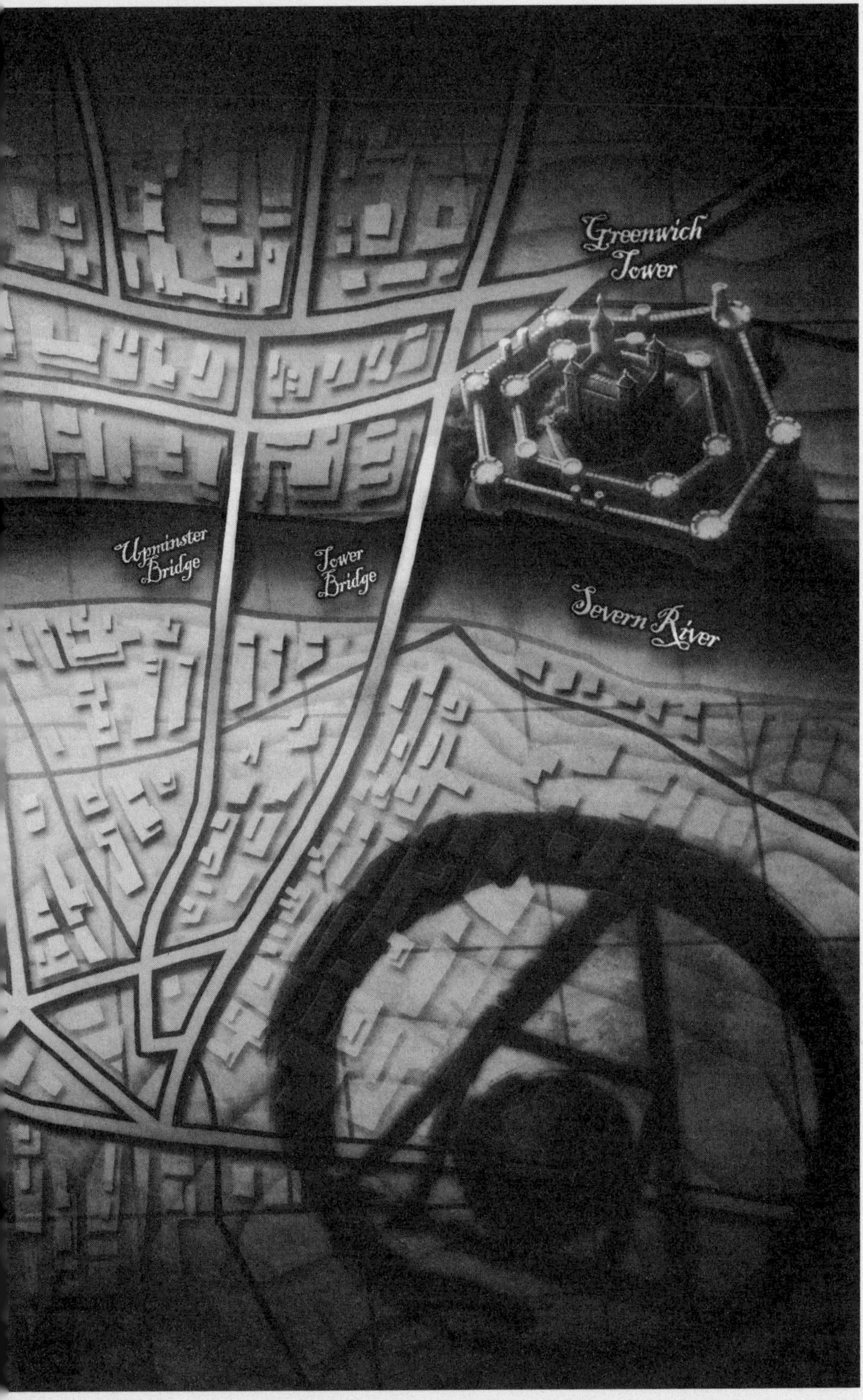
Greenwich Tower
Upminster Bridge
Tower Bridge
Severn River

1

I STAND AT THE EDGE of the crowded square, watching the executioners light the pyres. The two men, dressed for work in dark red cloaks and charred leather gloves, circle the narrow wooden platforms, their lit torches held high. At the top of each pyre, four witches and three wizards stand chained to a stake, bundles of wood heaped around their feet. They stare into the crowd, determined looks on their faces.

I don't know what they did; they weren't my captures. But I do know there will be no apologies from them. No last-minute pleas for mercy, no scaffold-step promises to repent. Even as the executioners touch their torches to the wood and the first of the flames leaps into the leaden sky, they remain silent. They'll stay that way, stubborn to the very end. It wasn't always like this. But the worse the Reformist rebellions get, the more defiant the Reformists themselves become.

It doesn't matter anyway, what they did. What magic they used. Spells, familiars, potions, herbs: It's all illegal now. There was a time when those things were tolerated, encouraged even. Magic was seen as helpful—once. Then the plague came. Started by magic, spread by magic—we were almost destroyed by magic. We warned them to stop, but they didn't stop. Now here we are, standing in a dirty square under a dirty sky, forcing them to stop.

To my right, about twenty feet away, is Caleb. He stares into the fire, his blue eyes narrowed, forehead slightly creased. By his expression he could be sad, he could be bored, he could be playing against himself a game of noughts and crosses. It's hard to tell. Even I don't know what he's thinking, and I've known him longer than anyone.

He'll make his move soon, before the protests begin. I can already hear the murmuring, the shuffling feet, the odd cry or two from a family member. People raise sticks, hold up rocks. They stay their hands out of respect for the men and women on the pyre. But once they're gone, the violence will begin. Against the executioners, against the guards who line the street, against anyone who supports the justice doled out in front of us. People are frightened of magic, yes. But the consequences of magic frighten them even more.

Finally, I see it: a gentle tug on a lock of dark blond hair, a hand placed slowly in his pocket.

It's time.

I'm halfway across the square when the shouting breaks out. I feel a shove from behind, then another. I pitch forward and slam into the back of the man standing in front of me.

"Watch it, you." He whips around, a glare on his face. It

disappears as soon as he sees me. "I'm sorry, miss. I didn't see you, and—" He stops, peering at me closely. "My word, you're just a child. You shouldn't be here. Go on home. There's nothing here you need to see."

I nod and back away. He's right about one thing: There's nothing here I need to see. And somewhere else I need to be.

I follow Caleb down a wide cobblestoned street, then through the Shambles, a maze of narrow, sludge-filled alleyways lined with squat, dark-timbered row houses, their pitched roofs casting a near-permanent shadow over the street. We wind through them quickly: Cow Lane, Pheasant Court, Goose Alley. All the streets in this area have funny names like this, originating from when the square at Tyburn was used for herding livestock.

Now it's used for a different kind of slaughter.

The streets are deserted, as they always are on a burning day. Those who aren't watching the burnings are at Ravenscourt Palace protesting them or at any one of Upminster's taverns trying to forget them. It's a risk, making an arrest today. We risk the crowds; we risk being seen. If we were arresting an ordinary witch, we probably wouldn't risk it at all.

But this is no ordinary arrest.

Caleb pulls me into an empty doorway. "Ready?"

"Of course." I smile.

He grins back. "Pointy things at the ready, then."

I reach under my cloak and pull out my sword.

Caleb nods in approval. "The guards are waiting for us down on Pheasant, and, just in case, I've got Marcus posted on Goose and Linus covering Cow." A pause. "God, these street names are stupid."

I stifle a laugh. "I know. But I won't need their help. I'll be fine."

"If you say so." Caleb reaches into his pocket and pulls out a single crown. He pinches the coin between his fingers and holds it in front of my face. "Shall we say the usual, then?"

I scoff. "You wish. I've got five times the quarry, so that's five times the bounty. Plus, these are necromancers. Which means there's at least one corpse, a bunch of blood, a pile of bones...that's a sovereign at least, you cheapskate."

Caleb laughs. "You drive a hard bargain, Grey. Fine. Let's make it two sovereigns and drinks after. Deal?"

"Deal." I give him my hand, but instead of shaking it, he kisses it. My stomach does a funny little tumble, and I can feel warmth rush into my cheeks. But he doesn't seem to notice. He just shoves the coin back into his pocket, then pulls a dagger from his belt, and flips it into the air, catching it deftly.

"Good. Now let's get going. These necromancers aren't going to arrest themselves, you know."

We edge along the front of the houses, our footsteps squelching softly in the mud. Finally, we reach the one we're looking for. It looks like all the others: a dingy white plaster thing with a wooden door covered in peeling red paint. But unlike all the others, given what's on the other side. The wizards I usually catch are still alive, still corporeal. Not so, today. My stomach tightens in the familiar way it does before an arrest: part thrill, part nerves, part fear.

"I'll kick it open, but you go in first," Caleb tells me. "Take charge of it. It's your capture. Sword up and out. Don't lower it, not for a second. And read the arrest warrant straightaway."

"I know." I don't know why he's telling me this. "Not my first time, remember?"

"I do. But this won't be like the others. *They* won't be like the others. Get in and get out. Nothing fancy. And no more mistakes, okay? I can't keep covering for you."

I think of all the things I've done wrong in the past month. The witch I chased down the alley who nearly got away. The chimney I got stuck in trying to find a hidden cache of spellbooks. The cottage I stormed that didn't house wizards brewing potions but a pair of aged friars brewing ale. They're just a few mistakes, true. But I don't make mistakes.

At least, I didn't used to.

"Okay." I raise my sword, my sweaty hands slipping off the hilt. I quickly wipe them on my cloak. Caleb draws his leg back and slams his foot against the door. It smashes open, and I burst into the house.

Inside are the five necromancers I'm looking for, huddled around a fire in the center of the room. There's a large cauldron perched above the flames, a foul-smelling pink smoke billowing from the top. Each of them wears a long, tattered brown robe, and oversized hoods conceal their faces. They stand there, moaning and chanting and holding bones— either arm bones or a very small person's leg bones—and shaking them like a bunch of damned Mongol shamans. I might laugh if I weren't so disgusted.

I circle around them, my sword pointed in their direction. "Hermes Trismegistus. Ostanes the Persian. Olympiodorous of Thebes—"

I stop, feeling like an idiot. These necromancers and the

ridiculous names they give themselves. They're always trying to outdo one another.

"You five," I say instead. "By the authority of King Malcolm of Anglia, I am commanded to arrest you for the crime of witchcraft."

They continue chanting; they don't even look up. I glance at Caleb. He stands by the door, still flipping his dagger. He almost looks amused.

"You are hereby ordered to return with us to Fleet prison for detention and to await your trial, presided over by the Inquisitor, Lord Blackwell, Duke of Norwich. If you are found guilty, you will be executed by hanging or by burning, as is the king's pleasure, your land and goods forfeit to the crown." I pause to catch my breath. "So help you God."

This is usually the part where they protest, where they say they're innocent, where they ask for proof. They always say this. I have yet to arrest a witch or wizard and have her or him say to me, "Why, yes, I have done illegal spellwork and read illegal books and purchased illegal herbs and thank goodness you've come to stop me!" Instead, it's always, "Why are you here?" and "You've got the wrong person" and "There must be some mistake!" But it's never a mistake. If I show up on your doorstep, it's because you've done something to draw me there.

Just as these necromancers have.

I keep going. "Tuesday, 25th October, 1558: Ostanes the Persian purchases wolfsbane, a known poison, at the black market in Hatch End. Sunday, 13th November, 1558: Hermes Trismegistus etches the Seal of Solomon, a talisman used for summoning spirits, on Hadrian's Wall outside the city. Friday, 18th November, 1558: All five subjects seen at the All Saints Cemetery in Fortune Green, exhuming the corpse of Pseudo-Democritus, né Daniel Smith, another known necromancer."

Still nothing. They just drone on and on, like a hive of old bees. I clear my throat and go on, louder this time.

"Subjects possess the following texts, each on the list of *Librorum Prohibitorum*, the king's official list of banned books: Albertus Magnus's *Magister Sententiarum*. Thomas Cranmer's *New Book of Common Spells*. Desiderius's *Handbook of a Reformist Knight*."

Surely they'll react to this. Wizards hate nothing more than finding out I've been inside their home, finding things in places they thought no one would ever look. Small hollowed-out niches under the floorboards. Beneath the chicken coop. Stuffed inside a straw mattress. There's nothing a wizard can hide that I can't find.

It occurs to me that it's rather pointless to recite their crimes, considering I've caught them in the middle of an even bigger one. I'm not sure what to do. I don't have all day to stand around listening to these old fools chant, and I can't let them finish their spell. But I can't exactly jump in and lay them out with my sword, either. We're supposed to capture, never kill. Blackwell's rule. And none of us would dare break it. Even still, my fingers tighten around the hilt and I'm itching to start swinging, until I see it: a shape beginning to form in the pink mist in the cauldron.

It rises into the air, swaying and undulating in a nonexistent breeze. Whatever this thing is that they're in the middle of conjuring—my guess is that it's Pseudo-Democritus, né Daniel Smith, who I watched them dig up—it's hideous. Something between a corpse and a ghost, translucent yet rotting, mossy skin, disjointed limbs, and exposed organs. There's a strange humming noise coming from it, and I realize it's covered in flies.

"Elizabeth."

Caleb's voice startles me. He's standing beside me now, his dagger held in front of him, staring at the thing in front of us.

"What do you think?" I whisper. "Is it a ghost?"

He shakes his head. "I don't think so. It's too, I dunno…"

"Juicy?"

Caleb makes a face. "Ugh. You know I'd rather you say viscous. But, yes. And a ghost wouldn't take five men to raise, so my guess is ghoul? Maybe a revenant. It's hard to say. He's not fully formed enough yet for me to tell."

I nod.

"We need to stop them before they finish," he continues. "You take the two on the left, I'll take the three on the right."

"No way." I turn to face him. "This is my arrest. I get all five. That was the deal. You can have the viscous thing in the pot."

"No. You can't take on five by yourself."

"Three more sovereigns say I can."

"Elizabeth—"

"Don't you *Elizabeth* me—"

"Elizabeth!" Caleb grips my shoulders and spins me around. The necromancers have stopped chanting, and the room has gone silent. They're staring right at us. Instead

8

of bones, they're clutching long, curved knives, all of them aimed in our direction.

I break free of Caleb's grasp and step toward them, my sword held high.

"What are you doing here, girl?" one of them says to me.

"I'm here to arrest you."

"On what charges?"

I tut in irritation. If he thinks I'm going through the litany of that arrest again, he's got another thing coming.

"That thing." I jerk my sword at the twitchy apparition. "That's the charge."

"*Thing?*" one of them says, looking affronted. "That's not a *thing*. It's a ghoul."

"Told you," Caleb whispers behind me. I ignore him.

"And it's the last *thing* you'll ever see," the necromancer adds.

"You wish," I say, reaching for my handcuffs. I look down, just for a second, to unhook them from my belt. But it's enough. One of the necromancers sends his knife flying.

"Watch it!" Caleb shouts.

But it's too late. The knife lands with a sickening thump in my chest, right above my heart.

"DAMNATION."

I drop my sword and rip the knife from my chest, throwing it to the floor. There's a flash of heat in my abdomen, followed by a sharp, prickling sensation. And in an instant, the wound heals. There's almost no blood; it doesn't even hurt—at least not much. Seeing this, all five necromancers go still. They know—the moment I came through the door they knew—but it's different altogether to see it work: the stigma branded into the skin above my navel, a scrawl of black. XIII. The stigma that protects me and shows me for what I am. An enforcer of the Thirteenth Tablet. A witch hunter.

They back away, as if I'm the one to be afraid of.

I *am* the one to be afraid of.

I lunge forward and punch the nearest necromancer in the stomach. He doubles over as I slam my elbow into the back of his neck and watch him slump to the floor. I turn to one of the others. Stomp on his foot, pinning it to the floor, and slam my other foot into the side of his kneecap. He drops to his knees, howling. In a flash, I snatch his hands and bind them tightly with the brass handcuffs. Brass is impenetrable to magic; there's no escaping for him now.

I round on the other three. They hold their hands in front of them, backing slowly away. From the corner of my eye, I see Caleb watching me. And he's grinning.

Snatching another pair of cuffs from my belt, I start toward them. Close up, I can see how old they really are. Gray hair, wrinkled skin, watery eyes. Each of them seventy if they're a day. I want to tell them they'd be better off going to church and saying their prayers instead of exhuming bodies and conjuring spirits, but what's the point? They wouldn't listen anyway.

They never do.

I grab a necromancer's wrists and clamp the manacles around them. Before I can get to the other two, they twist away, one of them muttering an incantation under his breath.

"Mutzak tamshich kadima."

The room goes still. The fire stops burning and the billowing pink smoke disappears, receding into the cauldron as if it never existed. The necromancer keeps muttering; he's trying to complete the ritual. I grab a dagger from my belt and hurl it at him to try to stop him. But it's too late. The spirit hovering over the cauldron above us, hideous yet harmless before, becomes solid. It drops in front of me with a thud.

Caleb swears under his breath.

Before either of us can move, the ghoul knocks me to the floor, fastens his cold, rotting hands around my throat, and starts to squeeze.

"Elizabeth!" Caleb leaps forward, but before he can reach me, the last two necromancers turn on him, their knives held high.

I grab the ghoul's hands. Tug at his wrists, scratch and beat on his arms. Try to suck in air, even if it does smell like dirt and rot and death. It doesn't stop him. I can hear Caleb shouting my name, and I try to call back, but my voice comes out a strangled whisper. I keep struggling, twisting back and forth to try to break his grip. But he's too strong.

My vision starts fading, disappearing into patches of black. I slap my hand against the stone floor, trying to reach my sword. But it's too far. And Caleb can't help me. While he's managed to get one necromancer on the floor in cuffs, he's still fighting off the other, who sends objects flying toward him: furniture and smoking logs and bones. I'm on my own. There's a way out of this—I know there is. But if I don't figure it out soon, this ghoul will strangle me to death. Not even my stigma can protect me against that.

Then I get an idea.

I summon the last bit of air I have, give what I hope is a convincing last gasp, and go still. Let my jaw go slack, allow a vacant look to slide into my eyes. I don't know if it will work, because this thing is dead and maybe the dead can't be fooled. When he doesn't stop squeezing, I think I've made a mistake, and it takes every bit of self-control I have to keep still.

Finally, he stops. In the second it takes him to loosen his

grip around my throat, I plunge my hand into the sack of salt on my belt, snatch a handful, and fling it in his face.

An unearthly shriek fills the room as the salt melts what's left of his skin and penetrates his skull, his eyes, his brain, dissolving it into a gray sticky mass. Warm, putrid chunks of flesh drip onto my face and hair; an eyeball unravels from its socket and dangles in front of me like a viscous ball of twine. Stifling a gag, I roll to the side, snatch my sword off the floor, and swing. The blade cuts neatly through the ghoul's neck, and in a swirl of hot air and another ear-splitting shriek, he disappears.

The last necromancer pauses at the sound, the objects he has spinning around the room dropping unceremoniously to the floor. Caleb doesn't hesitate. He grabs him by the back of the head and slams it into his knee, then punches him in the face so hard the necromancer staggers backward and falls into the fire. Before he can move, Caleb drops beside him and slaps bindings around his wrists.

He pauses there for a moment, head down, breathing hard. His sweaty blond hair is plastered across his forehead, his face smeared with blood. I'm still sprawled on the floor, my hands and clothes covered in dirt and rot and God knows what else. Finally, he lifts his head and looks at me.

And we both start laughing.

———————|•

Caleb steps outside and whistles for the guards. They storm into the house, clad in their black-and-red uniforms, the king's coat of arms emblazoned across the front and a red rose, the flower of his house, embroidered on the sleeve. One by one they haul the necromancers outside, toss them into the waiting hurdle, and chain them in. When they get to the last one, a look of dismay crosses their faces.

"He's dead," one says to Caleb.

Dead? That can't be right. But when I look over at the necromancer I flung my dagger at, I see him lying faceup, eyes open to the sky, the knife I'd meant for his leg impaled in his gut.

Damnation.

I shoot a horrified glance at Caleb, but he ignores me and begins speaking.

"Yes, he's dead," he replies calmly. "It's unfortunate, of course, but we got lucky."

"*Lucky?*" the guard says. "How d'you mean?"

"Lucky that only one of them died," Caleb continues smoothly. "They tried to kill each other the moment we arrived. I suppose they had some sort of pact. You know how necromancers are. Obsessed with death." He shrugs. "We spent half the arrest trying to keep them off one another. I mean, look at this place. And look at poor Elizabeth. She's a mess."

The guards look from Caleb to me, as if they had forgotten I was there.

"I'll have to report this to Lord Blackwell," one of the guards says. "I can't very well deliver a dead prisoner."

"Certainly," Caleb says. "In fact, I'm headed back to Ravenscourt myself. Why don't I accompany you? Less paperwork for us both if we go together, don't you think?"

"Paperwork?" The guard shifts uncomfortably. "On a Saturday?"

"Of course. After we deliver the report in person, we'll have to write it all up. Shouldn't take too long, a couple of hours at most. Shall we?" Caleb walks to the door and holds it open.

The guards look at each other and begin speaking in whispers.

"Maybe it can wait. Not as if he's going anywhere—"

"But what about the body? Someone's bound to notice if he's not moving—"

Caleb smiles. "I wouldn't worry about that. No one pays much attention to prisoners once they're inside. And you're right, he won't be going anywhere. After all, no one gets out of Fleet. Unless it's to the stakes."

The guards laugh, and Caleb laughs with them. But I feel a sudden shiver. I stuff my hand into the pocket of my cloak, clenching it into a fist.

Caleb escorts them outside, watches as they mount their horses. After a minute they shake hands and the guards ride away, the hurdles' heavy wooden frames dragging divots through the mud, the thud of the horses' hooves the only sound in the still-empty alley.

He comes back into the house, his expression once again unreadable. I watch as he begins righting the furniture, retrieving our weapons. I know he's mad I killed that necromancer—he's got to be. It was stupid and it was careless; it was a mistake after he warned me not to make one. Worse still, I have no excuse. At least not one I can give him. Any minute he'll start yelling. I can't stop him, but maybe I can soften the blow.

"Okay, I'll admit it. It wasn't my best work," I say. "But look at it this way: At least you don't have to pay me the two sovereigns now. I'll settle for just the one."

He sets down the chair he's holding with a thud and rounds on me.

"What the hell happened?"

"I don't know," I say. "I guess I made a mistake."

Caleb frowns. "I warned you about that."

"I know. And I'm sorry. I don't know what happened."

He peers closely at me, his eyes searching mine as if he might find a better explanation there. Then he shakes his head.

"You know that's not good enough. If anyone asks what happened today, you'll need to tell them the same story I told the guards."

"I know," I repeat.

"It's important," he continues. "If anyone finds out, it'll get back to Blackwell. You know what'll happen if it does."

I do. He'll call me into his chambers, stare at me with eyes as sharp and black and cunning as a crow's, and demand to know what happened. Not just what happened here, today. He'll demand to know everything. The things I've done, the people I've seen, the places I've gone. He'll demand to know how I lost focus. He'll wear me down with his questioning until I confess it all and he knows everything.

And he can't know everything. No one can. Not even Caleb.

"Let's get out of here," Caleb says. "The fire will be over by now, and we can't be seen."

He takes my arm and leads me out the door and into the streets. We wind through them the same way we came until we reach Westcheap, the wide, paved road that leads from Tyburn all the way to Ravenscourt Palace.

We're blocks away, but I can still see the mob stretching from the gates into the surrounding streets. Throngs of men—women, too—all of them shouting and chanting, denouncing the king, his advisors, even the queen for their unrelenting policy against magic.

"It's getting worse," Caleb says.

I nod. Burnings have never been popular, but they've never been protested before. Not like this. It used to be if you disagreed with the king's policy, you did it quietly: handed out pamphlets in the street, whispered your complaints over drinks at the tavern. It seems impossible that the entire city would now gather in front of the palace gates, armed with sticks and rocks and...

Sledgehammers?

"What are they doing?" I can just make out a group of men, hammers held high, spread out along a stretch of gate where twelve stone slabs hang: the Twelve Tablets of Anglia.

The Twelve Tablets are the laws of the kingdom, etched into stone and posted along the gates of Ravenscourt. Each tablet details a different law: property, crime, inheritance, and so on. After Blackwell became Inquisitor, he added the Thirteenth Tablet. It listed the laws against witchcraft and the penalties for practicing it. It gave rise to witch hunters, to pyres, to the burnings being protested today. It disappeared two years ago—vandals, probably. But even though it's gone, the laws, of course, remain.

Destroying the other twelve tablets won't bring about change. They have nothing to do with witchcraft; it wouldn't matter even if they did. But the men continue to pound away, though they haven't made a dent. No wonder. The tablets are huge: six feet high and at least a foot thick, solid stone.

Caleb shakes his head. "He's completely lost control," he mutters.

"Who?" I say.

"Who do you think? King Malcolm, of course."

My eyes go wide. This makes the third time in as many months Caleb's spoken against the king. He's never done that before.

"He's doing the best he can, I'm sure."

Caleb tsks. "Hard to put down protests or stomp out rebellions when you're too busy hunting or gambling or spending time with women who aren't your wife."

I gasp and feel my cheeks redden. "That's treason."

He shrugs. "Maybe. But you know it's true."

I don't reply.

"Malcolm's got to get rid of him," Caleb continues. "Or we do. It's the only thing that will end these rebellions."

Him is Nicholas Perevil, a wizard and the leader of the Reformists. That's what those who support magic call themselves. Not all Reformists are wizards, but all Reformists seek the same end: to reform the antimagic laws, to abolish the Thirteenth Tablet, to stop the burnings.

Nicholas Perevil should have been just another wizard we hunted and captured and tied to the stake. But before Malcolm became king, his father turned to Nicholas for help. Invited him to court, sought his advice, tried to find a way for Reformists and Persecutors—what Reformists call those who oppose magic—to coexist peacefully.

He soon became the most powerful wizard in Anglia. Not just in his magical ability, but also in his influence. He had the ear of the king; he was changing the policy of

Anglia. He was appointed to the king's council and even brought in his own men. It was unthinkable, his opposers said. Impossible.

They were right.

And five years later they were dead, along with half of Anglia. Killed by a plague Nicholas started, a plot designed to kill his enemies, weaken the country, and put him on the throne, all in one convenient curse. But Nicholas hadn't planned on Malcolm's surviving, on Blackwell's surviving.

And he hadn't planned on us.

"Maybe," I say. "But it's hard to catch someone you can't find."

"Then maybe we should try a little harder." Caleb glances down at his rough wool tunic and grimaces. "I didn't go through a year of training to dress like some broken-down squire. You can't be happy about wearing that thing, either." He points to my ugly brown maid's dress.

After the rebellions started, witch hunters became Reformist targets. It's why Blackwell ordered us to stop wearing our uniforms, to lie about our identity, why he sent us to live at Ravenscourt to blend in with the rest of the king's servants. And it's why I lost focus today, why I made a mistake. Because if I'd never come back to Ravenscourt…

I squeeze my hand into my pocket again.

We turn off Westcheap onto Kingshead Alley, a dark, dank street filled with tiny shops, their shutters closed and doors shut tight. At the very end is a battered wooden door, above it a green wooden plaque that reads THE WORLD'S END in gold block lettering. Caleb pushes it open. Inside, it's packed with people: pirates and thieves, drunks and vagrants.

Most of them are already drunk, even though it's not much past noon. There's a loud card game in one corner, a fight breaking out in another. A trio of musicians cowers between them, trying in vain to play above the brawl and the crowd that cheers every time someone gets punched.

We spy Joe, the old, white-haired owner, pulling drinks behind the bar, and we head straight for him. As soon as we walk up, he slides each of us a foaming glass of ale and watches as we take a cautious sip.

"Well?" He folds his arms across his chest.

Caleb chokes, sputtering ale all over the counter.

"Don't mind him." I jab my elbow into Caleb's side. "It's very nice."

Joe fancies himself an ale connoisseur, and each week he brews up different concoctions to try on his clientele, with varying results. Last week's brew, infused with the essence of roasted pig, was the worst to date. "Why eat supper when you can drink it?" he'd asked. Today's has a hint of rosemary—and something else I can't quite place.

"What is that?" I say. "Licorice?"

Joe snorts. "Not quite. I hope you two don't have much to do today."

We spot Marcus and Linus sitting at our usual table in the back and make our way to them. Caleb reaches around me to pull out a chair, and I flush with pleasure, thinking it's for me, until he slides past me and sits down. I stand there for a moment, feeling foolish. Then I pull out my own chair and sit down.

"What happened to you?" Marcus gestures at me with his glass.

"What are you talking about?"

"You look like the dead." He wrinkles his nose. "You smell like it, too. Did you arrest the necromancers before or after they killed you and dug you back up?" Marcus laughs at his own bad joke, and Linus joins in.

"Maybe if you cared less about the way I look and more about catching witches, you might be half as good as me," I snap.

Caleb laughs at this, but Marcus glares at me and mouths a filthy insult. I ignore him. But when he turns away, I quickly smooth my hair and tuck it behind my ears. I wince as a chunk of bloodied flesh falls from my hair into my lap.

"She was incredible. Her best arrest yet." Caleb lifts his goblet in a toast to me, but the other boys don't join in. Of course not. Linus hasn't spoken to me since the summer, after he cornered me in the palace gardens and tried to kiss me and got a punch in the face for his efforts. And Marcus... well, Marcus has never liked me. Tall, black-haired, and brutish, he never expected to find competition in someone like me: short, blond, and girlish.

Even still, Caleb doesn't seem to realize that the more he boasts of my success, the more the others grow to hate me. Besides, today's arrest was hardly something to boast about. I consider joining Joe back at the bar when Linus says something that stops me.

"We were just talking about the Yuletide masque," he says to Caleb. "Have you decided who you're taking yet?"

Caleb smiles and takes a sip of ale. "Maybe."

Maybe? My stomach twists into a hopeful little knot.

Marcus whoops. "Who is it?"

"I'll tell you after I ask her."

"It's Cecily Mowbray, isn't it?" Marcus says.

"No, it's Katherine Willoughby," Linus says. "I saw them together last weekend."

Caleb laughs. "We're just friends."

Friends? I think. *Since when?* Cecily is the daughter of an earl, and Katherine is a viscount's daughter. They're both ladies-in-waiting to Queen Margaret, both terribly snobbish, both terribly beautiful. Especially Katherine. Tall, dark-haired, and sophisticated, she's the kind of girl who wears gowns instead of trousers, jewelry instead of weaponry, who smells like roses instead of rot.

"You looked more than friends to me," Linus replies. "Unless you go around kissing all your friends," he adds, smirking.

I know this bit of spite is aimed at me. Right after I punched Linus, he accused me of liking Caleb. I denied it, but I guess he didn't believe me.

"Ah." Caleb scratches the back of his neck, and I'm shocked to see his ears turn pink. I've never seen Caleb blush before. "I guess my secret is out, then."

Something inside me goes flat.

Marcus and Linus start laughing and teasing Caleb, but I don't pay attention. *Caleb and Katherine Willoughby? How is that possible?* I know Caleb is ambitious, but he's always hated people like Katherine. People who were given everything, people who never had to fight for what they wanted, as he did.

I guess he changed his mind.

I'm so lost in my thoughts I don't notice the other boys getting up until Caleb is standing above me.

"We're going back to the palace," he says. "To visit the queen's rooms. There's supposed to be dancing later."

I shrug. I'd rather not think about Caleb dancing with Katherine Willoughby. Caleb doesn't even like dancing.

"What are you going to do?"

"Stay here," I say. "Listen to music. Drink ale."

Caleb raises his eyebrows. "Why? It's awful."

"I like it." But he's right. It is awful. It's heavy and flat and has a strange metallic taste that burns my throat when I swallow. Though it's nothing compared with the churning in my stomach and the terrible prickling behind my eyes, the kind I get when I'm about to cry.

"Okay." He frowns. "But be careful with it. It feels a little strong, and—"

"I'll be fine." I wave him off. "Don't worry about me."

"I always worry about you," he says. But then he leaves. I watch him go, wishing more than anything I was the kind of girl who could make him stay.

I MOVE FROM THE TABLE to a plush chair near the fireplace and order lunch—some bread and cheese and more of Joe's funny green ale. The burning sensation has gone away, and it's starting to taste pretty good. The other patrons seem to think so, too; they're downing it by the bucketful and are louder and more boisterous than usual.

I have no idea how long I've been here until a man at the bar stumbles to stand, knocks his stool to the floor, and starts retching. He bolts for the door, and when he flings it open, it's pitch black outside.

Have I really been here all day? It seems like only a couple of hours. I guess I should go back to the palace, but there's nothing waiting for me there. At least nothing good. Another ale sounds like a much better idea. I jump to my feet.

Big mistake. The world starts to spin—fast. I reach out to

steady myself, but as I place my hand on the wall, it disappears. Not the wall, my hand. Into the stone, right up to my wrist.

Fascinating.

I pull my hand out of the wall, then stick it back again. Over and over again, until someone speaks up.

"Something wrong with your hand, love?"

I turn around. The voice belongs to the man sitting across from me, his face hidden in a veil of smoke.

"Yes. No. I don't know. Only…hands don't usually disappear into walls, do they?" Through the fog in my head, I know I'm not making any sense. I start laughing.

The smoke lifts to reveal the man's face: curly black hair, short black beard. A long, curved pipe dangles from his mouth. It has a wooden stem and a white bowl carved into the shape of a dog's head. He speaks without taking it out.

"You're a little young to be drinking that stuff, aren't you?"

I laugh even harder. I've been on my own for so long that it seems absurd for someone to question my behavior. Especially when that someone is a pirate. I can tell by his pipe. Only well-traveled men, like pirates or the wealthy, own pipes like his. The rest make do with ordinary ones. Besides, the wealthy don't hang out in taverns like this. Which leaves pirates.

I stare at his pipe as it bobs up and down, then give a start when it transforms into a giant black snake. It slithers out of his mouth and winds itself around his neck. The pirate continues, seemingly oblivious to the enormous snake wrapping itself around his head.

"I wouldn't let my son drink this, and he's older than you. You can't be more than, what, fourteen?"

"Sixteen. Watch it!"

I reach forward and smack the pirate square in the mouth, knocking the snake to the floor. It lies there, coiling and shuddering, then bursts into a rainbow.

"Pretty." I wave my hands, trying to catch the ribbons of light spiraling in front of me. A chorus of voices fills the room then—they're coming from the rainbow. "Listen. Can you hear that? The rainbow is singing!" I open my mouth and sing along with it. *"Greensleeves, la-la-la who but my Lady Greeeensleeeeves…"*

"God's blood, you're a mess," the pirate mutters.

He picks his pipe off the ground and tucks it inside his cape, then he takes me by the arm and leads me to the door. I take offense to this. He really shouldn't be touching me, him a pirate and me a young girl and all. And I definitely shouldn't be letting a strange man lead me outside and to God knows where. But I can't seem to stop singing long enough to tell him this.

"Why don't we get you some air?" he says.

"There's air in here. I can see it! It's pink. Did you know air was pink?" I babble away, looking up at the pirate as he guides me out into the now-crowded alley. He's really tall. "What's your name?"

"I'm Peter." He turns away from me. "George, there you are. Thanks for coming so fast. So? What do you think?"

"Nice to meet you, Peter George. I'm Elizabeth Grey. Do you see the stars, Peter George? They're spelling your name in the sky. P-E-T…" I jab my finger at the twinkling lights that dance in front of my eyes. They're so close I can almost touch them.

"Aye, that's her," comes a voice in my ear.

I jump and give a little shriek. There's a boy standing next to me. Where did he come from? He's looking me up and down, and I stare back. Dark brown hair, light blue eyes. He's dressed well enough, in a green cloak, blue trousers, black boots. Something about him looks so familiar, but I can't seem to place it. I open my mouth to ask him, but instead start giggling.

"She drunk?" the boy asks.

"Roaring, and then some," Peter George says. "Absinthe. Damned Joe, put it in the ale and didn't bother telling her. She's too young to be messing with that stuff. But, you're sure?"

Absinthe! So that's why the ale was green. I've seen courtiers drink absinthe and get a little crazy afterward. Good thing it doesn't have that effect on me.

"She's a bit haggard at the moment, but it's definitely her," the boy says. "Think she's in any condition to talk?"

"I can talk," I blurt. "See, look. I'm doing it right now. I like to talk." This isn't true, really, unless I'm with Caleb or I've had too much to drink. Then Joe says I talk ten to the dozen, which is his way of saying a lot.

Peter George and the boy look at each other.

"Fine. Let's get her somewhere less crowded, see what we can get out of her."

The boy loops his arm through mine and guides me down Kingshead Alley and through a series of streets toward the river. I notice they take the long way, avoiding Tyburn.

"We're just going to help you back to the palace and have a little chat on the way," the boy says. "If you don't mind."

"Pinwheels," I reply, stumbling on a rock.

"That so?" He steadies me. "I don't see any, but I'll take your word for it."

"No, your eyes. They spin like pinwheels. What's your name again?"

"George."

"Funny. That other man is a George, too. Peter George—whoops!" I trip over the hem of my cloak and tumble to the ground.

"No, he's just Peter. I'm George. Here, let me help you up." He pulls me to my feet and I notice we're the same height.

"You're awfully short," I say.

"Short? Not me! Maybe *you're* the short one. Ever think about that?"

I consider it. "My God, you're right. You must be very clever."

George cracks a laugh. "If only everyone was this easy to convince."

Just Peter comes over, grips my shoulders, and peers down at me, forcing me to look at him.

"George says you live at the palace?" he says.

I nod.

"What exactly do you do there?"

"I'm a maid." The lie rolls easily enough off my tongue. I used to be a maid, I still sleep with the maids, sometimes I wish I still were a maid.

"A maid?" He blinks in surprise. "What kind? Chamber? Lady's?"

"Scullery."

I can't help but notice he looks disappointed. "For how long?"

28

"Since I was nine."

"Nine?" He frowns. "Where are your parents?"

"Dead."

"I see." Just Peter's scowl softens. "You've been in the kitchen this whole time?"

I nod again. "I can kill chickens, cook them, too, and ducks, peacocks, you name it. I make a good stew, decent bread; I can even churn butter. And my floors are so clean, you can eat off them." I wince, knowing how stupid that sounds. But I have my orders.

Just Peter waves his hand. "Very well. But besides that, is there anything about you that is, say, different from the other maids? Unusual?"

Only about a hundred things. Well, maybe not a hundred. Maybe just one.

"No, sir. I'm really very ordinary."

He turns to George. "Veda must have meant someone else. This can't have been who she wanted us to find. I thought for a moment, maybe, if she'd been a maid for the queen. But this girl, she can't help us. She's just a lass. George?"

George isn't paying attention. He's staring at me, the most curious expression on his face.

"Perhaps you're right," George says, turning away from me. "Let's take her back to the palace. It's late, and she'll be missed."

We start walking back to court, taking the graveled path by the Severn River to avoid the busy streets. We stumble along, me falling and George and Just Peter taking turns pulling me to my feet and dusting off my cloak until the path ends in a flight of steps that leads to the palace gates.

"Here we are," Just Peter says. "George, you ready?"

"Absolutely." George grins at me. I'm about to smile back when I see his teeth stretch into long black fangs. I squeeze my eyes shut.

"Elizabeth?" I open them to find Just Peter's face only inches from mine. "George will take care of you, make sure you get in all right. In the future, though, try to steer clear of the absinthe?"

I nod. For a pirate, he's very nice. I just wish his face would stop melting. "Okay, Just Peter." I close my eyes again. "I will."

He chuckles softly. "Not Just Peter, love. Just...uh, right, then. George, I'll see you later." He turns and disappears into the darkness.

George helps me up the stairs to the heavy iron gate at the top, which opens into the palace gardens. The guard unlocks it for us, and George leads me inside.

"We're home," he says.

"We?" I blurt, surprised.

George laughs. "Yes. I live here, too. You still don't recognize me, do you? I'm King Malcolm's new fool."

4

I THOUGHT HE LOOKED FAMILIAR. "You don't look like a fool."

"I should hope not. I'm a fool by occupation, not presentation. And only occasionally by reputation." He grins.

"You're too young to be a fool," I persist, swaying a little.

"Not at all." George takes me by the shoulders. "I'm eighteen, which is the most foolish age of all. All the troubles of a man, yet none of the excuses of a boy." He leads me down the dirt path that winds around the edge of the garden. "We need to get you to your room before anyone sees what condition you're in." He looks around. "But I don't know how—"

"Oh, I do." I grab his sleeve. "Follow me."

I drag him off the path and across the grass toward a vine-covered wall. I walk along it, trailing my hand through the leaves.

"Know what's funny about this palace?" I say. "All the

gargoyles. Lots of them are hidden, but when you find one, they're always next to something interesting. See?"

I stop and point to the little snout that's almost completely buried by the ivy. Stick my hand into the greenery and feel around for the door latch I know is there. Got it. I lift it and hear a tiny click, then pull apart the curtain of vines to reveal a small doorway.

He's doing it again: staring at me with that funny expression, his dark eyebrows raised, the tiniest smirk on his face.

"What?" I say.

"Nothing. But—you're a funny girl."

"Not really."

"Yes, really. I mean, what does a girl from the kitchen know about secret doors?"

I tut a little. "This is nothing."

"You don't say." He shakes his head, then gestures to the door. "Ladies first."

I squeeze through the tiny opening, and George climbs in after me. I lean out to rearrange the vines before closing the door behind me. Inside, it's pitch black.

"There's a staircase here," I say. "If you go all the way to the top, you'll come to a door. It opens up into the great hall, behind that huge tapestry, you know, the one with the owls and bats attacking the wizard on the table?" King Malcolm has a fondness for violent tapestries and paintings, and I hate them all.

"Aye, I know it. But what about you?"

"I'm going this way." I jerk my thumb over my shoulder, though it's so dark he probably can't see. "Behind me. The hallway leads to the kitchen. The maids' quarters are just past it."

I stand there for a minute, waiting for him to leave. But he doesn't. And even though I can't see him, I can feel his eyes on me. I can't figure out what he wants.

"I guess you can go now," I say.

But he doesn't move. "I would feel better if I saw you safely to your room."

I fold my arms. "I don't need your help."

"I didn't say you did," George says mildly. "I was just being friendly. Seems as if you could use a friend."

"What makes you say that?"

"I dunno. Hanging out in a dodgy tavern alone, drinking absinthe alone, stumbling home with a pirate and a fool, alone—"

"What's it to you, nosy parker?"

"Last name's Cavendish, actually. But come on. Let's be friends. I'm new around here. I could use someone to show me how things are done."

"You are a fool if you want a kitchen maid to show you how things are done," I mutter.

I wish he'd leave. I want nothing more than to go to my room and sleep. Forget this day ever happened. In the dark like this, the absinthe is starting to wear off and I'm beginning to remember everything. Accidentally killing that necromancer. Caleb's kissing Katherine Willoughby. Going to the masque with her while I stay home alone.

Then I get an idea.

"If you're King Malcolm's fool, then I suppose you know about his Yuletide masque."

"Aye. I've heard of it."

"If you really want to know how things are done around

here, that's a good place to start. Since we're friends now, why don't you go with me?"

George clears his throat. "Go with you?"

"Yes."

"To the masque?"

"Yes."

Silence. For the third time today, I can feel my cheeks getting hot.

"What?" I say irritably. "I suppose a fool is too good to go to a dance with a maid?"

"No. It's just...I didn't know maids were allowed to go to masques."

Damnation. He's right, of course. Maids can't go, but I wasn't going as a maid; I was going as a witch hunter. Not that it matters, since I'll be wearing a mask and no one will see my face anyway.

"We're not," I correct myself. "But you are. And as I say, I think you should take me."

He clears his throat again. "You know, you're very cute. And if I were at all inclined in that direction, you'd certainly be someone to consider."

It takes me a second to realize he's turning me down.

"A simple no would suffice," I mutter.

"Suffice it to say, my no isn't simple."

"I'm not in the mood for riddles," I snap. I'm starting to wish I hadn't drunk that ale. Or that I'd drunk more so I'd be passed out somewhere instead of babbling like an idiot to a fool.

"I'm going to go now," I say. "So, as I said, up those stairs, through that door, under the tapestry, and that's that." I turn around and walk down the hall. I'm almost to the end when I hear his voice.

"Maybe I'll see you around sometime?"

I don't reply. I just keep walking.

Soon the hall grows narrower and warmer, and I know I'm nearing the kitchen. Supper was over hours ago, but I can still smell the food through the wall, hear the commotion on the other side as they clean: pots banging, maids shouting, the footsteps of servants still carrying in trays from the dining hall.

My stomach starts growling, and I wonder if I can sneak inside and get something to eat without anyone seeing me. I drop to my knees and skim my hand along the wall until I feel a small notch, big enough to slip my finger through: the handle on the tiny door that opens into the kitchen between the wall and the bread oven.

I discovered this door my first week in the kitchen. I was only nine then and didn't have the courage to open it. I didn't know what was on the other side, but I imagined plenty: snakes, ghosts, vicious child-eating monsters. Time passed and I forgot about it, until one day Caleb came to keep me company while I did my chores.

I remember his sitting on the floor, playing against himself in a game of dice, left hand versus right. He wasn't supposed to be in the kitchen with me; the other maids found him distracting. Caleb was only fourteen then, but he was almost six feet tall, with dark blond hair that fell over his eyes in waves. He was good-looking and he knew it. I was only twelve and I knew it, too.

I also knew he was stubborn. No amount of whining or

pleading could make Caleb do something he didn't want to—or turn him off course once he'd decided to do it. If he wanted to stay in the kitchen and distract me, he would. The door is what finally enticed him to leave that day. He swept his dice from the floor, crossed the room, and pushed it open. There was a hall on the other side, dark and dank, leading to the unknown.

He asked me to go with him, to find out where it went. I didn't hate small, dark spaces then—not like I do now—but I still didn't want to go. I had work to do and knew I'd get in trouble if I left. But I always followed Caleb everywhere. There wasn't any place he could ask me to go that I wouldn't say yes to. But I never considered the possibility that one day he would stop asking me. Never realized that without him, I had nowhere to go.

Suddenly, I don't feel hungry anymore. I get to my feet and push through the next door, into the hall that leads to the maids' quarters. Here, it is dim, lit only by a single torch set into a bracket in the wall. But it's still bright enough to make my head start spinning again, just like it did inside the tavern. I lean against the wall and close my eyes to try to make it stop. I'm tired. So tired that when I hear his voice it takes me a second to respond.

"Elizabeth?"

I jerk my head up. There, at the end of the hall, is Caleb. He starts toward me, his hands clasped behind his back. My heart leaps at the sight of him.

"Where have you been?" He's standing in front of me now, his face half hidden in the shadows. "And what happened to you? You look terrible."

"Just what every girl wants to hear," I mutter.

"I didn't mean it that way."

"What are you doing here?" I say. "Shouldn't you be, I don't know"—I wave my hand around—"moving in circles and swaying oh-so-gently to the music?"

Caleb smiles. "It's midnight. The ladies have been asleep for hours."

Something about the way he says that grates on me. As if he's insinuating I'm not a lady because I haven't been asleep for hours. As if I didn't already know I was no lady without that.

"Well, tra-la-la," I say under my breath.

"I wanted to check on you before I went to bed, only you weren't here."

"I was busy," I snap. "I don't always sit around my room waiting for you to show up. If that were the case, who knows how long I'd be stuck inside?"

Caleb's eyes go wide. I don't think I've ever talked to him this way before. But I'm so angry I can't help myself.

"Besides, I don't need you to check on me. I'm perfectly fine." I move toward my door but get hit with another wave of dizziness. I throw my arms against the wall to steady myself, but my feet get tangled up in my cloak and I tumble to the floor.

"Yes, you seem perfectly fine," Caleb says. I can hear the amusement in his voice. I would be furious if I weren't about to throw up. "Just how much of that ale did you drink, anyway?" He helps me to my feet.

"I dunno," I mumble, leaning against him and closing my eyes again. Things don't spin as much when my eyes are closed.

"I don't know what's gotten into you," Caleb says. "First the necromancer, now this."

I crack open an eye to look at him. "Just having a bad day."

"But it isn't just today," he says. "Lately you've seemed a little..."

"A little what?"

"Unhappy."

I blink in surprise. I didn't know he paid enough attention to me to notice.

"What makes you say that?"

He shrugs. "I don't know. You just don't seem yourself. You're so quiet. Normally, I can't get you to shut up." He smiles. "And you say I never come to see you, but it's been a long time since I've gotten an invitation."

"You used to not need one."

"Yes. Well. We were kids then. I can't exactly show up at your room without an invitation now, can I? I shouldn't even be here now. What would people think?"

I know exactly what they'd think. My hand goes to my pocket again.

"Anyway, if something's bothering you, you can tell me. You used to be able to tell me anything."

I was able to tell him anything—once. But that was before he grew tall and I stayed short, he got handsome while I stayed cute, and he opened all the doors I wanted to keep shut.

"I'm fine, Caleb. I'm just tired. I'll feel better in the morning."

He's quiet for a moment.

"If you say so," he finally says. "Can I at least help you to your room?"

I nod. He slips his arm around my shoulder and I lean into him, and for a second, it feels as if it's just us. As if it's always been. I think for a second that maybe I can tell him what's happening with me, what's happening *to* me. I'm trying out the words in my head, and I actually open my mouth to say them. But when I look up, I see he's looking over my head and frowning.

I turn around just as he steps out of the shadows: one of King Malcolm's guards, standing next to my door in his crisp black-and-red uniform, holding his pike.

Oh no, I think. *Not now.*

A flicker of surprise crosses Caleb's face.

"Richard." Caleb nods. "Are you looking for me?"

Richard clears his throat. "No. I'm here to, *ah*, you know."

"No, I don't." Caleb's surprise turns into a scowl. "Care to tell me?"

Richard glances at me but doesn't reply.

"Elizabeth?" Caleb looks at me. "What is Richard doing here?"

I shake my head, too horrified to speak.

Caleb releases me and starts toward Richard. I slump against the wall, pressing my cheek against the cool stone. I hear his footsteps tap the floor as he moves down the hall.

"I'll ask you again: What are you doing here?"

Again, Richard doesn't reply. But I know Caleb won't let it go until he does.

"Answer me!"

"Caleb, stop." I peel myself off the wall. Start toward him. I don't make it more than a few steps before everything starts spinning out of control again. I pitch forward wildly and tumble to the floor in a heap.

"Elizabeth!" Caleb rushes to my side.

"I'm fine," I mutter. But I'm not. Every time I open my eyes, everything goes topsy-turvy. The air is dark and suffocating, and the walls feel as if they're closing in on me.

"Let's get you inside." Caleb pulls me to my feet. We start toward my room again, but Richard steps forward to block us.

"She's to come with me," Richard says.

"She's not going anywhere with you," Caleb snaps. "And if you don't get out of my way, I swear to you, you'll be sorry."

I wince, waiting for Richard to yell, maybe throw a punch. Instead, they both go quiet. Caleb releases me. I open my eyes to find him crouched beside me, clutching a bundle of herbs. I recognize them immediately: purple spiky pennyroyal, yellow flowering silphium. My hand goes immediately to my pocket but I already know it'll be empty.

He gets to his feet. "Elizabeth, where did these come from?"

"Her pocket. They fell out of her pocket." Richard's eyes are wide. "I saw them."

Caleb turns them over in his hand. Examines them closely. Frowns.

"This is pennyroyal," he says. "And silphium. Women use these if they're, you know"—I can hear the discomfort in his voice—"trying to prevent a baby. They're witches' herbs." He looks up at me. "Why would you have these?"

It's a long, silent, dreadful moment before he speaks, as he works out what he knows against what he wishes he didn't.

"Baby," he repeats, his face going pale. "And you...you're going with him." He jerks his head at Richard. "At midnight. To see the king."

I shake my head. Look for a denial. An excuse. Anything. Only there isn't one.

Caleb spins on his heel to face Richard.

"You didn't see anything," he says. "She was never here. She never had these. I've got money. I'll pay you to keep quiet...."

Caleb starts pulling coins out of his pocket. But Richard is already backing away, his thumb placed between his first two fingers: the old sign against witchcraft.

"She's a witch," he says. "I can't let her go." He reaches for his belt, pulls out a pair of handcuffs.

"She's not a witch," Caleb says. "She just—"

He cuts himself off, but I know what he was going to say: She's not a witch, she just has witches' herbs. Caleb knows the laws, just as I do. What I have, what I was using them for, it's enough to send me to the rack for torture, to prison for detainment, to the stake for burning.

I turn to run, but lose my balance again and slip to the floor. Caleb reaches for me, but Richard pushes him away and grabs the back of my cloak, hauling me to my feet. He yanks my arms roughly behind my back and slaps the bindings over my wrists.

"Elizabeth Grey, by the authority of King Malcolm of Anglia, I am commanded to arrest you for the crime of witchcraft. You are hereby ordered to return with us to Fleet prison for detention and to await your trial, presided over by the Inquisitor, Lord Blackwell, Duke of Norwich. If you are found guilty, you will be executed by burning, your land and goods forfeit to the crown." A pause. "So help you God."

"You can't take her to prison!" Caleb shouts. "You don't have the authority. Not without Blackwell's consent."

Richard considers this.

"Then I won't take her to prison," he says. I'm about to breathe a sigh of relief, but he adds, "I'll take her to see Blackwell."

PRISON WOULD HAVE BEEN BETTER.

Caleb takes my arm. "You're not taking her. Not without me."

Richard jerks me from his grasp. "I wouldn't if I were you," he growls. "She's in enough trouble as it is. Your trailing after her like a puppy isn't going to help."

"He's right, Caleb," I say. "You'll only make it worse. Just go to your room and wait for me. I'll be back soon."

Caleb glances between us, weighing his decision.

"Fine. I'll wait. But not in my room. I'll wait here. If you're not back in an hour, I'm coming for you."

Richard hauls me out the door, into the empty courtyard, across the grounds, and up a flight of stairs that leads to the living quarters. Ravenscourt is the main residence of the king and queen, but Blackwell keeps apartments here, too, more for status than necessity as his own home is a short boat ride down the river.

He thrusts me down the shadowed hall until it ends in a set of wide double doors: shiny dark oak, glittering brass handles, a pair of guards dressed in black and red. As we approach, they uncross their pikes with a clink, the blades flashing like lightning, reflecting the candles flickering along the wall.

The door swings open, and a boy slips out and scurries past me. A servant, maybe, though he seems little more than a child. The guards don't seem to notice; they act as if he's not there. Maybe he isn't—maybe I'm imagining him. Maybe I'm imagining this whole thing.

Inside, a fire crackles in the hearth; the scent of rosemary drifts from the fresh rushes strewn on the floor. Blackwell sits behind his desk, papers spread before him, working as though it were twelve noon instead of twelve midnight. If he's surprised to see me standing there, in his chambers, hand-cuffed and escorted by one of Malcolm's guards, he doesn't show it. His eyes flick from my face to my bound hands to Richard, then back to me again.

He's not an old man, nor is he young. I don't actually know his age, but he looks the same now as he always has: dark hair, uncut by gray, closely trimmed to his head. Short, cropped beard. A long, thin face, a nose that stops just short of being called big. Tall, well over six feet. He might be attractive were it not for his eyes, like chips of wet coal. Cold, hard, black.

"Uncuff her," he says to Richard.

"But—don't you want to know what she's here for before I release her?"

"I give the orders here, and I ask the questions," Blackwell replies. "Uncuff her."

Richard steps forward, unlocks my bindings. They snap open with a quiet click.

"I want to know why you're here," Blackwell says, his attention still on Richard. "Why you've brought one of my witch hunters to me in the middle of the night shackled like a common criminal. And why you"—he shifts his gaze to me—"allowed it to happen."

Richard glances at me, as if willing me to speak first. I look straight ahead and say nothing. If he thinks I'm indicting myself in front of this judge and jury, he's got another thing coming.

"You tell me," Blackwell repeats, his voice a quiet menace. "Now."

"I—I went to her chambers. To take her to the king. He requested her presence," Richard stammers. "And she had these. They fell out of her pocket."

He pulls out the herbs, drops them on Blackwell's desk. Green, fragrant; pretty, even; tied into a bundle with a snip of twine, like a simple posy a boy might give a girl. So innocent-looking. Yet so very damning.

I close my eyes against the deafening silence that follows, resigning myself to what comes next. I never imagined that coming back to Ravenscourt could lead to this. First I'm disguised as a maid, then I'm introduced to the king. Then I'm summoned before the king, and the next thing I know I'm on a skiff downriver at midnight, to a bathhouse in search of a wisewoman and a bundle of herbs. I paid that old hag three months' wages: two for her knowledge, one for her silence, for all the good it did me....

"Leave us," Blackwell says.

My eyes fly open. Richard glances at me, and I see a flicker of something pass across his face: It almost looks like guilt. He nods at Blackwell, spins on his heel, and leaves the room.

Blackwell leans back in his chair, a high-backed wooden thing padded in crimson velvet. It could be a throne. By the power he has over me, it may as well be one. He clasps his hands on the desk in front of him and stares. This is his way. He will stare at me until I have no choice but to say something.

But I won't say anything—I swear I won't. There's no point anyway. I'm in trouble and nothing I can say will change that. Seconds turn into minutes and, still, he remains silent. I begin to sway on my feet: tired, my head fuzzy from the absinthe, my gut churning with nausea and nerves.

Maybe I'm making things worse by not speaking. Maybe Blackwell sees my silence as defiance. And the last thing I need right now is for him to think I'm defying him.

Again.

"It wasn't anything I wanted. With the king, I mean." I begin like this, preemptively, the words harsh against the silence in the room. There's no way to mitigate the truth of them, so I don't even try. "I didn't encourage it, if that's what you're thinking. He sent for me. With a note."

That's how it started: with a note. Written in the king's own hand and given to his guard, passed to a page to a servant then to me, dropped into my lap one night during dinner. I remember unfolding the thick parchment with a smile, thinking it was from Caleb.

It wasn't.

"He asked me to wait in the hall outside my room at midnight. But I didn't. Not at first. Why would I? It was a mistake—it had to be. What would the king want with me?"

But it's a lie. I knew what he wanted. How could I not? There were too many sidelong glances, too many invitations to sit near him and talk about nothing, too much interest paid to someone who should have been no one. Even without all that, I would know. As Caleb always reminded me: Nothing good comes to a girl after midnight.

"The notes kept coming, and I kept ignoring them. Then one night he sent one of his guards for me. I had to go with him. To him. What else was I supposed to do?"

Blackwell doesn't reply. I didn't expect him to. Still, I go on. Now that I've started I can't seem to stop.

"I couldn't stop it from happening, but I could make sure nothing else did. I couldn't have the king's child." I swallow. It's the first time I've admitted it out loud, the possibility of it, what I was trying to prevent. "I knew he'd send me away. That he'd shut me in an abbey, to live behind walls forever. Everyone would know. I didn't want that. I don't want that. I want to stay. Here, with you."

If Blackwell is moved by my plea, he doesn't show it. He continues to stare at me, his face cold, hard, carved in stone. I can read nothing from it.

Finally, he speaks. "How long have you known?"

"How long have I known what?"

"That you're a witch."

"A witch?" I shriek the word as if I've never heard it before. "I'm not a witch! I'm not—"

"You. Had. Herbs." His words are a growl; they may as well be a shout. "Witches' herbs. As far as I'm concerned, that makes you a witch."

"I'm not a witch," I repeat. "I mean, I did have witches' herbs. And I did take them. But I'm not a witch." Even to me, this sounds weak.

"What else do you have tucked away, besides these herbs?" Blackwell flicks his wrist at them, still lying on his desk. "Wax dolls? Witch's ladder? Spellbooks? A familiar?"

"Nothing! I have nothing tucked away. I hate witchcraft, just as you do!"

"Not as I do." His voice is a shower of winter rain down my back. "Not I."

He falls silent. The only sounds in the room are the crackle of the fire, my own heavy breathing, my own thudding heart.

"I'm not a witch," I say again.

Blackwell opens a drawer in his desk, pulls out a sheet of parchment. Takes up his pen, dips it in ink, and begins writing. I can hear the nib scratching the paper.

"I'm disappointed in you, Elizabeth." A pause. "Very disappointed."

I take a breath. Hold it.

"You have spent years with me, have you not? You were one of my best witch hunters, were you not?"

"Yes," I whisper.

"I had my doubts, you know," he continues, still writing.

"When Caleb first brought you to me, he said he could make something of you. I didn't believe him." Another pause as he signs the paper, his hand looping out his waving, scrawling signature. He scatters sand on the ink to dry, shakes the excess onto the floor. "But you surprised me. I didn't expect you to live past the first week."

I shiver at his bleak analysis. At his thoughts about my chances of surviving, at his tone that tells me it didn't much matter to him if I hadn't.

"But you did. And here you are."

Finally, Blackwell looks up at me, takes me in with a sweep of those cold, black eyes.

"I expected more of you. What I did not expect is this." He waves his hand. "You broke one law by possessing those herbs. Another when you killed that necromancer"—he gleams at me, so he knows about that, too—"and you have become a liability. I cannot have witch hunters breaking my laws. These are laws I created—your king created—to keep this country safe. You break them, you will be punished for them."

Punished.

I knew it was coming; there was no way it wasn't. I imagine the things he could do: demote me, send me back to the kitchens, shut me behind the walls of a nunnery, just as I feared.

I don't say anything. I just nod.

He stands then, abrupt. It's then I notice he's dressed for daytime: black trousers; black doublet, the wrists ringed with dark fur; his collar of office draped around his neck, heavy and gold. Clothes to remind me of his power, his influence. Of his power to do anything, to anyone.

As if I needed reminding.

He lifts the parchment from the desk, holds it up. It looks official enough: long and scrolled, his signature just above the royal seal at the bottom. I can just make out a rose, the flower of his house—same as the king's house—pressed into the hard red wax.

"Do you know what this is?"

I shake my head.

"It's a Bill of Attainder." With a flick of his wrist, he tosses it onto the desk. It slides across the slick wooden surface, curls onto the floor. It's this: this momentary loss of control that tips me to his anger, simmering below the surface like a pot left to boil too long. And I know that whatever this Bill of Attainder is, it isn't a pardon. "It proclaims your sentence."

"My...*sentence*?" The word sticks in my throat. "What sentence?"

"The sentence I have given you, in punishment for your crime."

My crime. I suck in a breath.

"You are accused of witchcraft. You have admitted to practicing witchcraft. This is treason. The punishment for witchcraft, and for treason, is death."

"*Death?*" I repeat the word, I whisper it.

"Yes."

"Me?"

"Yes."

"But...I'm a witch hunter," I cry. "Your witch hunter! You can't just send me to prison, to the pyre...you can't just burn me alive in front of everyone! You can't!"

Blackwell shrugs, careless. "I can, and I have. It's done.

You will be taken to Fleet to await your execution at Tyburn, where you will be burned alive at the stake." He flicks his hand toward the fire roaring in the grate. "Alongside the rest of the lawbreakers and heretics."

The floor rocks underneath me then, as if I were standing on the deck of a ship. I stumble backward, search for something to hold. But there's nothing. Nothing to save me. Nothing at all. I crumple to the floor in a heap.

"I lived with you," I whisper against the lump rising in my throat. I can't cry, I won't cry. It won't help. "I did everything you asked me to. I was loyal to you. You said it yourself: I was one of your best witch hunters—"

"Then you betrayed me. Disobeyed me. Now you're nothing to me. And I am finished with you." And he doesn't have to say it, but I know he's thinking it: *What's done is done; it cannot be undone.* His steadfast motto, the one he lives by.

The one I will die by.

Blackwell snaps his fingers. Before I can get up, two guards burst in, haul me to my feet. I struggle, but it's no use. Terror has sapped my strength, and shame has robbed me of my determination to fight. Because I know—deep down, I know—I'm getting what I deserve.

They take me to Fleet.

Less prison than purgatory: a state of waiting, of suffering; a place where people wait with no hope, wait to die; a place to pass through before you reach the end of the world. It ends the same for everyone here: in fire and ash, disgrace and dishonor.

There's no special treatment for me. They take my cloak, my shoes. They throw me in a cell with the rest of the criminals and heretics, as if I were a criminal or heretic.

I am a criminal and heretic.

To my right, a small window is set into the wall, a slice of early-morning sky visible through the small iron bars. To my left is another set of bars and a door that leads out into a dark hallway. The floor is caked with dirt and rat droppings and completely devoid of furniture.

In the cell with me is another woman, a witch by the looks of her. She lies across from me, stretched out on the floor. She looks like a rag doll. Her arms and legs are broken and disjointed, sticking out at odd angles. Her chest whistles as she breathes in and out. Every now and again, she moans. She's been pulled apart on the rack. Shredded. I back away from her, as far as the cell will allow me. Away from her suffering, as if it were contagious.

I hear footsteps then, echoing down the dark stone hallway. Someone is coming. I jump to my feet, push down my mounting panic, and step to the door. I won't let them take me. I won't let them torture me. I will kill them or I will die trying.

When he emerges from the shadows, I nearly collapse in relief.

"Caleb!"

"Elizabeth. Oh my God—" Caleb grips the bars of my cell, his eyes wide. "Are you okay? No, of course you're not."

He pushes his hair off his forehead in a frantic swipe. "Are you hurt?"

"No." I shake my head. "I'm okay."

"I got here as soon as I could. I waited for you, outside your room, as I promised. And when you didn't show up, I went looking for you. I found some guards, and they told me what happened. But by the time I found out you were here, they wouldn't let me in."

I notice his hands then, still wrapped around the bars, the knuckles scuffed and raw and bloody.

"What happened?"

He shrugs. "I told you. They wouldn't let me in."

His eyes meet mine and we both fall silent.

"What am I going to do, Caleb?" I say, finally. "Blackwell sentenced me to death. To be burned alive. I'm going to die—"

"No, you're not." He reaches through the bars, grips my shoulders, gives them a little shake. "Do you hear me? You are not going to die. I won't allow it."

"But Blackwell—"

"Isn't thinking," Caleb finishes for me. "He's been under a lot of pressure lately, these damned Reformist protests..." He shakes his head. "When he realizes what he's done, he'll issue a pardon. I'm sure of it."

I frown. Blackwell has never been one to forgive. To apologize. To admit when he's been wrong, if he's ever been wrong. Caleb knows this as well as I do.

"I'll go to him today," he continues. "Plead for you. Remind him how valuable you are. How good you are."

"But I haven't been good," I say. "Not lately. You've had to cover for me four times in as many weeks. You've never had to do that before."

"No, but there's a reason for that, isn't there?" He looks at me, eyes narrowed, jaw clenched in a hard, tight line. "Why didn't you tell me? About the king, I mean? If you'd told me, I could have helped you. Stopped it, maybe—"

"You couldn't have stopped it," I say. "You know that."

Caleb goes quiet.

"I guess not," he admits, finally. "But I knew something was wrong with you. I should have tried harder to find out what it was." He winces and looks away. "I'm sorry."

"It's not your fault. It just happened."

"Because I wasn't paying attention." Caleb turns back to me. "I didn't see what everyone else saw. What *he* saw. If I had, I would have seen that you..." He looks at me as if he's never seen me before. "That you're not..."

"That I'm not what?"

"That you're not a girl anymore." Caleb gestures at me with a sweep of his hand. "You grew up."

If this were a different time, or a different place, I might have felt something. Pleased that he finally saw me. Displeased, maybe, that it took him so long. I might wonder what he thinks of me now, if things might change between us. But it isn't. So I don't.

"If I didn't notice, I guarantee Blackwell didn't," Caleb continues. "He probably still sees you the way you were when you started. A small, scrawny little thing. Far more trouble than you were worth."

He means to be reassuring, I know. But it's so close to the

way I see myself—the way I fear Caleb still sees me—that I wince.

"I'll never forget the look on his face when I first brought you to him."

I find a smile from somewhere. "Horrified."

"I pleaded with him to give you a chance," Caleb says. "I swore to him I'd make a good witch hunter out of you."

"You were ruthless," I say. "Waking me up in the middle of the night to train. Making me run until I threw up. Throw knives until I had blisters. Throwing punches at me over and over again until I could block them."

He turns serious. "I know. You must have hated me for it."

"I didn't hate you."

"I had to do it," he says. "I had to make sure you'd survive. And you did. Look how strong you are now. Look at what you've become."

What have I become?

Caleb grins then. And despite everything, I start to feel better. Start to feel foolish for doubting him, for thinking he couldn't get me through this. He got me through training. He can get me through anything.

I smile back.

"That's my girl." He glances out the window, then gives my arm one last squeeze before pulling away. "I better go. I want to be first in line to see Blackwell."

"Okay," I say, though I can't stand the thought of spending another minute in this cell. I glance at the witch in the corner. She's lying still, her eyes closed, silent. I wonder if she died.

"I know it's hard, but try to stay calm," Caleb continues. "It might take some time to persuade Blackwell to free you; you know how stubborn he can be. But whatever you do, don't do anything crazy, like try to escape. That'll only get you into more trouble. I'll be back as soon as I can."

I nod.

"I'll come back for you," he says again. "I promise."

Then he's gone.

ONE DAY PASSES, THEN TWO.

Three.

Four.

No visitors and no guards, except when they came to collect the dead witch in my cell, her body stiff and cold and blue. If I've counted correctly, I've been in prison for nearly a week now, which means tomorrow's Saturday again. Another burning. If Caleb doesn't come back soon, they'll be burning me. My stigma can't protect me from turning into a pile of ash.

I kept my promise and haven't tried to escape. For all the good it's done. Caleb said it would take time; but time, I think, is running out. I have doubts about my ability to get away now, even if I wanted to. I've been without food for nearly a week. The only water I've managed is from the rain that blows in through my window. On top of that, I can feel a fever coming on. My hands are clammy and my throat hurts.

Illness. Something else my stigma can't protect me from.

Rain pours steadily outside the bars; it hasn't let up in days. My cell is wet, probably freezing. I wouldn't know. I'm burning up with fever. I started coughing last night, and there's a strange rash all over my arms and legs. I hope it's not sweating sickness. That would kill me before the fire gets a chance to.

I'm exhausted but can't sleep. I tell myself it's because I want to be ready when Caleb shows up, but, in truth, I'm too scared to sleep. Because every minute that passes, as the day wears on and the shadows inside my cell grow longer, I can feel hope giving way to fear. The other prisoners aren't helping. The noises from their cells—moans of pain, weak crying, murmured prayers, the occasional panicked shriek—are wearing on me. Even if I hadn't kept track of time, they have.

They know what's coming.

I'm hunched in the corner of my cell, my dress pushed up as far as it'll go, trying to cool off. I'm drenched in sweat; even my hair is wet. But I can't tell if that's from sweat or the rain that continues to come through the tiny window. The cold water feels like needles on my skin, but it gives a little relief.

I must have drifted off at some point, but I'm awakened by the sound of footsteps in the hall. Caleb! He's finally come for me! I climb to my knees but get hit with a fit of coughing and fall to the floor, hacking. The footsteps stop in front of my cell.

"Caleb?" I whisper when I finally stop coughing.

"I'm afraid not," comes a voice I don't recognize.

I pull myself up until I'm sitting, the effort leaving me panting.

"Who are you?" My voice is so hoarse.

A tiny flicker of light appears. It's a man. I've never seen him before. He's very tall and very thin, wearing a long red robe knotted around the waist with a thick black rope. A black cloak falls over his shoulders down to his feet. His short hair is a mix of black and gray like his short, pointed beard. He stares at me curiously, his dark eyes intense but not unkind.

He's not a guard—I know that. He's not one of the king's men; I don't see the royal standard. He's dressed almost like...almost like a priest.

Oh, God. A priest. Come to give me the sacrament, the last rites. Which means I slept too long, which means Caleb came and couldn't wake me and left without me...

Then I see it. The light. It's coming from his hand, a single flame flickering from his outstretched fingertip. He flicks it into the air, where it hovers next to him, a tiny, pulsating sun. He's a wizard.

"Get out of here!" I croak. If Caleb sees me talking to a wizard, he'll be furious.

"I won't hurt you," he says. "I'm here to help you."

"I don't need your help!"

"Oh?" The sympathy in his voice infuriates me.

"Caleb! Caleb!" I scream before dissolving into another coughing fit.

The wizard grasps one of the bars on the cell door. He murmurs something under his breath, and the door begins to glow a soft pale blue. It starts to shudder, and with a small noise like snapping bones, it falls into a pile of smoking dust.

He's by my side then, kneeling over me.

"Child, you're sick," he says. "Come with me. Let me help you."

"No! Get away from me!" I shuffle to my knees and crawl away from him. I don't get more than a few feet before my legs give way and I collapse into the straw.

"The guards will be coming for you soon," he says. "The burning is scheduled for this morning."

"You're lying." But when I lift my head and tilt it to the window, I see pale streaks beginning to cut through the night sky. A sharp surge of panic pushes strength into my limbs, and I manage to stumble to my feet, grasping the wall for support.

Where is Caleb?

"I promise you, I am not." The wizard walks toward me, his hand outstretched. I shift away from him, my back sliding against the rough stone wall.

"What do you want with me?" I glance at my now-demolished cell door, the wide opening into the dark hallway. There are no guards to stop me, still enough darkness to conceal me. The only thing standing between me and freedom now is him.

I take a step toward the door. He anticipates it, steps forward to block me. I shift direction, take another step, then another. He follows. A dance.

"I'm not sure," the wizard says. "But I was told to find you. We thought it was a mistake at first, but it turns out it's not."

His voice is calm, as if he doesn't know I'm trying to escape. As if he doesn't know he's trying to stop me. "Please, Elizabeth. Come with me. You'll be helping me as much as I'm helping you."

What on earth could a wizard want my help with? Doesn't he know what I am? I look at him closely. Pale, drawn skin, bags under his dark, bloodshot eyes, his face heavily lined. He looks old, he looks ill, he doesn't look dangerous at all. But then, neither do I. You can't always go by looks in these matters. I suppose if he wanted to hurt me, or see me dead, he wouldn't be here. But I'm not taking any chances.

"I doubt that." I lunge to my right, as if I'm about to run past him. Again, he anticipates it, reaches for me. But it's a feint: I pull back and spin to my left, bolt for the door. I'm not fast enough. The wizard reaches out and snatches my arm, his grasp surprisingly strong for an old man. I don't think. I pull back my other arm, make a fist, and swing.

My hand connects with his face…then passes right through it. I stumble forward, I nearly fall. The wall catches me, and when I turn around, there are two of him. Two identical wizards in two identical sets of robes, speaking identical words:

"I wouldn't do that if I were you."

I don't listen—to either of them. I push down my fear as I launch myself off the wall, lunging for him again. Swing, again. My hand hits nothing, but immediately, two wizards become four.

"Stop," they croon. "Come with me."

A scream rises in my throat. I won't go with him, with

them. I won't go anywhere with a wizard. They step toward me. I swat at them, lash out, hit nothing. Six, eight, ten wizards now: dark cloaks, dark eyes, dark magic. I spin around, looking for a way out. But they surround me, twenty hands reaching, a hundred fingers grasping. I drop to my knees, cover my head.

"I can help you," they chant. "You'll be safe with me."

A wizard can't help me; magic can't help me. There's nothing about magic that doesn't end with you tied to a stake with flames licking at your feet, or on your knees with your head on a block. Straw for kindling, straw to catch your blood...

Straw.

I reach out, snatch a handful of the damp, stinking stuff from the floor and hurl it at him—at them. Watch as they flinch from it. In the split second it takes for them to turn from me, I reach down, pull up the last bit of strength I have, crawl to my feet.

And I run.

Through them, past them, out the door, into the hallway. I don't make it ten steps before my chest seizes up and I start coughing, so hard I can't breathe. I fall to my knees, sucking in air so desperately it sounds like a scream.

I force myself to my feet, stumble another few steps. Through the darkness I can just make out a set of stone stairs, maybe thirty feet away. I can make it thirty more feet....

In a swirl of a black cloak, he appears, faster than I could have imagined, standing before me—just one of him now—his hands outstretched.

"No," I say. It comes out a whimper.

A *whoosh* of warm air surrounds me and I feel myself

start to fall. But the warmth disappears as quickly as it appeared—his spell either stopped or broken—and I regain my footing. The wizard mutters something, impatient. He raises his hand again. But instead of surrounding me with more air, he reaches for me. Grasps my arm.

"Come with me," he commands. *"Now."*

I start to yank away, but then I pause, thinking fast. I need to get out of here. But maybe if I capture this wizard, it would be enough to prove to Blackwell he still needs me. Enough to make him reconsider my sentence.

Enough to make him decide not to kill me.

The wizard takes my arm again, and this time, I let him... until I'm hit with stomach cramps so strong I collapse to my knees again. He reaches down and scoops me into his arms, lifting me easily. I'm too weak to fight it. He carries me down the hall, toward the stairs. I can see the other prisoners in their cells now, watching us pass. They'll start shouting soon. Screaming. The guards will be on us within seconds.

But as we pass each cell, the prisoners that can still stand rise to their feet and nod their heads at him. Some call murmured blessings to him, others reach out through their bars to try to touch him. Their reverence startles me.

"Who are you?" I whisper.

"I am Nicholas Perevil," he says. "Forgive me for not introducing myself earlier. But you didn't give me much of a chance."

I stiffen in his arms. *Nicholas Perevil! The most wanted wizard in Anglia!* I can't believe my luck. If I brought him in, Blackwell would certainly pardon me. He might even honor me. I give a little nod, force myself to relax. I don't want to tip him to my plan.

63

We reach the end of the hall, pass through a narrow archway into one of four circular towers that surround the main prison building, then down a flight of narrow, winding steps.

We go down, farther and farther, until we come out underneath the prison. The walls here are damp, the air cold and foul. He must be heading for the sewer drains. It's where I'd have gone, too. They're easy enough to find and always unguarded. For obvious reasons.

How will I do it? I run through plan after plan. I'm weak, yes. But I could stun him with a kick or two. How will I restrain him once he's down? His rope belt: perfect. I look around for something I can knock him out with—a brick, stone, anything. If I had to, I could jam my thumbs into his eyes.... Oh, no—

The stomach cramps are back. They're agony. I begin to moan.

"Elizabeth? Are you all right?"

I start retching. There's nothing in my stomach but bile— it burns my throat as I vomit all over him. I can't stop shaking. Surely he'll dump me on the ground now, and I'll get my chance. Instead, he holds me tighter and walks even faster.

"Hold on. We'll get you help soon, I promise. Just hold on."

Finally, we reach the entrance to the sewer tunnel. It's a small hole in the wall, about three feet square and covered with thin iron mesh. That's to contain the rats.

Nicholas kicks it open and immediately they start pouring out. Hundreds, maybe thousands of them, crawling over the floor and across the walls. A writhing mass of greasy fur and tails, chittering and squeaking, claws scratching on stone, the overpowering smell of sewage…I give an enormous shudder and start retching again.

"We'll have to go in one at a time." His voice, deep and clear, sounds very far away. "I'll go first, then help you after. Can you do it?"

I nod. As soon as he climbs inside, I'll attack.

"You're a brave girl." He sets me down against the wall before crawling through the hole into the sewer. Seconds later his head pops out, arms outstretched. "Come on."

All I have to do is kick him. I can crush his windpipe. I can break his nose. I can knock him down and tie him up and take him in. This is my chance. I pull my leg back and take aim.

In the distance, I hear shouts. Footsteps. I can hear them coming down the stairs. The guards, they know I've escaped. The unending stream of rats must have tipped them off.

"Elizabeth!" Nicholas whispers. "Now!"

I hesitate, my leg still poised to kick. There are a hundred reasons I should hurt him. A hundred ways I could do it. Instead, I do the one thing I could never have imagined.

I reach for him.

He gently pulls me through the opening and into his arms. I curl into them like a child. I'm shaking so hard now. Nicholas tightens his grip and draws me closer. I rest my head against his shoulder and close my eyes. I can't help it. I'm so very, very tired.

He carries me through the endless maze of tunnels, through the rats and the filth and the stench. After what seems like hours, we emerge, the tunnel emptying under a bridge by the river. Near the opening is a horse, waiting to take us to freedom.

He takes off his cloak, wraps it tightly around me, and lifts me into the saddle. Then he climbs on behind me.

"You'll be all right now." He holds me steady and urges the horse forward.

Why didn't I capture him? I don't know. I only hope I can escape before he finds out what I am. Or that whatever illness I have will kill me before he can.

Will Caleb miss me when I die?

It's the last thing I think before I close my eyes.

7

I HEAR VOICES AROUND ME, quiet and whispered. But everything is still dark. I will my eyes to open, but they refuse.

"Is she going to die?" A boy. He sounds familiar.

"Ugh. Smells as if she already did." A girl this time.

"Fifer..." Another boy, sounding exasperated. "George, hand me that bottle."

"What? It's not my fault she looks terrible." The girl again.

"Aye, she's scrotty now, but she's quite lovely when not covered in filth." A pause. "What? She is."

"She's doing remarkably well, considering. Jail fever—she's lucky she didn't die."

"She's lucky she has you to help her, John. No one else could go near her! Honestly, I don't know how you stand it."

"Since you're so concerned with the way she smells, you can be the one to clean her up, then."

"Ugh."

This time, my eyes open first. They take a minute to adjust: Everything is blurry around the edges. I stare at the ceiling, blinking hard. Slowly, it comes into focus. Whitewashed plaster, dark green vines painted across the surface, tiny leaves and curlicues trailing down onto the white walls. An iron chandelier hangs by a chain, its many candles unlit. In a daze, I follow one of the vines down the wall, as it winds around a window covered in green velvet curtains. They're pulled tightly closed, no light at all coming in behind them. *Where's the light coming from?*

I turn my head to the other side and see it: a single candle sitting on an otherwise empty table, flickering softly. I watch the tiny column of smoke drift upward from the flame. My eyes begin to close again when I realize I don't know where I am.

I bolt upright, then give a little start when I see I'm not alone. There, sitting in a chair at the end of my bed, is George, the king's fool. I thought his voice sounded familiar.

His feet are propped up on a stool, a blanket draped across him and tucked under his chin. He's sound asleep. Without thinking, I scramble out of bed. To him or away from him, I don't know. But my legs are weaker than I expected and I tumble to the floor.

"Going somewhere?" he murmurs, watching me through one half-opened eye.

"Yes. No. I don't know." I crawl to my knees, clutching the bedcovers around me. "What are you doing here?"

"Ah, yes. The age-old question." He casts his eyes skyward. "Theologists have long believed our time here on earth is—"

"Not that," I snap, and he laughs. "I mean, do you always sleep at the foot of people's beds?"

"Easy." He sits up and drops his feet to the floor. His dark hair is sticking up in all directions, making him look younger than he is. "John said you'd probably be waking up soon. Didn't want you to come to alone, strange place and all."

"Where am I?"

"Nicholas's house. He brought you here after…you know." He shakes his head. "You don't make things very easy, do you?"

Nicholas! I'm at Nicholas Perevil's house. Everything comes back to me in a rush then. The arrest. Being thrown into Fleet. Caleb coming, then failing to return. Then Nicholas showing up, looking for me. Bringing me here.

Wait a minute.

"You're a fool," I say. "Malcolm's fool. What are you doing at Nicholas Perevil's house?"

George stands up and stretches.

"Where are you going?"

"To get Nicholas."

"What? No. Why?"

George gives me a look I can't quite read. "He just wants to talk to you. Asked me to get him as soon as you woke." He crosses the room and reaches his hand down for me. I stare at it a moment, then let him pull me to my feet. "He'll explain everything. I'll be right back." The door closes behind him with a quiet thump.

I pace the room, trying to control my nerves. *I'm in the home of the most dangerous criminal in Anglia, and all he wants to do is talk? Right.*

If George had said Nicholas wants to tie me to a chair and beat me until my eyeballs roll, that I could believe. Drench me in water and put me outside until I freeze to death? Sure. Pour molten lead on my skin. Split my knees, crush my fingers in a thumbscrew, saw off my limbs. Really, the possibilities are endless. Talking is the least likely one of all.

Worse still: What if he performs some kind of spell on me? I think about his coming to me here, the way he came to me in my cell. Multiplying, surrounding, overpowering. I've never seen magic like that before. Never known it was possible. I give a little shiver. Because as much as I hate to admit it, it frightens me.

He frightens me.

I sit back down on the bed then. Look around. There's a fireplace behind the chair where George was sleeping, the fire low but warm. A soft carpet covers the wood floor. The bed is big and soft, the bedcovers lavender-scented and clean. Then I realize, so am I. My filthy dress is gone, replaced by a simple linen shift. It dawns on me that however long I've been here, whatever Nicholas Perevil wants from me, I haven't been ill-treated.

Yet.

I don't know what to do. I can't run, can't hide. My first instinct is to fight, but I can't do that, either. Not without giving myself away. I don't know what they know about me; I don't even know what they want with me. But if I want to get out of here, I'd better find out both.

There's a soft rapping on the door, and before I can respond, Nicholas walks into the room, George close behind.

He's rumpled from sleep and looks even older than I remember. He's got a dark blue dressing gown on, pulled tightly at the waist. He looks me over, then gives me a quick nod. He's so thin I can see the cords in his neck, the sharp angles of his cheekbones.

"How are you feeling?"

"Fine," I say. It's true. Maybe a little weak, and my chest hurts when I breathe. I'm pretty thirsty. Okay, I could eat. But other than that, I really am fine.

Nicholas smiles, as if he's reading my thoughts.

"We have John to thank for that," he says. "He has a gift." With a little groan, he sits in the chair where George had been sleeping. George hovers behind him, looking protective. "And so, Elizabeth, you want to know why you're here."

It's a statement, not a question. I nod.

Nicholas starts to speak when there's a soft tapping on the door. George goes to open it. In walks a young man carrying two pewter goblets. They're steaming slightly, sending tiny puffs of white smoke into the air. He hands one to Nicholas, who grasps it gratefully. Then he walks over to me with the other.

"Elizabeth, this is John Raleigh, our healer," Nicholas says.

Healer? I frown. I can't help it. For the most part, *healer* is just another word for *wizard*. He holds out the goblet to me. I don't take it.

"It's angelica and burdock," he tells me.

I shrug. If it's not an herb that can poison or kill, I don't know it.

"It's just a blood purifier. Plus something to help your stomach. That's all." A pause. "Well, I added in a little cucumber for your fever, some burnet and elm for your cough. A bit of oat for your rash. Mugwort, too, because you have fleas. And a couple of drops of poppy, just to help you relax. But that really is it. I swear."

He smiles then. It's a nice smile, warm and friendly. Not the smile of someone who wants to fill me with poison and watch me drop to the carpet and foam at the mouth and twitch out a slow, agonizing death in front of him. Still, when he offers the goblet again, I don't take it.

Maybe he knows what I'm thinking, because he says, "If I wanted to harm you, I wouldn't have given you anything at all. You've been drinking it since you got here."

I look at George. I don't know why, but I feel that if I were about to drink a fat batch of poison, he would tell me. Or at least make a joke about it beforehand.

He nods.

I snatch the goblet from the healer's hand and drink the whole thing in one swallow. It tastes like celery.

John laughs a little, as if I've done something funny. He doesn't look like a typical healer, at least the ones I've seen. Most of them are old, gray, and toothless. Not to mention female. But he's young, my age. Maybe a bit older. Longish dark curly hair, hazel eyes. Tall. A little scruffy, as if he needs a shave. But maybe that's because it's the middle of the night. When I hand him back the goblet, I notice his shirt is buttoned up wrong.

He takes it and goes to check on Nicholas, who doesn't

need an explanation of what's in his cup. But I wonder what is. He places his hand on Nicholas's forehead, then around his wrist. He frowns.

"Not too long, all right?" John looks at me. "That goes for you, too."

I raise my eyebrows.

Nicholas smiles at me. "He's very strict." He nods at John.

"Like a priest on Sunday," chimes in George.

John responds with something a priest on Sunday definitely would not do. George and Nicholas crack up with laughter. I start to smile, but stop immediately.

"I'll check on you both in the morning," John says, walking to the door.

"You don't have to do that," I blurt. Healers make me nervous. And the idea of this too young and far too male healer coming into my room—alone, when I'm in bed—makes me even more nervous.

"Whyever not?" George asks, mystified. "He's only been checking on you every hour since you got here. If we're down to twice a day now, that's a vast improvement."

I feel my cheeks grow hot. Every hour? Was he the one who changed my gown? Cleaned me up? No, that was the girl. God, I hope it was the girl.

"It's not necessary, that's all. I'm fine," I say again, but John isn't even looking at me. He's scowling at George.

Then he turns to me with a small smile. "Don't argue with the clergy." He closes the door quietly behind him.

Nicholas leans back in his chair and sips his drink. I wait for him to say something, but he just sits there, tapping his fingernail on the goblet and staring at its contents. Finally, he speaks.

"Elizabeth, up until now, you have been a good and loyal subject of King Malcolm, have you not?"

"Yes."

"As such, you have, up until now, abided by the rules and laws of his kingdom, correct?"

I hesitate a little, then nod. *Where is he going with this?*

"Whether or not you believed his rules to be fair."

That's where. "Yes."

He drains his goblet and hands it to George. "As you may know, not all of King Malcolm's subjects are as loyal as you. Not all of them abide by his rules. Many of them, myself included, believe his rules are wrong. How could it be right that an innocent girl such as yourself be thrown in jail and sentenced to death? For nothing more than possessing herbs?"

The herbs.

I guess I'm not surprised he knows about them. He knew my name, knew I was in prison. It stands to reason he would know why. And what I used them for.

Who else knows? That healer? The girl? George? A glance at him confirms it: He doesn't meet my eyes, intent now on examining his fingernails. A hot blush works its way up my cheeks again, and I duck my head in hopes of hiding it.

"It's all right," Nicholas says, his deep voice quiet. "You needn't fear recrimination here. There's no one here who will judge you, or harm you. You're safe now."

Safe. It's the same thing he said in prison. Right after he multiplied on me and converged on me and used magic to subdue me. It's enough to remind me of burnings, of death, enough to remind me who my enemy is. I was a fool to forget it, even for an instant.

A fool.

"You." I turn to George. "You're not a fool at all, are you? You're a Reformist. A spy." I can't believe it took me this long to figure it out.

George looks at Nicholas, who nods. "Aye. It's true," George says. "I am a spy. And a Reformist. But believe me, I'm still a fool," he adds, winking.

I can't believe Nicholas managed to place a spy right under Malcolm's nose. More than that, I can't believe he admitted it. This is too much, even for me. I have to get out of here. And the sooner I get this wizard talking, the sooner I can figure out how.

"At Fleet, you told me you were sent to find me," I say to Nicholas. "Who sent you?"

"From time to time we consult a seer. She helps us by telling us things. Things that have not yet happened, things that have already happened but we don't yet know about. Everything she has ever told us has proved to be true, so we take her visions very seriously."

Already, I don't like the sound of this. But he continues.

"The last two times we saw her, she said we had to find you—you, specifically—and bring you here."

"Me?" The fear I felt earlier is back. "Why?"

He shakes his head. "We don't know. She hasn't been able to tell us, at least not yet. Seers can be roundabout at times.

It can take several visions for their meaning to become clear. But now that you're here, that will change. We'll take you to her, and she'll be able to tell us everything."

It may not be clear to Nicholas, but it is to me. This seer, she's finding witch hunters. Because if they're really looking to stop the burnings, killing witch hunters is a good place to start. As soon as they realize that's what I am, they'll start with me.

I can't kill him: Blackwell's rule. I can't fight him or capture him: I'm still too weak and I'm not about to risk his performing any more magic on me. Which leaves only one choice:

Escape.

Out of this house, back to Upminster. Find Caleb and tell him what happened. Lead him straight back here, along with every witch hunter we've got. It's the only hope I have of earning back Blackwell's favor. The only hope I have of getting out of here alive. So I do the only thing I know that is guaranteed to drive both George and Nicholas out of this room: I bury my face in my hands and pretend to cry.

"I'm sorry," I whisper, innocent girl voice. "This is a lot to take in. I think I'm still sick. Perhaps if I had a bit more rest..."

"Of course," Nicholas says, moving to stand. George helps him to his feet. "I understand this has been very trying for you. We can talk in the morning."

"I think I'll feel much better by then," I say. When I'm halfway to Upminster, that is.

George walks Nicholas to the door. "Good night, Elizabeth," he says quietly. "Sleep well." Then he's gone.

I look down to hide my smile. No wonder these Reformists haven't been able to take over. They're far too trusting.

When I look up, George is watching me intently.

"What?"

"Nothing," he says, closing the door. From the inside.

"What are you doing?"

"I thought I'd stay. You know. Since you're so upset and all." He settles back in the chair, propping his feet on the stool and pulling the blanket over him. Then he closes his eyes. I swear I see him smirk.

Not too trusting at all, then.

8

I COULD KILL HIM, OF course; Blackwell has no rule against killing fools. Especially when the fool isn't a fool at all but a Reformist and a spy. I could do it here. I could do it now.

But George won't go down without a fight. He'll call for help and there's no telling who will answer. Wizards, undoubtedly. Reformists, naturally. Spies, witches, healers, God only knows who else is in this house. No matter what, there are more of them than there are of me. I'm not strong enough to fight all of them at once, then make it back to Upminster. Not the way I am now. I have no clothes, no coat, no weapons. I don't even have shoes. It's one thing to escape under these conditions. To fight in them, another thing entirely.

All I can do now is watch and wait. Watch my surroundings, watch my back. Wait to get stronger, wait for an opportunity to present itself. It always does.

Satisfied with my plan, I slip under the warm covers. Within moments, I'm asleep.

When I wake next, it's daytime. George is standing in front of the fireplace, poking at a log with his toe. He's fully dressed, wearing green trousers, a red-and-white-striped shirt, and some sort of vest.

"Good afternoon," he says without turning around.

I roll my eyes. "Am I ever going to get rid of you?"

"Is that any way to greet your new best friend?" He turns around and gives me a grin. The front of his vest is brightly embroidered in red, green, and blue, and he's wearing a gold brooch with an enormous red feather sticking out of it.

"You look like a Yule tree. You know that, right?"

"Wait 'til you see my hat," he says. "Now get up. I'm starving and tired of waiting around for you."

"What time is it?"

George sniffs the air hopefully. "Smells like supper. You hungry?"

"Not really," I say.

Oddly, I'm not as hungry as I should be, given that I haven't eaten in...I have no idea how long.

He nods. "John's been adding things to your potions— infusions and whatnot—so you wouldn't starve. I guess you're still full from breakfast."

I feel my eyes go wide. "Breakfast? He came in this morning?"

"Aye, he said he would. Remember?"

79

"I remember him saying he would. I don't remember him actually doing it." I frown. "How can you people come in and make me drink things without me knowing? Or remembering? That's not right."

George looks at me solemnly. "Maybe not. But the day you got here, we thought you were dead. You looked it; you were damn near to it. John stayed with you, made sure you didn't die. He didn't sleep for nearly three days."

Three days? My stomach twists with an uncomfortable mix of gratitude, guilt, and something else I can't name. I don't know what to say.

"Anyway, when he couldn't stay awake any longer, I stepped in," George continues. "He wanted someone with you, in case you had a relapse."

"It still doesn't explain why I don't remember any of this."

"Ah." George's mouth twitches into a smile. "As I say, you looked pretty bad when you got here, so John brewed something up. He held you, tried to get you to drink it. As soon as the cup touched your lips, you went completely mental."

"I did?"

"Aye. Started thrashing, screaming, cursing. You have a mouth like a pirate, you know that? It's not very ladylike."

In the most unladylike way possible, I tell him what he can do with his opinion.

He cracks a laugh. "Poor John. You kicked him in the stomach, drenched him with his own medicine, then banged him on the head with your cup. He brewed you more but this time added something to calm you down." He smirks. "Knocked you out a bit, but it worked."

"You don't say."

"Oh yes. No more privy-mouth Lizzie. Got real sweet after you drank it, all smiles and sugar. We decided that version of you was easier to manage, so we kept giving it to you. Do you know you talk in your sleep?"

"I do not," I say, horrified.

He nods. "I've been with you every night and getting an earful. Swoony little maid, you are, going on about running off with some boy. Caleb, is it?"

Damnation.

"It's nothing," I say quickly.

"It's the stuff of romance books. Who needs knights in shining armor or handsome princes when you have Ca-leb?" He draws out his name in a singsong voice.

"It's not like that." I feel my face go hot again. "He's a friend."

Then I stop. If George bothers to ask around, he'll realize exactly who Caleb is. And if he knows I'm friends with a witch hunter, it won't be long before he knows that's what I am, too. I can't exactly lie and say I don't know him, not after I talked about him in my sleep. The only thing I can do is put as much distance between us as possible.

"But I haven't seen him in years," I add quickly. "We grew up together. Worked in the kitchens together. I liked it; he didn't. So we went our separate ways." It's not too far from the truth, anyway. "I guess I just miss him sometimes. You said yourself it looked as if I could use a friend." This isn't too far from the truth, either.

George walks over and sits down next to me.

"I'm sorry," he says. "I shouldn't have said anything. But

not to worry. You'll make plenty of friends here. Charming girl like you, who can resist?"

"According to you, I kicked John and cursed out everyone in the room," I say. "I would hardly call that charming."

"It was." He laughs. "The cursing was the best part. It's funny to hear something so salty coming from someone who looks so sweet."

A smile tugs at the corner of my mouth.

George pulls me to my feet. "Come on. Get dressed so we can eat. There are clothes in the wardrobe. When you see John, be sure to tell him you're sorry. That kick you gave him knocked him clear across the room." Then he leaves, shutting the door behind him.

I cross the room, open the wardrobe. It's empty inside, save for a single stack of clothing. A pale green silk tunic; tan close-fitting trousers. A wide brown belt and a pair of sturdy brown boots, both a size too big. A hairpin. Bronze and delicate, one end tipped with glittering green jewels, the other tapered into a sharp, deadly point. I twist my hair up into a knot and work it in. Then I step back and examine myself in the mirror fastened to the back of the wardrobe door.

I don't like what I see.

The remnants of my illness are everywhere. In my skin, so pale I can see a network of bluish veins under the surface. In my eyes, the way the color seems to have faded, once bright but now a pale, watery blue. In my body, so thin I can see the ridges in my sternum, exposed by the deep V of the tunic. Even my hair seems muted: a weak, tired blond.

There's no hint of the strength I worked so hard to build. No hint of the training I went through to get it. Nothing at all to show that, for a time, I was one of the best witch hunters in Anglia. Instead, I look fragile. Sickly. If I look better now than when I arrived, it's no wonder they thought I was going to die. I think again of the healer and feel another pang of gratitude, guilt, and the feeling I couldn't place before that now has a name: doubt.

John used magic to heal me. If he hadn't, I'd be lying stiff and blue in that bed, the way that witch lay stiff and blue in my cell. Magic is wrong—I know this. Blackwell drilled into us, over and over, the danger of it. I spent two years fighting it, seven years recovering from it. I'm still not recovered. But if Caleb had been the one to pull me out of Fleet, if he'd seen how sick I was, would he have done whatever it took—even if it meant using magic—to keep me alive? Or would he simply have let me die?

I slam the wardrobe door harder than necessary and meet George in the hallway. It occurs to me that I have no idea how long I've been here.

"Two weeks, give or take," George says as we walk to the stairs.

Two weeks. Of course, Caleb knows I've escaped. Is he pleased? Worried? I don't know why he didn't come back to get me, but something must have happened. For the first time, it occurs to me he might be in danger. What if Blackwell thinks he had a hand in my escape? What if he's been arrested? What if he's being tortured?

The thought distresses me so much that I careen into the wall, smacking into a heavy, gold-framed painting.

"Easy." George reaches behind me to straighten it. "You all right?"

"Fine," I say. "I guess I'm just nervous. You know?"

The words come out without thinking, but I realize they're true. I am nervous. Facing all these people, dining with them. The wizard who rescued me, the boy who healed me, the girl who bathed me, the fool who befriended me. I'm indebted to each of them in some way, yet they are my enemies. They've shown me kindness, yet I'm prepared to kill them. The whole thing is so confusing that it curls my stomach into a hard, tight knot.

"Aye." He turns to me with a sympathetic smile. "If it gets to be too much, just excuse yourself. Say you aren't feeling well. Everyone will understand."

"I'll be fine."

George stares at me a moment.

"Take a look around," he says, spreading his arms. "I know you're used to the king's palace, but this is quite a fine home, too. Take this rug, for example." He gestures to the rug that runs the length of the hall. It's beautiful, woven in shades of dark blue, yellow, and green. "It was woven by a blind woman with a missing arm. Amazing, isn't it? It's over five hundred years old. Of course, it took her that long to finish it..."

"Is that so?"

"Oh yes," he says solemnly. "See, the key to investing in fine objects for your home is to find artisans with as many disadvantages as possible. Greatly increases the value."

I roll my eyes, but he keeps going.

"See this portrait here?" He points to the one I nearly knocked off the wall, of a sour-faced woman. "It was painted by a dwarf. Had to stand on a ladder just to reach the easel.

You know, paintings done by dwarves are triple the value of paintings done by regular-sized men."

I feel a tiny smile creep across my lips.

"And these—" George gestures to the brass candlesticks fitted along the dark wood-paneled wall. They're each shaped like a fleur-de-lis. "The blacksmith had no arms, no legs. Can you imagine? He used nothing but his teeth and tongue to forge those. That's extraordinary. You can't put a price on that."

I laugh then. I can't help it. George places his hand on my arm and we start back down the hall. He's halfway through a story about a deaf lute maker when I realize we're downstairs already, standing in the middle of an enormous entrance hall.

Directly in front of me is a set of wooden doors. They're flanked by large mullioned windows, each inset with a symbol in stained glass. A small sun surrounded by a square, then a triangle, then another circle that is actually a snake with its tail in its mouth.

The symbol of the Reformists.

It's an alchemical glyph; a series of symbols, each with its own meaning. The sun for illumination: a dawn of a new existence. A square representing the physical world. The triangle a symbol for fire: a catalyst for change. The snake—an Ouroboros—for unity.

Combined, the shapes form the symbol for the creation of the philosopher's stone: the substance for turning ordinary metal into gold. That's not what the Reformists are trying to achieve—that's for alchemists—but the end goal is the same: change. They're trying to create change in Anglia. Change in policy, change in mind-set, a change in the way magic is viewed.

And much like the idea of changing ordinary metal into gold, it's impossible.

"He can't hear the lute, so you'll never guess how he tunes it," George continues. "He takes the neck and sticks it in his—what?"

I look over his shoulder and see them sitting around an enormous dining table. I don't see who or what they are, or how many. I barely register them. Because what's happening in there, in that room, the magic, no.

I take a step backward, then another. My heart picks up speed and my stomach tightens, the way it does before a hunt. Only there's no one to hunt, not without giving myself away. I can't even run, though I want to. I want to get as far away from this as I can.

Where there should be a ceiling, there isn't. Just a vast expanse of sky, the entire universe spinning in the darkness above me.

9

I STARE AT IT.

At the sky, black and dark and empty as the moonless night I was arrested on. At the stars that spin against it: some white and bright, some small and glowing pale. At the planets that bob among them like colorful marbles, revolving in wide, lazy circles around a bright orange sun.

Then at Nicholas, who sits beneath it all: arms stretched upward, a benevolent God—or perhaps not—flicking his hand this way and back; a conductor, the planets and stars dancing to his tune.

I watch in horrified fascination as a line appears across the sky, a series of tiny numbers and glyphs appearing beside it. Nicholas turns to the man beside him. He's dressed in all black like a clerk, a fat leather book in one hand, a pen poised in the other.

"Transiting orb, two degrees, Neptune in trine with natal Jupiter," Nicholas murmurs. He pauses to allow the clerk time to write it down. "Tell him he'd be better off waiting. The fourteenth of next month, though no later. Whatever trifles he's got, they can wait. He might consider a few days of restful silence as well. His wife, I know, will be glad of the break."

Everyone around the table laughs.

It's astrology; I know that much from training. Many wizards consult astrology tables, looking to divine answers in the planets and stars. They're common enough; I've come across dozens in houses of wizards I've captured. But never, not once, have I seen a wizard create a full-scale replica of the sky like this. And, like the way he multiplied himself in front of me at Fleet, I don't know how he's doing it. I don't know how it's possible.

I back up another step. Then, just as if the stars directed him to, Nicholas looks up. His eyes meet mine across the table. He holds up a hand; the clerk stops writing. Silence falls. I don't need to look, because I can feel them, the eyes of everyone in the room on me.

"Elizabeth!"

The sound of my name, shouted across the universe, snaps me from my daze. At once, the sky disappears, the stars disappear, the planets and the sun disappear. Into nothing, winking out as if they never were. It's just an ordinary ceiling now, open to the rafters, a half dozen small chandeliers hanging at intervals over the table.

I look down to see a man striding toward me. I know him. Curly black hair, short black beard. Even without that dog's head pipe in his mouth, I know him.

"You!" I gasp. It's Peter. *What on earth is a pirate doing here?*

"Me." He laughs. He clasps my shoulders, then plants a loud smacking kiss on each of my cheeks. I can feel myself blushing. "Pleased to see me, love?"

I don't know. Am I? He seems harmless enough, kind even. But how harmless can a Reformist pirate really be? Before I can answer, Peter drapes his arm around my shoulders and pulls me into the dining room. Stone walls, stone floors. A row of stained glass windows on one side of the long, polished wooden table, a heavy cabinet on the other, piled high with food.

I stumble after him, uncomfortably aware of the stares still leveled in my direction, of the flush still on my face, of my heart still knocking against my rib cage.

"Looking so lovely, too," Peter continues. "Far better than when I saw you last. But then, it's hard to look good when your eyeballs are floating in absinthe, eh?" He thrusts me into the chair next to John.

"Father," John groans.

I forget my discomfort for a moment and turn to him, incredulous.

"He's your father?"

John nods. I notice he's blushing a little, too.

"Naturally!" Peter booms, walking around the table and throwing himself into the chair opposite mine. "Where else do you think the boy got his good looks?" He waves his hand in John's direction. "A specimen that fine can only come from the loins of a pirate!"

John groans again and buries his head in his hands.

"Dear God, please don't let him use the word *loins* ever again," George whispers, sitting down next to me.

"Why don't we move on to introductions?" Peter continues. "Now, there's Nicholas, of course. Him you know already."

Nicholas smiles at me. In the ordinary candlelight, he looks less godlike, more man, and an ill man at that. His face is drawn and haggard, his skin translucent and gray. He's clutching another steaming mug of something I'm guessing John made for him.

"Welcome, Elizabeth." His voice is warm. "I'm so pleased to see you're feeling better."

"Thank you," I say. My voice comes out weak and timid. I don't like it. I clear my throat and try again. "I am feeling better."

"I do hope I didn't startle you with my little display." He holds his arms wide again. "I take it you've not seen much magic before?"

It's a loaded question. If I say I have seen magic, he'll want to know where and who performed it. He might assume there are other witches—if that's what he thinks I am—living in the king's household. He might start asking questions. One question will lead to another, and...

"No," I lie at once. "That was only my second time. The first was at Fleet."

Nicholas nods. "I assure you that everything practiced in my home is harmless, if not beneficial. I know I said this before, but perhaps it bears repeating. I promise that no harm will come to you here."

His words, they're kind. But I don't believe them for a moment.

90

Peter claps his hands, moving on. "John and George you also already know, but this"—he gestures to the girl to Nicholas's right—"is Fifer Birch. She's a student of Nicholas's, been working with him for years. She's his star pupil!"

Pupil. I take this to mean witch. She's my age, maybe younger. Thin, with dark red hair and pale skin dotted with freckles. She looks me over, her eyes drifting from my face to my hair to my shirt—which I now realize is her shirt—then back to my face. Her eyebrows are raised, her lips pursed. Skeptical. Finally, she turns away from me and whispers something to Nicholas.

"Lastly, this is Gareth Fish." Peter points to the man still hovering beside Nicholas, his book still open, pen still poised. Tall, thin, cadaverous. He wears thin-framed spectacles and a thin-lipped pout, clearly irritated at the interruption. "He's a member of our council and serves as a liaison between Nicholas and, well, everyone. Mainly the citizens of Harrow, of course, but anyone anywhere, really. Anyone who needs his help."

Harrow. Short for Harrow-On-The-Hill, a village full of Reformists, of witches, of magic. It's hidden away somewhere in Anglia, only its inhabitants know where. It became a refuge once the Inquisition started, and if you had any magical power or Reformist leanings at all—and didn't go into exile or prison—you went there. It's the nexus of the Reformist movement, and Blackwell would give just about anything to find it.

Gareth gives me a curt nod before turning back to his book. Apparently, I'm not interesting or impressive enough for more than that. I'm glad he thinks so.

Peter turns to me. "Now that you're here, we can eat. I hope you're hungry." He gestures to the platters of food piled on the cabinet against the wall.

There's the standard fare: chicken, bread, a simple stew. But there's more exotic food here, too, the kind I used to make at court: roast peacock, redressed in its feathers; a platter of quail in what looks like fig sauce; a stargazer pie, the tiny fish heads poking out from under the crust. A platter of fruit, cakes, even an assortment of marchpane: roses, shamrocks, and thistles, all fashioned out of sugar.

I feel my eyes go wide.

"I thought you might be." Peter laughs. "Shall we?" he says to Nicholas.

Nicholas nods and gives his hand a little wave. At once, the platters rise and begin floating in the air. One by one they land gracefully on the table. Once again, I'm shocked. That level of magic is beyond anything I've seen before.

But when the quail lands in front of me, I decide it doesn't matter. I'm starving. I reach for the platter, but John grabs my arm and pulls it back.

"Wait," he says.

"Why?" I briefly wonder if he's questioning my manners.

"It's just that Hastings—that's Nicholas's servant—well, he's a ghost. You have to be careful when he's around." John gestures at the empty air. "He usually wears a white hat so we know where he is, but sometimes he forgets. I usually wait until everything goes still before reaching for anything. I've made the mistake of touching him before." He gives me a sheepish smile. "Hurt like hell."

Being a witch hunter, I've seen a lot of things: revenants,

ghouls, demons, and, yes, ghosts. But never ghost *servants*. Ghosts are known for destroying your home, possessing livestock, and suffocating you in bed, not pouring tea or fluffing pillows.

"I've never heard of a ghost servant before," I say.

"He came with the house," John says. "Used to work for the wizard who owned it before. Mostly cooking, but other things, too. Gardening, cleaning, things like that. Apparently, he was so good at his job that after he died, the wizard brought him back so he could keep doing it."

I think of those necromancers digging up that corpse in Fortune Green. Mossy, decaying, maggots, bones gleaming in the moonlight...

I smile weakly. "Well, you know what they say. Good help is hard to find and all that."

John laughs. Across the table, Peter looks from John to me then back to John again. He's smiling.

"Nicholas keeps offering to send him on, but he wants to stay," John continues. "And he's great, really. I mean, the not seeing him part takes some getting used to, plus he's hard to understand. Half the time it feels as if he's just blowing in my ear."

I manage another smile, a real one this time.

"Anyway, it looks all right now." John nods at the table. "I imagine you're hungry."

"A little." It seems rude to say yes, especially after all the trouble he went to brewing me those potions.

"Dig in, then. Hastings is an excellent cook."

I watch him pile his plate high with food. After a minute I do the same, taking huge helpings of strawberries and cake.

If Caleb saw this, he'd laugh and tell me to save room for supper. I always eat dessert first.

The mood at the table is relaxed, everyone eating and making small talk. No one speaks to me directly, and aside from the occasional glance from John, no one even looks at me. I relax a little, look around. Still amazed at what I see.

Before, whenever I thought of Nicholas Perevil, I imagined him holed up in a dank, drafty cottage somewhere. Tattered robes, matted hair, living off grubs and acorns and tea made from leaves. A fugitive. The most wanted criminal in Anglia.

The table in front of me tells a different story. I glance at my plate. Pewter, definitely valuable. The silverware. Finely wrought and highly ornate. A tablecloth made from soft-spun linen instead of coarse muslin. Fine candles made from beeswax instead of rushes dipped in tallow with a flame stinking of animal fat.

He's not foraging for food. He's not selling his possessions to raise an army. He's not wanting for anything. This is the kind of information Blackwell would want to know. Information he'd pay a king's ransom to know. Because he'll know, as I know, it means Nicholas is receiving help— and money—from somewhere. But from where? And from who?

I pick up my glass and examine it. It's thick and heavy, probably crystal. The stem is made up of three intertwined snakes, the bowl perched on top of their heads. I'm wondering what the disadvantage of the glassblower was—aside from having questionable taste—when Gareth speaks.

"Have you told her yet?"

Her. I set my glass down on the table with a thud. "Told me what?"

"I was going to wait until later to tell her, in private." Nicholas's voice is low, full of warning. Gareth seems not to notice.

"Tell me what?" I repeat.

Peter clears his throat. "The thing is, Elizabeth, Gareth just came in from Upminster," he says. "And things there, well, they're a little worse than they were three weeks ago."

Three weeks ago there were protests, burnings, and I was accused of witchcraft and sentenced to death. How could things possibly be worse?

"I know Nicholas already told you about Veda, our seer, that she sent us to find you," Peter continues. "But while she gave us your name, she didn't give us much else. Not where you were, not what you looked like. It was down to us to figure it out.

"We managed to locate two people named Elizabeth Grey. You and a witch from Seven Sisters. We thought for certain Veda meant her. I don't know what kind of magic she can do, but she was certainly more…formidable than you. She weighed about fifteen stone."

Beside me, George lets out a snort.

"So we let you go. A mistake in hindsight, of course, but we're not in the business of rounding up people for interrogation." Peter's dark eyes flash with sudden anger. "But if we had, we could have avoided"—he waves his hand—"all this."

"My arrest," I say.

"Among other things."

"What other things?" I look around the room. Gareth, suddenly interested in me; George, suddenly interested in the ceiling; John, turning his fork over and over in his hand; Fifer, looking somewhat gleeful.

Finally, Nicholas speaks.

"Your arrest, your escape. Your story, unfortunately, is all over Upminster. More unfortunate is what that story has turned into. That you're not just a kitchen maid, but a spy and a witch. A secret Reformist in league with me, spying on the king and queen while feeding us information. Conjuring spells against them, using herbs in an attempt to poison them. You're now the most wanted person in Anglia."

I gasp at this litany of accusation.

"They say this?"

Nicholas nods. "It's quite a scandal. The queen is said to be distraught, completely inconsolable." He smiles then: hard, ironic. "They're generating a lot of sympathy for it. Even to a public who is angry with their monarch, it's too much. They're calling for blood. Only this time, it's not the king's, the queen's, or even Blackwell's. It's yours."

I drop my head into my hands, stunned. That Blackwell accused me of this, that Malcolm believes it. That it went this far, this fast. And I know, with dreadful certainty, that whatever hope I had about regaining Blackwell's favor is gone. Maybe I should have known better; maybe I did. But it was the only thing I had to hope for. It wasn't the job I loved so much; it was never that. It's that it was the only home I had. Now there's no going home for me.

Ever.

"We know it's a lie," John says. I lift my head to find him watching me closely, his eyes dark but sympathetic. "They just needed something to divert the public's attention from the burnings. A scapegoat. You're safe with us. We'll protect you."

"But who will protect us?" Gareth says. Everyone's attention shifts to him. "She's exposing us to a great deal of danger when we don't know what she can do." He gestures at me with a long white hand. "Whatever it is, it better be worth it, considering the price on her head."

"How much?" I blurt.

"A thousand sovereigns."

George lets out a soundless whistle, then leans over to pour me a glass of wine. The most Blackwell was ever prepared to pay for Nicholas was five hundred. I reach for my glass.

"Yes, she's very valuable," Gareth continues. "But she'd better deliver on it. Otherwise, what's to stop us from sending George to turn her in and collect that reward? We could fund a nice army with that."

John drops his fork to the table with a thud.

"We're not going to turn her in," Nicholas replies, a sharp edge sliding into his voice. "There's no need to make threats."

"The charts—" Gareth begins.

"Are inconclusive," Nicholas finishes. "Veda will tell us what we need to know."

"The witch hunters—" Gareth tries again.

"Will come," Nicholas says. "As they always have. And we will be careful, as we always have. Elizabeth being here doesn't change anything. Blackwell will never stop hunting us."

"That's another thing," Gareth says. "It's not Blackwell after us now. He's sent someone else. A new Inquisitor. Someone called Caleb Pace."

I SQUEEZE MY GLASS SO tightly that it shatters in my hand. A lot of wine but very little blood splashes onto the cream-colored tablecloth, staining it a deep crimson. I let out a gasp and shove my hand into my lap.

Caleb is the new Inquisitor?

The others—except for Gareth and Fifer—look at me with alarm.

"Elizabeth!" Peter cries. "Are you all right?"

Am I all right? No. Definitely not. When did Caleb get promoted to Inquisitor? Why? And if he's the new Inquisitor, what does that make Blackwell?

"Let me take a look." John pulls a clean napkin off the table and reaches for my hand. Another problem. If he sees there's no blood…

"No." I yank my hand away. "Not here. It's the blood. I may faint." I look down, trying to appear sick. It's not hard.

"John, why don't you take her upstairs," Nicholas says. "Hastings, can you bring him what he needs?"

As John rattles off a list of supplies, I feel a surge of heat in my abdomen followed by a prickling sensation. The wound is starting to heal. I tighten my fist around the thick shards of glass, pressing them into my skin, wincing as they cut deep, down to the bone. But it gets the blood flowing again. John wraps his napkin gently around my hand and helps me to stand.

"Hold on." Fifer, so quiet throughout dinner, speaks up. Her voice is raspy, almost gritty-sounding, a surprising contrast to how young she looks. "This new Inquisitor. This Caleb." She says his name as though it were anathema. "You don't know him, do you?"

I feel George's eyes on me. Wondering if this is the same Caleb I talked about in my sleep, the same Caleb I said was my childhood friend. I spoke his name to Nicholas, too, when I was inside Fleet.

I think about denying it. Then I remember what Blackwell told us: If ever we got caught, tell the truth, as much as doesn't condemn you. The less you lie, the less chance there is of confusing your own story. Not that it mattered anyway. He also told us that if we ever got caught, we were on our own.

"Yes," I say. "I know him."

The table around me goes still.

"And?"

I take a breath. "And we were friends. Once."

"Friends," Gareth repeats. "You were friends with the Inquisitor, and you didn't think to tell anyone this?"

"I didn't know he was the Inquisitor," I say.

"Don't play games," Gareth snaps. His eyes fall to my hand. "Is that why you broke the glass? Because you're friends with him still, in league with him? Because you plan on escaping and leading him here? Is that why you stand there, looking so shocked?"

I feel a hot blush climb up my cheeks. That was my plan, of course, and now I feel caught. Cornered by the enemy and exposed by my lies and I don't know what to do.

"I did tell someone about him," I say, finally. "I told George. I told him Caleb and I grew up together, at the palace. That we worked in the kitchen together."

The others look at George for confirmation.

"Aye. She did tell me that. Only..." He clears his throat, uncomfortable. "You didn't tell me he was a witch hunter."

I take another breath, force down the tide of panic rising in my chest.

"No," I say. "I didn't tell you he was a witch hunter, because I didn't see any reason to."

"No reason—" Gareth sputters.

Nicholas holds up a hand. "Let her speak."

"We were very young when we met," I say. "We both lost our parents. And for a long time, we only had each other. Then we grew up. Caleb wanted to be a witch hunter; I didn't. So we drifted apart."

"You say you drifted apart," Nicholas says. "Yet you called out for him, the day I came for you at Fleet. Why?"

I feel Nicholas's eyes on me, and I turn to meet them head on.

"Because I was ill. Because I was in prison for a week and no one came for me. Because I"—my voice catches, and I hate myself for it—"I was hoping that the first friend I ever had would be the last person I ever saw. That's all."

No one says anything to this, so I continue.

"I didn't break the glass because I'm in league with him. I broke the glass because I don't like the idea of my childhood friend coming after me to try to kill me."

I look around the table. Nicholas and Peter watch me closely, George, too; but they don't look angry or suspicious. John is still behind me, his arm still pressed against mine. He hasn't moved or shifted backward. He's done nothing to make me think he's angry or suspicious, either. Only Gareth and Fifer look doubtful, but they looked that way the moment I walked into the room.

"I think she's one of them," Gareth says. "A plant. A way for them to try to infiltrate the enemy camp—"

"Five people is hardly a camp," Peter remarks. "Six, if we include you, and you've only just arrived."

Gareth waves it away. "Then what do you make of her being friends with the Inquisitor?"

"Elizabeth already explained that they're not," Nicholas replies. "The evidence of that is clear. Were they still friends, he wouldn't have left her to die in prison."

The baldness of his words, the simplicity of them, hits me like a slap to the face.

"Nevertheless, she's still acquainted with the enemy—"

"It was a long time ago," Nicholas interrupts. His voice is calm but final. "We can't hold her accountable for what her friend—former friend, rather—chose to become." He smiles. "Now, if you please, John, could you take Elizabeth upstairs? Her hand is in dire need of attendance."

I look down. The white napkin John used as a bandage is now stained through with blood. The glass. I didn't realize I was still squeezing it.

John steers me out of the dining room, up the stairs, down the hall, and past the endless expanse of paintings and sconces. I don't remember which door is mine, but he does. We stop in front of one halfway to the end. John leans around me to open it.

On the table beside the bed is a tray piled high: a bowl of steaming water, bundles of herbs, an array of tiny metal instruments, and a stack of clean white towels and bandages. There's even a pitcher of wine and a platter of food. Yet for all that, there's no place for us to sit. Well, no place except the bed.

I glance at John, who surveys the scene with a slightly furrowed brow. After a beat, two, he clears his throat and gestures toward it.

"Do you, uh, is that all right..." His gaze shifts around the room as if he were wishing a set of chairs would magically appear—or that he might disappear.

"It's fine," I say, and cross the room to the bed, made now—the green coverlet pulled smooth and tight across the mattress. I perch on the edge, my feet firmly planted on the floor as if this might somehow lessen the intimacy of sitting on a bed with a boy I don't know—or for that matter, one I do know.

But my discomfort is nothing to the worry that underneath the napkin my hand is beginning to heal, the skin stitching itself together by the second.

John closes the door, pauses, then moves to sit beside me, the mattress shifting under his weight and shifting me along with it. We're so close now our shoulders touch. He looks at me, hesitates, then takes my hand.

"Let's have a look." He peels off the bloodstained napkin.

"I thought it was magic," I blurt.

"You thought what was magic?"

"The platters. Downstairs. Before you told me about Hastings, I thought it was magic."

"Oh. I guess it would look that way." He takes a pair of tweezers from the tray. "Nicholas could do that, I suppose. But he wouldn't waste his energy, at least not now. Hold still." He pulls out the first shard of glass. I hold my breath, willing the wound not to heal. At least not in front of his very eyes.

"Why not?" I think of Nicholas's face, gray and drawn. Of the potions he's always drinking, of the last spell he performed on me inside Fleet, the one that faltered, then failed. "Is it because he's sick?"

John doesn't reply. He just keeps working on my hand.

But I keep going. "What's wrong with him? Can't you heal him? I mean, if you can heal me, and I had jail fever, then why not him? Jail fever is the worst thing out there. Except maybe plague, but he doesn't have that, I'd have noticed. Is it sweating sickness? No, if it were that, he'd be dead by now...."

I'm babbling, I know. Any second he's going to notice

something's not right. That my hand isn't as cut up as it should be. He's going to put two and two together, and when he does, I'm going to have to take him out. For some reason, I don't think I'll enjoy it.

"It's not an illness, at least not in the way you're thinking," John finally says. He drops the tweezers on the tray and picks up the herbs, crumbling them carefully into the water. I can't believe it. He doesn't seem to have noticed a thing. "It's a curse."

"Nicholas is cursed?" I'm surprised, but maybe I shouldn't be. Nicholas didn't get to be the head of the Reformists without picking up a few enemies along the way.

"Yes. That's what's making him sick. On the outside, it looks like pneumonia. Which would be bad enough. But on the inside, it's much worse than that. It's eating him up. There are things I can do to make him feel better, but I can't make it go away." He takes my hand and gently places it in the bowl. The water smells like mint and makes my skin tingle pleasantly. "If we can't find a way to stop it, eventually it will kill him."

If Nicholas died, the Reformist movement would probably die along with him. The rebellions and protests would end; things would go back to normal. Normal for everyone except for Nicholas, the Reformists, and the witches and wizards on the stake, I suppose.

And me.

I'm aware of John watching me, of my hand in the bowl of warm, tingly water, of him still holding it, his long fingers lightly wrapped around my smaller ones.

"I'm sorry," I say, because I can't think of anything else to say. "You seem very loyal to him. You all do. Your father—" I'm cut off by John's sudden grin. "What?"

"Well, when sentences start with 'your father,' they have a tendency to not end well."

I smile at that. I can't help it.

"Sorry," he continues. "What were you going to say?"

"Nothing, really. Just that I've never heard of a Reformist pirate before."

"Ah." John pulls our hands from the water and dries his with a flick of his wrist. "He's the only one, at least that I know of. Pirates aren't generally known for being political, are they?"

"I guess not," I say. "When did he join? And why?"

He hesitates before replying.

"It was about three years ago. Things were starting to get bad, you know? Malcolm had just become king; Blackwell had just become Inquisitor. The Thirteenth Tablet had just been created. The burnings hadn't started yet, but they would soon enough."

I swallow. I'm beginning to wish I hadn't brought it up.

"Piracy isn't exactly the safest profession anyway. He traveled a lot, would be gone for weeks at a time. So he quit. He didn't think it was safe to leave us alone until things got better."

He stops, reaches for a bandage. Looks down, his eyes resting on my hand, but they don't really see it. They're far away, somewhere outside this room. I'm left wondering who he meant when he said "us."

"Of course, things didn't get better," he says, finally. "My father wanted to help the Reformists fight back, but they didn't think he'd be useful. Or, if I'm being honest, they didn't think he was trustworthy. He's a good man, my father. A little different, I grant you. But a good man nonetheless. Nicholas saw that even if the others didn't."

"And now he's a Reformist."

John nods. "Committed. Nicholas has that effect, you know. He wants to change things. To help people. To bring the country back where it used to be, finish what Malcolm's father started. People believe he's the one to do it. They believe it so much they're willing to risk their lives to see him succeed."

"Or is it the other way around?" I regret the words as soon as they're out of my mouth.

"What's that supposed to mean?" John asks, his quiet voice turning sharp.

"I don't know."

"Of course you do."

"It's just..." I shake my head. "You say Nicholas is trying to help people. But all he's doing is helping them to the stakes." John's eyes narrow, but I go on. "Magic is against the law. You know this. Your lives depend on not doing it, yet you keep on. It seems to me that if he really wanted to help you, he'd make you stop."

John stands up then, so quickly he bumps into the table, nearly overturning the pitcher of wine. He reaches out without looking and steadies it.

"So you're saying that when Nicholas brought you to me, coughing and shaking and delirious and dying, it would have been better for me not to do anything? For me to stand by and watch you die, knowing all the while there was something I could do, and instead do nothing?"

"That's not what I mean."

"I think that's exactly what you mean." He swipes a hand across his jaw, frustrated. "Magic isn't something you can just stop. It's who you are. You're born with it or you aren't. You can make the most of it, as I do, as Fifer does, or you can ignore it. But you can't make it go away." He shakes his head. "I use it to help people. So I wouldn't stop even if I could."

Immediately, I'm reminded of the witches and wizards on the stake in the square, their expression mirrored in the way he's looking at me now: anger and defiance on the surface of an almost desperate sadness.

"What about you? You were arrested with those herbs"— his eyes meet mine, steady and unabashed, and I know immediately he knows what I used them for—"and if Nicholas hadn't come, hadn't broken you out using magic, you'd be dead now. If not by fire, then by fever. Does that seem right to you?"

"It doesn't matter what I think," I say. "Magic is against the law. I got exactly what I deserved."

John walks to the window and pulls open the curtain. It's completely dark outside now. He stands there for a long time, staring out the window. Finally, he speaks without turning around.

"Downstairs. You said you lost your parents. May I ask what happened to them?"

"Plague. First my father, then my mother a few days later. I was nine."

That's how I met Caleb. The plague that killed my parents killed his, too—along with a million others—during the hottest summer and the worst plague outbreak anyone could remember. It started in the crowded, hot cities and ran rampant, killing the young, the old, the poor, and the rich, before making its way to the country. It was less than a week before the population of Anglia had been decimated, leaving kids like Caleb and me to fend for ourselves.

The first time I saw him, I thought I was dreaming. I hadn't seen anyone—at least, anyone who was still alive—for weeks. It felt as if I were the only one in the world still left. Water was scarce and the food had long since disappeared. I survived by eating grass, tree bark, and the odd surviving flower, and I wished—more than once—that one of them would poison me. Kill me and put me out of my misery.

The day Caleb found me, riding by my house on a stolen horse on his way to court to beg for a job, I was a mess. The bodies of my mother and father were still in the house, and the heat and the stench of their decay had forced me to live outside. He approached me, talking slowly and quietly as you might to an injured animal. I was covered in dirt and filth, hunched over in the mud, eating the last of the raw vegetables I managed to dig up from the garden. I remember screaming and throwing a half-eaten parsnip at him. I was long past reason.

But he picked me up, more like a man than an eleven-year-old boy, put me on his horse, and managed to get us to the king's palace in Upminster. It was a three-day journey, but he got us there safely. And he managed to secure us jobs—not terribly difficult since the plague had killed off most of the servants, along with the king himself.

His only surviving son, Malcolm, was just twelve and wouldn't be able to run the country for four more years. So the business of running what was left of Anglia went to his uncle, Thomas Blackwell, who became Lord Protector of the kingdom. There was no queen to wait on then, but I wouldn't have been fit for that anyway. Instead, I did laundry, worked in the kitchen when they needed help, ran errands into town. I was content to do this forever, but Caleb had other plans for us.

"I'm sorry about your family." John turns to face me. "But if you could have done something to save them—even if it meant using magic, even if it meant breaking the law—wouldn't you have done it anyway?"

I shake my head. "Magic is what killed them. A wizard started that plague—you know that. Some say Nicholas did it. That he was the one who killed Malcolm's father—"

The fire roars sharply in the grate then, the flames shooting high into the chimney.

"Hastings, it's fine." John waves his hand toward the fire and it abruptly dies. "Nicholas didn't start that plague. And he didn't kill the king. He would never do anything like that."

"Then who was it?" I demand. "Only a very powerful wizard could start a plague and spread it like that. And Nicholas is the most powerful wizard in Anglia."

"What would Nicholas gain by wiping out half the country?"

I shrug. "Maybe being the most powerful wizard in Anglia isn't enough for him. Maybe he wants more. Maybe he wants the throne, too."

"If Nicholas wanted to be king, why didn't he make his move after he supposedly killed Malcolm's father? It would have been much easier to do then, only a Lord Protector and a boy heir to stand in the way."

"I don't know," I say. "Maybe he's biding his time."

John's eyes grow dark then, his thoughtful gaze slipping into anger.

"For what? So he could sit by and watch as his friends and family are forced to leave the country? Watch as they're arrested, tried, and sentenced to die? So he could bide his time?"

"I don't know," I repeat.

"Well, I do. Have you ever seen one? A burning?" His voice is quiet with intensity. "They're horrible. The worst kind of death there is. There's no dignity in it, only torture and spectacle and—" He breaks off. "They have to be stopped. And we can't stop them by walking away."

"The king—the Inquisitor—they'll never change the law," I say. "Surely you know that."

John turns back to the window and doesn't reply.

"And, yes, I've seen burnings," I add quietly. "They're terrible. It's a terrible death to die."

I was fourteen the first time I saw one. Threw up right in the middle of Tyburn; it even shook Caleb. But Blackwell wanted us to see it. He said we needed to see it to understand his laws, to know what it meant to be on the other side of them. I remember how Caleb and I huddled together that night, unable to sleep, afraid to sleep. It was months before the nightmares went away. But eventually I hardened myself against them, we both did. We had to.

John turns to face me. He starts to speak but is cut off by the door banging open.

"How are we coming on?" George stumbles into the room, holding a goblet. He looks drunk.

"Fine," John says, walking to the table and collecting his supplies. I notice his hands shaking as he piles everything back on the tray.

"What about you?" George walks over to me. I'm so busy watching John that I forget about my hand until he reaches over and grabs it.

"It still hurts," I say, but it doesn't matter. George doesn't really notice. He just glances at it and drops it back into my lap. He's definitely drunk.

"Nice work, John. As always." George reaches for the pitcher of wine, refills his goblet, then slumps into the chair by the fireplace. "I'm on night watch again," he tells me.

"Grand," I say.

"Isn't it?" He takes a drink and looks at John. "They want to see you."

"Who does?"

"Well, Fifer. She needs more"—George glances at me—"something for Nicholas. The usual. Peter wants something to help him sleep. And Gareth says he's got a headache."

John closes his eyes and nods, pressing his fingertips against his eyelids. He looks exhausted: deathly pale, circles under his eyes so dark they look like bruises.

George winces. "Sorry."

"It's fine," John says. "I'll go now. But see she wraps that hand, will you?" He plucks a bandage from the tray and tosses it to George. "The cut wasn't as bad as I thought it would be, but there's no sense inviting infection."

He slips out the door without another glance in my direction. I realize I never thanked him.

For anything.

I STAY THROUGH THE NIGHT.

I nearly didn't; that encounter at dinner was too close for my liking. But the news that I'm now Anglia's most wanted has complicated things. It's not enough to escape here and get back to Upminster—not anymore. Because it's not just Blackwell and his guards after me; it's every mercenary in the city. It's about as safe for me there as it is here, which is to say not at all.

Anglia's most wanted.

It's almost too much to believe. There's something about it all that is too much to believe. I know Blackwell wants me dead. But more than he wants Nicholas dead? Even if he does think I'm a witch, a spy, and a traitor, I'm still not as dangerous to him as Nicholas.

I can't go to Upminster, and I can't stay in Anglia. I suppose I'll have to escape to Gaul. It's close, just across the channel. Provided I can find a ship to stow away on, it'll be easy enough to get there. Their king is sympathetic to Anglican exiles; they won't turn me away.

Then there's Caleb.

I don't know what to make of his being promoted to Inquisitor. Was Blackwell planning to do that all along, even before my arrest? Or did Caleb ask for it afterward, as a way to protect me? But if he took the position to protect me, why didn't he come back to Fleet to get me? He didn't leave me there to die. I don't believe that. There must be another explanation.

Either way, today's the day I escape.

Last night, George let it slip that everyone would be gone all morning, something about going to the black market to get supplies. It's the opportunity I need to search the house. I can't leave for Gaul empty-handed; I need to prepare. Get my bearings, steal money and other valuables to trade with, arm myself with whatever I can find or make. Then tonight, when we make the trip to visit the seer, run like hell. And kill whoever gets in my way.

George is still asleep. He's splayed out on the floor at the end of my bed, completely passed out, a blanket tangled around his feet. He must have tripped over it at some point last night and fallen, either unwilling or unable to get up.

I dress quickly and quietly, putting on the same clothes I wore yesterday. It would be nice if I had something warmer or more practical. But they'll have to do. I snatch George's blanket from the floor and hastily tie it into a makeshift bag.

I glance at George. He doesn't look as though he'll be up for a while. I consider tying him up before I leave, just in case. But that might wake him, and then I'd have to hurt him. I don't want to do that. He's grown on me a little. So I let him be.

I open the door slowly, quietly. Tiptoe out, then down the hallway to the head of the stairs, and listen carefully. It's silent: no voices, no sound of footsteps or dishes at the table. Nothing. I hurry down the stairs into the entrance hall.

First stop, dining room. Pewter plates, silverware, I'll even take those ugly snake glasses if I have to. I rush to the cabinet where all the food was laid out last night and rip open the drawers, one after the other. They're all empty. *Damnation.*

I cross to the room on the other side of the entrance hall. It's a sitting room, very grand. Tall stained glass windows line the room, each pane in a different shade of blue. A large fireplace takes up one wall, a tapestry of a pleasant woodland scene covers another. A table sits underneath it, surrounded by chairs covered in blue brocade.

I race around the room, searching. Under the rug for a loose floorboard. Behind the tapestry for a secret alcove. The underside of the table for hidden drawers. The seams along the walls for a concealed door. Nothing. *Where the hell are all the weapons?* I'm in the home of the biggest traitor in Anglia—sorry, make that second-biggest—and there's not a single sharp, strung, or incendiary device in the whole place? It's not possible. Nicholas hasn't gotten this far by leading a rebellion with his bare hands.

The only place I haven't looked is the kitchen. It's risky. That's Hastings's territory. And servant or no, he's still a ghost.

I don't know how Nicholas managed to tame his destructive side, but it's there. With ghosts, it always is. Witch hunters are sometimes requested for hauntings, but it's pointless. We can't do anything except stand back and watch the chaos. The last haunting Caleb and I were called to, the ghost ripped a barn from the ground and sheared the entire flock of sheep inside. Scattered the wool for miles. Such a mess, it looked as if it were snowing in July. Caleb and I sat on a hill and watched, giggling like children.

I swallow hard and push him out of my head. I can't think about Caleb right now.

Next to the dining room is a doorway that opens into a narrow, dark hall. I can't be sure, but my guess is it leads to the kitchen. I step inside, pause, and listen. Silence. If Hastings is around, surely I'll hear him? The hall is cold, dank, and drafty. That could be because it's made entirely of stone, but it could also be Hastings. Ghosts make everything cold. I shiver a little and keep going.

Finally, the hall opens into the kitchen. I stop in the doorway and look around. It looks like a smaller version of the kitchen at Ravenscourt. To my left is the oven. It's huge. The opening is tall enough for a man of Nicholas's height to walk inside without having to duck. There's a fire burning inside, and something turning on the roasting rack. It looks like deer.

In front of me is a trestle table. On top are baskets heaped with fruit, vegetables, flour, spices. Underneath are more baskets filled with everything from firewood to onions to eggs. In one corner are caskets of wine, ale, and salted fish. In another, hanging by their feet from a rack, are dozens of dead birds: chicken and duck and quail and pheasant. And everywhere lie kettles and cauldrons, skillets and pans. It's a properly stocked kitchen. Which means somewhere there are knives, cleavers, meat forks, scissors. At this point I'd even take a cheese grater.

I watch the room for a few minutes. There's no movement. Nothing floating in the air, nothing stirring of its own accord. And didn't John say Hastings usually wears a white hat? I don't see that, either. Satisfied he's not around, I rush to the table and start digging through everything. Sift through the flour, pick through a pile of apples. Nothing inside but a spoon and a tiny three-pronged fork. I pocket them anyway. Crawl under the table and rummage through the other baskets. Nothing, nothing, and, *damnation*, now I've gone and broken a bunch of eggs. I wipe my hands on my trousers and get to my feet, looking around. Then I see the ladder leading below the kitchen. The larder.

Larders are used to store meat, cheese, butter, freshly caught fish. Things you need to keep cold so they won't spoil. They're tiny rooms, dark, freezing. Usually on the north side of a house, where they get the least amount of sun. Usually underground. Always terrifying. I hate small, dark spaces. But a larder is the perfect place to cure meat. And where there's meat, there are knives. I grab my bag and start down the ladder. My heart speeds up the second I'm plunged into the darkness. I breathe deeply, hum a little. Imagine the cache of beautiful, pointy weapons I'll find down here. It helps.

When I reach the bottom of the ladder, I realize my eyes are closed, so I open them. It takes a moment to adjust to the lack of light—there's only a sliver of it coming through the vent in the wall. When they do, I feel them grow round. There, hanging neatly along the wall, is the most gorgeous array of carving tools I've ever seen. Blunt cleavers. Curved skinning knives. Short boning knives. There's even a bone ax. I nearly squeal with glee.

I hook as many knives as possible on my belt and shove the rest into my bag. There are a couple of pairs of heavy gloves, and I take those, too. They may come in handy. I sling the bag across my shoulder and start back up the ladder. There's still plenty of room inside for pewter plates and silverware. Enough to trade for clothes, food, and weapons. My plan is coming together.

I poke my head into the kitchen. It's still quiet, but I check everything anyway. A neat pile of apples, a slightly skewed basket of onions. A dusting of flour on the tabletop. Everything is just how I left it. I scramble to my feet and head to the door opposite the one I came in through: the scullery. Where those valuable pewter dishes are washed and stored. I take about three steps, then it happens.

The temperature in the room plunges in a second. I suck in a surprised breath, and when I exhale, it comes out in a plume of white frosty air. A frigid wind begins to swirl around me, lifting my hair from my shoulders, whipping it across my face and into my eyes. Then I hear a whisper. Soft at first, like steam from a teakettle. As the wind grows stronger, the voice grows louder. I can't make out the words, but I can hear the anger behind them.

Hastings.

I lunge for the door, forgetting the scullery. The pewter

isn't as important as getting out of here. There's no telling what Hastings is capable of. I make it as far as the trestle table when a basket comes flying toward me. I realize what's in it a split second too late: flour.

It swirls into the air, flies into my eyes, my mouth, my hair. I'm coated in it. I drop my bag to the floor and start coughing and gagging, wiping the stuff from my eyes. I clear them just in time to see a dead pheasant flying at my head, beak first.

I snatch one of the knives from my belt and hurl it at the bird. I get a direct hit, and both bird and knife go clattering to the floor. I make it another step before more birds come at me. Three ducks. Two chickens. A peacock. A brace of quail. I empty knife after knife into them.

Finally, Hastings runs out of birds. I drop to my knees and crawl along the floor, trying to retrieve my knives. I manage to locate several and yank the blades from the birds' bellies. But when I get to my feet, the doors to the bread ovens fly open and hot loaves go pelting in my direction. I bat away most of them, but one or two clip my face, leaving white-hot welts on my skin. They heal quickly enough, but I'm getting annoyed. I've lost countless weapons, I'm a flour-covered mess, and the smell of all this food is making me hungry.

I turn on my heel and sprint to the fireplace. The deer is still on the spit, roasting nicely. Hastings takes pride in his work. If I'm right, he won't sacrifice a fine piece of meat just to taunt me. I scramble up the rack, all the way to the top, out of reach of the flames. Then I whirl around.

"Go ahead!" I shout. "Throw something! I dare you!"

I look around. The air is still thick with flour, but nothing comes flying at me. Everything's gone still. Smirking, I hop down from the spit. Saunter across the room, snatch my bag off the floor. Then I survey the scene.

Flour on every surface, bird carcasses strewn along the floor. Broken loaves of bread, smashed eggs, feathers everywhere. What a disaster. But I held my own against a ghost, and that's no small thing. Caleb would be proud. I start for the door. Then, through the haze of flour still hanging in the air, I see him. Standing in the doorway, arms folded, eyebrows raised.

George.

"Well, well," he smirks. "If it isn't our little maid, back in the kitchen."

My heart sinks to the bottom of my too-big boots. How long has he been standing there?

"I knew there was something funny about you." He steps toward me. "I couldn't put my finger on it. Are you going to tell me the truth now? Or am I going to have to drag it out of you?"

"I don't know what you're talking about." I drop my bag on the floor and kick it aside.

"No?"

"No."

"Suit yourself," he says. Then he pulls a dagger out of his jacket. My eyes widen.

"Don't," I say.

"Catch," he says. Then he hurls the knife at me.

12

THE KNIFE WHISTLES THROUGH THE air, heading straight for my head. It's less than an inch from my eye when I catch it, smacking the blade flat between my palms. Before I can react, George is at my side.

"We need to talk." He grabs my arm and drags me from the kitchen.

Upstairs, he pushes me into my room and rounds on me.

"You prowl around the king's palace like a rat in the rafters." George holds up a finger. "You crushed a glass in your hand, yet there's not a scratch on you. You're all moony over this Caleb, who just happens to be the new Inquisitor." He holds up three fingers now. "And where'd you learn to throw knives at birds like that? The circus?" He narrows his eyes. "You're a witch hunter."

I open my mouth, a denial on the tip of my tongue.

"It's a damned good thing I am," I snap. "Otherwise you'd have some explaining to do. I could have lost an eye."

George groans and pushes me away. He paces the room, hands clasped behind his head.

"I knew it," he says. "I knew there was something about you. The way you look, your face and all this." He gestures at me with a sweep of his hand. "I thought you were a Gallic spy." He flops down in the chair by the fireplace and buries his head in his hands. He looks so distraught I almost feel sorry for him. "A witch hunter," he mutters. "A bloody witch hunter."

"Just let me go," I say. "I can be out that door and gone within minutes. No one has to know. It's nothing to you."

"It's not nothing to me." He peers at me through his fingers. "You make it sound as if you're here by mistake. It's not a mistake. You're here for a reason."

"Yes. Because your seer is naming witch hunters," I say. "So you can find them and kill them."

"You're not here for that," George says.

"You don't know that," I say. "Nicholas said he didn't know why I was here."

"That's not exactly true."

I narrow my eyes. "What do you mean?"

"I can't tell you."

"Then I can't stay." I start toward the door.

"Stop." He sticks his leg out in front of me. "I'll tell you. You're here because Nicholas needs to find something. Whatever it is, it's important. According to Veda, you're the only one who can get it."

"What?" This makes no sense. "What could I possibly

find for him? He's a wizard and I'm a witch hunter, and—oh." I finally catch on. "It has to do with his curse, doesn't it?"

George scowls. "How d'you know about that?"

"John told me." He raises his eyebrows at that. But I go on. "So that's it, isn't it? There's a wizard cursing Nicholas, and you want me to find him and take him out?"

He shrugs. "I dunno. I mean, now that I know what you are, it seems the most likely possibility. We'll find out for sure tonight."

I shake my head. "I'm sorry," I say. "I can't find your wizard for you. In case you haven't noticed, I'm in a lot of trouble. I have to get out of here."

"How exactly d'you plan on doing that?" George says. "You're the most wanted person in the country. They'll be looking for you."

"I know that!" I say. "Why do you think I was trying to take Nicholas's stuff?"

"To fulfill your dream of opening a china shop?"

I glare at him. "I don't have time for this." I move toward the door again. "You'll just have to get someone else to find your wizard for you."

George gets to his feet and steps in front of me. "You know I can't let you do that."

I sigh. "I don't want to hurt you, George. But if you get in my way, I will."

He holds up his hands but doesn't move. "You want to leave. I get that. If I were you, I'd want that, too. But you have no clothes, no weapons. And no money to get those things."

"No thanks to you," I mutter.

"Even if you did, you have no safe way to get around.

123

With the reward they're offering, you'll have people after you everywhere you turn. Pirates, hirelings, mercenaries—"

"I can take them."

"Yes, but for how long? Long enough to make it across the country? All the way to Gaul? That's where you're going, isn't it?"

I don't reply.

"We can help you," George continues. "If you did this for us, if you helped us find the wizard cursing Nicholas and stop him, I reckon he'd give you whatever you want."

It's a tempting offer. Still, I hesitate. Finding the wizard isn't the concern; I could do that with ease. It's not that Blackwell is after me; he's after me anyway. It's not even Caleb.

There's something else bothering me. Finally, I land on it.

"Why me?" I say. "There are other witch hunters who could have done the job for you. Ones you wouldn't have had to break out of jail, or who weren't wanted criminals. I'm sure you could have found someone willing." Not Caleb, of course. But I can think of several others who might've done it. For the right price, anyway.

"I don't know why you, either," George says. "You heard Peter. We thought you were a mistake. If we'd gotten to you earlier, when we were supposed to, none of this would have happened. It didn't make it easy on us, either."

"Why didn't Nicholas just tell me this?"

George's eyes widen. "Didn't know you were a witch hunter, did he? Thinks you're an innocent girl, doesn't he?" He shakes his head. "I'll tell you, you had us all fooled. I thought you were a spy. Fifer and Nicholas think you're a witch. And John…"

"John what?"

"He just thinks you're a mistake. That's all."

"Oh." This bothers me for a moment, but I shake it off.

"As I say, Nicholas doesn't know what you're supposed to find," George continues. "He hasn't told you what he does know because he thought you were too fragile to take it."

"Fragile?" I scoff. "I could kill you right now, using only my thumb."

To my surprise, this makes him laugh. "Aye. But have you looked in the mirror lately?"

I ignore this. "So that's it, then? I just have to help him find this wizard?"

He nods.

I consider it. As much as I hate to admit it, I do need help. That much hasn't changed. I still need a way to leave the country and money to do it with. And it might not be a bad idea to have Nicholas's protection. He's been in exile a long time and managed to keep Blackwell at bay. Maybe he can do the same for me. If I had to guess, I'm going to be in exile for a long time, too.

"Fine. I'll do it. I'll find your wizard for you." George sighs in relief. "Not so fast," I add. "I have a few conditions."

"Oh?"

"First, I want a guarantee you aren't going to use me to get what you need, then turn me over for the reward."

"Nicholas would never do that."

I think Nicholas would absolutely do that, but I don't bother to argue. "Fine. Then after it's over, he won't have any problem escorting me wherever I want to go."

George nods. "If that's what you want."

"Second, I don't want anyone else to know about me."

This makes him frown. "Nicholas is bound to find out," he says. "If he doesn't figure it out on his own, the seer will surely tell him."

"I know. But it's not just Nicholas I'm worried about."

I think about the others. Peter's a pirate, no doubt skilled with a sword. Fifer is Nicholas's "star pupil." There's no telling how many ways she could curse me. Then there's John. He wouldn't hurt me, I know that. But I think if he were to learn the truth about me, it would be just as unpleasant, in a different kind of way.

"So do we have a deal?"

George nods. Then he sits back down in the chair and beckons to me. "So, can I see it? Your stigma, I mean? I've never seen one before."

"There's nothing to see." I touch a hand to my stomach. "It only shows itself when I get injured, then vanishes when I heal."

George grins. "I could stab you...."

I point my thumb toward his eye.

He cracks a laugh. "I'm joking. But that's clever, it disappearing like that. Keeps you from getting caught. Explains why Fifer didn't see it when she cleaned you up, or John when he examined you."

I feel a sudden jolt at the thought of John looking at—and possibly touching—my bare stomach.

"So what does it look like?"

"What?"

"Your stigma," George says. "Is it awful?"

"Oh. No. I mean, it's not as bad as you'd think." When

I found out we were getting stigmas, I panicked. I imagined the worst: a brand, a scar, something raised and raw and ugly. But it's small and delicate—elegant, even, like handwriting done with a fine pen.

"Did it hurt?"

I don't answer right away. The marking ceremony took place right after I took my final test as a recruit. That test is something I don't like to think about, much less talk about. I must have been in shock after it was over. I don't really remember if it hurt or not.

"A little." I don't want to talk about my stigma anymore.

George presses on. "It's magic, isn't it? I mean, it has to be. Don't you think that's strange? That a witch hunter uses magic? That doesn't seem right, does it? Who gave it to you, anyway?"

"Yes. No. I guess. I don't know."

And I don't. I've thought about my stigma, thought about it until my head spun. Why did Blackwell give us magic when he hates magic? When he blindfolded us and led us behind closed doors and had us marked, how did he know it would work? Caleb said one of the wizards we captured did it, but how did Blackwell know it wouldn't kill us?

This is when I usually stopped asking, because I knew he didn't. We were his experiments. His subjects. And if he killed one of us, he'd simply find a replacement. Just as he always did.

George looks at me for a moment. "How exactly did you get mixed up in this? Witch-hunting is a really serious business. And you're just a girl." He frowns. "How did this happen?"

I think back to the day Caleb first approached me about being a witch hunter. It started out ordinarily enough, but by sunset I had already taken my first frightened steps down a path I knew there was no coming back from. But the idea of Caleb walking it without me frightened me even more.

"Caleb convinced me to go with him. He was my best friend. The only family I had."

George looks skeptical. "Fine way to treat your family. Forcing them to do something like that against their will."

I shake my head. "It wasn't like that. He didn't force me."

"You wanted to be a witch hunter?"

"I—no. I wanted to be with Caleb. It was what he wanted. And I trusted him to do what he thought was best."

George makes a face. "The best for you or for himself?"

"What's that supposed to mean?"

He shrugs. "Seems to me he was more interested in advancing himself than he was in keeping you safe."

"You don't know what you're talking about," I say. "He's always taken care of me. He's always kept me safe."

"Didn't do a very good job of it, did he?" George replies. "Girls who are safe don't get thrown into prison and sentenced to death. He left you there to die—"

"He didn't leave me to die," I say. "He was coming back."

"Oh, aye, he was coming back. To escort you to the stakes."

"Stop."

"You know I'm right. Surely you know that."

"Stop," I repeat. "I'm serious, George. If you say another word against Caleb, I'll leave. I don't care what you offer, or what happens to Nicholas."

"Elizabeth—"

"Not another word!" I'm shouting now. "Or I swear, I'll—"

The sound of someone clearing his throat interrupts me. I jerk my head around and there's John, standing in the doorway. He's wearing a thick black traveling cloak, a large canvas bag slung over his shoulder, traces of rain still on his face and hair. He must have gotten back and come straight upstairs.

George stands up. "Didn't hear you come in."

John shrugs. "Sorry to interrupt. I knocked a few times, though." He looks at me, then back at George. "Nicholas wants to see you," he says. "He's downstairs."

George moves to the door, eyeing me warily. Probably thinks I'll try to escape again.

"I thought I'd clean up," I say.

"I'll ask Hastings to prepare a bath," George says. Then he leaves. John lingers, looking at me with the strangest expression. His eyes travel from my hair, which I know is still covered in flour, to my grubby, egg-stained trousers, then to my hand, which is fully healed now and still unwrapped, back to my face.

"We leave at five," he says. "Be sure to wear something warm."

13

WE LEAVE AT FIVE O'CLOCK, right on schedule. Peter and Gareth stay behind; apparently Veda has a fear of all old men, except Nicholas. I wonder why.

Outside, the night is cold and crisp, and I'm grateful for the clothes Hastings brought me to wear. Close-fitting green trousers and a soft white shirt. A long black velvet coat and knee-high black boots. Fifer's clothes. I knew by the scowl she gave me how much she hated having to give them over.

Nicholas says it's an hour's walk to get there, none of it on open road. He knows the path well, directing us around trees and over fallen branches, until we're deep in the woods. The moon is completely black tonight, not a single sliver of light to guide us. I walk beside George, and while I'm used to walking in the dark, he's having trouble. He stumbles every few feet, tripping over fallen logs and into potholes.

"A pity Veda can't see in the daytime." He pitches forward again, and I grab his arm to keep him from falling. "Honestly, is the bit about the moon really that important?"

"The bit about the moon?" Fifer tsks beside me. "The dark phase of the moon is only the most significant aspect to divination. The time when seers are at their most powerful. And you call it 'the bit about the moon.'"

"Well, not all of us are witches," he replies.

I feel Fifer's eyes shift to me when he says it.

"You said the phase lasts three days," George continues. "Can't Veda see at any point during that time?"

"Strictly speaking, yes," Nicholas replies. "But the energy is strongest in the first few hours. We want to take advantage of that. Anyone with any seeing power will be looking in these three days as well. It's best to be done before the energy starts to wane."

I knew some of this already. Witch hunters are always sent out during the dark moon. Not just to look for seers; it's also an ideal time to find witches and wizards performing dark spells and curses. They work best during this time, too. Then it occurs to me.

"They'll be looking for us, won't they?" I say.

"Undoubtedly," Nicholas replies. "But I've taken every precaution. Veda's home has a protective spell on it. No one will be able to see it, nor us once we're inside. Using Fifer's help, I've extended that spell so we can walk through the woods, virtually undetected."

"Why take the risk?" I say. "Isn't there another way to get there? One where we don't have to walk?" It's clear he's having trouble with that himself. He takes slow, cumbersome steps, clutching John's arm for support. Unlike George, I know that's not because of the dark.

"There are ways to use magic for travel," Nicholas says. "Lodestones, primarily, though they are few and far between, not to mention extremely difficult to procure. People have died for a lot less."

"Died?" I raise my eyebrows.

"Yes. Like from an excess of curiosity," Fifer mutters.

John shoots her a look. She sticks her tongue out at him.

"Lodestones are formed when lightning strikes certain types of minerals," Nicholas continues. "Typically they explode, which is why they're so difficult to find. But sometimes a wizard will attract the lightning himself and try to hold the mineral intact as it hits. Perhaps you can guess what happens next."

"I can?"

John nudges me and makes an exploding motion with his free hand.

I clap my hand over my mouth, stifling a laugh.

"It's not funny," Fifer snaps.

"No," John agrees. "But what else do you expect when you play with lightning?"

Nicholas gives an indulgent chuckle that turns into a horrible, hacking cough. John and Fifer exchange a worried glance.

"Quite right," Nicholas finally manages. "But there are other restrictions as well. A single lodestone can only be used once, and by two people at most. We'd need six to manage the trip here and back. I don't think I've come across six of them in my lifetime." He smiles at me. "Don't worry, Elizabeth. You're safe with us."

———————

We continue walking, the five of us falling silent. The only sound is that of leaves and twigs crackling beneath our feet. It's just as well. I don't feel like talking anyway. I'm nervous about meeting this seer. Worried about what she might see. Afraid of what she might say.

It's almost a certainty she'll name me as a witch hunter. To be found out that way, in a roomful of vengeful Reformists... what would happen then? I've got a few ideas, none of them good. And I have nothing to defend myself with. No knife, no ax, not even that tiny three-pronged fork. George took them all.

Still, I've been in worse situations and come out ahead. There's no reason to think this will be any different. So I try to relax. Tilt my head back, watch the sky. It's clear tonight, full of a thousand stars. I watch them as I walk, searching for constellations I know. It takes a minute, but eventually I'm able to make out a few.

First, I see Cygnus. He's a swan but is actually shaped like a giant cross. Easy to recognize. Left of that is Pegasus, the winged horse. He looks like a giant crab. Above him is Andromeda. She's the girl who was chained to a rock, a sacrifice for her mother's arrogance. Above Andromeda is her mother, Cassiopeia. Her constellation is simply five stars in the shape of a *W*. Caleb told me it's meant to depict her punishment. Because of what she did to Andromeda, the gods tied Cassiopeia to a chair and banished her to the heavens. She's stuck in the sky, forever.

I feel a hand on my arm, pulling me firmly but gently to one side.

"Careful," John says. "You almost walked into a tree."

"Oh," I say, feeling foolish. "Thank you."

"Stargazing?" He falls into step beside me.

"A little."

He nods. "I guess you didn't do much of that at court, did you?"

"Not really," I say. It isn't true, but I know what he means. In Malcolm's court, it was never a good idea to show an interest in stars. Because knowing astronomy might mean you have an interest in astrology. Charting stars, knowing the positions of planets, understanding the zodiac...that's too closely related to divination. Even if you can't replicate a full-scale model of the universe on your ceiling the way Nicholas can, it's still forbidden.

Oddly enough, though, Blackwell encouraged it. Part of our training as witch hunters included education. Of course, most of it involved mastering subterfuge, armament, and the subtle art of poisoning, but there was a softer side, too. Blackwell was nobly born, highly educated. He had the best tutors in the kingdom at his disposal, and he brought them in to teach us art, literature, arithmetic, languages, geography, and, yes, even astronomy.

When I first went to live with him, this surprised me. I thought his desire to educate us meant he was interested in us. That he cared. Eventually I realized that wasn't the case. He may have clothed us, fed us, housed us, and educated us, but we were not his children. We were his soldiers: indispensable, yet replaceable. He needed us smart because he needed us alive. But if he lost one of us in training, he never said a word about it. There'd just be one less place at the dinner table, and we'd never hear that person's name again.

But Caleb said it didn't matter. He jumped at the chance to learn. If it weren't for Blackwell, he never would have gotten an education. He studied everything he could, insisted I did, too. I resented it at first, but now I'm glad. I'm as educated as any man in the kingdom now. I can't help feeling proud of that.

John is still walking beside me, and I realize I haven't said anything in a while.

"I'm sorry," I say, finally. "For not talking, I mean. I guess I'm just worried."

"Not at all," he says. "But you have nothing to be worried about. Veda is very sweet."

Sweet? He must be joking. Trying to lighten the mood. Because I've come across my fair share of seers before, and they were all cantankerous, grouchy, sour old cats.

I start to reply, but Nicholas's quiet voice cuts me off.

"We're here."

We've reached the edge of the forest, the trees ending in a clearing. I can just make out a small village in the distance.

"Somewhere in there, then?" I whisper, pointing at it.

"A little closer than that." John directs my hand toward an old stone well about twenty feet away. It's about three feet high on one side, but the other side has collapsed and lies in a broken heap of stones.

"What, we have to go through it?" My chest tightens at the thought of crawling into such a small, dark space.

"Not quite." Nicholas steps up beside me, reaching into his cloak and pulling out a small object wrapped in cloth. He unwraps it, peeling away layer after layer until I can see what's inside. It's a stone, one from the well by the looks of it. He places his hand on top of it.

"Reveal."

In an instant, the broken-down well is gone, replaced by a small house. It's made from the same rough stone as the well and like the stone in Nicholas's hand. The house is tiny and ramshackle, but it's got a small garden out back, along with a pen filled with chickens and a single tiny pig. It's so quiet I can hear him snorting as he roots around in the mud.

"Fantastic," George murmurs. "I tell you, I never get tired of watching him do that."

A concealment spell is very difficult magic. It calls for a strong enchantment on not just one object, but two: the thing being concealed as well as the thing that links the concealed object to its illusion. Most wizards don't have the ability to execute a spell like that. If Nicholas is cursed—dying, even— and can still manage it . . .

I'm suddenly wishing for those weapons again.

"I'll let her know we're here," Nicholas says. "Stay here until I call for you."

He walks to the narrow wooden front door and scratches a soft knock. After a moment the door opens and Nicholas disappears inside. Minutes pass. I'm starting to get fidgety when Nicholas finally comes back out. He crooks his finger, beckoning us to come inside.

THE HOUSE IS DIMLY LIT as we enter. A small sitting room, sparsely furnished. A table in one corner with a couple of stools, a single bench, a few lit candles scattered on the surface. On the other side of the room is a fireplace. There's wood inside, only it's not lit. I wrap my arms tightly around myself.

"The ritual requires the house to be as cold as possible." Nicholas gestures to the dark fireplace. "We'll light it again after. Come. Meet Veda. You three, wait here."

He beckons me toward the only other door in the cottage. It's open slightly, revealing yet another dimly lit room. Fifer hops onto the table; George settles on the bench and pulls out a deck of cards. I glance at John, still standing beside me. He nods and gives an encouraging smile.

Nicholas and I walk into the room, and a woman approaches us.

"Avis, this is Elizabeth. Elizabeth, this is Avis. Veda's mother."

Veda's *mother?* I take another look at her. She's got brown hair tied back in a knot, no gray in it at all. She gives me a bland smile—no wrinkles around her eyes, either. She's twenty-five, if that.

"And this is Veda," Nicholas says. I look around but don't see her. "Look down," he tells me, and I do. Before me stands a tiny little girl. She looks to be around five years old. My eyes go round with surprise.

I crouch down to take a better look at her. Long brown hair, huge brown eyes. She smiles at me, and I notice she's missing her two bottom teeth.

"Hello," she pipes. "I know you already. I saw you in my head! I'm glad they finally found you. They kept looking for some ugly, old lady. But you're not ugly at all!"

"Well...thank you," I say, and Nicholas laughs.

"Veda, now that Elizabeth is here, we need you to tell us what she's supposed to do." It's a careful choice of words. Nothing at all about needing me to find something for him. "Can you do that?"

Veda nods.

There's a single wide bed pushed into the corner of the room, and next to it is a small table covered with a clean white cloth. On top is a scrying mirror, surrounded by six flickering candles. The elaborate silver frame is dull and choked with tarnish, but the glass is clear: deep, black, infinite.

Nicholas takes out five round, flat objects from his cloak

and places one at each corner of the table, the last one in front of the mirror. Each stone is inscribed with a different symbol, runes by the looks of it. Finally, he sets down a small hourglass.

"Are you ready?" Nicholas asks Veda.

"Yes," she crows, hopping into a chair.

"Elizabeth." Nicholas turns to me. "Please stand back. Veda shouldn't be able to see any shadows inside the mirror."

I move to the far wall of the bedroom, by the window. Nicholas settles into a chair beside Veda, and Avis hands him a sheaf of parchment and a pen.

"We're going to need absolute silence," he tells me. "No matter what you hear, you've got to remain silent. Do you understand?"

My stomach gives a little tug of unease. "Yes."

Nicholas clears his throat and begins speaking, reciting some sort of poem. He repeats it, over and over in a low monotone. Despite the cold in the room, I feel myself grow warm and relaxed. It has the same effect on Veda. Her little head droops forward, nearly touching the table. She sits like this for a moment, and I wonder vaguely if she's fallen asleep. Then she jerks her head up. Her eyes are wide open as she stares into the mirror.

"What is your name?" Nicholas asks her.

"Veda," she intones.

"How old are you?"

"Five."

"What did you tell me, last time I was here?"

> "Look beyond what you see, to one made blind.
> The thing you seek only she can find.

Betrayed, sent to a place of no return,
Elizabeth Grey, forsaken to burn."

At those words, I give a little gasp. But Nicholas turns to me, his finger on his lips. Then he tips the hourglass over. I watch the tiny grains of sand trickle to the other side.

"What is she supposed to find?"

Silence.

"Can you tell me where it is?"

Silence.

"How much time do we have?" Nicholas presses. His pen hovers over the paper, but he hasn't written a thing. The sand is a quarter way through the hourglass now. I'm about to dismiss this entire scene as a joke when she finally speaks.

"Upon this stone are etched meters of death.
From you it will draw your very last breath.
Come third winter's night, go underground in green.
What holds him in death will lead you to thirteen."

None of this makes sense to me. But Nicholas is hunched over the table, nodding and writing furiously. The room is so quiet I can hear his pen scratch the parchment.

"Trust the one who sees as much as he hears,
For always, things are not as they appear.
Betrayed by three, beholden to four,
One who lost two is loath to lose one more."

Nicholas's brows twitch together a little at this, but he keeps writing. Veda continues.

"Darkness comes; the circle closes its end.
The ties that bind do both break and mend.
The elixir of life will pass between,
Because she bears the numbered mark unseen."

Nicholas jerks his head in my direction, a look of surprise on his face. It takes me a moment to realize what just happened. *The numbered mark unseen:* my stigma. Veda just named me for a witch hunter. Just as I thought she would.

My first instinct is to leap out the window and run like hell. But where would I go? So I force myself to stand still and face whatever happens next.

The last grains of sand slip through the hourglass, and Veda slumps forward onto the table. Nicholas takes her by the shoulders and gently leans her back in the chair. After a moment she stirs, her eyes slowly coming back into focus. She looks at Nicholas.

"How'd I do?"

"Beautifully." Nicholas gives her a kind smile. "Now why don't you run and see Fifer? She has a gift for you." Beaming, Veda jumps off her chair and charges into the next room. He looks at Avis. "Would you mind if I spoke with Elizabeth privately for a moment?" She nods and leaves the room. I notice she avoids looking at me.

The door quietly shuts, and Nicholas leans back in his chair. He clasps his hands together, the tips of his fingers resting against his lips as he studies me. His gaze is hard; there's no hint of the levity or kindness I've seen before.

"You're a witch hunter," he says, finally.

I don't reply. My heart is beating somewhere in my throat, and my palms are damp with sweat. I slide them against my trousers, hoping he won't notice.

"I wouldn't have guessed it," he continues. "You don't look the part. Then, that's probably the point." He goes quiet again. "You wanted to kill me at Fleet, didn't you?"

I still don't reply. I quickly scan the room for something to protect myself with. The candlesticks, the stones on the table. The mirror I could break, use the shards as knives....

"I think we should have a little chat." He stands and pulls out a chair. "Sit."

I don't move.

"Sit," he repeats. "I won't harm you."

I hesitate for a moment before moving to the chair. I watch him closely, waiting for him to make a move. He just sits down and resumes staring.

"I thought you were a witch," he says. "An untrained witch. I thought it was how you knew to procure those herbs, how you survived jail. John said you should have died."

"I heard," I say.

"Your stigma protected you?"

"No. It protects against wounds, not illness. It makes me strong, so I can hold out longer than most. But if you hadn't found me and John hadn't healed me, I would have died."

Nicholas doesn't respond to this. Maybe he's wishing I had died; there'd be one less witch hunter in the world. He can wish it all he wants; but if he wants to stay alive, he needs me alive, too. Just as I need him.

"John said you're cursed. That you're dying." I don't bother dressing up the words into something more tactful. Nicholas grunts in disapproval—maybe at my impertinence, maybe at John's carelessness—but I continue. "Veda said the thing you seek only I can find. It's a wizard, isn't it? You need me to find the wizard who's cursing you and kill him."

"It's not a wizard," he says. "It's a curse tablet."

Now it's my turn to be surprised. "A curse tablet?"

"Yes. Do you know what they are?"

I nod. I've come across a few curse tablets before. The idea behind them is simple: Etch a curse onto a flat piece of stone, lead, or bronze, then dispose of it someplace it can never be found. Wells, lakes, and rivers are popular choices. But while the idea is simple, the execution is not. To create the curse, you have to use a specific material, a certain stylus to write with, the correct runes. If a single step is done incorrectly, it won't work.

And most of them don't. The curse tablets I've seen were always incomplete, abandoned at some point in the process. But if done correctly, it's one of the most effective ways that I know of killing another human being. The only way to break the curse is to find the tablet and destroy it. Which is nearly impossible.

"You may be looking for a curse tablet," I say. "But it still amounts to me finding a wizard. A wizard cursed it, a wizard hid it. One of your enemies, I presume." Nicholas raises an eyebrow at that, but I go on. "I find him, persuade him to tell me where it is. Then I destroy it. It's really not that difficult."

"You're very confident," Nicholas remarks.

"I'm good at finding things."

"Perhaps you wouldn't be so confident if you knew the curse tablet is the Thirteenth Tablet."

"What?" I gape at him. "That's impossible. The Thirteenth Tablet has been missing for years. If you were cursed by it, you'd be dead by now." No one can hold out against a curse tablet that long.

"The Thirteenth Tablet disappeared two years ago," Nicholas says. "My symptoms began around that time and have grown progressively worse. Still, I thought I was ill. I never suspected I was cursed, not until Veda told me a few months ago."

"But why?" I say. "It's a lot of trouble to go through. Stealing it from the gates at Ravenscourt, hauling it off, then there's the matter of disposal…"

"Yes. It would have been much simpler to create a traditional curse tablet, though for a curse of this scope, it would need to be quite large anyway."

He's right. If you want to kill a man's dog or make him lose all his hair, you can use a smaller tablet to write the curse on. But the bigger the curse, the more complicated, the bigger the tablet needs to be.

"That aside, I suspect using the Thirteenth Tablet was symbolic," Nicholas continues. "To curse a wizard using the very tablet written as an edict against witchcraft? It must have held some amusement to the wizard who performed the curse."

"Don't you know who it is?" I say. "Surely you have an idea. There can't be more than a handful of people who could manage a curse like that."

Nicholas looks at me, his gaze turning to steel again. "To

my knowledge, the only witch or wizard who could perform a curse like that was captured and tried and burned at the stake."

Something floods through me then. Fear? Shame? Guilt? I don't know. But whatever it is makes my insides twist and my cheeks grow warm. I knew this admonishment was coming, but I didn't know the effect it would have.

And I don't like it.

"I was doing my job." I return his look with equal force. "The job given to me by the king, enforcing the laws of the kingdom. Laws that were put in place for a reason." I gesture at him with a sweep of my hand. "As you can plainly see."

"It's curious that you defend these laws," Nicholas replies. "Considering you yourself are a victim of them." He mimics my gesture. "As you can plainly see."

Anger lances through me, quick and sharp. "I wouldn't be here if it weren't for you!"

"Indeed, you wouldn't."

"It's because of you I had no trial," I continue. "It's because of you I had no leniency. It's because of you I'm the most wanted criminal in Anglia!"

"That is how irony works."

"At least I did what I did for the country," I snap. "You did what you did for yourself."

"You are no patriot, Elizabeth. You do us both a disservice by claiming it."

"A patriot? That's what you call yourself?"

"I call myself a Reformist."

"You mean lawbreaker?"

"I don't seek to break laws. I seek to change them. I seek

145

fairness. Tolerance. For everyone, regardless of the side they align with."

I shake my head. "Impossible."

Nicholas waves his hand, and the candles abruptly die out. "Improbable," he says. He waves his hand once more, and they relight. "But not impossible."

We stare at each other across the table.

"Let me get this straight," I say. "A cursed wizard needs a witch hunter to find a tablet cursed by yet another wizard, so that said cursed wizard can rid the country of the laws that were created to prevent the curse in the first place." I smirk. I can't help it. "Yes. That is how irony works."

Nicholas's mouth twitches.

"I have terms, of course."

"Terms?"

"For finding your tablet."

"Ah." Nicholas raises a finger. "I didn't ask you."

Inwardly, I roll my eyes. These old wizards are so set in their ways. He probably wants to issue a scrolled proclamation for me to sign with a plumed pen in front of robed witnesses.

"There's no need to stand on ceremony," I say. "You can just ask me."

"I'm afraid it's not quite that simple."

Outwardly, I roll my eyes.

"If I ask you to help me, I'm asking a witch hunter to come into my home, to be around the people I care about. To put them in danger. As it stands, I have done that already. It simply cannot continue."

This, I was not expecting.

"It would be far better for me to die than to continue risking their lives on my behalf." Nicholas slides his chair back and stands. "I'm afraid this is where we part ways."

"You aren't serious," I say. "You don't want me to find your tablet because I'm a witch hunter? It's because I'm a witch hunter that I can find it." I shake my head. "You didn't really think an untrained witch could manage that, did you?"

Nicholas arches an eyebrow. "Why are you so eager to help me?"

I shrug. "It's a means to an end."

"Money, I presume."

"For starters. Enough to get out of the country and to live on for a while. And safe passage."

A pause.

"And?"

"And what?" I say. "That's it. Your life in exchange for mine. A fair deal."

Nicholas doesn't reply. He's still standing, gazing at the parchment on the table, Veda's prophecy written on it in his careful hand. I didn't understand it all—any of it, really—but I do see the word *death* written there. Twice. Other words jump out at me, too: *darkness, end, break, betrayed. Last breath.* I feel a momentary twist of fear. Are those words meant for him, or for me?

"I'm not going to hurt them," I say. "I don't even care about them." Though this isn't exactly true. I've come to like George, and Peter is kind. Fifer I could do without, but she's not worth the trouble I'd have to go through to kill her. And John saved my life. The idea of hurting him bothers me more than I care to admit. "Did Veda say I would?"

"No," Nicholas says. "She didn't. In fact, she implied the

opposite. That you may actually—" He breaks off, running his finger along Veda's words, lost in thought. "Even taking that into consideration, there's no guarantee. And the risk—"

"Becomes a certainty," I say. "You turn away my help, you die. Without your protection, Blackwell will find them. And they die, too."

Nicholas scowls at me. But it's the truth and we both know it.

"Blackwell always told us to remember the greater game," I say. "The greater victory. It's good advice. You should remember it, too."

He looks at me and shakes his head, as if he can't quite understand me or doesn't know what to do with me. "How exactly did you become involved in all this?"

It's the same question George asked me. So I give Nicholas the same answer: the truth. There's no reason to keep it from him now.

I start with the plague, with Caleb finding me and taking me to Ravenscourt. I tell him about working in the kitchen, about Blackwell asking Caleb to witch-hunt for him. About my going along. I even tell him about training, something I never talk about.

"We trained for a year," I say. "There were tests along the way. We had to pass them in order to move forward."

"What kind of tests?"

"Fighting, mostly. Swords, knives, archery, unarmed combat. We fought one another at first, then Blackwell brought in creatures for us to fight. At first, they were fairly regular. Snakes, scorpions, storks—"

"You fought a stork?"

"Yes. It was seven feet high, with bright red eyes and a steel beak. The scorpion was probably twelve feet long with a stinger that dripped poison that killed on contact. The snake had a head that if you cut it off, it grew two more in its place."

"These creatures were, as you say, fairly regular?"

"I just meant they were recognizable. After that, we had to fight things I couldn't name. Things that looked like giant rodents but had six legs and a head like a crocodile. Or reptiles with wings and metal feathers that would fly off their bodies and try to impale you. Something that, just as you started to kill it, changed its appearance so it couldn't die. So if you tried to poke its eye out, it would change into something that didn't have an eye. You see."

"I'm starting to," Nicholas murmurs.

"Then there were endurance tests. Like spending the night in a severely haunted house."

I particularly hated that one. I spent the night huddled into a ball, a foul-smelling, frigid wind swirling in the air, the ghosts' hateful voices echoing around me while they scratched frightening messages to me in blood on the wall. I thought it couldn't get much worse than that test. Of course, as I came to find out later, I was wrong.

"There was a hedge maze we had to figure our way out of. The walls would shift. Things would come after you. We had no food, no water. No supplies. It took me three days to get out." The only person who got out in less time than I was Caleb. It took him two and a half days.

"What happened if you couldn't get out?" Nicholas asks.

I don't reply. What does he think happened? We lost

three prospective witch hunters to the maze test. I never did see them again.

He's quiet for a while. His eyes shift from me to the parchment on the table in front of him, then back to me again.

"Well?" I say. "Do we have a deal or not?"

Nicholas starts to speak but is cut off by a knock at the door. It's George.

"We've got a problem."

Nicholas pushes past him into the other room, George and I behind him. Immediately, I see what's wrong. Veda is standing in the middle of the room, arms held stiffly by her sides. Her tiny body is rigid, but her head lolls from side to side, her eyes rolling into the back of her head. Avis and Fifer are kneeling next to her.

"What happened?" Nicholas demands.

"I don't know," Fifer says, looking frightened. "We were sitting on the floor, playing with the doll I brought her. Then she jumped up and started doing this."

Nicholas crouches in front of her. He's so tall that he's practically on his hands and knees to get eye level with her.

"Veda? Can you hear me?" He places his hand on her cheek and mutters something under his breath. Nothing happens. I take a step toward her to get a better look, but Nicholas glances up at me.

"Stay back, Elizabeth—"

At the sound of my name, Veda's head snaps up and her eyes stop rolling. She stares straight ahead and speaks, her soft voice ominous.

"They're coming. They're coming for her. They're coming." She looks at me. "They're here."

15

THE REACTION IS INSTANTANEOUS. Fifer and George race to the window, flinging back the lace curtains. Veda bursts into tears. John scoops her up, grabs Avis's arm, and pulls them into the bedroom. Nicholas joins Fifer and George at the window, and together they peer into the darkness.

In the distance, I hear male voices: shouting, laughing, catcalling. Soft at first, growing louder by the second. Pin-pricks of light flicker between the cottages in the village. Torches.

I rush to the window and quickly start to count. Two, six, ten, fourteen bobbing lights. Fourteen. I give a little huff of relief. It's only the king's guard. They always patrol in groups of fourteen. But what are they doing out here? We're too far from Upminster for this to be part of their route.

Then I see it: a fifteenth torch blazing to life, its bearer stepping from behind a house and into the empty street. He holds the torch high above his head, the bright flame illuminating his features. He's far away still, too far for me to hear him. But there's no mistaking who it is.

"Caleb," I whisper.

Nicholas lifts a hand and at once, Caleb's voice fills the tiny sitting room.

"I want this whole village searched," he barks. "I want every house torn apart until she's found."

I'm up against the window now, my fingers gripping the windowsill. Caleb and the other witch hunters make their way down the narrow, lamp-lit lane. I watch him kick down door after door, storm into house after house. Listen to his threats, his demands, the terrified screams of the people inside. Hear the anger in his voice as he shouts my name over and over. I know it's an act, a show he's putting on for the other witch hunters. There's no reason for me to be afraid.

But the pounding of my heart tells me otherwise.

I turn to Nicholas. "You said they couldn't find us."

Nicholas glances at me but doesn't reply.

"Well?" I say.

"Shut your mouth," Fifer hisses. "How dare you question him."

"Don't tell me what to do," I fire back. "I'll question who I want."

"Quiet," Nicholas says. "Both of you. They're heading this way."

I turn back to the window as the witch hunters approach Veda's home. Caleb leads the way, Marcus, Linus, and the others behind him. They point and gesture in the direction of the cabin.

"They know," George whispers.

He's right. Maybe one of the neighbors was frightened into giving them our location, maybe they're guessing. Either way, if they keep walking, they'll run right into us. The illusion acts like a veil: As long as the house stays behind it, it's invisible. But if they somehow manage to slip through it, it won't be. And neither will we.

The room erupts into silent movement. Nicholas whirls away from the window, points to the table in the corner. Fifer and George rush to it, pick it up, and move it quietly to the side. On the floor beneath it is a small door. George reaches down and, with a creak and a puff of dust, opens it to reveal a narrow staircase that descends into darkness. John emerges from the back bedroom, still carrying Veda. Avis is on his heels. One by one they start down the stairs.

I turn back to the window. Caleb is so close now I can see his face: his blue eyes narrowed, forehead slightly creased. I don't know what he's thinking. Is he worried about me? Is he afraid of what will happen if he finds me? Or what will happen if he doesn't?

"Elizabeth." The whisper in my ear makes me jump. It's John. "We need to go."

The cottage is empty now save for Nicholas and Fifer. They both stand at the window, muttering some kind of spell. Caleb and the others are having difficulty moving now, their quick strides turning slow and sluggish, as if they're walking through water.

John takes my arm and steers me toward the door in the floor, down the narrow wooden stairs. I go willingly, but when I reach the bottom, I balk. I'm in a tunnel. It's tiny: six feet high, three feet wide, carved entirely from dirt. I feel as if I'm standing in a grave.

I yank my arm from his grasp and lunge for the stairs. I make it to the bottom step before Nicholas and Fifer appear, closing the door from above and bolting it shut. I'm plunged into darkness, the dank smell of earth and decay surrounding me.

Immediately, I'm transported back to that last day of training as a witch hunter. The day I should have died. But somehow, miraculously, lived.

I sink to the ground, press my head to my knees, and try to stop the memories.

It was our final test, our final challenge as recruits. If we succeeded—the eighteen of us who had made it this far—we would receive our stigmas and become the most elite of the king's guard: a witch hunter.

None of us knew what awaited us, what we'd have to fight. Frances Culpepper thought witches. Marcus Denny was hoping for demons. Linus Trew guessed we'd have to fight one another. Only Caleb thought it would be more sinister than that. I saw the look on his face as Blackwell delivered his final speech, when he gave us the barest hint of what was to come.

"You'll be fighting whatever frightens you the most," Blackwell said. "In order to succeed as a witch hunter, you must learn to face your greatest fear and control it. Then—and only then—will you realize that your greatest enemy isn't what you fight, but what you fear."

Caleb betrayed no emotion—almost none. Only I knew him well enough to see the way he pressed his lips together, the set of his jaw, and recognize what it meant. He was afraid. And if Caleb was afraid, then I had cause to be very afraid indeed.

Guildford, one of Blackwell's guards, led me to my test. I couldn't speak, could barely breathe, terrified of what awaited me. My greatest fear. What could it be?

"We're here," Guildford's voice broke the silence. We stood at the edge of the forest, dying trees all around me, crackling leaves under my feet, the sound of water rushing somewhere in the distance. The shadowy, predawn light made everything feel all the more ominous.

Guildford bent over and unearthed an enormous brass ring. It was attached to a narrow wooden door set into the forest floor. He tugged once, twice, and on the third pull it opened to reveal a narrow wooden set of stairs. At the bottom was another door, as rickety and rotten as the stairs. There was no handle, only a smattering of iron nail heads, rust staining the wood like blood.

I started down the stairs, counting as I went. Two. Four. Six. When I reached the bottom, I placed my hands on the door, looked over my shoulder at Guildford.

He nodded.

With a shove, the door creaked open, the rusted hinges shrieking in protest. I could see nothing on the other side, but there was a smell: something sharp, rancid, rotting. I buried my head in my sleeve and started through the opening. I was halfway in when Guildford spoke.

"When you're down there, try to remember what you're fighting."

I paused for a moment, then slipped inside. The door slammed shut by itself, fast and hard, as if it sensed my hesitation, as if it knew I might try to escape.

Darkness descended on me like a shroud. I took a tentative step forward, then another, my hands held in front of me, palms outstretched. I touched something soft, crumbling. Dirt. I felt around me. Above, around, below. Dirt was everywhere. Where was I? A cellar? A tunnel, maybe? I started back toward the stairs when suddenly, inexplicably, the world turned upside down.

I pitched forward and landed on my stomach, hard. As I rolled onto my back, wiping dirt from my mouth, I saw it: the outline of a door far above me, ringed by the sun that had just cleared the horizon. And it was no longer that rotting, rusted, bleeding wooden door missing its handle. It was a stone slab.

I was inside a tomb.

I scrambled to my feet just as the first clumps of dirt fell on my head. And I started to scream. This was magic, I knew; Blackwell had used it in our tests before. But this time something went wrong. This was a mistake; it had to be. He didn't mean to put me in a tomb. Blackwell wouldn't try to bury me alive.

I was sobbing then, trying to get out. But the dirt was too soft to get purchase on, the walls too unstable to climb. Every time I tried, the dirt fell faster, harder. There was a way out—I knew there was. I just couldn't see it.

I heard Blackwell's voice in my head: *Your greatest enemy isn't what you fight, but what you fear.*

What was I afraid of? The falling dirt that now reached my waist? The magic that turned an ordinary tunnel into a grave? I didn't know. But if I didn't figure it out soon, I would die. The realization stopped me cold. As the dirt swirled around my face, sticking to my lips and eyelids, I just stood there, frozen with fear, as I contemplated dying there, in that way.

Alone, forever.

I thought of my mother. Of the lullaby she used to sing to me when I was a little girl. When I was frightened of thunderstorms and make-believe monsters under the bed, not dirt and tombs and magic and death. What use was a lullaby against those? But it was all I had. So I closed my eyes and began to sing.

Sleep and peace attend me, all through the night.
Angels will come to me, all through the night.
Drowsy hours are creeping; hill and vale, slumber
   sleeping,
A loving vigil keeping, all through the night.

The dirt continued to fall. It crept past my lips now; I stood on my toes, wiped clumps of it out of my mouth. I kept singing.

Moon's watch is keeping, all through the night.
The weary world is sleeping, all through the night.
A spirit gently stealing, visions of delight revealing,
A pure and peaceful feeling, all through the night.

Finally, the dirt slowed, then stopped. But I didn't dare stop singing.

To you, my thoughts are turning, all through the night.
For you, my heart is yearning, all through the night.
Sad fate our lives may sever, parting will not last
forever,
A hope that leaves me never, all through the night.

The dirt began receding around me, trickling down past my shoulders, my waist, my legs. I moved down with it, crouching lower and lower until the dirt was nothing more than a floor, me curled into a ball on top of it.

When Guildford finally came for me, he had to fetch another guard to pull me out. As he carried me across the grounds in his arms, I was still curled in a tight, little ball. My hands clapped over my ears, my eyes clamped shut. I kept singing. *All through the night.* Over and over. I couldn't stop. I was far beyond fear now, and I didn't want to come back.

A pair of hands encircles my wrists. Gently, they try to pry my hands from my head, but I jerk away. I hear voices. They're faint, far away. I press my hands harder over my ears to block them out. I don't want to hear anything but that song.

Hands slip around my back, under my knees. I'm being lifted up, carried. It can't be easy, holding me when I'm balled up like this. I'm deadweight. But the guard is strong. I bury my head in his uniform, grateful to breathe something other than earth and decay. He smells good. Clean, like lavender. Warm, like spices. I tuck my head against his shoulder and breathe it in.

I'm still singing, but my voice has dropped to a whisper. I'm so tired. I rub my cheek against the soft linen of the guard's shirt, wishing it were my pillow. His arms tighten around me, holding me close.

Finally, I feel safe.

VINES. THEY'RE THE FIRST THING I see when I wake. They trail across the ceiling and loop down the walls, their edges blurred in the room's dim light. I frown. My room at Blackwell's doesn't have vines. I blink once, twice. Then the memories come crashing down and I remember everything. Veda. Her prophecy. The test, the dirt, the darkness.

I take a breath and push the memories away, as far back as they'll let me. It's never far enough. They're always there, lurking in the corner of my mind like a cat in the dark, waiting for a chance to strike.

Caleb would tell me to think of something happy, to remember something good. But all my memories are about him. And right now, thinking of him doesn't make me happy. It makes me think of Blackwell. Of his determination to find me, of his using Caleb to do it. Of how I'm not sure what will happen if he does.

Nicholas seemed as surprised as I was that Caleb found us. But if anything, it's further proof he needs my help. Further proof I need his. On my own, with no weapons, no money, no way to get out of the country, I will certainly be caught. I escaped a burning once. I don't think I'll be so lucky a second time.

I feel a soft rustling by my feet and realize George must be here. Again. This time I don't mind. Maybe he can help me persuade Nicholas to let me stay. I fling off the sheets and bolt upright, a persuasive argument on my lips. But it isn't George.

It's John.

He's sitting in a chair at the foot of my bed, fast asleep. His head and chest are draped across the mattress, one arm curled over his head, the other stretched out to the side, fingers clenching and unclenching the blanket as if he's grasping for something. That was the rustling I felt. Next to his hand is an open book, the pages lying facedown. What is he doing here?

Of course.

It wasn't a guard who carried me; it was John. My stomach twists when I think about being curled up in his arms. Smelling his shirt. Tucking my head into his shoulder, then falling asleep. I flush a little at the memory.

He must have brought me up here and for whatever reason decided to stay. Why? After all of Nicholas's talk of my being a danger, why would he allow his healer—or for that matter, Peter his son—to be in a room with me? Alone?

I climb out of bed—John doesn't even stir—and walk to the window, twitch open the curtains. It's nearly morning now, the sun stretching rose and cream across the horizon. I consider the possibility Nicholas has decided to wait until today to deal with me, but it still wouldn't explain why John is here. Or why he let me spend the night in a warm room and a comfortable bed instead of tying me up, throwing me in the larder, and letting Hastings torture me all night. It's what I would have done.

Unless Nicholas hasn't told them about me. That after seeing Caleb and the witch hunters come for me, he came to his senses. Realized that if he dies, Blackwell will come for them next. And the only way to stop it is to hire me to find his tablet.

Maybe it's not over for me after all.

I turn from the window and start toward the door, eager to find Nicholas, eager to start planning. Then I stop.

Even if Nicholas does need me to find his tablet, it won't do for me to be too agreeable. I need things from him, too, and I don't want to sell myself short. After what happened last night, it's going to be harder to evade Blackwell than I had previously thought. It won't be enough just to go into exile. I'll need a way to keep moving, a way to stay one step ahead of him. I can never stop, never rest. Not if I want to live.

Both of us have our lives at stake here, only Nicholas is a lot more willing to sacrifice his than I am mine.

I crawl back into bed, careful not to wake John. He's still sprawled across the mattress, still sound asleep. Healing must be exhausting; I wouldn't know. He seems too young to be doing it anyway. My guess is he's around nineteen, but he still seems very boyish. Maybe it's because he's always so rumpled-looking. Like right now.

His white shirt is a wrinkled mess, unbuttoned too low at the top, the sleeves shoved up past his elbows. He still hasn't shaved. And his hair. It's completely wild, those soft dark curls sticking up everywhere, falling across his forehead and into his eyes. He's about six months past due for a haircut, obviously forgotten.

I always had to remind Caleb to cut his hair, too. I don't know what it is about boys, but unless there's a girl around to remind them, they forget even the simplest tasks. Like cutting hair. Or shaving. Or changing their damn clothes. I guess John doesn't have anyone to remind him about those things, either.

His hand shifts across the mattress then, and I spot a tattoo on the inside of his forearm. A black circle about two inches in diameter with a cross inside it: a sun wheel. The circle represents life, the cross triumph over death.

I start tracing the shape of it along the bedcovers with my fingertip. Watch the lines press into the blanket, then disappear. I do this over and over. Then I move to the shapes of the vines on the ceiling. The heart-shaped leaves, the long, looping vines that wind and curl down the wall. I'm so absorbed in what I'm doing that when John's finger reaches over and touches mine, I gasp. I didn't realize he was awake.

"Hi." He looks at me through one half-opened eye.

"Hi."

"You all right?" His voice is quiet, deep.

I shrug. "Fine."

He blinks, but he doesn't take his eyes from me. He's probably looking for an explanation for what happened last night. Why I collapsed as I did, why he had to carry me back. Just thinking about it makes my cheeks blaze.

"I don't like enclosed spaces," I say, finally. "Childhood trauma." It's true enough, anyway.

He props himself up on his elbow. "No need to explain. I was just checking."

"Okay," I say. "Well, thank you for bringing me back. And I'm sorry, I guess." I duck my head to hide the burning in my face again.

"No need to apologize, either. It's not every day I get to carry a girl fifty miles through an underground tunnel." His voice sounds serious. But when I look up, he's smiling.

"It wasn't that far."

"It was. Plus, you're really heavy," he goes on. "You know. Like a sack of feathers."

I shake my head, but I can feel myself start to smile.

John leans back in his chair, runs a hand through his hair. "Anyway, I'm the one who should apologize. I didn't mean to stay, at least not all night. I was waiting for George to come back, started reading, and"—he gestures at his book—"fell asleep."

I glance at the cover. *Praxis Philosophica: Alchemical Formulas for Transformation.*

"I can't imagine why," I say.

He laughs. "I don't know why he didn't come back. I guess I should find out." He gets to his feet just as there's a knock at the door. It's George. He steps into the room, his usual care-free expression replaced with something far more solemn.

"I was just coming to find you," John says. "What's going on?"

George jerks his head at me. "Nicholas needs her."

My stomach flutters with anxiety.

"And he needs you, too. He's not well. Last night took a toll."

John swears under his breath. "I'll go now. Can you take her?"

George nods and they both start toward the door. "We'll go when you're ready."

I still have on the clothes I wore last night: the dark green trousers, the white shirt. The velvet coat is draped across the back of John's chair, the boots underneath it. I draw them on, run my hands through my tangled hair, pinch some color into my cheeks. I was feeling confident about Nicholas, that he wouldn't throw me out of his house, that I'd get another chance. But now I'm not so sure.

George waits for me outside the door. He gives me a quick nod, and, without a word, he starts down the hall, the opposite direction from the stairs.

"What's happening?" I hurry to keep up with him.

He doesn't reply.

"He knows about me. Veda told him. Did you know that?"

George still doesn't reply. We walk along the hallway until we reach the double doors at the end.

"George, what's going on?"

"It's not my place to tell you. You'll find out soon enough

anyway." He gives a quick, staccato knock. My heart is beating a little too fast, my palms a little too damp. I swipe them against my trousers.

"How is he?"

"Cursed," George replies shortly. Then he opens the door.

Inside is an enormous bedchamber. It's dark, and it takes a moment for my eyes to adjust. When they do, I see Nicholas sitting in a chair next to the fireplace, John leaning over him, speaking to him in a low voice. Nicholas looks so frail, so fragile, and even from here I can see he's trembling. My stomach gives an uncomfortable twist.

"Please, come in," Nicholas says. His voice is hoarse, thin. George steps aside to let me through. John straightens up and makes his way to the door. He stops in front of me.

"He wants to see you alone," he says quietly. "It's important, I know, but try to keep it quick, all right?" He and George leave then, the door closing behind them with a quiet thump.

Nicholas beckons me to the chair opposite his. "Come. Sit."

I cross the vast bedroom. It's decorated entirely in shades of red: red carpet, red walls, red bedcovers. Even the candles are red, their flames flickering rhythmically off the walls. I feel as if I'm inside a beating heart.

I settle into the chair. Up close, Nicholas looks even worse. His skin is ashen, his hair is grayer than it was last night, even his dark eyes seem gray. For a moment, he just stares at me.

"I'd like to talk to you about what happened last night," he says, finally.

"Okay." I take a breath. "Which part?"

"About Caleb and the others showing up."

"How they found us, you mean?"

He nods. "How they found us, how they knew we were there. That was not guesswork, nor was it an accident. They knew the location down to the village, the time down to the hour. How do you suppose they knew that?"

"I don't know," I say. "But Blackwell always seems to know everything. As for how, it could have been as simple as using a spy, or as complicated as using magic."

"As complicated as using magic," Nicholas repeats. "Has it ever occurred to you how odd it is that the Inquisitor—former Inquisitor, rather—a man who spends his life rooting out magic and punishing those who practice it, uses magic himself?"

"Blackwell doesn't use magic himself," I say. "He… employs the use of magic, if and when it suits his needs."

"I fail to see the difference."

"There's a big difference. Blackwell had to use magic to educate us. To train us. We had to have magic in order to know how to fight it. He couldn't very well train us without it. It would be like trying to train an army without giving them weapons."

I repeat the answers Caleb gave me to the very questions I had asked, time and time again. But Nicholas just shakes his head.

"The things you describe, your experience, those were not simple spells or mere enchantments. The power it would take would rival my own. However, the lack of conscience…those creatures…"

"Blackwell called them hybrids; Caleb called them halflings. I jokingly called them cockatrices, after the dish I used to make in the kitchen."

He nods. "But creating living creatures like that is no joke. It is complex magic—highly difficult, attained through many years of practice and trial and error. It could not have been done by just anyone. How did he come by such magic?"

I have to admit I never questioned exactly how Blackwell made those things happen. Not that he would have told me even if I did. He did everything in secrecy, behind closed doors and blindfolds. I never even saw who marked me with my stigma. At the time, I didn't really care.

"Caleb said he used some of the wizards we captured to do things for him," I say. "There were plenty of wizards we arrested that I never saw burn."

Nicholas goes still.

"Why is he after you?" he says after a moment.

"What do you mean?" I say. "You know why."

He waves it away. "What is it about you that makes him so determined to find you? I'm a far bigger prize than a sixteen-year-old girl. Why did he go through the effort of trumping up charges for you? Do you really believe he thinks you're a witch? A spy? A traitor?"

"He told me I was a liability."

"He may have been telling the truth about that. At least, the truth the way he sees it. Rather, the way it has been foreseen."

"What do you mean?"

"I'm talking about the tablet."

I frown. "Are you saying Blackwell had me arrested because he knew I could find your tablet?"

"Yes."

I shake my head. "I don't see how he could possibly know that."

"No? You said yourself Blackwell used magic if and when it suited his needs. Wouldn't it be possible, then, that he used a seer?"

I shake my head again, but he presses on.

"It would explain how he found us at Veda's, how he knew you were here. Perhaps you saw one in his room, someone you mistook for a servant. Perhaps even a child?"

I think back to the night Richard took me to Blackwell, the boy I saw scurrying down the hall. He was about five years old, the same age as Veda. I look up to see Nicholas watching me. He just nods.

"So he has a seer," I say. "It doesn't mean anything."

Nicholas takes a breath, as though his words were a weight he was about to lift.

"Elizabeth, I've been watching Blackwell for a long time. I watched him go from duke and brother of the king to Lord Protector, as good as a king. Indeed, if Malcolm had died from plague, too, Blackwell would be king. I don't doubt a day goes by that he doesn't regret that."

I can't disagree. Malcolm knew Blackwell hated him; he never knew why. I didn't have the heart to tell him it was because his uncle wished he were dead.

"With Blackwell, change tends to precede greater change. A king dies, a duke becomes Protector. A prince becomes king, the Protector becomes Inquisitor. Now he's handed that title over to your friend Caleb. Do you think Blackwell will be content to go back to being a duke?"

169

I suck in a sudden, sharp breath. "Do you think he means to be king?"

"I think he's after the greater victory," Nicholas replies. "Whether that is king or something worse than king."

Something worse than king. The words send a chill down my spine.

"Whatever his plan, he needs me out of the way to achieve it," Nicholas continues. "He knew you would threaten that, so he was forced to take action. I believe it's why he's after you now. I believe it's why he cursed me."

"Why he had you cursed, you mean."

"No. I mean why *he* cursed me."

His words hang in the air, swooping and swirling above me like one of Blackwell's winged reptiles; and when they land, they pierce me like metal feathers: hard, sharp, burrowing deep.

"Why he cursed you," I repeat.

Nicholas nods.

"So you think…you think that…" I can't say it.

He says it for me. "Blackwell is a wizard."

I'm on my feet before he finishes the word.

"No," I say. "No, no, no." I shake my head so hard it hurts. "Blackwell is not a wizard. No. That's ridiculous. It's impossible. It's insane."

"He trained you, using magic. He marked you, using magic. He created things, using magic; and he, himself, uses magic." Nicholas marches through the evidence like a barrister before the bar.

"He didn't do those things," I say wildly. "It was the other wizards. The ones we captured, the ones we didn't burn. They did it. Not him." I cling to this scrap of possibility as I might cling to a scrap of rock to keep from falling off a cliff.

"No." Nicholas's voice is soft but firm. "I told you. The only witch or wizard who could perform magic like that is now dead. And they are dead: I witnessed their deaths myself."

"It's not true. Not true, not true, not true." I'm babbling.

"He led a life of lies," Nicholas says quietly, almost sympathetically. "He would have had to; a young wizard living in a household of Persecutors. At best, they would have sent him away; at worst, well. We know what they do to witches and wizards, don't we?"

I'm still shaking my head.

"By the time his brother became king, by the time he opened the door to the possibility of reconciliation between Persecutors and Reformists, Blackwell's choice was made. It wouldn't be enough for him to be able to finally use his power. He wanted to rule with it. To take control after all the years spent relinquishing it. I believe it's why he started the plague: to kill the king, to kill Malcolm, to give him the throne."

The ground shifts; everything shifts. The rock breaks and I'm off the cliff now, falling through the air, plummeting toward the hard earth and an even harder truth:

Blackwell started the plague.

Blackwell killed my parents.

Blackwell is a wizard.

I sink back into the velvet chair, bury my head in my hands. I don't know how long I sit here, in this red, beating room. It could be minutes; it could be hours.

"What do I need to do?" I say, finally. There's no point in

telling him I can't find the tablet, that I'm in enough trouble as it is, that helping him will only make things worse for me. There is nothing worse than this.

Nicholas nods. "First thing—and this is very important— you cannot let anyone know you are a witch hunter. I know that George knows. But he can be the only one."

I frown. "Surely they'll find out," I say. "If I get hurt, if I heal, if I'm somehow drawn into a fight...it's going to be really hard to keep it from them."

"Then I'll need you to try even harder to keep it secret," he says. "Don't get in any fights, and don't get hurt." A pause. "I've already told them you're a witch."

"What? Why?"

"Because they need a reason why you're the one to find the tablet. They need a reason why you survived jail. And because you were arrested with those herbs in your pocket, it's the reason that makes the most sense."

"And what about Blackwell? That he's a—" I swallow. I still can't say it.

"I think it's best we keep that to ourselves for now. The truth will come out soon enough."

I nod.

"Second, I'm sending you away. Today. You're to travel with the others to Stepney Green, to pay a visit to Humbert Pembroke."

I blink. Humbert Pembroke is the richest man in Anglia, next to the king. He's a great friend of Blackwell's and a big supporter of the crown. He's been a fixture at court for many years, though I haven't seen him in a while. *Why him?*

"He's one of us," Nicholas says before I can ask.

I'm so surprised by this it takes me a moment to respond. "Why Stepney Green?" I say. "Is that where the tablet is?"

"No," Nicholas says. "But you're not looking for the tablet there. Remember what Veda said? *Come third winter's night, go underground in green. What holds him in death will lead you to thirteen.* What you're looking for in Stepney Green is the thing that will lead you to the tablet, not the tablet itself."

"That's all I have to go on?"

"Yes. But it's enough, at least for now."

"How?" I say. "It doesn't tell me anything. Veda said more after that, a lot more. What did it all mean?"

Nicholas hesitates. "There is nothing I can tell you that you will not learn for yourself."

"So you do know, then. You know what's going to happen." It hits me then, what he knows. "You know I'm going to die."

"We all die," Nicholas says. "That's not a prophecy; it's a certainty."

"Don't mince words," I snap.

"Elizabeth, this is your prophecy. How it plays out is entirely in your hands. I can't tell you what to do or what to find, because I don't know. All I can do is put you in the right place at the right time and trust that you'll know it when you see it."

I feel a sudden surge of anger. At putting my fate in the hands of a child, into a string of meaningless words.

"I realize this seems far-fetched to you," Nicholas says.

"That's not quite the word I would use," I mutter.

"I've been deciphering prophecies for a long time," Nicholas replies. "Veda's for as long as she could talk, countless others' before her. Some are simple, some complex. Some are more riddle than vision. But regardless, all prophecies require a measure of conjecture."

There's a soft tapping on the door, and John steps inside. He's dressed in a heavy black coat, his bag slung over his shoulder.

"I'm sorry to interrupt," he says. "But we're ready to go. I need to check on you one last time before we do."

"We're nearly done," Nicholas says. John nods, glances at me, then closes the door.

I spread my hands. "So I go to Stepney Green. Look for the thing that will lead me to the tablet. Then what?"

Nicholas smiles. "I cannot tell you that, either. But the answer will present itself in time."

I bite back my frustration. "Is there anything you *can* tell me?"

"Use your judgment. That's very important. Do what feels right to you, in whatever circumstance you find yourself in, even if it seems improbable or even impossible. And have faith. Everything else will follow."

17

AN HOUR LATER PETER SEES us off. It's a six-hour walk to Humbert's home in Stepney Green. We can't ride; it would call too much attention to ourselves, make it harder to hide if we came upon unwanted company. It's just as well. Nicholas has only one horse anyway.

Peter rubs his face with both hands and sighs. "Stay off the main roads as much as possible. Stick together, but don't travel in a group. John, you lead the way. George can bring up the rear. Cover your tracks. If there's any sign of trouble, or you think you're being followed..."

"Father." John places his arm on Peter's shoulder. "We'll be fine."

Peter nods and lets out a series of short whistles. An enormous falcon swoops down from the sky and settles on John's outstretched arm.

"Send him back here the moment you arrive at Humbert's," Peter says. "If you don't, I'll assume something's happened. But if you don't send him and nothing's happened..." He looks at John sternly. "I swear to you, John Paracelsus Raleigh, when I'm through with you, you'll wish something had."

George gapes at John. "Your middle name is Paracelsus?"

"Shut it," John snaps. He turns to Peter, flushing slightly. "I'll send Horace. Everything will be fine. Please try not to worry."

"Hmph," Peter grunts. He wraps John in a tight embrace, patting his back softly. Then he releases him and looks at us. "We're taking Nicholas to Harrow so the healers there can watch over him. Once he's settled and we see Avis and Veda to a safe house, I'll meet you at Humbert's. I'll be there as soon as I can."

He unbolts the door and pushes it open, a flurry of snowflakes rushing into the hall. The first snow of the season. I pull my coat tightly around me and step outside.

"Be safe," Peter says, his face still etched with worry. "If you see anything, anything at all, just run."

The four of us trudge across the wide gravel path and the grass, into the woods. Fifer and John walk ahead of us, their heads bent toward each other, whispering. All the while Nicholas's voice is whispering in my ear: Blackwell is a wizard. Blackwell is a wizard.

Blackwell is a wizard.

"What's with you?" George falls into step beside me. "You've barely said three words since you left Nicholas's room." A pause. "Did he put a spell on you? You know. To keep you from getting all—" He mimes choking and stabbing motions with his hands.

I burst into a fit of giggles then. I can't help it. Maybe it's nerves. Maybe I've gone mad. The whole world has gone mad; seems right I should go down with it. My laughter echoes through the trees, the only sound in the otherwise silent forest. John spins around and flashes me a grin. Fifer punches him in the arm and he turns back to her, a scowl replacing his smile.

I compose myself. "No. I'm just...you know. I don't know."

"Mmm. Clarity is vastly overrated."

I shoot him a look. "You know what I mean. It's going to be hard enough finding this tablet without having to hide who I am from everyone."

George nods. "Aye. But it's important. Nicholas wouldn't ask it if it weren't."

"Why? You know and you aren't getting all—" I mimic his choking and stabbing motions. "Why does it matter if they know?"

He squints up ahead, in the direction of John and Fifer. It looks as if they're arguing now; Fifer is gesturing furiously while John shakes his head. She glances back at me and scowls.

"She doesn't like me, does she?"

George shrugs. "Don't take it personally. She doesn't like anyone except John. He's the only one who can put up with her anyway. He's got the patience of a saint."

I turn my attention to John then, watch as he walks through the trees up ahead.

He's so tall that he's having a hard time avoiding all but the highest branches. They brush against his face, the leaves and twigs getting caught up in his dark hair. When he stops to disentangle a cluster of leaves, he sees me watching him. He gives me a little wave, then yanks the leaves out and throws them to the ground, a grin lighting up his face. Suddenly, my stomach feels as if someone tied a knot in it. Without thinking, I smile back.

George elbows me. "Stop that."

"Stop what?"

"Smiling. You can't go around smiling at people like that. It's…" He trails off, searching for the right word. "Distracting."

"Don't be ridiculous."

"I'm not. Look, there's something you need to know." He glances at John, making sure he's not paying attention. He's not; he and Fifer are back to whispering again. "John's mother and sister were captured by witch hunters and burned at the stake for witchcraft. They were healers."

"What?" The knot in my stomach grows tighter. "When?"

George sighs. "Last year. One morning Anne and Jane—they're his mother and sister—left Harrow, presumably to see a patient. John and Peter didn't even know they'd gone. Anyway, they never returned. I guess you know what that means."

I shake my head. But, of course, I know.

"Peter and John knew, too. They both went to Upminster, did everything they could. But Anne and Jane went to the stakes anyway. At one point, John tried to get to them, in the fire…." George's voice breaks. "I don't know what he was thinking. He's lucky he wasn't arrested, too; I don't know why he wasn't. The guards got ahold of him, beat him senseless. He lay there in the dirt, beaten and bloody, and watched his mother and sister die right in front of him."

I stop walking. Remember what John told me back at Nicholas's about the burnings. I hadn't realized he was talking about his own mother and sister. Never imagined he had to see that. I feel sweaty, queasy. I wonder vaguely if I might throw up.

"I didn't do it," I whisper. "Capture them, I mean. I remember everyone I've ever arrested. It wasn't me."

"Even so," George says. "He can't know. He wouldn't kill you, but that's not really what I'm worried about. Do you understand what I'm telling you?"

"Yes," I whisper.

"On we go, then."

We keep walking. I keep my eyes on the ground in front of me, on the snow-dusted leaves and twigs that snap underfoot like breaking bones. I can feel George's eyes on me, watching me carefully. I ignore him.

But I can't ignore the feeling that's crept into my chest, that uncomfortable twist of guilt, like a vine curling its way inside, threatening to choke me. I may not have captured John's mother and sister, but I've captured others like them. I've been responsible for their deaths, for ruining families the way John's was ruined, and for what? I thought I was doing what was best for the country, to keep it safe.

It was all a lie.

After several hours the woods eventually break, giving way to pastures. Rolling green hills, wide swaths of browning, early winter grass framed by low stone walls and dotted with sheep, fluffy in their thick white winter coats. The land stretches ahead of us for miles, a narrow dirt road our only passage through. The snow has now switched to rain, accompanied by a low rumbling of thunder. After being ensconced in the relative safety of the woods, I feel vulnerable being out in the open like this.

"We split up, I think," John says. "I'll go ahead. George, you follow behind. If there's anything unexpected, Horace will let us know. So if you see him, run. Hide. I'll come find you when I think it's safe."

The falcon has spent most of the journey circling the sky over our heads, but he is now resting on John's outstretched arm. We agree, and he releases Horace and takes off in a slow run, down the road and over the first hill until he's out of sight.

George hangs back, letting Fifer and me walk ahead. She makes a show of ignoring me, so we're quiet for the next few miles, concentrating on the path in front of us. The rain is still coming down, turning the road into a river of mud. It's slow going, trudging through the ankle-deep sludge.

Fifer is shivering under her wet cloak, her lips nearly blue with cold. When she steps into a pothole and trips, I grab her arm to keep her from falling. She looks grateful, for a second. Then she yanks away from me and storms off, muttering under her breath.

"You're welcome," I say.

She whirls around, a look of disgust on her face.

"What are you doing here?"

I smirk. I can't help it. "Theologists have long believed that our time here on earth is—"

"Not that, you idiot," she flares. "What I mean is, can you do anything? Nicholas said you're a witch, so I'm asking you if you can do any magic."

"Oh," I say. "No."

"You've never done any spells? Curses?"

I shake my head.

"Not even by accident? Say, wished harm on anyone and caused it to come true?"

"No," I repeat.

"Well, do you get lucky a lot? That's what happens to untrained witches, you know. They do magic without realizing it and think they're just lucky."

"Do I seem lucky to you?"

Fifer snorts, her face softening a bit. "I guess not. Although you did survive jail fever. I guess now you know why." She purses her lips, thinking. "There must be something you can do. Otherwise—"

She's cut off by Horace, soaring toward us and clipping the tops of our heads with his outstretched wing.

"Run!"

We sprint across the muddy road, hurling over the wall and into the fields, searching for somewhere to hide. The grass is too low to offer cover. The only trees are in the distance, but if we're fast enough we might make it.

I grab Fifer's sleeve and start toward them when I hear it. Softly at first, then louder: the unmistakable thundering noise of horses, their hooves pounding through the mud. Whoever's coming, they're close. We won't make it to the trees before we're spotted.

Fifer grabs my arm and yanks me to the ground.

"What are you doing?" I say. "They're going to see—"

"No, they're not." She reaches into her cloak and pulls out a long silk cord with three knots tied in it. I recognize it immediately: a witch's ladder. Witches use them when they need to perform difficult or time-consuming spells quickly. Their energy and power are stored in the cord, and they're released whenever a knot is untied. Blackwell showed us what they were in training, how they worked.

I suppose he would know.

Fifer yanks a small tuft of grass from the ground and starts to untie one of the knots from the cord, her fingers trembling as the sound of the hooves grows louder.

"Enlarge." She flings the grass into the air. The blades expand and shoot upward, forming an enormous overgrown hedge. It's at least four feet high and ten feet long. The grass is so high it curls over on itself, thick enough for us to hide under.

We crawl beneath it, pulling our cloaks and bags tightly around us so they can't be seen from the road. In the distance, I see them: four men riding under the king's standard. Fifer watches them, wide-eyed. We both go still and wait for them to pass.

They don't. The horses slow to a canter, then a trot, then stop completely, less than fifty feet from us.

"I've had to piss for miles!" grumbles one man. I hear his feet splash in the mud as he dismounts his horse.

"Hurry up and have done, then. Nothing here is stopping you."

"I'm coming, too," says another, slipping from his saddle.

The two men make their way across the field, heading in our direction. They march straight up to our hedge, stop, and proceed to unbutton their trousers. Fifer grimaces; she looks horrified. I smile a little. I can't help it. Pissing men don't bother me in the slightest. I was the only girl among twenty male witch hunters. I've pretty much seen it all.

"So what do you think?" one guard says.

"Dunno," says the other. "Ten more miles, maybe?" He shakes his head. "Bloody Stepney Green, middle of nowhere—"

"Not that. I'm talking about her."

Her. They're talking about me. Fifer shoots me a look. She knows it, too. I stare at the guards through the hedge, willing them not to say more.

"Aye. But I wouldn't worry too much," the guard continues. "D'you really think Pace would send us if there was any chance of her being there?"

Fifer's expression turns to confusion.

Shut up, I plead silently. *Shut up, shut up....*

The other guard looks doubtful. "If you say so."

"I do. Look, she can't be in three places at once. And if you ask me, Stepney Green's the least likely of all."

Three places? Where else does Caleb think we are?

"Even still. You'd think they'd at least send a witch hunter with us."

"What for? You don't think we can take a little girl?"

"She's not just a little girl."

Fifer narrows her eyes at me. I shrug, as if I hear this sort of thing every day. But my heart is pounding so hard it's a wonder they all can't hear it.

"She's dangerous," the guard continues. "Who knows what she's capable of now that she's with Nicholas Perevil. I say we search the place as we're supposed to and get out of here. If we find her, we'll let Pace take care of her."

"You don't have to tell me twice." The men button up their trousers and turn to walk away.

I breathe a sigh of relief. *That was close*, I think. *Too close.*

"Hard to believe, isn't it? That she's a witch hunter *and* a witch?" He tuts. "Blackwell ought to be more careful about who he recruits next time."

Damnation.

I look at Fifer. She stares back at me, her expression blank as a fish's. I open my mouth to say—I don't know what—but she turns away, either in fright or disgust. Probably both. She sits, unseeing, unmoving, as the two guards join the others in the road. They mount their horses and ride away, kicking up a fountain of mud in their wake.

Damned bigmouthed idiots! I should have taken them out when I had the chance. Well, it's too late now. Nicholas won't be happy that Fifer found out about me, and neither will George. Where is he, anyway? I'm going to need his help managing Fifer when she snaps out of this daze she's in. She's still staring blankly through the hedge. I slide out from under the hedge to look for George. The second I do, she pounces.

"You're a witch hunter!" She shoves me to the ground and jumps on top of me. "A goddamned witch hunter!"

"Fifer! Stop!" She's hitting me now, punching my arms, my stomach, my face. I can't fight back, not really. I'll just hurt her. Or worse, I'll kill her. I grab her wrists to try to stop her, but she yanks away and slaps my face and rakes her fingernails down my cheek.

"I could kill you! I will kill you! You—" She lets out a string of obscenities so blistering and outrageous I actually start to laugh. Until she grabs a hank of my hair and pulls. Hard.

I let out a yelp, and for a moment I forget I'm not supposed to fight her. I grab her shoulders and fling her off me. She tumbles into the grass, but she's up in a flash, cuffing me across the head so hard my ears ring. I jump on top of her, and we start rolling around on the ground, both of us slapping and pulling hair and screaming.

There's a streak of movement in the distance, and suddenly George is there, standing over us with a horrified expression.

"Oi!" He hops around us, dodging our flailing bodies. "What the hell is going on?"

We keep fighting.

"Would you two quit? Quit it, I say!" George takes me by the waist and pulls me off Fifer. She jumps up and flies at me, her hands spread like claws. I catch her wrists, and the three of us stagger around, reeling like drunkards in a brawl before tumbling headlong into the hedge.

"Peace, for God's sake!" George shouts, prying us apart. "What the hell is going on?"

Fifer scrambles to her feet. "She's a witch hunter!" She lunges for me again, her hands tightened into fists.

George grabs her before she can get to me.

"What are you doing?" she shrieks. "Go get John! We've got to kill her. Right now! He can, or you can. Or I'll do it myself!" She pulls out her witch's ladder.

"You can't kill her," George says.

"Yes, I can!" Her fingers fumble around a knot. "I'll curse her into a thousand pieces—"

George yanks it out of her hands. "D'you want Nicholas to die?"

"What?" Fifer looks horrified. "No!"

"That's what will happen if you kill her. She's the only one who can find that tablet. You know that. So it shouldn't matter to you what she is. Witch hunter, demon, she could be the devil for all you care."

"She is. She is the devil." Fifer seethes. "And you." She rounds on George, jabbing her finger at him. "You're awfully calm about this. So help me, if you knew she was a witch hunter and didn't tell us…"

George and I exchange a rapid glance.

"You knew," Fifer whispers. "You knew and you didn't tell me. Why? How could you do that to me? Or John?" Her eyes go wide. "Nicholas—"

George holds up a hand. "He knows. Of course he knows. I didn't tell you because he told me not to. Didn't see any reason for you to know."

"No reason?" Fifer screeches. "No reason to tell us she's a vile, lying, barbaric *bi*—"

"Fifer." George raises his eyebrows.

"You don't really believe she's going to help us, do you?" Fifer says. "She means to run us in circles long enough for Nicholas to die, then turn us over to her friends!"

"I'm not going to do that," I say.

"She's not going to do that," George repeats.

"I don't believe you," Fifer says. "I don't believe her. I don't believe any of this." She's pacing back and forth, shaking her head. Finally, she stops. "I'm telling John." She turns and heads for the road.

"No." George grabs her sleeve. "We keep this among us."

"No!" Fifer says. "He needs to know. Do you know what he'll do if he finds out?"

"Aye. I do know. Which is why he can't." Fifer opens her mouth to argue, but George shakes his head. "The main thing is finding the tablet. You know that. Right now, we can't afford it to be about anything else. If we tell him, that's exactly what will happen."

Fifer doesn't reply.

"Look, when we get to Humbert's, you can write to Nicholas," George continues. "Ask him yourself. He'll tell you the same thing."

"Why would he keep this from us?"

"He has his reasons." George holds the witch's ladder in front of her. "Do we have a deal?"

Fifer lunges for the ladder, but George yanks it away.

"Fine," she rages. "It's a deal."

"Good. Now wipe that murderous look off your face. Here comes John."

I look over the hedge and see him coming toward us in a slow run. He's completely coated in mud.

"Oi, man. What happened to you?" George says, looking him over.

"Jumped in a ditch." John wipes his face with his sleeve. "Nice hedge," he says to Fifer. She shrugs and doesn't reply.

"Those guards, they're headed the same way we are. I suppose they're looking for us." He looks at each of us in turn. "Did you hear them say anything?"

None of us reply.

"I could have sworn I asked that question out loud," John says wryly. "Fifer?"

"Oh, don't ask me! I don't know anything!"

John raises his eyebrows. "What's wrong with you?"

"Everything! Nothing! I don't know!" She gives her witch's ladder a little shake. "It's just…I'm upset because I had to use one of my knots. I only have three. I didn't want to waste it on something so stupid." She gestures at the hedge.

"It's not stupid; it saved you," John says.

"It doomed us!"

"Don't be such a tragedy queen," I say irritably, rubbing my scalp. It smarts from where she pulled my hair. "So you used a knot. You can make another at Humbert's."

Fifer glares at me, and without a word, she stalks off toward the road. George hurries after her.

I look at John. "What was that about?"

"Fifer didn't make those knots—Nicholas did," John replies. "She's not quite powerful enough for that yet. He was going to make more, but…you know."

"Oh," I say. "That's too bad." I can see how those knots would come in handy.

But it's good to know Fifer isn't as powerful as she pretends to be.

18

ANOTHER HOUR PASSES, AND THE sky begins to grow dark. The rain that has dogged us most of the day has turned back into snow, coming at us in gusts and swirling around our feet. Eventually we reach a crossing, the road splitting into two lanes. One is wide and well paved, leading into town. The other road is barely that—footprints in an expanse of knee-high grass that looks as if it's been walked on maybe twice in the last month. John checks his map again and, of course, that's the road we take.

The snow falls faster and harder, and what little path we had is swallowed by snow and darkness. Every now and again I catch a flash of red in the sky, blinking in the darkness like a crimson star. Spook lights, I suppose; we must be nearing a bog or a marsh of some sort. I just hope we don't have to cross it. While bog spooks aren't dangerous, they are very irritating. They'll make you play a thousand stupid games before letting you cross the water in peace. I'm too tired to deal with that right now.

Finally, we come upon a series of hills, each steeper than the last. I lose my footing on the icy ground a few times, so John walks beside me, holding my arm to keep me steady.

"How much longer?" Fifer moans. "I'm cold, I'm hungry, my feet hurt—"

"We should be coming up on it now," John says. We crest another hill, the steepest one so far. When we reach the top, John points to the valley below. "There it is."

Humbert's house. It's more castle than home, really, built entirely from gray stone and surrounded by an enormous square moat. Only a pair of arched footbridges joins the house with the surrounding land. It might look like a fortress were it not for all the ivy, the leaves gone red for the winter, lacing the stones like veins. Multiple gardens fill the land- scape, cut through with ponds and more arching bridges. The whole thing is covered in a light dusting of snow, like a dream.

We scurry down the hill and cross the bridge that leads to the inner courtyard. The house is less imposing here, more domestic: half-timbered walls, diamond-paned win- dows, a large stone fountain. When we reach the front door, it swings open almost immediately and a doorman ushers us into an impressive entrance hall. Glittering brass and crystal chandeliers. Shiny black-and-white checkerboard floors. Rich wood-paneled walls, hung with a series of oil paintings. Tasteful nudes, nothing violent here at all. There's a particularly nice one of Venus and Cupid that takes up nearly an entire wall.

"Hullo!" booms a voice. I look around to see Humbert Pembroke waddling toward us, a large glass of brandy in his hand. He hasn't changed much since the last time I saw him: very short, very portly, dressed finely in a brightly colored silk jacket and velvet trousers. "What happened to you lot?"

He looks us over. John's still covered in mud. Fifer's got streaks of dirt on her face and grass tangled in her hair. I'm sure I look just as bad. George is the only one who looks moderately clean. How does he do that?

John—in an absurdly loud voice—fills him in about our run-in with the guards. Humbert nods and makes appropriate listening noises, but it's clear he's too distracted by me to really pay attention. He can't keep his eyes off me. The second John finishes, he turns to me.

"So you're her, hmm?" Humbert bellows.

"Who?" I say.

"What?"

John turns to me, a smile tugging at the corner of his mouth.

"Humbert's a bit deaf, so you'll have to speak up," he whispers. "And I think he just wants to know if you're the girl Nicholas told him about."

"Oh." I walk over to Humbert and stand directly in front of him so I don't have to shout. "Yes," I say. "I'm her."

Humbert smiles and snaps his fingers. Instantly a maid arrives. She takes one look at our dirty faces and mud-covered clothes and sends us upstairs to bathe and be ready for dinner in an hour.

———————•

Moments later I'm standing in an upstairs bedroom, waiting as a servant prepares me a bath. I look around, impressed. Beautifully appointed rooms. Rich drapes. Carpets so plush they're ankle-deep. Tester beds, fat with goose down mattresses, layers of linen sheets, and soft fur-lined blankets. This house is as fine as any of Malcolm's palaces, finer than Blackwell's, even. If he knew Humbert was a Reformist, he'd take all of it, along with his head.

As I undress and slip into the bath, Humbert's maid—an older woman named Bridget—comes in with a stack of clothing.

"I thought you'd prefer a dress for dining." She holds it up.

I don't, but I guess I can't complain. It's a pretty thing: dark blue velvet, the skirt overlaid with rich gold panels, the bodice embroidered with some kind of bird woven in silver thread. She lays it out, along with a pair of slippers and earrings, gold and sapphire to go with the dress. There's even a matching ring. I stare at them, wide-eyed. I've never worn anything this nice in my life. I never had any reason to.

After the bath, Bridget helps me dress. She tuts over the condition of my hair and insists on styling it: drying it with a bath sheet, pulling out all the knots, then patiently coaxing my unruly waves into loose curls before pinning up the sides with a pair of blue-jeweled clips.

"There you are, poppet." She thrusts me in front of the mirror. "Don't you look lovely."

I look at my reflection and my eyes go wide. The color is back in my face, my eyes, even my hair. The bodice of the gown is low and tight, and I expected to see nothing there, just skin and bones. I'm shocked by what's replaced it: curves.

I never had them before. Curves were soft and vulnerable, and that meant death to me, so they were trained out of me. Instead, I became thin and wiry and strong. My illness tore me down, but I've been built back up, not by force this time but by care: by soft beds and sweet potions and gentle hands and magic.

I don't know what to think anymore. About any of it. Magic killed my parents; Blackwell tried to kill magic. Blackwell is magic; Blackwell tried to kill me. John saved me with magic; now I'm trying to kill magic to save Nicholas. It goes against everything I've ever known, a betrayal of everything I've ever been taught.

But who betrayed who first?

Bridget leads me downstairs, into the dining room. I'm the last to arrive. Everyone else is seated around the table, pitchers of wine and goblets scattered across the surface. John gets to his feet as I walk in, but Humbert fairly leaps from his chair and rushes toward me.

"*Elizabeth!*" he roars. "*Do come in!*"

He hauls me across the room and thrusts me into the seat next to his. The table is huge; it could seat at least twenty people. But he had to put me next to him. I'll be as deaf as he is before the night is through.

Next to me is Fifer. She's in a dress, too, copper-colored silk with an embroidered green bodice. But the way she's scowling you'd think it was made from metal, lined with nails. Even still, I have to admit she looks pretty.

Across from me are George and John, both clean and dressed for dinner. As usual, George looks horrifying. Yellow shirt, purple vest, orange harlequin jacket. Beside him, John looks practically funereal. White shirt, dark green coat. Both already wrinkled, of course. And his hair. It's still damp from bathing but already running out of control. I'm seized with a wild urge to run my hands through it. Make sense of those curls, push them out of his eyes at least. I wonder what it would look like if it were cut. Although, I rather like it long. Besides, if it were any shorter, it might get even wilder, and—

He grins at me and I realize I've been staring at him too long. I flush and turn to Humbert.

"I'm sorry to keep you waiting."

"It was worth it, I see," he booms. "I'm pleased you decided to wear the gown sent up."

Well, it's not as if he left me much choice.

"It's beautiful," I say.

"Isn't it? It belongs to the Duchess of Rotherhithe, a dear friend of mine. She and her family came for a stay one summer, brought ten trunks full of gowns. Left that and several others behind. I doubt she even noticed them missing."

I shift uncomfortably. I know the duchess. She and her daughter are close friends of Queen Margaret. I served them dinner once, and they were both awful. Worse still, her granddaughter is Cecily Mowbray, one of Caleb's new friends. I don't like the idea of wearing her clothes, no matter how pretty they are.

"You see that bird on the bodice there?" Humbert continues. "It's the symbol of the House of Rotherhithe, embroidered using thread made from real silver. I shudder to think of the cost. But the duchess, she's not very economical—"

The mention of the bird jars my memory. "I'm sorry to interrupt you, sir . . ." I realize I don't know how to address him.

"Call me Humbert."

"Of course, Humbert. But I just remembered something. John"—I turn to get his attention but find I've already got it—"did you send Horace back to your father? Let him know you're okay? I don't want him to worry."

George and Fifer exchange a glance.

"I did, yes," John replies. "Thank you for remembering." He rakes his hand through his hair then, and I notice how green his eyes look tonight. Usually they're more brown than green, gray around the edges with a little bit of gold in the middle, and—

"*Elizabeth*," Humbert trumpets, jerking me to my senses. "I do hope you'll like what I've had prepared this evening. I understand you're quite an expert on court cuisine."

A pair of servants walks in then, carrying several platters between them. Manchet bread, salted beef, fruit tarts, cheese, and, of all things, a cockatrice—a dish made by combining one half of an animal with another before roasting and redressing it.

They were common enough at court; Malcolm in particular loved them. His cooks tried to outdo one another with increasingly outrageous combinations: body of a chicken, tail of a beaver. Head of a deer, rear of a boar. This one is half-peacock, half-swan: snow white and long-necked in the front, bright turquoise and plumed in the back.

"Well, then?" Humbert asks. "What do you think of this little one?"

I lean over and examine it carefully.

"It's very good," I tell him. The white feathers of the swan blend in seamlessly with the peacock's, no sign of the careful stitching underneath. That's the hardest part of presenting a cockatrice, getting the feathers or fur right. It's the difference between wanting to eat it or run from it.

By the time the servants reappear to clear away the plates, I'm struggling to keep my eyes open. I'm tired from the walk, full from wine and cockatrice, and I've got an awful headache from Humbert's screaming in my ear all night long. I'm thinking about excusing myself when he starts in again.

"*The Thirteenth Tablet*," Humbert shouts. "What a thing to be cursed by! And what a thing to find." He shakes his head, pours his fifth glass of brandy. I swear, he drinks more than George, and that's saying a lot. "You really have no idea where it might be?"

"No," I say. "I really don't."

He looks at me expectantly. "Then I suppose the next question is, what do you want to *do* about it?"

The room goes quiet. I feel everyone's eyes on me. There's a collective intake of breath, as if they're waiting for me to make a sudden proclamation, like some sort of damned prophet on the mount.

"I don't know," I say.

The disappointment is palpable.

"I could go out tomorrow," I continue because I can't bear the silence any longer. "You know, walk around a bit? I don't know the area, so I'd need a map, but what can it hurt? Unless you think it's better for me to stay put, I guess—"

"*No!*" Humbert howls. "That won't do at all! This is a prophecy, Elizabeth. There can be no guessing. No hemming, no hawing. No shilly-shally!" He pounds the table with his fist. "You must be decisive! Whatever happens, you must really feel your decisions, my dear. Know them. *In here.*" He thumps his fist against his chest.

"Besides," George says, rolling his eyes at Humbert. "You can't just go wandering about, not with those guards looking for you."

"Then what are we supposed to do until Peter gets here?" I ask.

"Sleep?" Fifer mutters.

"For now, I thought I could show you all my cathedral," Humbert says.

Fifer gets up abruptly and starts stretching. John gives her a disapproving look, which she ignores. I'd rather go upstairs and sleep, too, instead of being dragged on some god-awful nocturnal pilgrimage. But I really can't resist.

"That sounds lovely," I say. Fifer gives me a filthy look. Humbert beams.

"I didn't know you had a cathedral," George says.

"Oh, well. It's not really a cathedral," Humbert says. "That's just what I call it."

"What is it, then?" George asks, politely stifling a yawn. "It wouldn't happen to be a privy, would it? Or a wine cellar? Either one would go down a treat right about now—"

"Certainly not, dear boy. The cathedral is where I keep all my artifacts."

"Artifacts?" George's yawn grows wider.

"Oh yes. It's quite a collection! Naturally, I've kept it quite secret. I've got spellbooks, grimoires, alchemy tools, and other bits and bobs, even an alembic once owned by Artephius himself! An athame made from whalebone and some other rare weapons. I'm a bit of an expert, I'll have you know. I've got spears and staffs and swords and knives—"

"Swords?" Fifer whirls around. "Knives?"

Humbert looks surprised. "I didn't know you were interested in weaponry, my dear."

"Of course I am," Fifer says.

John raises his eyebrows. "Since when?"

"Since now." Fifer shrugs. "You never know when you may have to defend yourself." She gives me a nasty look. "As Nicholas always says: There are enemies everywhere."

19

HUMBERT LEADS US OUT OF the dining room, back into the checkered entrance hall. He walks straight to the largest of the portraits, the one of Venus and Cupid I admired on the way in. At the bottom of the painting is a pair of masks, their empty, hollow eyes staring blankly in the distance. He reaches out and pokes his finger inside the eyehole, and I gasp—*Is there really a hole in the canvas of this priceless painting?*— then hear a tiny click. On the other side of the hall, a door swings open, just a crack. I'm impressed. The door is tiny, narrow; the seams so well disguised by the intricately carved walls as to be nearly invisible. That, or I'm losing my touch.

Humbert crosses the hall and pushes the door open, silent on its well-oiled hinges.

"Come on, then." He motions for us to enter. Fifer slips through the door first, followed by George. I go next. But what I see on the other side makes me stop. A narrow stairway leading down, into darkness. John slides through the door, glances at the staircase, then at me.

"Humbert, maybe Elizabeth and I will wait up here—"

"No, it's okay," I tell him.

"Are you sure?"

I nod. I'm a little curious to see Humbert's collection. And more than a little curious to see what Fifer's up to. My guess is she's going to try to steal one of Humbert's weapons. She can't hurt me, of course, but I worry about her getting her hands on something anyway. The last thing I need is for her to hurt John, or George, or even herself in some foolish attempt to protect them against me.

I look at John. "Walk with me?"

He nods, and together we start down the tiny staircase. Humbert squeezes through the door then, bolting it shut behind him. Immediately, my hands start sweating.

"Feel free to start singing any time you like," John whispers. I attempt a laugh, but it comes out sounding more like a groan.

When we reach the bottom of the stairs, I immediately see why Humbert calls it the cathedral. It's a large, circular room with arched, vaulted ceilings taller than the room is wide. One curve of the wall is made entirely from stained glass; another curve holds a large cabinet. The remaining wall space is lined with shelves, crammed with objects, all alive with movement. Jars that bubble and hiss. Clocks that tick and hum. Globes that whirl and spin. Books stacked upon one another; some leather-bound, others loose-leaf and tied together with string. The tools he mentioned are scattered everywhere: bowls, mortars and pestles, scales, bags of herbs,

and jars of various animal parts floating in solution like grotesque fish in a bowl. In the center of it all is a brick furnace, a
tiny blue fire dancing inside.

"Well, don't just stand there," Humbert says. "Have a look
around."

George walks off to examine the spinning globes, while
Fifer and Humbert head straight for the cabinet. That must
be where the weapons are. I start to follow, but John guides
me toward the furnace instead. There are several glass flasks
set on stands over the fire, brightly colored liquids bubbling
inside.

"What is that?" I ask.

John examines the largest flask, dark red liquid boiling
within.

"Aqua vitae, by the looks of it."

I raise my eyebrows. "Humbert's an alchemist?".

He smiles. "Well, he's not trying to turn lead into gold or
anything. He's just making wine. Rather, he's making wine
stronger. This flask over here"—he points to a smaller one
filled with orange liquid—"is brandy. It'll be strong enough to
melt paint off walls when he's done with it." He watches the
liquid boil, then reaches over and lowers the flame. "No sense
in his melting his insides, though."

I laugh, then remember the book he was reading the night
he fell asleep in my room.

"You're an alchemist, too?"

"Not quite," he says. "I thought about studying it at uni-
versity next year, though."

"Where?" Alchemy is far too close to magic for that to be
allowed in Anglia.

"Probably Iberia. Or maybe Umbria. I don't know. I haven't decided yet."

"So, no pirate apprenticeship for you, then?"

He laughs. "No, though my father would love that. He's been trying to talk me into it since before I could walk."

"No good?"

"No. I mean, it's fine. I just prefer healing."

"Better wenching in the pirate trade," I point out.

He snorts. "Yes. Because I am all about the wenching." I laugh again. John motions to the shelf holding all the animal parts. "Want to take a look?"

I nod, and we both rush over and start pulling jars off the shelves.

I read the label on a jar that holds what look like tiny gray raisins. "Mouse brains!"

"Oh, that's good." He peers at it closely, then holds out a jar for me to see. "Look at this one."

"Frog eyes," I say. "Look at them all. Staring at us. They're so..."

"Judgmental?"

I start giggling. He puts it back and reaches for a bigger jar, this one filled with something yellow and soft.

"Cow pancreas." I wrinkle my nose.

"Ugh, it looks like cheese."

"Trust me, you do not want that melted on top of anything," I say. And then we're both laughing, and he looks at me and I look at him, and suddenly the space between us seems very small and I feel a little thrill...until I remember what George told me. About his mother, his sister. Then that thrill turns into something else entirely and I take a step back.

John doesn't seem to notice. He just keeps pulling jars off shelves and examining them, completely engrossed. I should probably leave. Go see what Fifer is up to. I glance at her, standing with Humbert at the weapons cabinet—*Look at all those weapons!*—deep in conversation. George is still over by the globes, carefully not watching me, which only tells me he is. I should definitely leave.

"How did you become a healer?" I say instead.

John carefully sets the jar he's holding—sheep intestines—on the shelf and turns to me. "My mother was a healer," he says. "She ran an apothecary near our house in Harrow. When my father wasn't dragging me out to sea, I would help her. Sometimes my sister would help, too, but she was usually too busy getting into trouble with Fifer to be of much use." He smiles a little at that.

"Anyway, when I was about nine, she suspected I had the magic to be a healer, too. So one day she took me to her shop, told me to make potions for two of her patients. One had green fever, the other pemphigus. A very unpleasant skin disease," he adds in response to my raised eyebrow. "And then she left."

"She left?" I feel my eyes go round. "What did you do?"

"Panicked, of course." He smiles. "I'd been helping her for years, but I'd never made a potion on my own before, and never anything that complicated. I had no idea what to do. I couldn't reach the upper shelves without a ladder. I didn't even know how to light the furnace. I thought for sure I'd burn the shop down, or, failing that, I'd turn a potion into poison and kill her patients and I'd have to live with that forever. But then…" He trails off, glancing at the ceiling for a moment as if lost in thought.

"What?"

"I just knew what to do." He looks down at me again, his eyes bright. "It's hard to explain. But there was something about the shop, the smell of the herbs, the way the light filtered in through the windows, all dusty, all the jars and books and the tools." He gestures at the shelves in front of us. "The magic took over then, and it told me what I needed to do."

I'm quiet for a moment, enchanted by the idea of something stealing over you, settling into you, and telling you, with absolute certainty, who you are and what you're meant to do.

"That sounds lovely," I say, and I'm surprised to find I mean it.

"I don't think it looked lovely, though." He laughs a little. "The shop was a disaster. There were herbs and roots and powders on the counter, the floor; I broke at least three flasks, so there was glass everywhere, too.... My sleeve caught fire when I lit the furnace, so I doused myself with rosewater. I was covered in wet petals....I must have looked like a lunatic."

I start to laugh, too.

"And now it's just me," he says, and I stop laughing. "I thought about quitting, but magic isn't something you can just quit. Besides, someone had to carry on after she..." He turns away then, busying himself with the jars again.

I'm quiet for a minute, unsure of what to say.

"George told me what happened," I finally manage. "I'm so sorry. I know how you feel." And I do. I wish there were something I could say to make him feel better. But there's really nothing. I could tell him what's done is done, but I know that would never be enough for someone like him. John's a healer. He knows the difference between a bandage and a cure.

John turns back to me and nods, as if he knew what I was thinking. For a minute we look at each other, neither of us saying a word. The thrill I felt earlier comes rushing back. I should move. George would want me to. I should want to, too.

Except I don't.

I hear someone clear his throat and I turn around. Humbert is smiling at us, but Fifer is glaring and George just shakes his head.

"I need a drink," he mutters.

Humbert steps over to the flask with the orange liquid and unhooks it from the stand. "I've got just the thing."

20

THE NEXT DAY PASSES WITH no word from Peter. I'm anxious to begin searching for the tablet—rather, for the thing that will lead me to the tablet—but Humbert is dead set against our wandering around without Peter's protection. He's worried about the guards; he's worried about us, me in particular—"the frail little thing," he calls me.

I don't push it. Not because I'm worried but because I don't know what to do. I spent the morning with John walking Humbert's property, poking through his endless number of rooms, but came up empty.

I don't think whatever I'm supposed to find is here, at least not in this house. It's not that simple. If it has to do with Blackwell, it can't be. Either way, I won't find it with Peter and the others trailing behind me. I've got to find a way to search on my own.

That evening after supper we move into Humbert's sitting room. He summons a musician from somewhere, possibly the last century, by the look of him. Skeletal, wispy white hair, bony hands clutching a lute. He perches on the edge of a chair and begins to warble out a dusty tune.

George and Humbert, absurdly, start dancing. Fifer paces in front of the window, watching the spook lights I saw the evening we arrived, only tonight they're green instead of red. Every now and again she'll glance at John, mutter under her breath, and then turn back to the window again.

The musician plucks away, hitting more wrong notes than right. I glance at John, sitting in the chair across from me. His head is tipped back, eyes closed, a look of intense pain on his face. Finally, he looks down and sees me watching him.

Help, he mouths.

I press my hand to my mouth, stifling a laugh. He grins and points at the door. I nod. He uncrosses his long legs, rises from the chair, and slips from the room. I wait as long as I can stand, thirty seconds, maybe, then do the same. He waits for me down the checkered hall, in front of a set of wide double doors inset with stained glass panels. The library. It's the only room we couldn't visit this morning, closed for cleaning and reshelving.

"Well, that was completely awful." He points to the door. "Want to go in?"

"Won't we get in trouble?"

"I think it'll be all right," he says. "Besides, what's the worst that could happen? I don't think Humbert will arrest us."

"I didn't realize you were such a troublemaker," I say, but I'm smiling.

"You have no idea." He smiles back. "Come on. There's something I want to show you." He presses his hand against the door and, with a heavy creak, pushes it open. "After you."

Inside is a vast, cavernous room, with vaulted stone walls as tall as the room is wide, inset with oak shelves and filled entirely with books. The floor is laid with bright green and blue tile, arranged in a complicated geometric pattern. The ceiling is a glass dome, open to the starry sky like an oculus.

But it's the enormous tree in the center of the room that commands the most attention. It sprouts from the floor, a massive thing, the trunk at least five feet in diameter, its many leafless branches extending like arms into the night sky.

"Is this what you wanted to show me?"

John nods. He's watching me closely.

"How did you know it was here?"

"My father told me about it," he says. "But I thought he was exaggerating."

We make our way toward the tree, our footsteps echoing off the hard tile floor. I don't make it more than a few steps before the dark room bursts into light, the candles in the many sconces fitted along the wall flickering into flame. I flinch a little.

"It's just an enchantment," John says. "The lights come on when the room is safe. If it senses danger, they go off—or don't come on at all. It's security, I guess you could say."

"It's a library," I point out. "Why does it need security?"

"Because it's a library with a very magical tree inside," John replies.

"The tree is magical?" We're standing in front of it now.

Up close it's a curious gray color, entirely stripped of bark. It almost looks like bone.

He nods. "If Humbert were to get visitors—say that duchess friend of his—and they happened to stumble inside..." He shrugs. "That's probably why the library was closed this morning, so Bridget could top up the spell. She's a witch, you know."

I'm surprised, but I guess I shouldn't be.

"What does it do?" I say, finally. "The tree, I mean."

"Oh." John runs a hand through his hair. "I'm not sure, exactly." But something in his expression tells me he does.

Suddenly, I want to touch it. It's bold; stupid, even, to want anything to do with magic, especially in front of John. But I want to see what it does. And since those enchanted lights seem to think I'm safe, maybe I am.

I reach out, tentatively, touch the withered gray trunk. Feel the smoothness of the wood beneath my hand. The tree shudders slightly under my palm, and with a sound like striking matches, it flares to life. Leaves bud, sprout, then unfurl, thousands of them—more—in shades of green so bright and vibrant they don't seem real.

I let out a surprised gasp, then start to laugh. The leaves continue to come furiously, spreading through the branches until the once-dead tree now looks as alive as a summer day. I turn to John.

"Why did it do that?" I say. "What does it mean?"

John swipes his hand through his hair. "They—I don't know." Again, something in his expression tells me he does.

"What would happen if you touched it?"

He looks away from me and doesn't reply. I could swear he's blushing.

But I don't let it go. "Go on, then."

He shoots me a look: half-annoyed, half-amused. After a moment he lifts his hand and presses it against the trunk. Nothing happens at first. But then, with a sudden pop and a soft rustle of leaves, a tiny bird appears on one of the topmost branches. It opens its beak and lets out an unnaturally loud chirp. He shuts his eyes, looking relieved and flustered all at once.

I start to giggle then. I can't help it.

"Now you have to tell me," I say. "Surely you know. I know you—"

The bird goes still then, stops chirping. And without warning, the candles in the sconces flare out, plunging the room into near darkness. Without thinking, I grab John's arm, spin him around, and pull us both behind the tree.

"Don't move," I whisper.

"All right," he says back. "But...what are you doing?" His back is pressed roughly against the trunk, and I'm pressed roughly against him, my fingers digging into the front of his shirt. He's so close I can smell him: clean and warm, lavender and spice.

"I—you said the lights go out if it's not safe," I say, and I'm the one blushing now.

"Ah." His lips twitch into a smile and I wait for him to tease me, to get back at me for making him touch that tree. But he doesn't. His smile disappears and he just looks at me. His gaze travels from my eyes to my lips, lingers there, then moves back to my eyes again. I look at him right back, and for a moment I think he means to kiss me. I feel a fierce rush of warmth at the thought of it—which gives way to a cold snap of fear.

I pull away from him. Take one step back, two. John doesn't move, doesn't try to stop me. But he doesn't take his eyes from mine, either. He holds them, steady; and after a long moment he simply nods. He knows about the herbs I was arrested with, knows what I used them for. It occurs to me that maybe he's figured out a lot more than that.

The library doors slam open then, echoing through the silent room like a shot. Fifer stomps toward us in a whirl of red hair and indignation.

"Here comes danger now," John murmurs.

"Oh ho! Exactly what is going on here?" She plants her hands on her hips and taps her foot. "Hiding in dark, shadowy nooks, are we?"

John rolls his eyes. "We're not hiding."

"And it's not dark. Or shadowy," I add. Except it's both. Fifer glares at me; John ducks his head and laughs under his breath. A stray lock of hair falls over his forehead, and I feel that urge again to brush it away.

"Is there something I can do for you?" John glances up at Fifer. "You look rather upset."

"Upset?" Fifer shrieks. There's a sharp rustle of leaves overhead and the tiny songbird lets out a loud, indignant chirp. "Is that a bird?" Fifer points at it as if it were a dragon. "What is that doing here? And why is this tree full of leaves?"

"I don't know anything about the leaves," I say, a bit too loudly. "We just came in here to look at the lights." I point at the shower of green sparks, shining through the oculus overhead.

John winces.

"Yes. The *lights*." Fifer turns to him. "We need to talk about that."

"No, we don't," he replies, sounding weary all of a sudden.

"Yes, we do. You know what it means. The prophecy—"

"That's not what it means."

"What about the prophecy?" I say.

"Says you," Fifer continues, ignoring me. "But what if you're wrong?"

"I'm not wrong," John fires back. "You're just not thinking clearly—"

"Oh, please! You're the one with your head in the clouds, ever since—" She stops at the warning look on John's face. "Fine. But why else are we here if not for that? It's not to walk around aimlessly, or to poke around Humbert's cathedral, and it's certainly not to go hiding in libraries under trees with girls, making *birds*—"

"That's enough, Fifer."

They glare at each other.

"Fine. But you have to come with me now, anyway," Fifer says. "Humbert needs you. Something about a tonic for that lute-playing crypt keeper of his."

"You really are as sweet as poison, you know that?"

She sticks her tongue out at him.

We follow Fifer back into the sitting room. The lute player is lying on the settee, hands folded in his lap, breathing heavily. George sits beside him, his lips pressed together as if he's sealing off a laugh.

John blinks. "What happened?"

"He's had a bit of a spell, that's all," Humbert crows. "Transported by the beauty of his own artistic expression."

The corners of John's mouth twitch. "I'll take care of it."

"I'm going to bed now," Fifer announces. She stalks out of the room, nearly colliding with Bridget, who walks in carrying a tray of tea. She sets it on the table and begins pouring.

Fifer stops in the doorway. Turns around. Glances at the tea, at John, then back at the tea again.

"Will you be needing your bag, John?" Fifer asks. Her voice is kind, helpful…and utterly unlike her. John doesn't seem to notice. He's too busy attending to the lute player.

"Uh, yes. Thank you."

Fifer ducks into the hall and comes back a few minutes later, carrying his bag. She sets it in front of him and smiles.

"Maybe I will have some tea, after all." She walks to the table. Hovers over the tray. Reaches for a cup but doesn't pick it up. Does it again. What is going on with her? She's acting strange, even for Fifer. "On second thought, I don't think I will, after all. See you in the morning." She darts up the stairs, her red hair flying.

"*Such a sweet girl*," Humbert roars.

No, she's not. And I'm suspicious. I've seen girls in the maids' chamber behave like this before. Usually because they've got a boy stashed in their room and are afraid of getting caught. That's not happening here, of course, but whatever Fifer's up to, it's guaranteed to be a lot worse than a boy hiding under her mattress.

I get to my feet. "I'm going to bed, too."

John looks up at me. *Lucky*, he mouths.

I grin and head for the stairs, straight to Fifer's room. I stop in front of her door, my hand on the door latch. Then I pause. Maybe I don't want to know what she's doing. Maybe it'll make things worse between us if I try to find out. And things are bad enough as it is.

The second I step away from the door, it flies open and Fifer yanks me into her room. She slams the door and pushes me against it, a weapon from Humbert's cabinet clutched in her hand: a spring-loaded triple dagger, by the looks of it. She holds it to my throat.

"Do you even know how to use that?" I say.

"Shut it. Why were you lurking outside my door?"

"I thought you were up to something. I wanted to see what it was."

Fifer pokes my neck with the blade again. "*You* don't get to suspect *me* of anything."

"But something's going on, isn't it? Outside, with the spook lights. And the tea downstairs. What is it?"

She pushes away from me and starts pacing the room, muttering to herself. "Should I tell her? No. But the prophecy... and I can't exactly show up with a bloodthirsty maniac—"

"I'm not a bloodthirsty maniac."

"Shut it."

"Show up where?"

"I said, shut it."

She walks from the door to the window, back and forth, chewing her fingernail. Finally, she turns to me. "I don't like you."

"I realize that."

"And I don't trust you. But the prophecy seems to think I should."

"What does that mean?"

Fifer marches to her bed, pulls a piece of parchment out of her bag, and thrusts it into my hand. I recognize it immediately: Veda's prophecy.

"Read the third line."

"Come third winter's night, go underground in green, what holds him in death will lead you to thirteen." I hand it back. "What about it?"

She stares at me a moment. "I'm going to tell you something, but I need you to hear me out before you say anything. Can you do that?"

Somehow, I don't think I'm going to like what I hear. But I nod anyway.

"Winter's night. Nicholas, John, everyone else thinks it's a date. The third night after the winter solstice, which is a week from now. But I think it's something else." She pauses. "Winter's night isn't just a date. It's also a party."

"A party," I repeat.

She nods. "It happens every year. Different places, different times. It lasts for three nights. This year's party happens to be in Stepney Green. The very same place Nicholas sent us to. And see those lights?" She points out the window, at the twinkling green lights in the distance. "They're not spook lights. They're nymph lights. Sent into the air every night during Winter's Night. The first night is purple, the second red, the third green. *Come third winter's night, go underground in green.* Get it?"

"I guess," I say. "But Veda didn't say anything about going to a party."

Fifer narrows her eyes. "What are you, fluent in seer now?"

"Are you?"

"As it so happens, yes. It's my specialty." She says this rather haughtily.

"Let me guess," I say. "You wanted John to go to this party, and he didn't want to. That's what you were fighting about on the way here. That's why he was so angry tonight."

Fifer shrugs. "He thinks it's a stretch. He thinks I just want to go to the party and I'm using the prophecy as an excuse."

"Are you?"

"If I were, I wouldn't be telling you about it," Fifer fires back.

I ignore this. "What kind of party is it?"

"Just a little get-together. Well, maybe not so little. A bit of food, a bit of drink, a lot of chaos. It's fun. Everyone goes."

"Everyone?" I don't like the sound of that. "Who's everyone?"

"Witches, of course. Wizards. Revenants, hags, demons... mostly the nondangerous variety, but not always. Ghosts. We try to keep them out, but, you know, that can be hard. Don't always know they're there until it's too late."

"Are you saying you want me to go?"

"Of course I don't want you to go," Fifer snaps. "You think I want to bring a witch hunter to a party like that? You're even more insane than I thought."

"I'm not insane. I'm not going to hurt anyone."

She waves it off. "I don't *want* you to go to the party. But after hearing what I've told you about it, if you feel as if you

216

might *find* something there"—I notice the emphasis on the word—"I can't stop you."

I'm about to tell her to forget it. John's right: It is a stretch. The words all line up, but I have a hard time believing Veda's prophecy amounts to no more than a party invitation.

Yet…there is a ring of truth to it. At the very least, it's a lot of coincidences. And Blackwell always says there are no coincidences.

"Yes," I say. "I think we should go."

Fifer goes quiet. Then her eyes flutter shut in an expression that almost looks like relief.

"That was good," she says, finally. "Very decisive. I could tell you really felt it. *In here.*" She thumps her chest in imitation of Humbert.

"No shilly-shally," I agree, and I almost see her smile.

"What should we do about the others?" I say. "If John didn't want you to go and finds out we both did—what?" A look of guilt flashes across Fifer's face.

"That's the other thing." A pause. "I drugged them."

"You *what*?"

"I took something from John's bag and slipped it in their tea."

"That's really dangerous!" I say. "You can't go around putting herbs in people's drinks like that. Each dose has to be measured exactly! The amount you'd need to knock out someone Humbert's size would be enough to kill poor George—"

"Poisoned a lot of people before, have we?"

"What? No. Well, sort of. But that's not the point."

Fifer shakes her head. "They'll be fine. A little groggy, maybe, but I know what I'm doing. And why do you care what happens to them, anyway? Or maybe you just care what happens to one person in particular."

I feel my cheeks burn. "I have no idea what you're talking about."

Fifer smirks. "Right."

I turn away from her. "We should go. We don't have all night to stand around talking." I walk to the window, push it open. "Look, there's a trellis here. We can climb down."

"Hold on," Fifer says. "We can't go dressed like this."

I glance at our clothes. More of the duchess's dresses: mine pale pink and brocade, hers mustard yellow and velvet. "Why not?"

"Because we look like someone's moldy old grandmother." She walks to her bed and starts sifting through a pile of clothes. "I thought about the party before we left, so I packed accordingly. I couldn't decide what to wear, so I brought a few things. Here." She pulls out a dress and hands it to me. "Put this on."

It's long and formfitting, made from white silk and patterned with tiny black, blue, and orange flowers. The neck, shoulders, and waist are decorated with shimmering blue and black beads. I've never seen anything like it before.

"It's pretty," I say.

"Too pretty for you, that's for certain." She wrinkles her nose. "All right. Jewelry. Where's the stuff you wore at dinner the other night?"

"My room."

She dashes across the hall and comes back with the sapphire earrings and ring.

"Put these on." She stands back and studies me. "I love this dress," she sighs, a dreamy look stealing across her face. Then she scowls. "If you get it dirty, I will kill you myself. Got it?"

"I won't."

Fifer nods and starts getting dressed. She pulls on a shirt—a tight, black, strapless thing, more like a corset than a shirt—a long black skirt, and a pair of tall black boots. She glances in the mirror, gives her reflection an approving nod, then marches to the open window and leans out.

"What is taking so long?"

"What?" I say, startled. "What is *what* taking so long?"

"Keep your hair on," comes a voice from outside. A boy's voice. *What is going on?* I hear a rustling of leaves and the voice grows louder. "You expect me to just drop everything and run every time you call?"

"Exactly so," Fifer replies, stepping away from the window. In a flash, a boy swings himself up and over the windowsill, landing gracefully beside her.

"Lovely to see you, too." He grins and kisses her on the cheek.

Okay, so Fifer didn't have a boy hiding under her mattress. But she did have one hiding outside in the bushes, which is just as bad. For some reason, I'm filled with a sudden, immense dread.

"Schuyler, there's someone I'd like you to meet."

Fifer takes the boy by the arm and spins him around to

face me. I suck in a breath. I should have known by his speed, by the way he leaped through a window two stories off the ground. But it's his eyes that tip me off. The second they meet mine: feral, hard, and knowing—too knowing—I know who this boy is. Rather, what he is.

He's a revenant.

And I'm in a lot of trouble.

21

I LOOK AT HIM, TRYING to figure out what kind of revenant he is. Is he the seventh son of a seventh son, relatively harmless? Or was he brought back by witchcraft, dangerous only to whom his necromancer bids him to be? Or is he the cursed undead, buried in unconsecrated ground, and dangerous to everyone? I don't know. It's difficult to tell just by looking.

The only thing I can tell by looking is that he's possibly the most attractive boy—living or dead—I've ever seen. Bright blue eyes, wicked grin, shaggy blond hair that falls to his chin. He looks to be around eighteen, but he could just as easily be a hundred and eighteen. Revenants usually favor clothes from the time they were alive, but his are too plain to offer any clue: black trousers, black shirt, long black coat ending in a pair of heavily scuffed black boots.

"This is Elizabeth," Fifer says.

"All right, love?" Schuyler extends his hand to me, but I don't take it. Revenants can tell a lot about a person through touch alone. They're like seers in that way, but worse. Because a single touch from a revenant grants them access to your thoughts and feelings—forever. And I know exactly what he'll see the second he touches me.

Fifer knows it, too. "Go on, Elizabeth. Shake his hand." Her eyes are alight with anticipation.

Damnation.

I give him my hand.

"Nice to meet you." He curls his fingers around mine. I can feel his immense strength even in the tiny squeeze he gives me. "Any friend of Fifer's—" He breaks off and narrows his eyes at me, his gaze flicking to my abdomen.

He knows.

I take an involuntary step backward. What is he going to do? Attack me? I have no way to defend myself against him. No knife and no sword, though neither of those things would make a dent in him anyway. Salt can kill off the freshly conjured undead, but the longer they've been around, the more indestructible they become. And judging by his strength, he's been around a while. He could tear my throat out or rip me limb from limb before I could utter a scream.

Instead of yanking my arm out of the socket, Schuyler leans closer, peering into my eyes. I watch as a variety of expressions cross his face. He frowns, raises his eyebrows, purses his lips, shakes his head. It's like watching someone read a book. Right before they rip it to shreds.

Finally, he releases me and turns to Fifer.

"D'you want me to kill her?"

"Unfortunately, no. I need her."

"Oh?" He gives her a delighted grin. "Do tell."

Fifer tells him everything: Nicholas's curse, the prophecy. The tablet. Caleb chasing us to Veda's, the guards chasing us to Humbert's. The thing we're hoping to find at the party.

Schuyler is silent for a moment.

"What'd you call me for, then, if you didn't want me to kill her?"

Fifer looks affronted. "What do you mean? We always go to this party together."

"Last I recall, you said you'd rather lick poison from a privy than go anywhere with me again."

"Last *I* recall, you said you'd changed," Fifer fires back. "Or did you lie about that, too?"

"You know you're the only one for me, love."

Fifer rolls her eyes. "Fine. But there is just one thing. John didn't want us going, so we'll have to be back by dawn. Quite a bit before dawn, actually..."

"Better hurry, then," Schuyler says. He leaps onto the window frame, his movements so light and fast it's as if he has wings. Then he's over the edge, slipping like quicksilver into the darkness.

I whirl around to face her. "A revenant?" I say. "What'd you call a revenant for?"

"You heard me," Fifer says. "We always go to this party together. Besides, I'm not going anywhere with you alone. I need him to protect me against you."

"Protect you against me?" I repeat. "That's like asking a wolf to protect you against a mouse!"

"You dare call yourself a mouse?"

"Never mind that! My point is, he's dangerous. He's liable to rip my hand off just for putting it in my pocket."

"Better keep your hands where we can see them, then."

I let out a groan of frustration.

"I'm not going to hang around all day," Schuyler calls from outside. I can hear the amusement in his voice. He probably heard every word we said. Damn revenants. And damn Fifer for bringing one here.

She grabs her bag off the floor and slings it across her shoulder. Then she turns to me, a malicious glint in her eye. "Just because I'm taking you to this party doesn't mean I've changed my opinion about you."

"Which is?"

"That you'd be better off dead," she says flatly. "Racked, hanged, burned at the stake. It's what you deserve. I guarantee no one would miss you."

I flinch at the hate in her words, at the truth of them.

"But until you find this tablet for Nicholas, you're better off alive. And for the next few hours it's up to me to keep you that way. So when we get to this party, stay close to me. Be pleasant to people, but don't talk too much. Not about magic, or curses, or, for God's sake, witch hunters. Don't say anything about Nicholas, or about his being ill. Don't mention Humbert. Or John, for that matter, or George."

"Maybe I just won't talk at all," I mutter.

"And whatever you do, stay away from other revenants," she continues. "I can protect you against Schuyler, but you saw how fast he had you figured out. If any of the others realize what you are, I don't know what might happen."

I do. It happened to a witch hunter, once. He tried to take

on three revenants alone and wound up torn limb from limb, eviscerated. There wasn't even enough of him left to bury.

"Scared?" Fifer smirks.

"You wish. Now get out of my way." I push past her to the window, climb up on the ledge—hard to do in this dress—and look down. Schuyler is standing below me, grinning.

"Go on, then, little mouse. This wolf isn't going to hurt you."

I scowl. Schuyler laughs. Then I jump.

With a muffled thud, I land securely in Schuyler's arms. He stares at me a moment before setting me down. "Not as heavy as you seem, are you?"

I don't know what he means by that, but there's no time to figure it out. He sets me to my feet and catches Fifer, who leaps out the window without hesitation. Then the three of us take off across Humbert's vast property in the direction of the nymph lights.

We walk along for several miles, Fifer on one side of me and Schuyler on the other. I feel like a prisoner. A tortured prisoner at that, since I'm forced to listen to their inane flirting. For a boy who's been around as long as Schuyler probably has, you'd think he'd have more interesting ways of talking to a girl.

"Where've you been hiding, love?"

"I haven't been hiding."

"Then why haven't I seen you?"

"You know why."

"No, I don't."

"Yes, you do."

"No, I don't."

On and on they go. Eventually I start daydreaming of different ways I could kill him. I'm halfway through a plot that involves a tree branch, a knife, a length of rope, and a sock full of gravel when Schuyler turns to me.

"So, Elizabeth"—the way he says my name sounds like "Elizabef"—"you're a bit bijoux for a witch hunter, hmm?"

I haven't a clue what he means, but Fifer leans around me and slaps his arm.

"Did you just call her cute?"

He shrugs. "She is a bit twee. Doesn't look as if she could harm anyone."

"She's a violent, deranged, lunatic murderer!"

Schuyler laughs. "So am I. But you still think I'm cute."

"No, I don't."

"Yes, you do."

"No, I don't."

I go back to plotting his death.

Eventually the nymph lights grow closer and brighter. When a shower of them erupts in the sky directly above us, Schuyler lets out a little whoop and takes off running.

When we catch up to him, he's lounging against a tree, an enormous grin on his face.

"I hope you're ready, Elizabeth. 'Cause this here's an eye-opener." He takes me by the shoulders and pushes me forward. I suck in a breath. I can't help it. I've seen a lot in my life. But never anything like this.

Through the trees is a valley, like a bowl sunk into the middle of a forest. Inside is a dizzying array of people, creatures, magic. And somehow, it's not dark here. It's as bright as a summer day: blue skies, dotted with puffy white clouds and brightly colored birds.

I don't know where to look first. At the beautiful naked women lounging in the lake? The lush grass that grows around the water, dotted with brilliantly colored flowers I know only grow in spring? Or the trees that sprout lemons, limes, and figs, fruits I know don't grow here at all?

Music drifts through the air, so beautiful, like nothing I've ever heard before. *And are those butterflies?* I watch one flutter by, its blue wings unnaturally bright, even against the unnaturally bright blue sky. Fifer looks around, nodding approvingly.

"How is this happening?" I ask.

"Nymphs," Schuyler says, still grinning. "I love when they're in charge of decoration."

We make our way down the hill. The vast space below is crowded; there are witches and wizards everywhere. Where did they all come from? Shouldn't they be in hiding somewhere? How are they not afraid? And with this much magic in one place, why haven't I heard of this party before?

"Doesn't anyone worry about getting caught?" I wonder aloud.

Schuyler shrugs. "Who in their right mind would try to take on this crowd?" He looks relaxed, bouncing on his toes and looking around. But Fifer seems wary, looking from me to Schuyler to the crowd then back to me again, as if she's afraid I'm going to charge in and start attacking.

"Settle down, love." Schuyler turns to her. "She's not getting stabby, so stop worrying."

"She'd better not. But if she does"—she glances at me, a nasty gleam in her eye—"you have my permission to rip her to shreds."

Schuyler winks at me and blows a kiss.

Finally, Fifer spots a group of people she knows. They see her and wave.

"Fifer, where have you been hiding?" says one boy as we approach. He's got dark hair and a nose that looks as if it's been broken several times. "We were worried something happened to you."

Fifer laughs. "I'm fine, fine. Just keeping my head down."

"Studying, I imagine," says another girl, short and blond.

"How is it coming along? He as tough as he seems?" asks a plump, brown-haired girl. She looks at Fifer with admiration.

"Is he well?" asks another boy. "We heard rumors he was sick—"

Fifer grabs my arm and pulls me next to her. "I haven't introduced my...friend." She nearly chokes on the word. "This is Elizabeth." She proceeds to tell them a story that paints me out to be some kind of nitwit: too dumb to know I was a witch until recently, too foolish to hide it once I did. The only truth she does tell them is that I came from Upminster, where apparently I spent my time wandering the streets like an idiot magical vagrant until Nicholas came along and rescued me.

They look at me with sympathy.

"We're so glad he found you," says the blond girl, Lark. "Imagine if you'd been caught! I hear the burnings are getting worse—"

"And all those rebellions," adds Bram, the boy with the crooked nose. "Just adding fuel to the fire, so to speak."

Another girl, who has been glaring at Fifer ever since we walked up, breaks in.

"Where's John?" she demands.

"Hello to you, too, Chime." Fifer gives her a cool look. "He couldn't make it this year. He's attending to some patients."

A shadow crosses the girl's face, then she smiles. "That sounds just like him. So responsible! Well, that's too bad. We had such a wonderful time together last year."

I look at her. She's tall and pretty, with long, straight black hair and big blue eyes. Tall enough that she wouldn't have to stand on her toes if she wanted to kiss him. I push the thought away immediately.

"I've got a letter for him," Chime continues. "Would you mind passing it on?" She pulls out a carefully folded piece of paper and hands it to Fifer. It's got a bright red wax seal on it in the shape of a heart. Ugh.

"A letter?" Fifer holds it gingerly between her thumb and index finger, as if it were a dead rat.

"Yes. We've been writing each other since last year! Didn't he tell you?"

Fifer raises her eyebrows.

"No? Well, John never was one to kiss and tell. As I say, very responsible!"

I've got half a mind to grab a fistful of that black hair, drag her into the woods, and cram that letter down her throat, but then Fifer speaks.

"Oh, Chime. I can't believe John didn't tell you. Well, so

229

much has been going on, all the preparations. It's been so whirlwind...but then, that's what makes it so romantic!" She looks at me, a gleam in her eyes. "Go on, tell her the news!"

I look at her blankly. Surely she doesn't want me to talk? Especially when I have no idea what she's talking about?

"Oh, Elizabeth," Fifer says. "You know I'm talking about you and John getting married!"

My mouth drops open. It feels as if a thousand of those bright blue butterflies have flown down my throat and into my stomach, beating their wings inside. Lark and Reverie shriek with glee and start hugging me.

Chime looks at me with undisguised hatred. "I don't believe it."

"No? Elizabeth, show her the ring!" Fifer grabs my hand and shoves it in her face.

Chime reaches over and snatches that hateful note out of Fifer's hand and stomps off. Lark and Reverie besiege us with questions.

"When is the wedding?"

"We'll be invited, won't we?"

"I can't give away all the secrets!" Fifer laughs. "I promise, you'll all know soon enough. Now, if you'll excuse us, I want to introduce Elizabeth to some more people!"

Fifer loops her arm through mine and leads me away.

"Ugh, I hate that girl," she barks once we're out of earshot. "I saw her and John together last year, but I didn't know they'd been writing. And all year, too." Fifer shudders, then bursts out laughing. "I can't believe I told her John was getting married. It was the ring that gave me the idea. He's going to kill me when he finds out! Serves him right, though, for not telling me about her."

"What are you going to tell them when there's no wedding?"

Fifer stops laughing, then pushes me away as if she'd forgotten who she was talking to.

"Never you mind. Besides, if you don't find that tablet, I'm going to have bigger problems than a fake wedding." She turns away from me. "Where'd Schuyler go?"

We see him standing by the lake talking to the nymphs, who are naked save for a piece of fabric tied strategically around their hips. They giggle and toss their hair at him.

"I swear, I can't leave him alone for a minute!" Fifer stomps off toward him. Schuyler sees her coming and breaks away.

"Why are you talking to them?" Fifer demands.

"What, can't I?"

"Why do the girls you talk to always have to be naked?"

"They're not always. You aren't."

"Not today!"

"Fifer, I was simply admiring their—"

"Don't say it!"

"Decorations. I was going to say decorations."

They carry on arguing. I stand there, fidgeting and waiting for them to stop when Bram and another boy walk up. They're both carrying cups of something giving off purple steam.

"They're at it again, eh?" Bram laughs. "You might be here for a while. I figured you might need a drink." He hands me a cup.

"Thank you." I take a tentative sip.

"What does it taste like?" Bram's friend asks eagerly.

I stop drinking immediately. "Why, what is it?"

Bram laughs. "Relax. He just means it tastes different to everyone. It's supposed to be the essence of who or what you want the most. Mine, for example, tastes like ginger." I notice his eyes flick to Fifer as he says this.

"What is it, some sort of love potion?" I peer inside the cup.

"More like a truth potion. The fun part is figuring out the truth." They both drink deeply. "Careful, though. It's strong stuff and a little goes a long way."

I shrug. I know a thing or two about strong drinks. I've been drinking Joe's ale since I was eleven. But a truth potion? I'd just as soon drink poison. Even still, I take another sip just to be polite.

"Congratulations on your wedding," Bram says, and the two boys walk off.

"Thank you," I say again, and take another sip. I have to admit, it tastes good. Spicy and tangy, almost like shandygaff, a mixture of ginger beer and lemons that Joe sometimes serves. Caleb always joked it was the most normal thing on the menu.

Caleb. Is that what the potion is trying to tell me? That I want him more than anything? That may have been true once. I don't feel as if it's true now. I can't forget how he never came back for me at Fleet, or the things he said about me at Veda's. I can't forget that when I needed him the most, he was nowhere to be found.

I dump the rest of the potion in the grass.

I settle down onto the ground to wait. I examine my ring, holding it up to the light, the sun penetrating into the deep blue stone. As I tip it back and forth in the light, I notice some sort of marking on the bottom. I take it off and turn it upside down and there, etched into the underside of the stone, is a tiny heart. I slip the ring back onto my finger. Too bad Fifer hadn't known that was there. That would have driven Chime crazy.

I'm back to pondering the allure of shandygaff when Fifer walks over in a huff.

"What's wrong?" I stand up and dust myself off.

"He is impossible," she fumes. "Impossible! He always says he'll change. But he never does." She looks at my empty cup. "What was that?"

"Bram gave it to me. Said it was some sort of truth potion."

"Oh. What does it taste like?"

"Lemons. And spice." Fifer gives me a sharp look. "Why? Have you ever had it before?"

"Yes." She grimaces.

"And?"

"And nothing. Mine only ever tastes foul."

I raise my eyebrows. "Speaking of foul, where'd Schuyler go? Isn't he going to help us look around?"

"Who knows," she says irritably. "As if I can ever guess what he'll do, or why. He told me I was being unreasonable."

"You? Unreasonable?" I fight the urge to laugh. "I can't imagine."

"That's what I said!" Fifer says. "I told him, if you think taking one girl to a party and going home with another is reasonable, you've got another thing coming. Then he said, why'd you go home with another boy last year? Then I said, John is *not* another boy. He's like my brother, which Schuyler very well knows. Then *he* said…"

As Fifer rages on, I search the crowd for Schuyler. Most of the boys here are dressed normally, but since he looks as if he just came from his own funeral, he shouldn't be hard to spot. I do see some boys all in black standing around a fire, but on closer inspection, they've all got bloodred eyes, not revenants but definitely some sort of demon.…

I'm about to give up when I spot a figure in black trudging up the hill by the nymph-filled lake, the coattail of his long black coat flapping in the wind.

Schuyler.

I turn to Fifer.

"Then *I* said, if you want to go home with a nymph, don't bother calling on me again. As if I care what they can do underwater—"

"Fifer."

"What?"

"There he is." I point at the hill. We watch for a minute as Schuyler winds his way around the water, the trees to his left, the lake on his right.

"Where does he think he's going?" Fifer murmurs.

I shrug. "Who knows. But we really need to start looking around. If he's not coming with us, that's fine, but we've only got a few hours, and this place is huge, and—what?"

Fifer is shaking her head and muttering under her breath. Her face is like thunder.

"What's wrong?"

"Oh, nothing. Just thinking about Chime again." She rips open the flap on her bag and starts pawing through it. "Do you know what her specialty is? *Love spells.* Can you believe that?" She pulls two necklaces from her bag and snaps it shut. "What a waste of magic. I'll bet anything that letter for John had a love spell on it. Well, I warned him not to mess with her. Never trust a girl with three last names."

I blink. "Fifer, I have no idea what you're talking about."

She reaches over and drops one of the necklaces over my head, then puts the other one on herself. She lets out a huff of relief.

"Finally. Now we can talk."

"What do you mean? What is this?" I hold up the necklace. It's long and delicate, with a series of odd-looking charms hanging from the end.

"Do you have any idea what it's like being involved with a revenant?" Fifer demands.

"Uh, no."

"They hear everything you say, know everything you think. They know what you're going to do before you do it. They can even manipulate your actions. They have all the power, and you have none. I think you'll agree that's not right, yes?"

There are about a million reasons being involved with a revenant isn't right without adding that to the list, but I don't say this.

"Right."

"That's why I came up with this." She holds up the necklace. "Brass chain. Ampoules filled with salt, quicksilver, and ash. Alone, they're nothing, especially to a revenant with Schuyler's power. But together, they act as a sort of shield. A barrier. With this on, he can't hear me or feel me or penetrate my thoughts. Yours either."

"Okay…but why do you need this now? I mean, why not wear it all the time?"

"I don't wear it all the time because I don't want him to know I have it. And I'm wearing it now because I'm going to follow him."

"Why?"

We watch Schuyler trudge up the hill until he disappears into the trees.

Fifer scowls. "Because he's up to something. And I want to know what it is."

22

FIFER STARTS MARCHING AROUND THE LAKE. I hurry after her.

"Are you sure this is a good idea? Following him like this?" I stumble over a branch and nearly fall. My dress is so tight it's hard to keep up with her.

"Good for us, not so for him," she says.

"What's that supposed to mean?"

Fifer doesn't reply.

We've reached the other side of the water now. It's eerily quiet here: The noise from the crowd has fallen away, muffled by the thickening trees. It's growing darker, too, the halo of sunlight above our heads fading the farther we move into the forest.

"You said you think he's up to something," I continue. "What is it?"

It could be anything. Revenants aren't exactly known for

having wholesome pastimes. Before he started recruiting and training witch hunters, Blackwell used revenants to find witches for him. It was a disaster. Unreliable at best, terribly violent at worst, they'd kill them and dismember them and bring back body parts as trophies. Blackwell said they were like cats dumping their kill on his doorstep for approval.

Finally, she speaks. "Stealing."

"Oh," I say, somewhat relieved.

"He promised me he'd stop. And he did for a while. But then I didn't hear from him for months, and I found out he'd been arrested. They put him in Fleet." She looks at me, her eyes wide. "I thought I'd never see him again. I prepared for the worst...but then he was let go. Well, he said he escaped, but I don't know if I believe that."

I don't know if I believe that, either. No one escapes Fleet. No one except me, and I had a lot of help. And Blackwell would never let a revenant go. Unless...

"You think he was let go so he could steal something?"

She nods.

I think a moment. "You think Blackwell wants him to steal something?"

She nods again.

"Like what?"

"Who knows. With Schuyler it could be anything. He's stolen money; he's stolen horses; he even stole a crate of chickens once—"

"Except Blackwell wouldn't have him steal chickens."

"No," she replies. "And that's what I'm afraid of." She glances in Schuyler's direction. Only his bright hair is vis-

238

ible now; the rest of him fades into the darkness of the trees around him.

Fifer turns back to me. "I didn't just bring Schuyler here to protect me against you. There's another reason, too." She takes a deep breath. "The prophecy. Remember the line that says, *trust the one who sees as much as he hears*? Well, I think that's about Schuyler. And I think that whatever Blackwell wants him to steal is the same thing we're here to find."

Her words come fast now, as though she's afraid I'm going to cut her off, to tell her she's wrong, to say I don't believe her, the way John did.

I don't.

"I wasn't sure, at first. But then when I saw him talking to those nymphs—" Fifer breaks off. "They know things, too, you know. They're connected to the earth the way revenants are. If there's anything hidden around here, anything out of the ordinary, they'll know it."

"Is that why you brought two necklaces?" I say. "Because you knew we'd have to follow him and you didn't want him to know?"

Fifer shrugs. "I always carry two necklaces. If I need to talk to someone else he's touched, doesn't do me much good to only have one, does it? Schuyler's smart enough to figure out what I'm saying even from half a conversation."

I smile a little at the lengths she goes to, to hide things from him.

"Anyway, even if I'm wrong about Schuyler being part of the prophecy—which I'm not—whatever Blackwell's got him doing, whatever he wants Schuyler to steal, it can't be good, can it?" Fifer goes silent. And when she speaks again, her voice is very quiet. "I always think of Schuyler as invincible. But I think he's gotten in over his head this time."

Immediately, I wonder if Schuyler knows about Blackwell. Then I dismiss it. Revenants need touch to gain access to people's thoughts: The more contact they have with a person, the deeper they can read into them. I doubt Blackwell would have allowed even a handshake.

I consider telling her then that Blackwell is a wizard. But Nicholas said not to, that the truth will come out in time. And if Fifer is right about Schuyler, that time will come soon enough.

"I think you're right," I say.

If Fifer is surprised by my agreement, she doesn't show it. We keep walking up the hill, pushing our way through the thickening trees until the path gradually narrows, then disappears. We've lost sight of Schuyler, and there's nothing around us but trees now, no way to know which direction he may have gone.

"What do you think?" Fifer asks.

I look around. While I'm used to hunting at night, I almost always had some sort of light. If not from the moon, then a torch. The moon is just a tiny sliver, too dim and too low in the sky to be of use. I keep walking anyway. Fifer trails behind me, silent. But I don't see anything. Just a typical forest floor, spongy with moss, brown with wet leaves and fallen branches. Unremarkable.

I start to wonder if Fifer's necklace doesn't work. That Schuyler heard us and outsmarted us and purposely led us astray...then my toe hits a rock and sends it clattering into a nearby tree. I reach down and pick it up. It's mossy, too, but green. Bright green. It looks out of place.

It is out of place.

Soon I see another green rock, then another. They're getting bigger, piling up along the ground until the forest floor disappears beneath them. We pick our way over them until they end at the entrance to a small tunnel, neatly hewn into the side of the hill.

Fifer shoots me a look. There's a challenge behind it.

I shrug, but I feel my heart pick up speed. I hate small, dark spaces but I'm not about to back out now. I take a breath and step inside, Fifer behind me. There's a faint light at the end, glowing soft and green. It has a strange, shimmery quality to it, almost like water.

We follow the tunnel to the end, where it veers sharply to the right, and peer carefully around the corner. About ten feet in front of us is an enormous stone slab, propped open like a door. I hear noises from inside. A grinding noise, like stone on stone. A shuffling, like footsteps.

Schuyler.

I turn to Fifer. "Stay behind me. Whatever he's doing in there, he won't like being surprised." It occurs to me that while I don't think Schuyler will hurt Fifer, he won't have any problem hurting me.

Fifer reaches into her bag, pulls out Humbert's spring-loaded dagger, and hands it to me.

"I don't think this will help," I say.

"Maybe not," she says. "But there's no sense going in empty-handed."

I take it and press the button in the handle. With a tiny

click, the single blade splits into three. Fifer pulls a small canvas sack from her bag and ties it around her waist.

"Salt," she whispers. "Just in case. It won't stop him, either, but it'll slow him down if we need to get away."

We slip through the narrow opening into a small room unlike anything I've ever seen. A thick carpet of moss covers the floor and the walls. Long tentacles of it hang from the ceiling, and the air smells damp and earthy, like a forest after a storm. In the center of the room is a single, moss-covered tomb. Schuyler stands in front of it, holding an enormous sword. His head whips around as we enter the room, and immediately he takes a swing.

Fifer screams and I drop to the ground, feeling a rush of wind as the blade skims the top of my head.

"Flamin' hell, Elizabeth!" Schuyler lowers the sword. "I coulda killed you. And you!" He looks at Fifer. "What are you doing here?"

"What am I doing here? What are *you* doing here?" Fifer steps over me and advances, pointing her finger at him. "Explain yourself!"

An unmistakable look of guilt flashes across Schuyler's face.

"Ah. Yes. Well, it's all a bit of a faff, really—"

"It looks pretty simple to me." She points at the sword. "You're stealing that, aren't you?"

Schuyler scratches the back of his neck. "It's not what it looks like."

"What is it, then?"

Schuyler doesn't reply.

"Tell me," Fifer says.

"I can't," he says.

"Tell me now," Fifer repeats. "Or I swear to you I'll walk out of here and you'll never see me again." Her words are angry, only she doesn't sound angry. She sounds upset.

Schuyler looks at her for a moment, then steps forward and takes her hand. Fifer doesn't move. They stand there, hands clasped, staring at each other in a way that makes me think I shouldn't be here.

She rises on her toes and leans against him, her lips moving toward his, as if she's about to kiss him. Schuyler's eyes are as round as mine feel; he looks as if he's about to devour her on the spot. Then, in a flash, she snatches the sword from his hand.

It takes a moment for him to snap out of his daze.

"What the hell are you doing?"

Fifer backs away from him, pointing the sword at his chest.

"Taking this. Until you tell me what you need it for."

Schuyler's eyes gleam with anger, and I feel a prickle of fear. I can't decide if Fifer is ridiculously brave or ridiculously foolish.

He whirls around then—the movement so sudden and fast it makes me jump—and reaches into the tomb. He yanks out a scabbard. It was once brown leather, I suppose, but now it's as green as everything else around us.

"Do you know what this place is?" He fastens the scabbard around his waist.

Fifer shakes her head. She's standing close to me now; I can feel her trembling.

"It's the tomb of the Green Knight," Schuyler says. "Heard of him?"

243

Fifer shakes her head again.

"What about that?" Schuyler points at the sword. "Called the Azoth. Lots of fairy tales told about it. Elizabeth, surely you've heard one or two."

Fifer looks at me; we both look at the sword. The blade is huge: made of silver, cut through with swirls of bronze, three feet long at least. The hilt is solid bronze, encrusted with emeralds of every shape, size, and shade of green.

"Blackwell didn't spend much time tucking me in and reading me bedtime stories, so no. I've never heard of it."

Schuyler raises his eyebrows. "Funny. Because it was Blackwell who hired me to bring it to him."

Fifer and I exchange a rapid glance.

"Perhaps hired is the wrong word," Schuyler continues. "I think his exact words were 'bring it to me or I'll drag you to the gallows in chains, hang you 'til you're near gone, then slit you from breath to belly, pull out your innards and set them alight while you watch—'"

"Stop," Fifer whispers, her face ashen. "Stop."

"What does Blackwell want with this sword?" I say.

"They say this sword is the most powerful of its kind in existence," Schuyler replies. "It can cut through anything. Stone, steel, bone—" He breaks off with a nasty grin. "They say whoever possesses it can never be defeated. Not by weapons, not by magic, not by anything."

"The most powerful of its kind in existence?" Fifer glances at the sword. "What kind?"

Schuyler flashes her a look. "The cursed kind, of course."

Fifer lets out a squeak.

"You can't be cursed just by holding it," he says. "You have

244

to use it. That's how the sword works. The more you use it, the more powerful you become, until you're invincible. That's when the curse takes hold."

"How so?" I say.

"The sword starts to take its power back. It gets stronger, the man weaker, until he's dependent upon it to survive. Once our knight here realized that, it was too late. Because the only way to get rid of the curse is to get rid of the sword. And the only way to do that is to lose it in battle. Only he couldn't do it. He was too powerful."

I'm drawn into the story despite myself.

"So how did it end up here?"

"Dying with the sword is the only other way to break the curse," Schuyler says. "So the knight found a witch, had her entomb him here, even had her put a spell on it so that no one could free him as long as he was still alive. I suppose that was in case he changed his mind."

I give an involuntary shudder.

"What does Blackwell want with a cursed sword?" Fifer says.

Schuyler shrugs. "I don't think he cares about being cursed. At least not as much as he cares about being invincible."

"You can't let him have it," I say.

"Interesting request, coming from a witch hunter," Schuyler says.

"She's right," Fifer says. "You can't."

"You want me to die?" he fires back.

"Of course not!"

"What would you have me do, then?"

"Leave it! Just leave it and walk away."

"And go where? If I don't bring him this sword—"

"You might live," Fifer says. "But if you bring it to him, he'll kill you anyway. Surely you know that."

"He gave me his word," Schuyler says.

Fifer whirls to face me. "Elizabeth, what do you say to that? What is Blackwell's word worth?"

I hesitate. I was loyal to Blackwell for so long that even now—even after he threw me in jail and sentenced me and turned his back on me, after he lied to me—I still hesitate to speak against him.

So I just shake my head.

Schuyler swears under his breath.

"And is that what you really want?" Fifer continues. "For Blackwell to become invincible?"

"It doesn't matter what I want," Schuyler says. "I have to do this."

"No, you don't!"

Schuyler marches toward us. Eyes narrowed, reaching for the sword. A thrill of fear rushes through me as I reach over, plunge my hand into the bag of salt hanging at Fifer's waist, and fling a handful of it in Schuyler's face.

He lets out an agonized shriek—uncomfortably reminiscent of the sound that ghoul made when I threw salt on him, too—and falls to the ground, covering his face and rolling around, his movements slow and sluggish from the salt.

Fifer looks momentarily stunned. She grabs another handful and flings it at him, then drops beside him and pulls out a fistful of something green and sweet-smelling—*Is that peppermint?*—shoving it down his shirt, into his boots, even down his trousers. Eventually Schuyler stops moaning and falls still.

She puts her mouth to his ear. "I'm doing this for your own good," she whispers. Then she jumps to her feet. "We've got about twenty minutes before he comes to. Believe me, we want to be long gone before he does. So grab that torch and let's go." Clutching the sword, she dashes to the door and slips through the opening.

I retract the knife and slip it into my boot. As I pass the tomb to get the torch, I pause to look. Inside is the perfectly preserved body of a knight. True to his name, he's completely green: green hair, green skin—even his armor is green.

Fascinating.

Fifer sticks her head back in the door. "Elizabeth!"

"Coming." I snatch the torch off the wall, and, as I pull away, the flame lights up the stone slab enclosing the knight's tomb, and I notice something I didn't see before. Markings. Etchings of some sort. Some are letters, some symbols. Runic alphabet, I suppose, very ancient magic. I don't understand them, though their meaning is clear enough: This knight was buried beneath a curse tablet.

I slip out the door, and Fifer and I start running, out of the tunnel, over the stones, and down the hill.

"That was quick thinking," Fifer says. "With the salt. I thought we were done for."

"What was that you stuck in his trousers? Was that peppermint?"

She nods. "It gives him terrible hives. He'll be covered in a rash for weeks. And in a very painful place, too."

I start laughing then. I can't help it. After a moment, Fifer joins in.

We stop a moment to get our bearings. We're somewhere halfway up the hill now. Below us are the lake and the party beyond, still going strong.

"Well?" Fifer holds up the Azoth. "This is it, right? The thing you were supposed to find?"

I shake my head. "No. Nicholas said I'd know it when I saw it, and this sword doesn't mean anything to me at all."

Fifer looks from me to the sword then back again. "Are you sure? Here. Take another look." She thrusts the sword at me; I take a quick step back.

"Watch it," I snap.

"Sorry," she says, not sounding the least bit. "But—the prophecy. *What he holds in death will lead you to thirteen.* The knight was holding the sword. And it's the reason Schuyler is here." Fifer makes an exasperated noise. "This has to be it."

"I'm sorry," I say. "But this isn't it." Fifer looks so disappointed I almost feel sorry for her. "Look," I continue, "it's not all bad, is it? Blackwell wanted it, and now he's not going to get it. Especially if it really does what Schuyler says it does."

"I guess." Fifer shrugs. "What should we do with it? We need to keep looking, but I don't want to drag it down there with all those people. Even if they don't know what it is, they might take an interest in it for no other reason than all these jewels." She twists the Azoth in her hand, the emeralds glinting even in the muted torchlight.

"Let's take it back to Humbert's," I say. "We can leave it in the cathedral and come back. How long does this party go on?"

"A while," Fifer says. "Especially on the last night. Could go 'til dawn, at least."

"Okay," I say. "I don't know what we'll do about Schuyler—"

"I have more peppermint," Fifer says. "And more salt. I brought enough to stun a revenant army. And I'm mad as hell. If he knows what's good for him, he'll stay away."

23

WE MAKE OUR WAY THROUGH the woods, back in the direction of Humbert's. I toss the torch on the ground and stamp it out: If Schuyler does come to, there's no sense in making it easy for him to follow us.

Fifer walks beside me, swinging the Azoth back and forth. Maybe I should be thinking about Blackwell, about his wanting the sword, if it really does what Schuyler says it does. But for some reason, my mind is on the knight, still and green in his tomb.

"Why do you suppose he was so green?" I say. "The knight, I mean? I've never seen anything like that before."

"Me neither," Fifer says. "But it was definitely a curse. Either from the sword or from the witch who entombed him. Did you see that slab on top? All the marks on it?"

"Yes," I say, shifting my attention to the treetops ahead of us. I just saw a pair of owls shoot into the sky. Might be nothing; owls hunt at night. But birds flying out of trees are also nature's way of telling you there are people nearby. Maybe it's just us. "It was a curse tablet."

Fifer nods. "You never see them disposed of that way. They're usually thrown in wells, dumped in lakes, rivers. The ocean. You know. But to put one in a tomb—"

I feel a jolt of warning down my spine.

"Tomb?" I stop and grab Fifer's arm. "What happens if you put one in a tomb?"

Fifer frowns. "For one, it makes for a more effective curse. The tablet draws upon the dark energy of the dead and strengthens the magic. Especially if the person died violently."

"Violently?" I feel cold, sick.

"But it's crazy," Fifer continues. "I mean, it's one thing in theory, burying a curse tablet with a corpse. Entirely another in practice."

"Practice?" I'm starting to sound like a popinjay, those ridiculous talking birds that pirates sometimes have. They can't really talk, of course. All they do is repeat the last few words you say to them. Stupid, useless creatures.

"Well, yes. Think about it. To do it you'd almost have to plan it all along—perform the curse, kill someone, and then bury the tablet in with the person you just killed. How would you do it otherwise? Not many people are going to run around town looking for freshly dug graves to put their curse tablet in, keeping their fingers crossed that the person buried there died a violent death. No one wants to get their hands that dirty, pardon the pun."

My head is spinning. Inside, words float around, disjointed and nonsensical. Curse tablet. Tomb. Violent death. Plan. Corpse. Grave. Dirty hands. But then they start to weave together like a tapestry, forming a picture I wish I didn't see.

Come third winter's night, go underground in green. What holds him in death will lead you to thirteen.

Fifer was right, but she was also wrong. It wasn't what the knight holds in death; it was what holds *him* in death. Not the sword, the tablet. The stone slab that entombed him. Just like the stone slab that nearly entombed me.

Suddenly, I know. I know where the Thirteenth Tablet is.

"Fifer," I whisper. My mouth is dry as dirt. "The Thirteenth Tablet. I know where it is. I—"

I hear it whistle through the air before I feel it: the fist attached to the arm of the guard that just connected with my face. There's a sickening crunch as my nose breaks and a gush of hot blood comes pouring out.

Next to me, Fifer screams.

"This was almost too easy," the guard mutters, shoving me aside before going after Fifer. The skirt on my dress is so tight I lose my footing and stumble to the ground, sprawling face-first into a pile of leaves and dirt. My stigma fires hot against my abdomen as my nose snaps back into place. I barely feel it.

Before I can get up, two of the guards flip me over and grab my wrists while a third clamps a pair of manacles around them. I recognize them immediately: They're the guards we ran into on the road to Humbert's.

"Not so dangerous now, are you?" one of them mutters.

I struggle wildly, trying to get to my feet. But my hands

are bound in iron, my legs in silk. The guards force me back to the ground, one of them driving his knee into my spine, hard.

"You're not going anywhere," he says. "Except to prison, where you belong."

I struggle more. He slams my face into the ground; the force of it makes my head spin. "We'll stay with her," I hear him call out. "You go help with the other one."

I hear a shuffle of leaves, then Fifer's panicked scream. I turn my head to the side and see the guards circle around her, taunting and laughing.

"Get away from me!" Fifer shrieks, holding the sword in front of her. She jabs it at the two men but keeps missing.

"Look at that little girl with the big sword!"

"You know, *witch*, you're lucky we caught up with you instead of Blackwell's boys. Your pretty face would be roasting on the spit before sunrise."

"Isn't that going to happen anyway?" the other guard says.

They laugh some more.

I've got to get us out of here. I've got one guard on my back, the other standing next to me. I've got that triple dagger in my boot, but since my hands are pinned beneath my chest, what good is it? I'm almost tempted to call for Schuyler. Then I remember the necklace and realize he won't hear me. Which means I'm on my own. I've got to get out of these manacles, but I don't know how.

Then I get an idea.

Quietly, slowly, I break my own thumbs. First one, then the other, gritting my teeth against the pain. I slip my hands out of the bindings, hear a quiet *crack* as the bones snap back into place. Then I go still. Have the guards noticed? No, they're too busy calling encouragement to the ones still teasing Fifer. They're such idiots. Now they're going to pay for it.

I flatten my hands underneath me. In a flash, I buck the guard off my back. Land in a crouch and yank the dagger from my boot. The guard who rolled off me, I grab him by the hair and stab him in the neck. He falls back to the ground, dead. Before the other one can open his mouth in protest, I pull the dagger from the dead guard's neck and send it flying toward him. It lands directly between his eyes and he slumps to the ground. Also dead. The whole thing is over in seconds.

The sudden silence gets the other guards' attention. Their eyes go from me to the two dead men and back to me again. They look stunned. I yank the blade from the guard's head and start toward them.

"Fifer, get behind me."

She stands there, dazed.

"Fifer! Now!"

Slowly, she steps around the guards, lowering the sword a little as she goes.

"Don't!" I shout, but it's too late. One of the guards leaps forward, grabs a hank of Fifer's hair and punches her square in the face. Then he drives his fist into her stomach and she drops to the ground. The sword falls limply from her hand.

The other guard picks it up and rounds on me.

I lunge forward and seize his free arm, twist it behind his back and jerk it upward, hard. I'm rewarded with a loud snap as the bone breaks. Still holding his wrist, I yank him to me and drive my dagger into his gut. He falls to the ground as the other guard leaps forward and snatches the sword before I can get to it. He swipes at me with it and I pull back. He does it again, then again, missing me both times.

I drop to the ground, swinging an outstretched leg underneath his feet, swiping them out from under him. As he crumples to his knees, I jump up and smash my foot along the side of his kneecap. I hear a crunch and he screams in pain. He falls toward me and takes a final swing with the sword.

The blade slashes across my abdomen, the cold silver red hot as it sears through the silk, all the way to my flesh. Immediately, it starts gushing blood. I feel the flash of heat in my abdomen and wait for the familiar, tingling healing sensation. But it doesn't come. Just more heat. And a lot more blood. I clutch my hand to my side and feel it spurt between my fingers.

It's not healing.

The guard lies awkwardly on the ground, his injured limbs sprawling uselessly beneath him. I stumble to him, snatching the sword from his hand and thrusting it into his chest. He gives a muffled grunt and falls back into the grass. Dead.

I hear Fifer groaning. I stagger to her side.

"Are you okay?" Her eye is starting to swell, and even in the pale predawn sky I can see a bruise blooming under the skin.

She looks at me, her pupils dilated so large her eyes look nearly black.

"You're hurt."

I nod. "I guess the sword has some power after all."

"Will you be able to make it back?"

"I think so." The blood is flowing hot and fast now, spilling through my fingers. I'm starting to shake. Fifer wraps her arm around my shoulders and, slowly, we make our way back to Humbert's.

I don't speak at all. Whether from pain or terror, I don't know. All I do know is that my stigma isn't healing me. What does that mean? Is it just this wound that won't heal? Or what if the Azoth has somehow undone the stigma's power permanently? If I've lost my stigma, I don't stand a chance of getting that tablet.

I may as well die right here.

Dawn breaks, weak threads of light pushing through the thick blanket of clouds that is already filling the sky. As we reach the edge of Humbert's property, Fifer is practically carrying me. I've lost a lot of blood and I'm so dizzy I can hardly walk. The ground swoops in giant waves below me, and things start to blur around the edges.

Soon we see the turrets of Humbert's house in the distance, poking up through the treetops like tiny teeth. As we draw closer, I can see servants in the courtyard, already going about their morning business. And I hear Humbert shouting.

"Keep your eyes peeled! If you find them, bring them to me, sharpish! I won't have them ruining my roses again, climbing down the bloody wall—"

Fifer shoots me a look. For the first time since we left the party, I start to worry about what waits for us inside. This might be bad.

Bridget is in the courtyard as we walk up. She takes one look at me and screams.

"Master Pembroke! Come quickly!" She rushes over to

me. "Oh my goodness, miss, what's happened to you? So much blood…" She clucks around me like an overexcited hen.

Humbert comes barreling through the door, his plump face flushed with anger. He's still wearing the clothes he had on last night, a bright silk doublet over a ruffled linen shirt, both now wrinkled and wilted. His spare gray hair sticks up at all angles, revealing patches of baldness underneath. He looks completely mental. I might laugh if I weren't about to faint.

He takes one look at us and stops dead in his tracks.

"My God," he stammers. "What—what happened? My God," he repeats, his eyes darting back and forth between Fifer and me in horror. He seems not to notice the enormous sword she's holding at her side.

Between the two of us, there's a lot to be horrified by. Fifer's red hair is matted and dirty, embedded with grass and twigs and broken leaves. Her shirt is mud-stained and her skirt hangs in tatters. But none of that compares with her face. Her eye, nearly swollen shut now, is a brilliant shade of purple. It stands out like a beacon against her pale skin.

But however bad she looks, I look a hundred times worse. I catch a glimpse of myself in one of Humbert's many diamond-paned windows and start at the reflection. My face is coated in blood and dirt. My arms are covered in moss and mud. But my stomach is the worst. Fifer's beautiful white dress has been torn clear open, revealing an enormous, oozing slash across my midsection. She said she'd kill me if I ruined her dress, but I'm wondering if the sword might beat her to it. My stomach lurches and the ground slides precariously under my feet.

"John!" Humbert rushes to my side. "George! Come quickly! We need help!" He and Fifer slowly lead me inside the house.

John and George run into the hallway. I lift my head to look them over. Unlike Humbert, they've changed into fresh clothes from yesterday, both wearing long wool coats, heavy gloves, and boots. Their faces are flushed with cold, as if they've been outside for a while.

"Oh," I whisper. I'm surprised at how weak my voice sounds. "Were you out all night, too?"

"We've been looking for you," George says. He can't tear his eyes away from my stomach, from the blood that drips onto Humbert's pristine black-and-white floors. Then he looks at Fifer, at the sword dangling from her hand. "Did you do that?"

"Don't be ridiculous," she snaps. We take another step forward and I stumble. "John, help her."

John steps forward and scoops me up in his arms.

"Take her to the dining room," Humbert instructs. Dimly, I hear him call out to Bridget. She rushes over, and John quickly rattles off the things he needs. I don't really listen. Can't he do whatever he needs to do upstairs, so I can sleep? I'm so tired. I lean my head against his chest and close my eyes. He smells like outside. Leaves and cold, crisp air.

"Bring me whatever sewing needles you have, and a spool of your strongest thread. No, I don't care what color," he adds. He carries me into the dining room, Fifer and George on his heels.

"You're going to sew my dress back together?" I open one eye and squint up at him. "That's nice of you."

"No. I'm going to sew your skin back together."

258

"What?" Fifer and I exchange a frantic glance. My injury is right above my stigma. If John tries to help me, he'll see it. I can feel the heat of it blazing into my skin, still trying to heal me. "No. You can't."

"I have to," he says.

"No, you don't. Just put me down. I'll be fine." I start struggling in his arms. But the pain is so intense it makes me gasp.

"Stop moving," he orders. "You're making it worse."

In the dining room, John lays me on the table, now covered in a clean white sheet, and then shrugs out of his heavy black coat. Bridget rushes around, carrying trays of things and setting them out for him. Fifer and George hover behind her, identical expressions of fear on their faces.

"No," I say again. "You can't do this." I roll to my side, try to get away from him. But John pins my shoulders to the table and leans over me. His face is inches from mine.

"If you don't let me do this, you will bleed to death," he whispers. "Do you understand me?" I look into his dark eyes and I can see fear there, lurking just beneath the surface. And I know he's telling the truth.

I let out a shaky breath. "Okay. But there's something I need to tell you."

"Tell me later." John grabs a bottle of spirits off the table, then pulls back the frayed edges of silk from my gory midsection. "This might sting a bit," he says. Then he dumps the clear, cold liquid all over my stomach.

The pain is sharp and penetrating. I stifle a groan, biting my lip so hard I taste blood. He presses a clean cloth to my side and begins cleaning off my skin. Any second he's going to see my stigma.

I glance at Fifer. She holds my gaze for a moment, a look of resignation crossing her face. Then she nods.

"John." She walks forward and touches his sleeve.

"Fifer, please. Not now." He lifts up the cloth.

"I need to tell you something."

"Fifer, I told you—" He glances at my stomach. Frowns. Peers in closer. Then he sucks in a sudden, sharp breath. I don't need to look to know what he sees: a black XIII, scrawled across my abdomen, burning bright against my pale skin.

John stumbles away from the table, his eyes wide, the color draining from his face.

"That's a... you're a..." He can't bring himself to say it.

I open my mouth to say something, anything, but nothing comes out. I start to reach for him, then think better of it.

"I'm sorry," Fifer says softly. "You weren't supposed to know."

John doesn't reply.

"None of us were," George adds. "It was Nicholas's order. Fifer and I only found out by accident."

John still doesn't reply. He just stands there, staring unseeing at the floor in front of him. An interminable silence passes, and I wonder for a moment if he's just going to walk away. Leave the room and let me bleed to death.

"I know what you're thinking," Fifer says. "But she's not like the others. She saved my life tonight." She quickly fills them in about our run-in with the guards. "If she hadn't been there, they would have taken me in. Or killed me. Or worse."

I stare at her, shocked by her words, by her defense of me.

"And she knows where the tablet is," Fifer continues.

"She does?" Humbert and George say at once.

George steps up beside me. "Where is it?"

"It's—*ah*." A bolt of pain shoots through me, making me gasp. "It's at Blackwell's."

"What?" Humbert looks stunned. "How is that possible?"

I open my mouth again, groan in pain again.

"She can tell you about it later," Fifer says. "But she can't if she's dead." She looks at John. But he's looking at me now, his jaw clenched, a flush of anger coloring his cheeks. Eyes so dark they're almost black.

"Hand me the needle and thread."

George lets out a small sigh of relief.

Bridget steps beside John, looking apologetic. "I tried to thread it myself but my hands were shaking too hard. I don't take to the sight of blood too well." She presses the needle and thread into his hand, then quickly moves away from the table, as if I'm going to jump off it and attack her.

John threads the needle without hesitation, as if he's done it a thousand times, pulling it through and tying the ends together in a tight knot. I see the slightest tremor in his hands. If I hadn't already seen how steady they can be, I might not have noticed. Without a word, he picks up the bottle of spirits again and offers it to me.

I take two huge swallows. The sharp, strong liquid burns my mouth and throat. I shudder as it hits my empty, roiling stomach.

John holds the needle up, a long length of thread trailing behind it. Green. The same shade as the knight in his tomb.

I close my eyes just as the sharp needle penetrates my flesh.

MY EYES FLUTTER OPEN. John is leaning over me, his palms spread across the table, his head bowed. I must have passed out for a moment, but I don't think he noticed. I can hear him breathing: long, slow, deep breaths, as if he's fighting to control them.

"I'm sorry," I say. My voice weak and hoarse, but I need to say it. "I'm so sorry."

He jerks his head up. Snatches the spool of thread off the table, hurls it across the room. It hits the wall and clatters to the floor. Then he spins on his heel and storms away.

George starts after him, but Fifer grabs his sleeve.

"Let it go," she says. "Just—let him be."

Fifer and George turn to me, and Humbert steps up beside them. They stand over me, watching me, silent. I feel vulnerable, lying here like this. My dress in tatters, my stomach exposed, my secret exposed. I'm trembling from cold and fear and loss of blood and a hundred other things I'm too weary to contemplate. But I need to tell them about the tablet. I need to tell them I have no idea how I'm going to destroy it. And I need to tell them about Blackwell.

"The tablet," I start.

"Is it really at Blackwell's?" George says.

I nod.

"That's a very serious accusation." Humbert frowns. "I've known Blackwell a long time. He's capable of some unpleasant things, certainly. And he certainly has reason to get rid of Nicholas. But breaking his nephew's rules to do it, the rules he himself created…are you absolutely sure?"

"Yes." I take a deep breath—hard to do without making my stitches hurt—and look at them each in turn. "There's something else you should know about him, too."

"What?" It's Fifer who speaks. "What is it?"

"Blackwell is a wizard."

The words seem to change as they leave my mouth. They shift and grow into monsters of their own, a hybrid of fear and truth and horror and lies: reaching, grabbing, shaking, shrieking. The others, they don't speak. They don't move. They just stand there, allowing themselves to be devoured.

"Nicholas…I think he suspected it for a while," I continue. "And after what happened at Veda's, after she told him what I was, after I told him all the things I'd done, the things I did…" I pause, swallowing back the lump in my throat. "He knew."

Then I tell them everything.

I tell them about Caleb. About my training, about my

final test at Blackwell's. How they took us one by one into the darkness, maybe to live, maybe to die. How Guildford marched me into the woods and into the tomb, where Blackwell tried to bury me alive with my own fear.

"After it was over, after the dirt receded and the tomb righted itself, it was already morning. I saw the light coming in through the edges of that door, and I remember thinking it looked different. That it didn't look like the same door as before. It wasn't wooden at all, but stone. But I didn't think it mattered. All that mattered was getting out." I take another breath. "Finally, Guildford came and got me. My eyes were shut. I was still singing. Still curled up in a ball. I wasn't in my right mind."

"Just like at Veda's," George whispers at last. His eyes are as round as trenchers. Fifer's face is vellum pale, and she goes a long time without blinking.

I nod. "As we left, I opened my eyes to take one last look. I don't know why. Maybe I wanted to see where I almost died, maybe I wanted proof I was still alive. But when I opened my eyes, I saw it. It was the Thirteenth Tablet."

Fifer sucks in a breath.

"Of course, I didn't realize it was the Thirteenth Tablet until we had the sword and I saw the Green Knight's tomb. I didn't know you could dispose of curse tablets in tombs, not until Fifer told me…." I shiver. "But now I know. And if I'm going to destroy it, I have to go back into the tomb at Blackwell's to get it."

"How are you going to do that?" George says. "Blackwell has more protection on his house than is on the king's. Guards, gates, a moat, and that's just to get to the main entrance. Inside, he's got archers stationed in towers around the clock. They don't fire warning shots."

Humbert sinks into a chair. He seems to deflate before my eyes: his face sagging, his posture sagging, the shock setting in.

"I thought you were a witch," he whispers. It's a surprise to hear him speak in anything less than a shout. "Nicholas said you had herbs, and I just assumed..." He trails off, shaking his head.

"I'm sorry," I say. "No one was supposed to know. Nicholas thought it was better that way."

Humbert considers it, then nods. "I understand the need for deception. I should; I live a life of it. Distasteful, perhaps. But necessary."

He motions to Bridget. She's hovering in the doorway, watching us, eyes wide.

"Please prepare a bath for Elizabeth, some food and clean clothing." He turns back to me. "We need to get you on the mend. Then we can figure out how to get you inside Blackwell's."

George helps me to sit, and Fifer wraps a blanket around my shoulders. We make our way down the hall, up the stairs, into my room. John is gone, nowhere to be seen. I saw the look on his face, when he realized what I am. He probably never wants to set eyes on me again.

After Bridget finishes the bath, she and George excuse themselves. Fifer helps me undress and I slip into the hot, fragrant water. And immediately, embarrassingly, I start to cry.

I'm weak. I'm tired. I'm injured. I'm confused. I'm ashamed of what I've done, afraid of what I've got to do. I am what I always feared I'd be: alone. I'm going into that tomb alone; I'm going to die alone. This is what Nicholas knew, what he didn't want to tell me. He didn't have to. Because deep down, I knew it, too.

"You're not going to die," Fifer says quietly. She's kneeling next to the bathtub, her hands gripping the edges. Watching me. "I know that's what you think. But you aren't. I've read the prophecy a thousand times. It sounds bad—I know that. But you aren't going to die."

"Why do you care?" I say, my voice cracking. "As long as I find the tablet, what does it matter to you if I die? You said I'd be better off dead. You said it's what I deserved."

"I don't—I didn't mean that," she says. "Well, yes, I did. But I don't anymore. I don't think you deserve that." She goes silent for a moment. "I understand what it's like, you know," she says, finally. "To have your life torn apart by magic."

I jerk my head up to look at her. "What?"

She sighs. "I started studying with Nicholas when I was six. Everyone—well, everyone outside this house—thinks it's because I'm so exceptional. A prodigy. For him to take on someone so young, I'd have to be, right?" She looks down, tapping her pale fingers against the tub. "Do you want to know the real reason?"

I nod, but she doesn't see me. "Yes."

"It's because my mother gave me to him. She wasn't a witch herself, and she was scared of me. Of the things I could do. My father had just died; she thought somehow I killed him. I don't know if I did. To this day, I still don't. All I know is she somehow found Nicholas, gave me away, and never came back."

I wince at the familiar tale of yet another broken family. "I'm sorry."

Fifer shrugs. "What could I do? I cried, I screamed, I ran away. But it didn't bring her back. I hated being a witch. I hated magic. Hated that it turned my family against me. If Nicholas hadn't taken me in, hadn't raised me as his own, things might have turned out very differently for me. I might still hate magic, as you do."

"I don't hate it," I say. "Not anymore. I've seen the worst it can do, but I've seen the good it can do, too. What Nicholas does, what John does—" I stop. "I guess I don't know what to think anymore."

Fifer nods. "Nicholas says that magic isn't inherently good or bad; it's what people do with it that makes it that way. It took me a long time to understand that. Once I did, I realized it isn't magic that separates us from them, or you from me. It's misunderstanding."

She holds up a finger, then plunges it into the tepid water. At once it becomes deliciously hot.

"Besides, magic does come in handy sometimes—I can't lie." She grins at me. "I guess the tree downstairs was right about you after all."

"What do you mean?"

"It's a tree of life. Didn't John tell you?"

I shake my head.

"Your making those leaves appear like that means...well, it means a couple of things," Fifer says. "It's mainly a sign of strength and power. But it also signifies change. New beginnings, I guess you could say."

"Oh." Maybe I should be pleased by this, by the chance to

start over—whatever that means. Instead, I'm left wondering how much it even matters anymore. Then I remember something else. "What did the bird mean?"

Fifer raises her eyebrows, the tiniest smile crossing her face. "I think John should be the one to tell you about that."

I shake my head, a sudden ache filling my chest. I don't think John is going to be telling me about anything anymore.

Fifer helps me out of the bath and into a clean nightgown. I look at her and feel a twinge of guilt. She's a mess, still dressed in her clothes from the party, her hair matted and dirty, her eye a brilliant shade of purple. She's so tired she's swaying on her feet.

"You should go sleep," I say.

"Okay." She yawns and walks to the door. "You should, too. You look terrible. You can't expect to destroy the tablet in this condition." She shuts the door behind her.

The tablet. It's the last thing on my mind as I fall into a fitful sleep, tossing and turning throughout the day and night, and the first thing on my mind when I wake up.

I ease myself out of bed—the pain in my side considerably less than it was yesterday—go to the window and throw open the curtains. Outside, the ground is covered in a thick, fog-like mist. Another cold winter day in Anglia. I consider crawling back into bed when there's a knock on the door.

"It's me," Fifer says. "Let me in."

I open the door and let out a yelp. Fifer is standing in the hallway holding a goblet, wearing a black glittery mask with a plume of bright pink feathers shooting from the top.

"What do you think? Do you like it?" She pushes her way

inside and prances around, making ridiculous poses. Her red hair clashes horribly with the pink feathers.

I wrinkle my nose and shake my head.

"I knew it!" She tears the mask off and flings it onto the bed. "It was George's idea. He said he couldn't stand looking at my face without it. He's such a baby."

I see what he means. Even though the swelling around her eye is gone, it's still a bloody, mottled purple.

"Here." She pushes the goblet into my hand. "It's medicine. John made it. You're to drink all of it, no complaints, and I'm to report back that you did."

I wince. There's no telling how bad he's made this medicine taste. I take a tentative sip. But instead of something sour or pungent, I taste strawberries. I think back to the night when I first dined with Nicholas, when I piled my plate high with strawberries and cake. John must have noticed and remembered. I feel that ache in my chest again.

"What's wrong? Why are you making that face?" Fifer demands.

"No reason," I say. Fifer raises her eyebrows. "Anyway, where did you get this?" I reach over and pick up the mask. It's pretty, black satin with tiny black jewels sewn all over it. The feathers are overkill, but I've seen worse.

"Humbert has a whole trunkful. That duchess friend of his, you know. They're left over from some masquerade ball they went to. I can't imagine how strange those parties must be. I mean, what's the point of getting all dressed up if no one knows who you are?" She tuts. "Have you ever been to one?"

I nod. "Two, actually. Would have been three if I hadn't been arrested. Malcolm has them every Christmas. This year's must be coming up soon."

It takes a moment for that to set in. Malcolm's masquerade ball is coming up. The one Caleb was going to invite Katherine to, the one I drunkenly invited George to.

I tear off my nightgown and fumble around on the floor for some clothes.

Fifer watches me, her eyes wide. "What's wrong?"

I tug on a pair of trousers and a shirt, shove my feet into a pair of boots, and stagger out the door.

"Where are you going?"

"I'll explain downstairs," I say, working my way down the steps. "Where's Humbert?"

"Sitting room."

Shuffling down the hall, I catch a glimpse of myself in the mirror. My shirt is buttoned up wrong, my hair is tangled. I look wild, unhinged.

I finally reach the sitting room, Fifer on my heels. Humbert is at his desk, writing a letter. "*Elizabeth!*" he crows. "It's nice to see you up and—"

"Humbert, what day is it today?" I demand, cutting him off.

"I'm sorry, dear—what day?"

"Yes. What day of the month?"

"Well, it's Wednesday, of course," he says. "The fourteenth of December." He smiles. "Oh, you must be talking about the weather. It does seem as if it came early this year, doesn't it?"

I ignore him, thinking. Today is the fourteenth. Malcolm's masque was to be held on the third Friday of the month this year. What day is that?

"I need a calendar," I blurt.

"Yes, well, fine." Humbert opens a drawer and pulls out a ledger. "Here you go."

I snatch it from his hands and flip the pages until I land on December 1558.

"Oh my God," I whisper.

"What's going on?" George says, walking into the room.

"I know how I'm going to get into Blackwell's." I hold up the calendar, point my finger to a date: Friday, December 16, 1558. Two days from now. "I'm going to be a guest at Malcolm's masquerade ball."

"What are you talking about?" Fifer says.

"Every year at Christmas, Malcolm has a masquerade ball," I say. "He invites everyone. It's a huge crowd. There's a performance, music. Food and dancing. People come from all over Anglia." I turn to Humbert. "You go, don't you?"

"Not lately," he admits. "Difficult for me to dance, what with my back. And my foot—" He stops. "But, yes, I did receive an invitation a while back. I tucked it away, didn't give it much thought." He pauses. "But Malcolm's Christmas masques are normally held at Ravenscourt, aren't they?"

"Yes, normally," I say. "But with all the rebellions, he thought it would be safer to move it. Keep it secret until the day before. Then all the guests would receive a second invitation with the location."

"Then how do you know where it is?" George asks. "I don't."

"I—" I feel my cheeks burn. "The king told me."

The three of them frown, confused. Of course, they don't understand how or why the king would tell me something like that. And I'm not about to explain it to them, at least not now.

"Anyway," I continue. "I've got a lot to figure out in two days. The biggest problem is how to get there. It's too far to ride, so I'll have to take a boat. I can sneak aboard. I've done it before; it's not terribly difficult. Granted, it'll take some doing to persuade the captain to drop a stowaway at Blackwell's doorstep, but—what?"

Fifer, George, and Humbert are all staring at me as if I'm as deranged as I look.

"I don't know, Elizabeth," Humbert says. "Walking into Blackwell's house, uninvited—"

"I'm not uninvited," I say. "I'll take your invitation."

"But poking about his grounds with all those people around? I don't know. It sounds potentially dangerous."

"It's dangerous no matter what," I say. "But the masque is by far my best opportunity to get inside. There will be hundreds of people around. My face will be hidden. Blackwell will be distracted. No one will notice one wandering guest."

I look at George and Fifer for support, but they avoid my gaze.

Humbert gets up from his chair. "Elizabeth, the four of us spoke at length about this last night, and we think you should consider waiting until Blackwell's at court. He's scheduled to be there within the week, presumably after he hosts the masque. Then, when his house is empty, you can go in. Peter will go with you, and he'll bring men with him."

"No," I say. "That's exactly what Blackwell will expect us to do. He'll expect us to come when he's gone. Then he'll set a trap for us, and it'll be over. He'll never expect us to show up at the masque."

Behind me, someone clears his throat. I turn around and see John standing in the doorway. He looks as he did the night I first met him: face pale, eyes shadowed, clothes wrinkled as if he slept in them. Or didn't sleep at all. The sight of him makes my stomach tumble wildly.

"How are you feeling?" he says to me.

"I—I'm fine." I'm surprised he'd bother asking. "Thank you."

He nods and turns to Humbert. "Horace returned with some news." He holds out a letter. "It's not good."

Humbert takes the letter and scans it briefly. Then he sinks into a chair, his head bowed.

"What is it?" Fifer says. "What's going on?"

"It's Nicholas," John says. "He's dying."

25

IMMEDIATELY, FIFER BURSTS INTO TEARS.

"What happened?" I say.

"He took a turn for the worse," John says. "The healers in Harrow say he won't make it through the week."

"We have to do something," Fifer wails. "We can't let him die!"

"He's not going to die," I say. "Because I'm going to the masque to destroy the tablet."

"Elizabeth—" Humbert starts again.

"No," I say. "You have to do what I want, remember? That's how the prophecy works. Whatever I want to do, we do. And I want to go to the masque."

Humbert is quiet for a minute. Then he nods.

"Good," I say. "I'll need a dress, a mask, and your invitation. And a horse to get to port." I turn to John. "Where's the nearest one?"

John thinks a moment. "There are a couple. Hackney is closest, but Westferry is the better bet. It's safe harbor for pirate ships that stop for provisions before heading south. My father knows all the captains and I've met a few. I could probably get us on one of them without too much trouble. If we left tonight, we could catch one in the morning."

"*We?*" I say. "There is no *we*. Just me."

"Wrong," John says. "I'm going with you." I open my mouth to argue, but he holds up a hand. "I heard what you said. But if you try to sneak aboard some ship, and they find you and decide to make an example of you, not getting to Blackwell's will be the least of your problems."

"I can take care of myself," I say.

"Fine," he snaps. "But who's going to take care of your stitches? Who's going to make your medicine? Who's going to keep you from dying?" There's an edge to his voice, something between anger and frustration.

"No one!" I shout, brought to anger and frustration myself. Maybe because I know it's true.

The room goes quiet as we glare at each other.

"I'm going with you," John says again.

"I'm going, too," Fifer says.

"No, you're not," John and I say at once.

"I am, and don't you dare try to stop me," she fires back. "I have a sword, and unless Elizabeth wants a matching set of stitches and you want some of your own, I'm going with you."

George raises his hand. "Count me in, too."

"This is ridiculous." I turn to Humbert, and I don't need to raise my voice for him, because I'm already shouting. "They cannot go, and you have to stop them. It's too dangerous. You know it and I know it. They could get captured. They could get killed, and—what?"

Humbert is shaking his head.

"It's Nicholas," he says simply. "We all care too much what happens to him to sit back and do nothing. So for me to try to stop them from helping would be wrong, not to mention unfair."

I start to argue, but Humbert speaks first.

"And you're going to need help," he reminds me gently. "You can't do it alone."

I snap my mouth shut, gritting my teeth against this foolishness; against the idea that they can help, against the idea that I am anything except alone. But I know that for now, arguing will get me nowhere.

Then I get an idea.

"I guess that settles it," I say. "Can you help us get ready?"

Humbert nods, then motions for John and George to follow him upstairs. When they're gone, I turn to Fifer. She's not crying anymore, but she's still sniffling, and now both her eyes are swollen and red.

"This is a terrible plan, you coming with me," I say. "Surely you know that."

"I do," she says. "But Humbert's right. You're going to need help."

"But you can't help me," I say. "And if something happens to you while I'm in there, I won't be able to help you."

"Let us worry about that." She starts toward the door. "We should probably go and get ready."

"You go ahead," I tell her. "There's something I need to do first."

I go to Humbert's desk, pull out a pen and some paper. While I may not be able to keep the others from going to Blackwell's with me, I can at least make sure they get out.

When I'm done, I fold up the pages neatly and seal them, dripping melted wax over the edges and pressing Humbert's signet, a falcon, into the pool of crimson.

I find Bridget. "Give this note to Humbert the moment we leave," I say. "It's very important. Do you understand?"

"Yes, miss, I do," she says, alarmed at my urgency. "I understand."

"Good. And make sure Horace doesn't go anywhere. Humbert's going to need him."

Several hours later we're all in Humbert's stable, loading our bags onto four of his horses. We're dressed in Humbert's servants' livery, pale gray trousers and tunic with an orange falcon embroidered across the front.

"It's a bit suspicious, your riding at night," Humbert says. "So if anyone stops you, tell them I'm expecting a shipment of fruit from Iberia at dawn, and you're going to port to wait for it."

"Fruit?" George says, climbing onto the mounting block. He's so short he can't get on his horse without it.

"Of course! How else would I get oranges, limes, and lemons in the dead of winter?" He slaps his hand on John's shoulder. "Just got one last week. It's a good thing, eh?"

John gives him a weak smile and climbs onto his horse.

"There's an inn at Westferry called the Nutshell. My servants always stay there. Ask for Ian. He'll give you a couple of rooms and not ask too many questions."

Humbert leads us outside. It's only four o'clock, but night is already falling. I can already see the moon, a shining crescent in the dusk. As we prepare to ride off, I feel his hand on my arm. I turn to him and he motions for me to come closer. I lean down.

"What is it?"

"Do you still have the ring?" he whispers.

"Yes." I feel embarrassed about packing it. It's probably valuable, and I suppose he's realized if I die, he'll never get it back. I reach for my bag. "It's right here, just give me a minute to find it—"

"No." He puts his hand over mine and squeezes. "I would like it very much if you wore it at the masque," he says. "Can you do that?"

"Yes, I suppose so," I say. "But why?"

"It's a lucky ring," he says. "I know, it's an old man's silly superstition. But I would feel better if I knew you had it on."

He's right; it is a silly superstition. Even still, I'll take all the luck I can get.

"Okay. I'll wear it," I say. "Thank you." He gives my hand one last squeeze and I'm about to ride off when it dawns on me. "Hang on," I say. "You can hear me. I've been whispering this whole time, but you can hear me. Can't you?" I stare at him as it sinks in. "You're not deaf at all, are you?"

Humbert winks. "Oh, I don't know. We're all a little hard of hearing in our own way, aren't we?" He laughs at the shocked look on my face. "It's a wonderful disadvantage to have, I'll tell you. One learns so much being deaf. You'd be surprised at what people will say when they think no one is listening."

Trust the one who sees as much as he hears. Fifer thought that was about Schuyler, and it was—but it was also about Humbert. I wonder if she knows.

I shake my head and laugh, too. I can't help it.

"Our little secret?"

I nod.

"Good girl. Now you'd better get moving."

The four of us ride away. But before we can even make it all the way through Humbert's vast estate, I see a falcon circling the sky. He hovers over us before swooping away, a rolled-up note clutched in his tiny feet.

"Isn't that Horace?" George says.

"Yes," John confirms. "I figured Humbert would write my father to tell him where we were going. But I thought he'd at least wait until we cleared his property first."

I smile. So far, things are going according to plan.

It's dark when we reach Westferry. We find Humbert's friend Ian easily enough. He takes our horses to his stable, feeds us, and shows us to our rooms, all without question. Fifer and I fall into our beds immediately. I'm exhausted, and my side throbs painfully. John wrapped it up tightly before we left, but three hours on horseback has left it aching.

The next time I open my eyes, it's morning. To my surprise, the sun is shining. Fifer and I dress and go next door to John and George's room. John is standing at the window, watching the ships that line the harbor. He's fully dressed and ready to go.

"See it?" Fifer asks, setting her bag on the floor.

"Not yet," John says, shielding his eyes against the bright sun.

"*It?*" I repeat. "I thought you said we could take any one of those ships."

John shrugs, but he doesn't turn around. "We could. And we might have to. But I'd rather take one I know. It'll make it easier, given where we're asking them to take us."

George comes in with food, and the three of us eat while John continues to monitor the window. Then Fifer and George play a card game on the bed while I sit in a chair in the corner, trying to rest. Even though I slept well last night, I'm still tired. I guess it's my stitches. I can't remember the last time an injury left me so exhausted.

Next thing I know, there's a hand on my arm, gently shaking me. "Elizabeth. Wake up." I blink and see George standing over me. "Time to go." He helps me out of my chair and hands me my bag.

John stands by the door, waiting. He hasn't spoken to me, at least not voluntarily, since we left Humbert's. Every now and again I catch him watching me when he thinks I'm not looking. But when I try to meet his gaze, he always looks away.

Outside, the dock is crowded with people, stevedores mostly, loading and unloading crates from the ships that line the quay. For a moment I stand there, letting the warmth from the sun sink into my skin. I should be feeling safe—as safe as someone like me could feel, anyway. But for some reason, the hairs on the back of my neck start to prickle, the way they do when I know I'm being watched.

"Which one is it?" George says. There are several ships along the pier. Some are massive, hulking things, all masts and rigging, billowing sails, and cargo stacked high. Others are low and sleek, with nothing on board but cannons, poking from the gun ports like tiny black eyes.

"There. At the very end." John points to one of the smaller ships docked at the end.

"It's smaller than I thought it would be," Fifer says. "Don't you think we'd be better off in one of those?" She motions to one of the larger ships.

John shakes his head. "Blackwell's house is off the river. Something that big will never be able to get us close enough without running aground. I don't really want to row in, do you?"

Fifer shakes her head.

We step into the jostling crowd and make our way toward it. We're about halfway there when someone bumps into me, knocking my bag off my shoulder. I stop to adjust it. In that moment, one man's heavy shoulder slams against mine as another man steps in front of me, and I lose sight of the others.

The sunlight bounces off the water and into my eyes, so bright I can't see where they went. I spin around in a circle, searching the crowd. When I still can't find them, I feel a little jolt of panic until a hand lands on my arm. I turn around, thinking it's George, maybe John. But it isn't.

It's Caleb.

"Hello, Elizabeth," he says, as calmly as if we'd met at the palace grounds, or the World's End, or any place besides this dock, the last place on earth I'd ever expect to see him.

"Caleb," I gasp. "What are you—how did you—"

"How did I find you?"

I nod, too stunned to speak.

"It was difficult—I won't lie. Easier, perhaps, once we found the dead guards in Stepney Green. As soon as I saw them, I knew it was you. I'd recognize your handiwork anywhere." He smiles then, but it doesn't quite reach his eyes.

I start to shiver. "Caleb, I—"

He holds up a hand. "I need to talk to you, and we don't have a lot of time. Marcus is here; so is Linus. They haven't seen you, at least not yet." I whip my head around, searching the crowd for them. What if they found the others?

"Don't worry, they're not here for your friends. I told them specifically to leave them alone."

I freeze.

"Don't look that way. I'm glad you made friends. I'm happy to see you were taken care of. The tall one, in particular, seems as if he's taking very good care of you."

I let out a strangled gasp.

"Elizabeth, I want you to come back with me."

It takes a moment to find my breath.

"What?" I say finally. "No, I can't go to prison, Caleb. I won't—"

"You're not going to prison," Caleb says. "I'm the Inquisitor now, haven't you heard? What I say goes. I want you to come back and be a witch hunter again."

"What?" I say again. I can't believe I'm hearing this. "No, Caleb, I can't do that."

He frowns. "Why? What else are you going to do? You can't tell me you want to stay here"—he waves his hand dismissively—"with them?"

"Yes. No. I don't know." I realize then I don't know what I want to do. Or what I can do.

"What has he told you?" Caleb reaches for me, takes my arm. "What did Nicholas Perevil tell you to make you think you would be safe with him? Safer with him than with me? What makes you think he won't kill you once you're done doing...whatever it is he's got you doing?"

I wrench myself from his grasp. "It's not Nicholas. It's you." I feel a sting of tears behind my eyelids. "You didn't come back for me. At Fleet. You left me there to die. You left me with no other choice but to do this."

"Says who? Nicholas?" Caleb says. His blue eyes flash with anger. "I was coming back for you. I told you to wait for me. You promised me you'd wait." He takes my arm again. "But when I came back, you were already gone."

The tears are threatening to break now. I don't know who to believe. I don't know what I want to believe.

"I almost died in there. Did you know that? I caught jail fever, and I almost died." I think of John then, how he saved my life. Of Caleb, how I'm not sure he would have done the same. "If you really were coming, why did it take you so long?"

"Because we knew Nicholas would show up for you," Caleb says. "Blackwell's seer told him he would. The whole thing was a setup. Your arrest, everything. It was to get you in jail to lure Nicholas in. Blackwell told me when I went to plead for you."

My stomach gives a sickening lurch at his betrayal.

"And you went along with it?" I whisper. "You must have known how scared I was. I almost died, Caleb." I repeat it because it needs to be repeated. "You almost let it happen."

"I did what Blackwell told me to do," he says. "I'm your best friend. Do you really think I'd leave you to die?"

I don't reply.

"Are you saying you don't believe me?"

I look at him. He's the same Caleb I've always known. Restless, ambitious, always yearning for more. It's only now I realize how deep that plague of ambition has spread inside him. Like a disease, it rules him now: his thoughts, his actions, the things he chooses to see, the things he chooses to ignore. And, like a disease, one day it will be the death of him.

It was very nearly the death of me.

"I believe you," I say. "But I don't believe Blackwell."

"What are you talking about?" Caleb says. "We'd be nowhere without him. We'd still be in the kitchen, or God knows where else. He gave us a chance when no one else would." His voice rises with conviction. "You owe him your life. We both do."

I shake my head. I don't want to think about what I owe Blackwell.

"Why did he make you Inquisitor?" I say instead.

Caleb doesn't answer, not right away. He turns away from me for a moment, but not before I see something flicker across his face, an expression I recognize but haven't seen in a long time: uncertainty.

"He made me Inquisitor because I'm his best witch hunter," he says finally. "Because he knows he can trust me. Because..."

"Because he knew if he made you Inquisitor, you'd be able to find me."

Caleb throws me a look, but we both know it's true.

"There are things about Blackwell—things you don't know," I say. "Things that, if you knew, might make you change your mind about him—about what you're doing for him."

"What are you talking about?"

"I'm talking about Blackwell's being a wizard."

Caleb goes still. Then suddenly, inexplicably, he starts to laugh.

"You don't really believe that."

"I didn't. Not at first," I say. "But it explains so much. It explains everything. About our stigmas, about training, about his plans."

"And what plans would those be?" He's still laughing.

"He plans to take over," I say. "To overthrow Malcolm and take the throne for himself. And he means to use magic to do it."

Caleb abruptly stops laughing. "That's treason," he says. "Nicholas has got you talking treason. What you just said could land you on the pyre before sunrise."

"Blackwell already tried that, remember?"

Caleb scoffs. "I told you already, that was just part of the plan."

I shake my head, but he continues.

"Come back with me." His voice is low, persuasive. "We could be back at Upminster by morning, and it'll be just as it's always been. Just you and me."

"No."

"What?" His eyes go wide, stunned. It's the only time he's asked me to follow him and I've refused.

"I can't go back," I repeat. "And I don't want you to go back, either. I'm afraid for you, Caleb. I'm afraid of what Blackwell is doing and I'm afraid of what he's doing to you." I swallow. "I'm afraid you're in danger."

"I'm in no danger," Caleb says. "But you will be, unless you come with me."

The warning is clear, but I back away anyway. For a moment I think this is my real test: a test of strength and will and a command of fear, every bit as real as the test in the tomb. A test not of Blackwell's design but one he contrived anyway, to make me choose between my best friend and my freedom, my family and my life.

"If you don't go back with me, I can't help you," he says, his voice tight. "No matter what happens, I won't be able to save you. Not this time. Do you understand?"

I nod. I do understand.

He steps forward and grasps my forearm for a moment, then quickly lets his hand drop, almost as though it's not his place to touch me anymore. And it's this: this small forfeiture of custody that makes me realize he's releasing me. Letting me go. That now, after spending half our lives together, we're going to spend the rest of them apart.

He backs away from me, nods his head in a little bow. A good-bye.

"I'll tell the others I lost you." His voice is gruff, and in it I can hear all the emotion he despises, all the emotion he's trying so hard to contain. "And it won't be a lie."

THERE ARE PEOPLE ALL AROUND, pushing into me. But I'm so stunned, I don't move. I'm so stunned, I don't do anything. I just stand there. Staring unseeing at the crowd around me, Caleb's words echoing inside my head.

I feel a hand on my arm and jump.

"There you are." It's George. He's standing in front of me, John and Fifer beside him. They're frowning. "What happened? We turned around and you were gone."

"I—I'm sorry, I—" I shake my head, still unable to think. "It's bright out here," I finally manage. "I guess I just got turned around."

George tuts. "Well, come on, then. We've got a ship to board." He and Fifer set off down the dock. But John just stands there, looking at me, brows raised. A question.

I could tell him that Caleb showed up, what he said to me. But what's the point? It doesn't change that I said good-bye to my best friend. Most likely forever. Tears fill my eyes again, and this time I don't bother to push them away.

John's eyes widen in sudden understanding.

"He's here, isn't he?" He spins around, searching the docks. "Was he alone? Are they sending more?"

"Yes. But they're not—he didn't." My voice breaks. "He let me go."

He turns back to me, surprise etched on his face. After a moment he nods.

"Let's go." He touches his hand to the small of my back and guides me through the crowd to the gangway, where Fifer and George are waiting. They give us both a curious look but say nothing.

The four of us start up the narrow wooden bridge. A bearded, heavyset pirate stands at the top, sword in hand. "Stop right there," he commands. He aims the blade at John's chest.

"I want to speak to the captain," John says.

The man laughs. "They all want to speak to the captain. I tell them all no. What makes you any different?"

"Because this is my ship," John replies. I shoot a surprised look at George; he shrugs. "I assume that makes me different enough?"

The man peers at John. Then his eyes widen and he lets out a sudden bellow.

"John Raleigh!" He grabs John's arm and hauls him onto the deck. "I should have known. You're the very spit of your father. What are you doing here? Don't tell me you've decided to trade a life of virtue for a life of debauchery?"

John smiles. "Not quite. My friends and I need a lift into Upminster. Greenwich Tower?"

The man raises his eyebrows. "I hope you came prepared."

John pulls a sack from his bag and gives it a shake. By the heavy, dull clank I can tell it's full of coins. "Of course."

The man turns around and motions for John to follow. "Come on. You can plead your case yourself. Your friends can wait here."

John follows the man to the upper deck of the ship, into the captain's quarters. We wait by the railing, trying to ignore the overly interested stares of the other sailors.

Finally, John emerges. He looks furious, and my heart sinks. The captain must have refused us passage. I don't see how it's possible, especially if this really is John's ship. I step forward, ready to find the captain and force him to let us on, when I see why John is so angry.

He exits the cabin behind John, a boy dressed entirely in black; shaggy blond hair, bright blue eyes, wicked grin.

Schuyler.

He's come back for the sword, and Blackwell sent him. It's the only explanation for his being here. I spin around, snatch the Azoth by the hilt from under Fifer's cloak, and advance on him, pointing the blade directly at his throat. Behind me, Fifer gasps.

Schuyler doesn't even flinch. "Ah, my little mouse, my bijoux. I knew we'd meet again someday. Though this is not at all how I hoped it might go. I imagined less weaponry, less hostility, less clothing—"

"Shut up," I say. "Turn around and walk away. If you can do it without opening your mouth again, I might let you keep your head."

"Elizabeth, put it down," John says.

"No!" I say. "That's what he wants. He wants the sword, and he can't have it. He'll take it to Blackwell. We can't let him have it—"

"He's not here for that," John interrupts. "He's here because Fifer called him. Last night. Told him to meet us here." He gives her a furious look. "He stole a crate of lemons from Humbert's and bribed his way on board with it."

George chokes back a laugh. "Lemons?"

Schuyler shrugs. "Scurvy."

I keep the sword on Schuyler's throat, my eyes on his face. "Fifer, why did you call him here?" I think a moment. "And how? Revenants have to be close to hear someone's thoughts. If he was in Stepney Green last night, he couldn't possibly have heard you all the way from here."

John makes a face and spins around, as if he can't bear to hear what's coming next.

"He—well, he didn't hear my thoughts as much as he, uh, felt them," Fifer finally manages. Her face turns as red as her hair. "We have a connection."

"A connection?" At once, I remember the way they looked at each other inside the knight's tomb. The way she almost kissed him, the way he looked as though he'd eat her alive. My face goes as red as hers. "Oh."

Schuyler shakes his head and tsks. "How you belittle our love."

"Shut up or I'll let her run you through with that sword," Fifer growls. Then she turns to me. "I called him here because I think he can help you get the tablet."

"I already told you—"

"I know what you told me," Fifer says. "But there's something we need to tell you."

"So tell me," I say.

George steps forward. "Might I suggest we do this somewhere else? Perhaps somewhere where we don't have half the ship watching?"

I turn around and see at least two dozen sailors clustered around us, clutching handfuls of coins.

"Don't stop," one of them says through a mouthful of broken black teeth. "I've got ten crowns that says the revenant rips your arm off."

"Double that says she takes his head."

"A sovereign says the revenant rips her arm off first, *then* she takes his head."

They start cheering and throwing more coins around.

"Come on," John says. "I had to give the captain nearly everything I've got just to let us on board. If we keep this up, he'll throw us right back off." He looks around. "Let's go to the back. You"—he points at Schuyler—"if there's even a hint of trouble out of you, I'll throw you off this ship myself. Got it?"

"Always so pleasant, John," Schuyler mutters. "No wonder she likes you so much."

A flicker of surprise passes over John's face. Then he scowls. "Go."

I pull the sword away from Schuyler's neck and the five of us thread through the men, who boo and catcall after us, around crates and cannons until we reach the back. One by one we climb the narrow wooden stairs to the upper deck. It's quiet back here, nothing but piles of rope, more cannons, and barrels of gunpowder.

I look around at all of them. "What is going on?"

Fifer sits down on a coil of rope. "It's about your test."

"What about it?"

"That night after you told us about it, and after you went to sleep, Humbert, John, George, and I talked about it. How it works, the magic of it."

"And?"

"Well, from what you've told me, the test sounds like a combination of spells. Rather, a spell within a spell. The first was concealment, obviously: hiding the tablet behind a simple wooden door. Then there was the illusion."

"It wasn't an illusion," I say. "It was real."

"It was an illusion," she says. "But that doesn't mean it wasn't real. You saw it, felt it, reacted to it. That's what made it real. Your fear is what made it real."

"Then there's no difference."

Fifer shakes her head. "Yes, there is. There's a big difference. Because when you're inside an illusion, you can—if you're very skilled or very lucky—make yourself believe it isn't real. By doing so, you eliminate the fear, which eliminates the illusion. Wasn't that the point of the test? To eliminate your fear?"

"Yes."

Fifer nods. "That's what happened when you sang. You calmed yourself down long enough to see it wasn't real. That's why you saw the tablet instead of the door. You saw through the illusion. You're going to need to do that again."

"Okay," I say. "So I do the exact same thing I did before, only now I do it knowing how the spell works."

I look around at the others. George is sitting now, knees tucked under his chin. John is staring out at the water, arms folded, jaw clenched. Schuyler looks from Fifer to me, his eyes going wide.

"Is there something I'm missing?"

Fifer takes a breath. "Do you know if the other witch hunters had the same test as you?"

"I—no. Everyone had something different."

None of us talked about our tests, but it wasn't hard to figure out what they were. The things people screamed in their sleep, the things they avoided when they were awake. Caleb never told me about his, but I guessed it had to do with drowning. It was a solid month before I could get him to bathe, and even now he cringes when it rains.

"That means the test is a spell that responds specifically to a person's fear. That's really advanced magic, you know. Blackwell must be extremely powerful—" She breaks off with a grimace. "What was yours? Your fear, I mean?"

"I already told you."

"I know, but...are you really afraid of being buried alive?"

"Well, I am now," I snap. "But no. At the time, I—" I hesitate. I don't want to tell them what I'm afraid of. It feels like admitting to something bigger.

"What was it?" Fifer presses.

I turn away from them, toward the water. I can feel their eyes on me anyway.

"I was afraid of being alone." My voice is quiet, small. I don't know if they can hear me over the sound of the men shouting on deck or the waves lapping against the ship's hull, but I keep going. "Of dying alone. Caleb says we all die alone, but I don't think that's true, not really. It's different to face it alone. To know that no one is coming, that no one will ever come. To know it's just you and that's all it'll ever be—"

I break off then, turn around to find the four of them staring at me, a chorus of horror and fear and sympathy on their faces.

"Are you still afraid of that?" Fifer says. Her voice is as quiet as mine.

"I don't know." I close my eyes against their unrelenting stares. "I don't know what I'm afraid of anymore. I don't see why it matters, anyway."

"It matters a lot," she says. "Because what if the tomb isn't the same this time? What if your fear isn't? There's no telling what you'll have to face in there. What happens if singing doesn't work?"

I feel my eyes go wide. I hadn't considered that. I never imagined the tomb might be different. Never imagined it might be worse.

"I don't know what condition you're going to be in, after it's over," Fifer continues. "You're also weaker now than you were then, when you were training every day, and you're hurt. If Schuyler is there, he can help you destroy the tablet. Besides you, he's the only one strong enough to do it."

I turn to him. "You agreed to this? Why?"

Schuyler sighs. And for once he doesn't look amused or indifferent. For once I can see the years and the things he knows flash across his eyes, a dark shadow behind the blue.

"Because Fifer asked it of me," he says. "Because I don't want her going in there alone. Because I don't want Nicholas to die. Because I think Blackwell is more dangerous than any of us knows. Because if I don't, I'm going to be hunted as much as you are." He shrugs. "I've got a very long life ahead of me. I don't want to spend it running."

I sink down on the deck and draw my knees to my chin. No one says anything; there's nothing to say. But after a minute George scoots next to me and puts his arm around my shoulder.

"You're going to be fine," he says firmly. "I told the others: Anyone who can take on Hastings and live to talk about it can take on anything."

I let out a shaky laugh. "Maybe that's what the test will be. A ghost, a basket of flour, and a brace of dead fowl." Fifer and Schuyler smile.

But when I look at John, he's not smiling at all.

The sun begins to set. The waters around us go calm, but the sailors on board grow loud. A few bring out instruments, a violin and a lute, and begin warbling off-key tunes. Others begin a loud game of cards on deck. Another group starts throwing dice.

George stands up. "I think I'll try to get in on that card

game," he says. "Try to win back our passage money. Anyone feel like staking me?"

John pulls out a couple of coins and tosses them to him. "This is all I have left. Try not to lose it all in the first hand."

George looks shocked. "Me? Lose? I think not. I'll have our money back within the hour—just you wait." He winks at me and gallops down the stairs.

"I think I'll go for a walk around deck," Schuyler says. "Gaze at the moonlight and all that. If that's all right with you." He looks at John. "Wouldn't want to anger the warden."

John shrugs. "As long as Fifer goes with you. And as long as she keeps a sword on you at all times."

Fifer snatches the Azoth off the deck and pokes the blade against Schuyler's back.

"Feisty." Schuyler grins. "Shall we?" He holds his arm out for Fifer. They walk down the stairs and across the deck, their heads together, whispering.

I turn to John. "You let them go off together?"

"Clearly, they go off together all the time. I haven't been able to stop it yet and I'm not likely to. At least I can make sure she's armed."

I smile. Then I realize he's left here alone with me. No doubt the last place in the world he'd want to be.

"I guess I'll just go to sleep now," I say.

John lifts an eyebrow. "Are you trying to tell me to leave?"

"I—no," I say. "I guess I'm just saying you don't have to stay."

"I'm fine," John says. "But I am hungry. Are you?"

"I guess. Maybe. I don't know."

He smiles a little. "It's really a yes or no question."

"Yes."

"All right. I'll be back." I watch him go. I don't know why he cares if I'm hungry or not. I guess because he knows in order to keep Nicholas alive, he needs to keep me alive. Which includes keeping me fed. I can't take it to mean anything but.

He returns a few minutes later, carrying a bundle of cloth. He unwraps it and lays the contents in front of me. Cheese, figs, apples, ham, a loaf of bread, a flask of water.

"No cake," he says. "Sorry. But I did ask."

I blink. "No, this is perfect."

"Dig in, then."

After we eat, he clears everything away and settles on the deck beside me, his back against the wooden railing. He takes a drink of water from the flask and passes it to me. We're quiet for a while, listening to the music on the deck and the sound of the water washing against the hull.

"How did Caleb know you were here?" John says, finally.

"He said Blackwell had a seer."

John nods. "We knew that. Or figured it, anyway. Does he know we're going to the masque? Was that why he was here? To try to stop you?"

"No. And I don't think Blackwell knows, either. If he did, he wouldn't have sent Caleb. He would have just waited. Caleb came because he wanted me to witch-hunt for him again. He said if I went against Blackwell, he wouldn't be able to save me. He said—" I stop.

"What?"

"He said if I didn't come back with him, I was on my own."

"What did you say?"

"I—" I swallow hard. "I said good-bye." I look at my feet and go quiet. John doesn't say anything. But I can feel his eyes on me in the moonlight.

"Do you love him?" he asks suddenly.

The question startles me so much that I drop the flask to the deck, water splashing on my feet. John quickly scoops it up and recorks it.

"He was my family," I say. "Of course I love him."

"I didn't mean in that way."

I think about it. Caleb was my best friend; he was my whole life. There was a time when I thought I loved him as more than a friend, hoped he might love me back. But I knew he found me lacking. Not pretty enough, not ambitious enough. Not enough, period. For all I fought it, I knew we were becoming different people. That the only thing that kept us together was my dependence on him and his sense of duty to me. And when I said good-bye to him today, I knew—deep down, I knew—he was relieved to see me go.

I glance at John. His eyes are fixed on the deck in front of him, but I know he's listening. I can see it in how still he is, the set of his shoulders, the way he grips the flask in his hand, that he's listening.

"No."

He looks up then, and for a minute we just look at each other.

"Why did you ask me that?"

He takes a breath. Looks out at the water, a crease forming between his eyebrows. When he looks back at me, his eyes are as dark and still and deep as the sea around us.

"I wanted to know. That's all. I guess I just needed to know."

"Oh," I say. We fall quiet again. And even in the silence it feels as if he's trying to tell me something and I him, but neither of us knows what. Or if we do, we're too afraid to say it.

"You should get some sleep," he says, finally. His voice is very quiet. "I brought you a blanket." He pulls it out of his bag and hands it to me. It's thick and gray and smells of salt and cedar, like the ship.

"Okay," I say, my voice equally quiet. "Thank you."

I lie down on the deck, tuck my bag under my head, and pull the blanket up to my chin.

But I can't sleep. My thoughts are full of Caleb and John and Blackwell and the tomb, wondering what's going to happen. But there's no point. Every time I imagine one thing, something worse comes along to replace it. I don't want to think about it anymore. I open my eyes and look at John. He's sitting with his back against the railing, his legs stretched out in front of him, head tipped back, watching the sky.

"Is this really your ship?" I say.

He lowers his head to look at me. "Yes."

"How?" I say. "I mean, I thought you didn't want to be a pirate."

"I don't." He shrugs. "But when my father joined the Reformists, he got rid of all his ships. All except this one. It was his favorite. He gave it to me, I guess in hopes I'd change my mind. I didn't, but I still didn't want to give it up. So I hired someone to run it for me."

"Oh." I think a minute. "But if it's your ship, why did you have to pay the captain to come on board?"

A small smile crosses his face. "Because he's still a pirate," he says. "He's ruthless and crass, and he's not known for his charity. But I trust him, and I like him. In the end, that is all that matters."

I close my eyes again. Finally, with the soft rocking of the ship, the strains of off-key music, and John's steady presence beside me, I fall asleep.

27

I'M JOLTED AWAKE, THE SUDDEN rocking of the ship rolling me off my bag. I open my eyes and peer through the railing. The skies are cloudy and gray, the waters choppy. Around me, the others are just starting to stir. Fifer and Schuyler are huddled together, talking in low voices. George is yawning, buried underneath his blanket and shivering.

I sit up and pull my own blanket tighter around my shoulders. A sharp, cold wind blows across the deck, lifting my hair and whipping it across my face.

"Where's John?"

"He went to get food," George replies. "And to find out when we arrive. I hope it's soon. If this boat doesn't stop rocking like this I'm liable to get sick."

John appears then, the boat lurching as he walks up the

stairs. He winces and grabs the railing to steady himself. He sets the food down in front of us and hands me a goblet.

"Medicine," he tells me. "It's not very good, but I didn't have a lot to work with. Might want to drink it while it's still hot. I can't promise it'll taste any better cold."

"Thank you." I take it from him. "What did you find out?"

"We're about four hours from Upminster. But there's a storm coming in, so it might take longer. Either way, we should be there by sundown."

John hands out the food—some bread and hard cheese—and sits next to me.

"I asked the captain to drop us off a mile downriver from Blackwell's," he says. "I know there will be other ships around and we could probably blend in, but there's no sense in taking a chance." He looks at me. "I hope that's all right."

I nod. "That's good. Thank you." I tear off a piece of bread but don't eat it. I'm too nervous to have much of an appetite. Judging by the way the others pick at their food, I guess they're not hungry, either.

"It should be easy enough to get in," I say. "We only have one invitation, but we can pass it back and forth. Once we're inside, we just need to blend in with everyone else."

Everyone else.

Malcolm, Blackwell, Caleb. Every witch hunter I've ever known. Not to mention guards and servants and a hundred other people who might recognize me. I suppress a shiver and keep going.

"Once we're inside, don't try to hide. Blackwell is alert to that sort of thing. Stay in the open, but try to avoid talking to people as much as possible. The performance starts at nine, and that's when we'll go down to the tomb."

Schuyler puts an arm around Fifer. I don't know what she's thinking, not the way he does. But by the way she chews on her lip, I can guess.

"Then you wait," I say. "You can't do anything but. Stay close by, but not too close. Act like guests and you'll be fine. No one will bother you. There are too many important people at this masque for Blackwell to risk irritating anyone. But if there's any sign of trouble while I'm in there, Schuyler, get them out."

"But what if something happens when you're still inside?" George says.

"Then he'll come back and get me." I look at Schuyler. "Right?"

Schuyler looks at me, his bright eyes darkening with sudden understanding. "Whatever you want, bijoux."

I turn to the others. "It's not the best plan in the world, but it's good enough. As long as everyone sticks to it, we should be fine."

Except it's all a lie.

Everything I'm telling them is a lie, and only Schuyler knows the truth. He heard me thinking last night, listened to my thoughts, just as I wanted him to. He knows what my real plan is. Knows that to keep the others safe, it's the only thing to do.

We sit in silence for a while. The ship continues to rock back and forth, sails flapping furiously. A handful of men run around the deck, roping down barrels and crates and cannons to keep them from sliding overboard. Abruptly, John jumps to his feet and walks away, striding quickly across the deck and into the captain's cabin. I look at George, but he just shrugs.

Soon I see the dark shape of land in the distance and know we'll be arriving soon.

"We should probably get ready," I say. "Fifer, we'll have to change, but I don't know where—"

"You can use the captain's cabin." I turn around to see John standing above me, holding his bag. He looks awful. His eyes are bloodshot and his face is pale. Even his lips are pale. "But I need to check your stitches first. We could do it here, but I thought you'd be more comfortable inside."

"Okay." We walk across the deck, the boat still pitching back and forth. I have to stop a few times to steady myself, but John plows ahead. I follow him into the cabin.

Inside, it's nothing but luxury. A carpet covers the floor, velvet drapes surround the wide, square windows. A wide oak table sits in the middle, surrounded by chairs. At the far side of the cabin there's a bed built into the wall, covered in plush bed coverings in different shades of blue, and next to it, a small desk with a mirror mounted on the wall above it.

"Where do you want me?" I say.

"The table is fine."

I climb on top of it and lie down, and John stands over me. He looks at me a moment, then clears his throat.

"I'll, uh, I'll need to see it."

I pause, then pull up the hem of my tunic, exposing my stomach. He's seen me before. He's a healer; he's seen a lot of people before. But this feels different. The cabin feels warm, but maybe that's the blush I can feel creeping up my neck, into my cheeks. I turn toward the window so he can't see.

John leans over me and begins to unwrap the bandage, his fingers brushing my skin like a caress. My heart is pounding so furiously, it's a wonder he can't hear. Or maybe he can.

"This looks good," he says after a minute. "I expected worse. Maybe your stigma helped after all. I don't know. But for someone with thirty-two stitches—"

"*Thirty-two?*" I turn to face him. "You gave me thirty-two stitches?"

He nods. "It was bad. I thought you were going to die. If that blade had gone half an inch deeper, you would have. If you had, I—" He stops, busying himself with bandaging me up again.

"What?"

"I don't know. I just didn't want you to die." He looks at me. "I know what you are now, but that doesn't change anything. I still don't want you to die."

The ship gives an enormous lurch then, pitching forward and rocking from side to side. I grip the edge of the table to keep from rolling off. John places his hands firmly on the surface, his head bowed. I can hear him breathing. Deep, slow, even breaths, the way he did after he stitched me up.

"What is it?" I say. "What's wrong?"

He doesn't answer. But there's another lurch and he slumps into a chair beside me.

"Do you mind if I sit?" he whispers. He reaches under the table and slides out his bag and starts digging through it. He pulls out a knife and—of all things—a lemon. He quickly slices it in two, holding one half to his nose and breathing deeply.

I watch him, my eyes wide. "What are you doing?"

He still doesn't answer. He just sits there, breathing in the lemon. The sharp, tangy scent fills the tiny cabin. Finally, he speaks.

"Remember when you asked why I wasn't a pirate, like my father?"

"Yes."

"It's because I get seasick." He looks at me then, his face as gray and colorless as the sky and sea outside. "Horribly, violently seasick. In fact, it's all I can do not to throw up on you right now."

He sets the lemon on the table and smiles a little, so I know he's joking. But probably not much. He looks awful.

"My father and I tried everything. Drafts, spices, herbs. But nothing worked. The only thing that takes the edge off is a lemon. When I was a kid, I used to squeeze the juice all over my clothes. It helps a lot, but it stains them terribly. It would make my mother crazy."

I remember the drink Bram gave me at the party. The one he said would taste like the one thing I wanted most in the world. The one that tasted like lemons and spices, the one I thought tasted like shandygaff. The one I thought was meant to remind me of Caleb. But it wasn't Caleb. It was John.

I feel a sickness then, one that's got nothing to do with the sea. There's a churning in my stomach and a terrible, hollow ache in my chest. I need to say something to him, but I don't know what.

"Whatever happens tonight, I just want to say thank you," I finally manage. "For taking care of me. For saving my life. I know that can't make up for what I've done, but I wish—" I stop. There's no point in saying what I wish. "Chime is very lucky," I blurt instead.

"What?" John jerks his head up. A stray lock of hair falls into his eyes, but he doesn't bother to push it away. "What did you say?"

"Chime," I say again. "I met her at the party. Fifer introduced us. She said you were—" I stop. A wave of pure jealousy surges through me, so strong it makes me dizzy.

"No." He shakes his head. "She's not. We aren't—" He breaks off.

"It's okay," I say. "I understand."

"Do you?"

I don't. I don't know what's happening. The only thing I do know is that when I look at him, his face pale and drawn, eyes shadowed and dark, he looks as miserable as I feel. Without thinking, I reach my hand up to his face and brush the hair off his forehead.

At my touch, his eyes widen in surprise. I freeze, feeling foolish. What am I doing? I start to pull away, but before I can, he catches my hand fast between both of his, wrapping his fingers around mine and holding them tight.

We stay that way, just staring at each other, neither of us speaking. I don't feel that familiar sensation of fear or the need to pull away. This time I feel something unfamiliar: the need to hold on tighter.

Someone clears her throat. I look up and see Fifer standing in the doorway, holding both of our bags. She looks from John to me then nods, as if she's come to some kind of understanding.

"I'm sorry to interrupt," she says. "But we need to start getting ready."

John drops my hand. He leans over his bag and hastily shoves everything inside: the lemon, the knife, the bandage. Then, without a word, he gets up and leaves, pushing past Fifer without a glance at either of us.

Fifer steps inside the cabin and shuts the door. She drops our bags on the ground and begins pulling things out: undergarments and gowns and slippers and jewelry.

I help her dress, lacing her into the same gown she wore the first night at Humbert's, the copper silk with the green bodice. She moves to the mirror next to the bed and fixes her hair, pulling it away from her face, little ringlets falling down around her freckled cheeks. Her bruise is still evident, but she manages to hide most of it with powder.

She spins to face me. "Well?"

"You look pretty," I say.

"We've got some work to do on you, though." She eyes me critically. "You're pale and your hair is a fright." She snatches my things off the floor: the blue dress with the bird embroidered on the front, the matching hair combs, the jewelry. "Let me see what I can do."

After what seems like forever, Fifer finishes with me. I look at my reflection in the mirror and, I have to say, I don't look too bad. By some miracle, she's managed to tame my hair. It's smooth and shiny and falls over my shoulders in soft waves. She pinned back the sides with the combs, just the way Bridget did, even added a bit of color to my cheeks and lips to hide how pale I am.

"Don't forget these." She hands me the sapphire earrings and matching ring. The one Humbert asked me to wear. I slip it on my finger. In the cabin's dim light, I can just make out the tiny heart etched underneath.

"Thank you," I say. "For someone marching to her untimely demise, I don't look half bad." I mean it as a joke, but Fifer scowls.

"We won't leave you there," she says.

"I might not make it out," I say.

"But we won't leave you there." She gestures at the door. "Come on. The others are waiting."

Outside, dusk is approaching and the clouds are beginning to part, revealing the bright moon behind them. John, George, and Schuyler stand by the door.

Schuyler is dressed in his usual black, George in all blue. Without all the feathers and brooches and bright-colored clothing, I almost don't recognize him. John has on black trousers and a white shirt under a black jacket trimmed in red. But his hair is still tousled, the wind blowing curls across his forehead and into his eyes. I realize I'm staring at him, but then he's staring right back at me.

Schuyler tips his head back and groans. "Not this again," he says. "I don't know how much more of it I can take."

"What are you talking about?" I turn to him.

"You. Him. This." Schuyler waves his hand between John and me. "All these *feelings*. Flapping about the ship like frantic birds in a cage. Love! Hate! Lust! Fear! *Ugh*. I feel as if I'm trapped inside an Aegean tragedy." He glances at George. "You're not going to start singing, are you?"

George grins. But I look away, my face flaming.

"Shut it, Schuyler," Fifer says softly. "Let's just show them and get on with it."

Schuyler pulls several pieces of paper from his coat. A piece of parchment, a wilted ticket, fragments of a map.

"How many?" Fifer says.

"Four," Schuyler replies. Then he takes the parchment and rips it in half. "Now five."

"Good." She reaches into her bag and pulls out a sheet of thick, creamy paper. I recognize it immediately. The delicate black script on the front, the bright red rose stamped on the top: the invitation to Malcolm's masque. She takes the ragged pieces of paper from Schuyler's hand and stacks them on the deck, one on top of the other. Then she takes the invitation and places it on top.

"What are you doing?"

"We need an invitation to get inside the masque," Fifer says. "I know you said we could pass the one back and forth, but I figured out a better way." She reaches into her bag again and pulls out her witch's ladder. "Two knots left." She holds up the length of black silk cording. "One of which is going to come in really handy right now."

"Ah," George says. "That is a good idea."

"I thought so, too." Fifer unties the knot and places her hand on top of the stack of paper. *"Alter."*

I watch as the map fragments, the ticket, and the two torn pieces of parchment shift and grow, changing shape and color until they become exact copies of the original invitation. Fifer starts passing them out.

"What kind of spell is that?" I say. "Is it like the one you did on the road to Humbert's, turning the grass into a hedge?"

"The principle is the same, yes." She hands me an invitation. The paper is slightly warm to the touch. "The idea of taking something and turning it into something else that's similar. It's called transference. It's actually a very handy spell. It needs a great deal of magic behind it, though. I couldn't do it without Nicholas's help." She holds up the cord and gives it a little shake. "He can transfer almost anything into anything else. It's pretty amazing."

Just then a man comes up behind us. He claps John on the back, and they shake hands. This must be the captain.

"We dock in about fifteen minutes," he says. "Best to get your things and wait by the plank. It'll be a quick stop. No need to stay here any longer than we need to." John thanks him, and then he's gone, striding across the deck and barking orders at his men.

We gather our bags and the Azoth—I've got it fastened under my skirt; it's so long the blade nearly grazes the floor— and cross the deck to the railing, watching as Blackwell's house looms into view.

From the river, it looks like a fortress. Four massive stone slabs, impossibly tall and straight, form the outside walls. On each corner is an even taller domed tower, topped with tiny flags, each emblazoned with a bright red rose. Blackwell's standard. Surrounding the house is another enormous stone wall. It lines the riverbank, stretching on for what seems like miles before turning inward to enclose the rest of the house.

Set in the middle of the wall is a single, small iron gateway, leading from the river into the moat within. Most of the time it's closed. But this evening it's open, like an enormous, gaping iron-toothed jaw. I can almost feel it waiting to devour me.

Normally Blackwell's home stands empty. But tonight it's crowded with ships of all sizes and shapes, carrying passengers from all over Anglia. Farther upriver are smaller barges, carrying people from their homes in Upminster. As they grow closer, I can hear the oarsmen beating time on their drums. *Thump. Thump. Thump.* It sounds like a heartbeat.

We slide into port. Two men rush over and quickly lower the gangplank, and it lands with a muffled thud on the dock below.

"Quickly, please," one of the men says, waving us on.

"This is it," George whispers. "Masks on." He slips his over his head: a plain black one. That took some convincing. The mask he wanted to wear was turquoise and covered in peacock plumes. "If you wear that, it'll take anyone five seconds to realize it's you," John had pointed out.

I pull my mask out of my bag, the black one with the pink feathers, and tie it on.

The five of us walk down the bridge. The second we step foot on the dock, the gangplank is whisked back up and the boat glides away, disappearing down the river, back to sea.

28

"INVITATIONS?" A DARK-UNIFORMED GUARD EXTENDS a white-gloved hand to us.

We're standing at the top of a wide set of stone stairs that lead from the dock to the entrance of Blackwell's home. The walls loom over us, damp and black with mold.

John hands over our magically altered invitations. I feel a squeeze of fear—*What if he can tell somehow?*—but he only nods.

"Enjoy your evening."

"Thank you," John says. He takes my arm then, steering me down the path in front of us.

I look around, impressed despite myself. Before tonight, this landing was never anything special. Just an expanse of dirt and scattered rocks, a nothing space that led from the water gate to the second gate of the inner ward. But now it's covered in grass and a freshly laid gravel path, lined with enormous potted trees and lit with a thousand candles. Musicians are stationed in the center of the clearing, strumming lutes and playing the pipes. The light, cheerful music seems completely out of place here.

John looks around, his eyes wide through his mask. His is plain black, too, just like George's. Humbert was able to round up only two like that. The rest were covered with feathers or jewels or fur. George got the first plain mask; John and Schuyler threw dice for the second. Schuyler lost. Somewhere behind me walks an annoyed revenant sporting a hideous, furry, cat-shaped mask.

For a moment I feel relief that we made it safely inside. I half expected Blackwell's guards to be on us by now, slapping us in irons and hauling us away, into the dungeon or God knows where else, never to be seen again. But that's not his way. If he knows we're here, he'll wait. Wait until we're cornered and helpless and then—only then—will he strike. Hard and fast to knock us to our knees, to make us beg, make us wish we were already dead.

That is his way.

We pass through the second gate, into the rose garden. This garden is Blackwell's most treasured possession. There are over a hundred species of roses here, carefully cultivated to bloom year-round, even in wintertime. Normally, they're kept under blankets in the cold months to keep away the chill. But tonight they're uncovered, beautiful and bright in shades of red, pink, yellow, and orange.

Guests stroll along the gravel paths that wind through the bushes, pointing and gasping at the array of topiaries that spring from the ground. Enormous shrubs carefully trimmed into towering pyramids, perfect circles, boxy squares, sometimes all three, one shape stacked on top of another. Others are pruned into animal shapes: owls, bears, even elephants, and their enormous green eyes stare unblinkingly as we pass. The hedge maze generates a lot of excitement, too. But after training, I rather lost my taste for them.

Soon the servants appear and begin ushering us inside. We follow them from the garden down a long stone walkway and through an enormous stone archway, into the main entrance hall. We trudge up the long staircase, through one of the many sets of doors that open into the great hall.

The great hall is just that: great. Three hundred feet long, a hundred feet wide. I can't begin to guess how tall the ceilings are. The walls are covered in rich tapestries: scenes of hunters on horseback, carrying spears and bows and arrows. But instead of the usual quarry—deer, boar, or wolf—they're hunting people. Specifically, witches and wizards. There's even one that features witch hunters roasting their kill on a spit.

I wish I could spare John the sight of that.

We push through the room. An energetic tune fills the air, but it's nearly drowned out by the sound of hundreds of guests milling about, gossiping, dancing, or huddled in groups along the window seats.

There are masks of every shape and type. Some are plain or lightly decorated, like George's and John's. Others resemble the heads of bears, wolves, and tigers, their mouths opened wide in toothy snarls. Some masks are covered in feathers of every color imaginable, others adorned with precious stones:

315

rubies, emeralds, sapphires, and even diamonds. I even see a few full-face masks, their fixed expressions grotesque, almost sinister. Especially since you don't know who might be underneath them.

I glance at the ornate clock mounted above the stage. Eight fifteen. In thirty minutes, I'll put my plan into place. That's when I'll excuse myself, tell the others I'm going to the privy. In reality, I'll be going to the tomb. At nine, just as the masque starts, Schuyler will tell the others I've called for them. He'll lead them outside, only instead of finding me, they'll find Peter, waiting with a ship outside the gate. Then Schuyler will have slipped away to meet me, and he and I will destroy the tablet. Afterward, if I'm alive, Schuyler and I will catch up to them.

But I don't count on being alive.

"I don't like this." Fifer looks around. "All these people, I feel as if they're all looking at us."

"They're not," John says. "It just feels like it because you're nervous. Try to calm down."

"How can I calm down? Have you seen all these tapestries?" Fifer bites her nails. "I feel as if I might be sick. Maybe if I get some air—"

"You can't," John replies. "We stick to the plan. And that means staying put until the masque starts."

"Let's find a place to sit," I say. "Somewhere close to an exit so we can slip out unnoticed." I spot an open area by the set of doors we came in through. You can't see or hear much from this far away, but that doesn't matter.

We push through the crowd, and I feel people's eyes on me as we pass. Fifer is right—they are watching us. Then one boy—man? Hard to tell through the mask—after another steps up, sketches a quick bow, asks me to dance. As politely as I can, I turn them down. But the attention is starting to make me nervous.

"What's going on?" George whispers.

"I don't know," I whisper back. "Maybe they think I'm someone else? I'm not sure—"

"It's your dress," John says. "The bird on the front. It's that duchess's symbol. Humbert's friend. Remember?"

Of course. The silver bird embroidered on the front of my dress, the symbol of the House of Rotherhithe. How could I have forgotten? That's who everyone thinks I am: Cecily Mowbray, the Duchess of Rotherhithe's granddaughter. A lady-in-waiting to Queen Margaret, a lady in her own right, Caleb's friend. Blond and petite, just like me.

Another boy approaches me. But before he can finish his bow, John grabs my hand and pulls me into the throng of dancers. He places one hand on my back, takes my hand with the other, and pulls me to him. Together we move slowly, quietly, in time with the music.

I should be thinking about Malcolm, who is somewhere in this crowd. I should be thinking about Blackwell, about Caleb, who is here, too. I should be thinking about my plan, the tomb, the tablet....Instead, all I'm thinking about is John. The smell of lavender and spice, the faint trace of lemons. The way he looks at me, the press of his body against mine, so close I can feel the rapid beat of his heart. It matches my own.

"I'm sorry," I blurt.

"What are you sorry for?" he says softly.

I shake my head. I'm sorry for nothing, I'm sorry for

everything; I'm sorry for the impossible way I feel about him, for the impossible hope he might feel the same. But I know I can't tell him that.

"I know how hard it must be for you to help someone you hate," I say instead.

He pulls back a little, tilts his head down, looks at me.

"I don't hate you," he whispers. "Maybe I should. But I can't. Because I know you now. And the you I know—brave and strong, but still so frightened and vulnerable—isn't someone I can hate. That person, I can only—" He breaks off, unable to find the words.

"It's okay," I whisper back. "I understand."

"Do you?" He looks down at me. Slides his hand along my cheek and lifts my face to meet his, so close our lips are an inch apart. Less. He dips his head. I can feel his breath on my skin.

Then he kisses me.

I forget about everything: my fear, my plan—I even forget about the tablet. All that matters is the feel of his lips on mine, his hands on my face and in my hair, the sense of safety he gives me. I never want it to end.

At the sound of applause, we leap apart; I hadn't realized the music had stopped. John stares at me, eyes wide through his mask, his lips parted, the shock on his face evident. Shock at what? That he kissed me? Or shock that he felt something, the same thing I felt? Still feel: thrill, desire, hope, all tangled together in a breathless little knot.

He reaches for me; I step toward him. I feel a tapping on my shoulder, but I ignore it, not wanting to turn away from him. And when I feel it again, I turn around, a refusal on my lips, thinking it's another stranger confusing me with someone else. But it's not a stranger. Because the moment I see his eyes, black as a snake's even under his wolf-shaped mask, I know who it is. I would recognize him anywhere.

Blackwell.

I feel the blood drain from my face, my arms, my legs. It pools around my feet like cement, rooting them to the floor.

"Miss Mowbray, I presume?" Blackwell says. "I know it's not the done thing to call you out before the unmasking. But I simply couldn't let a cherished guest go by without offering a word of condolence."

John sucks in a sharp, quick breath.

"Thank you," I say. I keep my voice soft, hoping he won't recognize it.

"I was so sorry to hear about your grandmother," he continues. I nod, remembering Humbert mentioning the duchess was ill. "Such a pity." I nod again, waiting for him to excuse himself. But he doesn't. John steps forward and takes my arm, but Blackwell's undeterred. "Might I persuade this young man to allow me one dance?"

John pauses a beat too long. "Of course," he says, his voice tight.

"I'll have her back soon," Blackwell adds carelessly. He takes my arm and pulls me into the crowd. I look back at the others, their masks unable to hide the horror on their faces.

"Enjoying your evening?"

"Hmm," I reply, too horrified to speak. All I can wonder

is, does he really believe he's dancing with one of the queen's ladies? Or does he know it's me? Did he somehow figure it out? I realize how stupid we were to think we could outsmart him. Blackwell knows everything that happens in his home. He knows everything that happens everywhere. I feel like a fly, fluttering on the edge of a spider's web. I could escape, unharmed. But one false move and I'm dead.

"Good," he says, seemingly oblivious to my terror. We dance along the hall, and I try my best to appear adept. Or at least not trip over my feet. But he seems oblivious to this as well. He barely seems to notice me. Instead, he looks around the room, craning his neck as if he's searching for something. Finally, the music begins to wind down. He leads me back to the doors, only on the opposite side of the room from where the others stand waiting. I can see their anxious faces bobbing through the crowd, looking for me.

"It was a pleasure," he says, releasing me. "Now if you'll excuse me, I've got some matters to attend to." I nod and dip a curtsy, and Blackwell turns to leave. As I back away from him, he turns around. "Oh, and Miss Mowbray?"

"Y-yes?" I stammer, too frightened to remember to disguise my voice.

He pauses, and I see a flicker of something cross his eyes.

"If you're going outside for some air, do be careful. As I understand it, we may have some unwanted guests this evening. But don't worry. My men are on it." Then he's gone.

For a moment, my mind goes blank with terror. Does he know we're here? Are we the unwanted guests? I don't know. But I know I need to get the others out of here. Now. I don't have time to wait until the masque starts, and I don't have time to wait for Peter. And if I've got any hope of destroying the tablet, I've got to do that now, too.

I look to where the others are standing and catch John staring at me through the crowd. *I'm sorry*, I mouth. Then I turn around. And I run.

I hurtle down the stairs, into the entrance hall. Lining the walls is a series of arches, set about a foot or so into the stone. They're purely decorative, all except one. I go to the third archway, place my hands against the flat stone surface, and push. It slides open to reveal a wide stone tunnel running the length of the great hall and beyond, all the way to the other side of the palace.

I gather my dress and squeeze through, pulling the door shut behind me.

"Schuyler," I say. "Blackwell knows we're here. Get the others out and meet me in the woods in ten minutes."

The tunnel ends in a simple wooden door. On the other side is another staircase leading downstairs, into the dormitory. I pause a moment, listening for voices. It's just a precaution; no one lives here anymore. But you never know.

I don't hear anything, so I run down the stairs and into my old room. It's somewhat of a shock to see it again. Tiny, windowless, dark. I never realized how much it looks like a prison cell. I haven't been here in nearly a year, though you'd never know it. My bed is still unmade; one of my uniforms lies crumpled on the floor. There are a few weapons laid across the trunk at the end of the bed. It's almost as if I never left.

Quickly, I pull the Azoth from the scabbard under my

skirt. Strip off my dress, yank the jewels from my ears and the combs from my hair, grab my uniform off the floor. I don't really want to wear it, but I can't destroy the tablet in a dress. And the last thing I need is for someone else to mistake me for Cecily Mowbray.

I pull on the tight black trousers, the wrinkled white shirt, the knee-length black boots. Draw on the long tan leather coat, fasten the leather straps across my chest. After refastening the Azoth around my waist, I strap my weapons belt over my shoulder and holster everything I can find. A couple of large, serrated knives, a handful of daggers. An ax and an awl. It's not as much as I'd like, but it's better than nothing.

As I slip in the last dagger, my hand snags on something. I look down and realize I'm still wearing Humbert's sapphire ring. I start to pull it off, and then remember what he told me. *It's a lucky ring.* I keep it on, just in case.

I climb the stairs and follow the tunnel to one of several doors that lead outside. I can hear the bells in the courtyard clock begin to chime.

Nine o'clock.

I move quietly across the shadowy grounds, past the tennis court and the archery butts, the stables and the hedge maze, until I reach the edge of the grounds. It spreads out before me, vast and dark. I remember all the things I've faced out here and feel a tug of fear. There's no telling who or what is prowling around tonight.

When I reach the forest, I take a sharp right, walking along the tree line, heading in the direction of the river. The last time I took this walk, I was on my way to my test. I still remember hearing the echoes of ships as they passed, the waves slapping against their hulls. The tomb is somewhere near the water.

I hear the tiniest rustle of leaves, and I whirl around, dagger drawn.

"Easy, bijoux. It's only me." Schuyler steps up beside me.

"What happened? Did they get out?"

He nods. "On the dock as we speak."

I huff a sigh of relief. "What did you tell them?"

"The truth. Said Blackwell knew you were here, and you were off to get the tablet."

"And?"

He shrugs. "And that's it. They're gone. Peter will be here soon, and they'll be safe. Just as you planned."

It is what I planned. But what I didn't plan was how their being gone would make me feel. Empty. Hollow.

Alone.

I look up to find Schuyler watching me carefully. He doesn't say anything. He only nods.

We're getting close to the tomb now; I can feel it. The air is getting colder, my breath coming in little plumes, and the woods are eerily silent. No crickets chirping, no owls hooting, no mouse or rat rustling the odd branch or two. There's only silence.

Then I see it. From the outside, it's harmless. A simple wooden door set into a patch of dying winter grass, partially covered in a carpet of leaves. It's so unremarkable that if you weren't looking for it, you would miss it.

"Schuyler," I say. He had walked right past it.

He turns around, following my gaze. When his eyes land on the door, he swears under his breath and exhales loudly.

I guess that's just for emphasis. Revenants don't need to breathe.

I start to pull the Azoth from the scabbard. It's half-way out, the silver blade and the emerald hilt glinting in the moonlight, when Schuyler holds out a hand to stop me.

"Don't," he says. "Use it to break the tablet, but not for anything else. Not unless you absolutely have to. You already killed that guard. You don't want to give the curse another chance to take hold."

"Okay." I ease the blade back down. "I don't know what shape I'll be in…after. I'll do what I can from the inside, but in case I'm not able, I need you to attack it from the outside, too."

Schuyler nods.

"Don't come for me until you hear me call for you," I continue. "If you hear me scream, ignore it. It's just…part of it. And if they come for you—for us—don't wait for me. Run."

I walk to the door and reach down, grab the heavy iron ring, and pull. I yank once, twice. On the third try the trapdoor creaks open. Down the wooden steps to the other door, the door that only after fear, after magic, after illusion, and after death, is the Thirteenth Tablet.

Pressing my hands against the splintered wood, I push the door open. A crack at first, then wider, the hinges shrieking into the silence. Rancid air comes pouring out, the smell of my nightmares. Beyond that: dank, dark nothingness. I slide through the opening, pausing once to turn around and look at Schuyler. That dark shadow passes before his bright blue eyes again.

"Be careful," he whispers.

29

THE DOOR SLAMS SHUT BY itself, and I'm plunged into darkness. It's not long before the world tilts and I'm thrown onto my back. I get to my feet and stand as still as possible, hands clenched into fists at my sides. I wait for the dirt to start falling. One heartbeat. Five. Ten. My palms are sweating and I'm breathing too hard, too fast. But still, nothing happens.

I see something flickering. Pale, yellow, like a faraway candle. It grows brighter, and as it does, I see I'm no longer in the tomb. I'm in a tunnel. I move in the direction of the light, but slowly. I've taken maybe ten steps when I hear a noise so loud it makes me jump. A thundering sound, like an angry fist on a wooden door. I ease a dagger from my belt and keep moving. The noise continues. Pounding, over and over. A splintering sound of breaking wood, the heavy tread of boots crossing a threshold. A shout. Then a scream.

My body reacts before my head does, and I start running toward the sound. I stumble along in the darkness, bumping into the walls, tumbling to my knees, and climbing to my feet. I follow the screams until the light grows brighter and the ground beneath me harder. I look down, and I can just make out flashes of black and white underneath the dirt. There's a door up ahead. I push through it and find myself standing in the middle of Humbert's entrance hall.

The black-and-white-checkered floors are dirty and chipped, the paintings torn off the wall. Cobwebs in the chandeliers, crystal vases shattered. The many diamond-paned windows broken. I take a tentative step, then another, glass crunching under my feet.

I feel my heart pick up speed. I know this is an illusion. Isn't it? I can't be in Humbert's home. It's miles away, and I'm here. At Blackwell's. I try to recall Fifer's voice, reminding me it's an illusion. But she feels long ago and far away. This feels here; this feels now.

This feels real.

"Is anyone here?" I call. "Humbert?"

I check the sitting room, the dining room. They've been torn apart: tables upended, chairs toppled to the floor, curtains pulled from the windows. I back away, back into the hallway, and I trip over something: John's weathered, brown canvas bag.

"John?" I dash up the stairs, into the bedrooms. Clothes lie in shreds everywhere: Fifer's beautiful dresses, John's dark green coat, even George's hideous orange harlequin jacket.

"George? Fifer?" I can hear the panic in my voice as I call their names. I run back downstairs, to the library. The door is gone, ripped off its hinges. Inside, it's dark. But I don't need to see to know that it's in ruins, too. A cold breeze blows through the broken glass ceiling, ruffling the pages of the books that lie in heaping pyres on the floor. In the moonlight, I can just make out the felled tree: its gray branches scattered through the room like bones in a graveyard, the leaves I made blowing through the air in swirling gusts.

I stand for a moment in the dark, broken library, trying to control my mounting fear. Trying to remember what Fifer said about illusion. Is it illusion that makes fear real? Or is it fear that makes the illusion real? And what does this illusion mean? It's meant to show me fear, but I don't know what I'm afraid of. Not yet.

I run back into the entrance hall. But instead of the black-and-white-tiled hallway I came in through, I'm somewhere different. Filthy stone floors, rugs shoved into the corner, more broken windows, stained glass this time. I can just make out a snake's tail in one of the shards, dangling precariously from the frame.

"Nicholas!" I run through the house the same way I did at Humbert's. The sitting room. The dining room. The bedrooms. They're torn apart the way they were at Humbert's. The kitchen. It looks as it did the last time I saw it: pots and pans and knives and food strewn everywhere. "Hastings!"

But no one answers. The house is quiet.

I turn in slow circles, my breath coming in gasps, my limbs numb with terror. What does all this mean? I don't know. I just know I want to get out of here. I run back into the entrance hall, push open the heavy front door.

And I freeze.

I'm standing at the edge of a crowded square, watching the executioners light the pyre. They circle the narrow wooden platforms, their lit torches held high. At the top of each, chained to the stake, bundles of wood heaped around their feet, are John, Fifer, George, and Nicholas.

I sway on my feet; I actually swoon in horror. And even before the executioners touch their torches to the wood, I start to scream. Push my way through the jostling crowd, trying to reach them. I scream their names over and over, but they don't hear me.

I lunge for the platforms, but the guards grab me and throw me to the ground. I scrabble in the dirt, trying to get back up, but they hold me down, and I'm screaming and sobbing too hard to fight back. But I need to get to them, to save them before it's too late, but then it is too late: There's an enormous whoosh of flames and a billow of smoke as the fire engulfs them and they're gone, forever.

Somehow, I stumble to my feet and push my way through the crowd and into the street. And I start to run. I don't know where I'm going, just away from this. Away from the smoke and the fire and the screaming and the death. Eventually I reach an empty alley and collapse in a doorway, trembling and crying and completely terrified.

So this is it—my worst fear. It's not dying alone anymore. It's watching the people I care for die in front of me and not being able to stop it. Being responsible for it. Knowing that if I don't destroy the tablet, this is what will come of it.

My heart is pounding too hard, my breath coming too fast. I have to make it stop. I remember what Fifer said: I have to eliminate my fear. That eliminating the fear eliminates the illusion. But how? I start to sing, but I can't remember the words. I take a breath, but I can't stop sobbing. I try to think of something else, but I can't seem to do that, either. I don't know how to do anything but be afraid.

Some men pass by me then, their arms looped around one another. They're singing some kind of drinking song. I smell the ale wafting from them as they go by and wrinkle my nose. They're drunk and it can't be past noon, and—

Then I get an idea.

I leap to my feet. Skirt through the alleys: left, right, left again, until I see the familiar green sign that reads THE WORLD'S END. I shove the door open and it's just as it usually is, just as it was the last day I was here. Crowded and loud, musicians playing, Joe pulling drinks behind the bar. As I approach, he slides me a glass of ale and watches me, his hands folded.

"Well?" he growls.

I take a tentative sip. But instead of the usual horror— roasted pig or absinthe or God knows what else—this time it tastes like ale. This time, it's actually good. And just like that, my heart slows. My breathing slows. I know without a doubt that this Joe and this ale aren't real. This is an illusion.

I start to laugh.

"What's so funny?"

I don't answer him. Instead, I turn around and rush for the door of the tavern, flinging it open. There, on the other side, is the tomb, dark and dank. I'm right back where I started.

I step inside and go still. For a moment I fear dirt will start falling, that the illusion still isn't over. But after a few moments when nothing else happens, I make my way to the entrance. The moon is bright enough that slivers of light work their way through the cracks, illuminating what is no longer a rickety wooden door but the edges of a massive stone slab, the number XIII etched at the top.

The Thirteenth Tablet.

It's big; I knew that. But standing in front of it, I realize just how huge it really is. Six feet tall, three feet across. Solid stone, at least a foot thick. It's been down here a while, buried in the dark and the damp, the edges beginning to turn green with moss.

I stare at it a minute. Run my fingers along the words etched down the length of the stone. I can just make out runes along the edge, along with Nicholas's name, written over and over among all the symbols and marks.

Nicholas said Blackwell did it. That Blackwell cursed him, that Blackwell is a wizard. I didn't want to believe it then, and, despite everything, I don't want to believe it now. It was just speculation, just a guess. There was no way of knowing for certain if it was true.

Until now.

There should be a signature on the tablet. The wizard's name, a symbol, a pseudonym like the ones necromancers take on. Something to identify but not incriminate. A curse tablet won't work without it.

I crouch to my knees. If there is a signature here, it will be somewhere along the bottom. But it's hard to see. The moonlight's not as strong down here, and there's dirt clumped around the edges. I brush it away, and I see part of a symbol. Words. I keep brushing until, finally, it comes into view. A rose. And his motto: *What's done is done; it cannot be undone.*

I fall back against the crumbling wall. Press my head into my hands, and I give myself a minute to feel it again. The betrayal, the disbelief, the horror, the truth: somehow sharp and numb, all at once.

Blackwell is a wizard.

I jump to my feet. Yank the Azoth from my belt. And, using every ounce of strength I have, I swing.

The silver blade sings against the stone, the sound echoing through the tomb like a scream. I can feel the power of it crawling through my limbs, filling my heart, my head, so strong I'm drunk with it. I swing again, and again, and again, the impact of silver on stone sending sparks that ignite the darkness.

"Elizabeth!" Schuyler's voice cuts through the clatter. "Can you hear me?"

"Schuyler!" I call back. "I'm here! The door—it's the tablet now. Help me break it, okay?"

There's a pause, then an enormous, resounding thud that shakes the tomb, showering me with dirt. There's another thud, then another.

I swing the Azoth, over and over, until a narrow crack appears in the center of the tablet. It's beginning to break. I keep swinging; Schuyler keeps kicking. The split grows longer, wider, until a bright green light issues from its center, snaking through the opening in tendrils: down the tablet, up the walls, across the ceiling, squirming and undulating as though it were alive. I step back, away from whatever magic the light possesses, but it's no use: The trickle of light grows until it's nearly blinding. Then with a rush of wind and a shattering noise—like ice breaking across a frozen pond—the tablet crumbles.

I leap out of the way, but I'm not fast enough. Pieces of the broken tablet fall on top of me, and the weight of them throws me on my back, knocking the breath from my lungs and the Azoth from my hand and burying me in a heap of rubble and stone. I wriggle under the debris, shifting the stones off my stomach and limbs.

"Schuyler." I cough, my voice raspy from the dust. There's no answer. "Are you there?" I wait for him to reply. But there's nothing. Just the sound of my own ragged breathing and a soft, steady rushing noise. It sounds almost like...almost like rain.

I feel a sudden chill. It wasn't raining when I went into the tomb. And there was no sign of it, either; the sky was crisp and black and full of stars. What does that mean? It could be that I've been in here longer than I thought. It is Anglia, after all, and the weather changes fast. But it could mean something else, too.

I'm still in the illusion.

I get to my feet. Retrieve the Azoth from beneath the dust. Step carefully over the debris, make my way up the stairs and through the trapdoor until I'm outside again. It's pouring. Icy rain is coming down in sheets. There are puddles everywhere. It's been raining for a while. And Schuyler—whose voice I heard just seconds ago—is nowhere to be seen.

I feel a rush of disappointment, then terror. Because if I'm still in the tomb, still inside the illusion, it means I didn't really destroy the tablet. Worse than that, it means whatever my biggest fear is, it's still to come. And if my biggest fear isn't dying alone, or watching John and everyone else die in front of me, then what is it? What could be worse than that?

It also means I was tricked into using the Azoth when I didn't need to. I can feel the power of it still thrumming through me, whispering to me. Wanting me to use it. To take the power it offers me: to destroy, to break, to kill.

I thrust it back into the scabbard, exchanging it for a pair of serrated knives. Then I step into the rain.

I'm still at Blackwell's, I can tell that much. I can see the flag-topped spires on the towers, the looming stone walls. A jagged flash of lightning brightens the sky. Thunder rumbles in the distance. I take a few tentative steps, my feet sinking softly into the mud. I scan the grounds carefully: the hedge maze in front of me, the trees that surround me. Something is out here, waiting. I know it; I can feel it.

Finally, I see it: a pair of yellow lamp-like eyes staring through the trees ahead. Then with a rustle of leaves and the snap of a branch, it comes for me.

The creature lumbers into the clearing, a huge, ratlike thing, the size of a horse but with six legs instead of four and a long, barb-tipped tail, filled with poison. Another of Blackwell's creations. I've seen it before, in training. It's slow and clumsy, but what it lacks in speed it makes up for in numbers. It travels in packs, as rats do. Which means there are more of them.

I send both knives flying, aiming directly for the eyes.

333

That's the only way to kill it, to put out both of its eyes. I manage to hit one but miss the other, and the rat stumbles onto its side and lets out an ear-splitting shriek. It's calling the others. I pull out another knife and run toward it, leap over the whipping tail, and plunge it into the other eye. The rat shudders and dies, but I feel the ground trembling and know more are coming. I whip around to see three of them heading right for me.

I've got four knives left. I hurl them at the rats. And even though it's dark and still pouring, I manage to hit each one in the eye. Not enough to kill, but enough to slow them down. I snatch the ax from my belt and rush to them as they lie flailing and shrieking on the ground. I get hit several times with their barbed tails, and although the wounds heal instantly, I feel the effect of the poison anyway. It makes me see double. And through the dark and the rain, I can't tell one rat from another. I follow their shrieks and keep hacking away at them and getting hit with their tails over and over until, finally, they go still.

I collapse on the ground, letting the rain wash over me, shaking and dizzy from the poison. I consider for a moment that the poison may not be real, that it may be part of the illusion. I suppose it doesn't matter. Because, like any illusion, it's real enough. And either way, I need to move. If there are more creatures around, they'll come for the dead rats. Blackwell could never figure out how to feed these things he created, so he simply allowed them to feed on whatever it was we killed. I asked Caleb once what happened to the bodies of the witch hunters who were killed in training, but he said it was better not to know.

Through the rain, I spot the outline of the hedge maze. I don't want to go there. I've been through it once and almost didn't make it out. But I also know that if I go inside, whatever else is out here won't follow me. They're scared of what's in there, too.

I roll onto my hands and knees and start crawling along the edge of the forest near the trees, where I won't be so easily spotted. Finally, the tree line ends at a stretch of open ground that leads to the maze on the other side. I huddle there a moment, shivering and soaking wet, my head still swimming. I need to stand. I need to run. I need to make it into that maze before anything else finds me. But I'm so tired. I lie back in the mud and go still, just for a moment, my breath coming in deep, heavy gasps. Close my eyes against the freezing rain that splashes around me.

"Elizabeth."

When I hear his voice, deep and quiet, I think that's the poison, too. That it's worked its way into my head and is making me hear things that aren't there. But when he says my name again, I sit up so abruptly my head spins. And I see him, standing in the clearing next to the hedge maze.

John.

I get to my feet, stumbling a little.

"You're hurt," he says, a frown crossing his face. He sounds so real.

He's not real.

Is he?

I make my way toward him. As I grow closer, he flinches at the sight of me: tattered trousers, torn shirt, covered in mud and blood and God knows what else. My hair unpinned and falling in tangled knots around my shoulders.

He's dressed as he was at the masque: white shirt, black pants, black jacket trimmed in red. Tousled hair, hazel eyes that look at me so intently. He looks so real.

He's not real.

Is he?

"It isn't really you," I say. It comes out a whisper. "I know that."

John—the illusion of John—glances over his shoulder, a brief shadow crossing his face.

"It is," he says, turning back to me. "It is me. Why would you think it isn't?"

I shake my head. "I don't know. Maybe because it's raining. I'm soaking wet and you're completely dry."

"It was raining, but it stopped." I look up. Illusion John is right. It has stopped raining. "And I'm not wet because I just got here."

I brush this off and continue. "Fine, then. I know you aren't you because you left. Schuyler told me. You're on a boat with Peter and everyone else, and you're going home. You left." I swallow back the lump in my throat.

"I never left." His voice is as quiet as mine. "You left me, remember? You ran away and I didn't want you to go. So I came to find you." He glances behind him again.

Something seems to bother him, this illusion John. He keeps looking over his shoulder as though there's something there. Something lurking in the shadows, waiting to attack him. I ignore it. It's not real.

Is it?

"Why would you leave the others to come after me?" My voice rises, angry because I want it to be true, angry because I know it's not. "Why would you do that?"

He steps toward me. "Don't you know?"

I shake my head.

He looks at me. Dark eyes, moonlight. "Because I'm in love with you."

I close my eyes, the fight draining out of me. I'm so tired. Tired of this illusion, tired of the truth, tired of the lies. *Blackwell is a wizard. Because I'm in love with you.* I don't want any more. I want to wake up.

I open my eyes. Snatch the last remaining knife from my belt and drive it, hard, into my leg. "Wake up!" I scream, not at John, or his illusion, but at myself.

He's in my face before I can finish pulling it out. Yanks the knife from my hand, flings it to the ground. Then he's got both of my hands in both of his, pinning them behind my back. He leans in close. I can feel his breath on my cheek.

"Stop."

I struggle in his arms. Try to get away before this illusion changes and he disappears or dies or turns into anything but what he is, dark eyes and soft curls and warmth and safety.

But when he pulls me back to him, I let him. And when he dips his head and brushes his lips against mine, I let him do that, too. They're warm and soft, as I remember. Slowly, he moves his lips from my mouth across my cheek, then to my ear, lingering there. I can feel him and hear him and smell him, and it's all *so real*. For a moment I close my eyes and give in to it, in to the shivers and the thrill he gives me, until I hear his hoarse, ragged whisper.

"Run."

I yank away from him with a gasp; and when I do, I see Blackwell standing beside John, slowly pulling a knife out of his side.

"THAT WAS A VERY TOUCHING SCENE," Blackwell says. He wipes a handkerchief across the blade and slides it back into his belt. John lets out a muffled groan and staggers backward, pressing his hand to his waist. Blood pours between his fingers.

"No," I whisper. "This isn't real."

"Oh, it's quite real, I assure you." Blackwell steps toward me. I look at him, hoping to see something that will show me he's just part of the illusion. But he looks the same. He's wearing the same clothes I saw him in at the masque: dark trousers, red brocade jacket embroidered in gold. His chain of office is gone, but then that belongs to Caleb now.

"You did destroy the tablet," he continues. "And you dispatched my hybrids quite handily, too." He gives a low chuckle, like an indulgent father. Only I know better. A chill races down my spine. "I taught you well. You really were one of my best witch hunters."

I shake my head. This isn't real—it *isn't*. I turn away from him then. Look around, search for something—anything—to show me what's really happening. Where I really am. I see the broken tomb, the dead rats. The rain is gone, the sky is clear, my clothes are wet, and here I am.

At Blackwell's. Right where I started.

It's all real.

"John!" I lunge for him just as Blackwell lunges for me. Quick as a snake, he snatches the Azoth from my scabbard. I reach out a hand to stop him, but it's too late. He holds it up, the emeralds in the hilt glinting menacingly in the moonlight.

I start for John again, but Blackwell stops me, thrusting the blade against my chest.

"You can't help him," he says. "He's got thirty minutes at most. He'll know it, too. He's a healer, isn't he?" John is on his knees now, still clutching his side.

"Why?" I shriek. It's all I can think to ask.

Blackwell shrugs, indifferent. "Why did I stab him? I assume you need a better reason than his trespassing on my property? Or do you mean why did I try to kill Nicholas Perevil? I assume you need a better reason than his being a Reformist, a traitor, and a threat to my kingdom?"

"*Your* kingdom?"

"Yes. My kingdom. My fool nephew may be king of this country, but I am the one who rules it. I work while he plays. Gather armies while he hunts, deploy them while he dances. I set policies and enact laws and plan rebellions while he drinks and gambles and wastes his time with women." He gives me a terrible, hard look. "You of all people should know this."

It takes a moment to find my voice.

"You knew," I finally manage. "You knew and you didn't stop him."

Blackwell gives my arm a rough shake. "Of course I knew. Malcolm was married at sixteen to a woman twice his age. He was bound to fall in love but never with her. When he took a liking to you, I used it to my advantage. I encouraged him. Told him you liked him back." He shrugs, dismissive. "I knew where it would lead."

Behind him, John makes a noise halfway between a growl and a groan.

"You were meant to do your duty—to do what I trained you to do—and kill him," Blackwell continues. "I needed him gone, and you were meant to do it. Caleb all but told you to do it." His voice rises. "How many times did he have to point out the ways Malcolm was losing control of the country? How many times did he have to tell you we'd be better off without him?"

"And I was supposed to take that as instruction to kill the king?" I say, incredulous. "That's insane. You're insane."

"Manners" is all he says in reply.

"You can't kill Malcolm," I say. "You can't."

Blackwell shrugs. "It's done. At midnight tonight, it's done. The mask will finally be lifted and I will unveil myself as the new ruler of Anglia." He smiles. "It's a bit theatrical, I know. But I really couldn't resist."

"It will never work," I say. "The whole country is in revolt against you—"

He laughs, a deep, rumbling laugh that stuns me to hear it. I've never heard him laugh before.

"The country is in revolt against Malcolm. I was simply carrying out his orders. He is king, as you pointed out."

"But you created the laws!" I say. "You were Inquisitor. They were your rules—"

"I created the laws Malcolm commanded I create." He spreads his arms. "I was a victim of his treachery as much as anyone. Perhaps more, as I was commanded to put hundreds of witches and wizards—my own kind—to death." He shakes his head in mock sorrow. "But tonight all of that will end. I will take the throne, and I will do it with an army so powerful no one will dare stop me."

"Army," I breathe. "What army?"

"The army you built for me, of course."

I let out a gasp. Then I realize. I realize what he's been doing all along, what he's done.

"I trained you to hunt witches and wizards," he continues. "Hunt them and bring them to me. Didn't you wonder why I never wanted you to kill them?"

"But you did," I say. "You burned a dozen a week. I was there. I saw it."

"I had to burn some of them," Blackwell says. "Malcolm would have been suspicious had I not. But surely you noticed the only ones on the pyre were healers and kitchen witches? I had to sacrifice someone, and I had no use for them. They're about as useful as he is." He waves his hand dismissively at John. "But the necromancers, the demonologists? The wizards practicing black magic? I had use for them, certainly. I do have use for them."

"You can't do it," I say.

"I can, and I will. There is no one to stop me now. And with this"—he holds up the Azoth—"I will be invincible."

"Nicholas," I blurt. "He's going to live. He can stop you...."

"Oh, I think not."

That's when I hear it. A girl's choked sob, a boy's muffled groan. It makes the hairs on the back of my neck stand up.

Caleb comes into view then, followed by Marcus and Linus, and I see where the noise is coming from. It's Fifer and George, both of them bound and beaten. Linus leads Fifer by the hair, and it's clear she's fighting to stay conscious. George's eye and mouth are bruised, and there's blood running down his cheek.

I let out a gasp.

"Did you really think you could get away with it? Did you really think you could simply walk away?" Blackwell advances on me. Grabs my shoulders and looks down on me; his black eyes boring into mine. "Did you really think you could stop me?"

I look at Caleb and he looks back, his face impassive. "I warned you," he says to me. "I told you what would happen if you didn't come back with me. I told you I wouldn't be able to protect you."

There's a terrible silence as we stare at each other; I can feel everyone's eyes on us. I search his face for something— a hint of sympathy, a shade of compassion—anything that shows that my friend is still there. But I see nothing. And I know—with painful certainty, I know—I'm on my own. That in this, his final test, when faced with the choice between family and ambition, Caleb chose ambition.

I turn back to Blackwell.

"What are you going to do?" I whisper.

Blackwell releases me then, so abruptly I stumble. "Bring me the girl."

Linus steps forward with Fifer, pushing her roughly in front of him. I can hear John's weak protests and George's muffled shouts, but they barely register. I can't take my eyes off her. Her dress is torn along the top; it keeps slipping over her shoulders. Her shoes are missing, and she's trembling so hard her teeth are chattering.

I turn to Linus. "What did you do to her?"

"Nothing." Linus gives a terrible smile and runs a finger down the back of her neck. Fifer and I both shudder. "Yet."

I'm so disgusted I don't think, I just launch myself at Linus. He pushes Fifer away and jumps me. We hit the ground, both of us punching and kicking and screaming horrible things at each other. He pulls out his dagger and stabs me repeatedly with it, aiming for my neck, my heart, my stomach. He's hitting something, but I can't tell what. The second I feel pain it disappears, followed by pain somewhere else. My whole body is so caught up in the loop of pain and healing, I can't tell where one begins and the other ends.

"Enough." Blackwell's voice thunders across the clearing. Linus leaps away from me like a trained dog, still in the habit of obedience. I get to my feet, but slowly. I'm not healing as fast as I should be; I'm still weak from the poison and from the wound in my stomach.

"What do you want me to do?" I whisper. "Whatever it is, tell me and I'll do it. Just don't hurt them." I lock eyes with him. "Just tell me what you need."

"I needed the king dead, and I needed Nicholas dead," he says. "You were meant to do both, and you failed. At both." He steps toward me. "Fortunately, I have these two now." He glances at George and Fifer. "They will tell me where Nicholas is; they will lead me to him. They will"—he repeats, louder, over John's protests—"if they do not wish to suffer—unduly—before I dispose of them."

Fifer lets out a moan.

"As for the king, he will be taken care of. It may already be done." He glances at Caleb, who nods. "So, as you can see, I don't need you to do anything." He steps up to me, his black eyes glittering with madness, boring into mine. "I don't need you at all."

The storm of his fury breaks. He throws up his arms and it begins to rain again, the way it was when I stepped out of the tomb. It comes down like an assault: I can't see beyond it, can't hear beyond the sound of it drumming into the ground. It's just Blackwell and me now; everything and everyone else has disappeared. I back away from him; I would look for somewhere to run, but I'm afraid to take my eyes from his face. Besides, I know there's nowhere to go.

"I would throw you into the maze," he says, not shouting—but I can hear him perfectly over the rain—"if I thought it meant I'd be rid of you. But I did that before and you came out. I'd send more of my hybrids after you, but I know what would happen with that, too."

He stops, his expression turning into something almost... curious.

"How did you do it? You weren't strong, not like Marcus. You weren't ambitious like Caleb. Not vicious like Linus." He

345

looks me over, shakes his head, as if the very sight of me baffles him. "How did you survive?"

He's asking me the question I've always asked myself. How an unremarkable girl like me could live through unimaginable danger like that. I didn't know then, not really, and I'm not sure now. I offer up my best guess anyway.

"Because I was afraid to do anything except live."

Blackwell nods, as if this were an interesting viewpoint he'd never considered before. "And now? Are you afraid now?"

I consider telling him I am. I consider that confessing weakness might buy me time, or clemency, or a chance to escape. But even as I think it, I know there's no chance. Of any of it.

"I'm not afraid." I say this because it's the last act of defiance I have against him and I say it because—and I'm shocked to realize it—it's true. "I'm not afraid of you."

Blackwell smiles. "Good. I might be worried if you were." He steps toward me, arm outstretched, the Azoth raised high. And, before I can register what he's doing, he swings.

I pull back, as he knew I would. He misses by an inch, as I knew he would. He draws back, then advances on me again, and again. I avoid blow after blow. Dodging, twisting, turning. He's not hitting me, but he's not trying. Not really. He's playing with me, as a cat might play with a mouse. To tire me, to weaken me. Then, when I start to stumble, begin to wear out, he will strike. And he will kill me.

I've got to end this. Now.

I step back, stagger away, as if I'm trying to run from him. Blackwell seems to expect this, too, and advances. At the last second, I turn to face him and I charge. He doesn't expect this; he hesitates—a split second—before raising the blade. It's enough. I lunge forward, slam my foot into his leg. He stumbles. I rise up, clasp my hands together, and bring my entwined fists onto his forearm, hard. Once, twice. The Azoth loosens, then falls from his grip. It lands with a thud on the rain-soaked ground. I drive my toe into the hilt, send it sliding through the mud, out of his reach.

Blackwell stops. Hesitates. Me or the Azoth? He can have only one of us.

He chooses me.

Fast—faster than I imagined he could be—he lunges at me. Fastens his hands around my throat. And with a growl of disgust, hate, and rage, he begins to squeeze.

I slap at his hands, tug at his wrists. Scratch and beat on his arms, his face. But I'm weak. I'm more tired than I need to be, and he doesn't stop. He just squeezes harder, looking me straight in the eye, his gaze merciless and unremorseful. I try to shout, to scream. But I can't. Even if I could, I wouldn't be heard above the pounding rain.

My legs go weak and collapse beneath me; I'm on my knees now, then my back. The rain pours down on both of us, and I thrash around in the mud, but Blackwell keeps squeezing. I can feel my eyes roll to the back of my head, and I'm blinking in and out of consciousness, almost in time with the lightning that flashes in the sky. My body starts jerking uncontrollably as it fights off the inevitable.

There's no one to save me this time.

Then I remember: Schuyler. He's here; he's somewhere. I shout his name inside my head. I scream it. Over and over.

Schuyler. The Azoth. It's here. Come get it, and come save them.

There's a shouting noise then, a screaming. It breaks through the rain and the dullness in my head—and Blackwell's concentration. He lets go of my throat. I take a ripping, searing breath and I still can't move. But the screaming continues.

Abruptly, Blackwell leans back and gets to his feet, swearing under his breath. He waves his arms and the rain around us stops. I turn my head to the side to see what's happening and feel my eyes go round.

It's carnage.

Schuyler stands in the clearing, the Azoth held in front of him. Marcus and Linus lie on the ground, the two of them flayed open, blood and innards pouring from their wounds. That was the screaming I heard. Schuyler's got the blade turned on Caleb now. Caleb holds Fifer in front of him, a dagger held to her throat. Across the clearing, George is huddled over John, who is still lying on the ground, still unmoving, still bleeding.

Blackwell storms toward Schuyler. "You," he growls.

"Tell him to let her go," Schuyler says, not taking his eyes off Caleb. "Tell him to do it now."

Blackwell advances on him. Throws his arms in the air and, at once, the rain starts up again, accompanied by a crackle of lightning and ear-splitting thunder. I lose sight of them all now, and I can't hear what's happening. But I know I need to move.

Slowly, I roll onto my side. I hurt in a thousand places at once and I'm bleeding from a hundred. I've got so many wounds my stigma can't heal them all. I get to my hands and knees but stumble to the ground again, face-first into the mud. I get up again, but it's so hard, so painful; even breathing is painful. Finally, I stagger to my feet and start toward them. I don't know what I think I can do. I can barely move. I don't even have a weapon.

I stumble over something then. I look down. It's the knife. The one I stabbed myself in the leg with, the one John flung to the ground. I reach down, pry it loose, and keep moving. Blackwell is directly in front of me now, his back to me. Schuyler twitches the blade between Blackwell and Caleb. Caleb digs his blade into Fifer's neck so hard I can see the blood rising. But his focus is slipping. His eyes dart around wildly, from Schuyler to the sky, then back again, blinking furiously against the downpour. Only I know how much Caleb hates the rain; I can almost hear him pleading for it to stop.

There's another crack of thunder and Caleb winces, closing his eyes for a moment against the sound. I don't think. I pull back my arm, take aim, and let my dagger fly, right at Caleb. It lands with a sickening thump in his neck and he jerks away from Fifer, a look of surprise on his face. The delay is enough. Schuyler lunges forward and snatches her from his grip. Caleb wrenches the blade from his neck, the wound instantly healing. Blackwell whirls around, as surprised as Caleb to see me standing there. He hesitates, just for a second, unsure of what to do. But that's enough, too.

The Azoth.

The second I think it, Schuyler throws it to me. I snatch it out of the air, and as Blackwell rounds on me, I swing. The blade slices down his face and across his shoulder. He pitches forward, stumbling to one knee, his hands pressed against his face, his shouts of agony piercing the air. I swing again. As the sword comes down, Caleb dives between us. Before I can pull back, the full force of the blow lands on his chest.

I step back, almost drop the blade. Caleb falls to his knees, clutching his wound, blood pouring between his hands.

"Caleb," I whisper. I look at him and he looks at me; and if I expected to see sorrow or regret in his eyes, I would be mistaken. I see nothing but determination.

"We owe him our lives," he says, his voice hoarse. He looks at his chest, at the blood, and he knows he's dying.

"No, we don't," I say, and I'm crying now. Dimly, I realize that the rain has stopped, but it's growing darker. Everything around me is fading into black, as if the world were dying instead of Caleb. Then there's no light at all and no noise, just the sound of me crying.

"Elizabeth!" The sound of Fifer's voice breaks through my sobs. "Elizabeth!"

I open my eyes. Look around. Caleb is gone; Blackwell is gone. In the spot where they stood lies a stone, faintly smoking on the ground. A lodestone. He disappeared, along with Caleb, along with the storm, along with his magic. It's clear again, the sky bright enough for me to see the others across the clearing, huddled over John.

I stumble to him, my legs weak with grief and injury and then, when I see him, terror.

"Oh my God." My knees give way and I collapse next to him. He's ghostly pale, his skin slick with sweat and blood. "We have to get him out of here." I reach for him, try to lift him. But the moment I do, John groans in pain and blood blooms brighter across his shirt.

"You can't move him; we already tried," George says. "He's lost too much blood. Every time he moves, he loses more."

No, I think. *This can't be happening. I can't let this happen. I can't let him die.*

Then I get an idea.

"Fifer." I look up at her. "Your witch's ladder. Where is it?"

"What?"

"Your ladder. Where is it?"

Fifer reaches into her boot and pulls out the black cord. Only one knot left.

"You said you can transfer things using Nicholas's power." My words come out in a rush. "Can you use it to transfer my ability to heal over to John? As you did with the grass and the invitations?"

"I—I don't know," she stammers. "I've never tried anything like that before. What if it doesn't work? It doesn't seem to be working on you."

She's right. I have so many injuries that it's taking much longer for them to heal. Stab wounds, broken ribs, punctured lung. Poison circulating through my veins.

"What if it doesn't heal him? Or worse, what if it hurts him more?"

John starts coughing then, his body shaking. He's lost too much blood. If we don't do something soon, he'll die. He told me he loved me. Do I love him back? I don't know. But all I know is that I cannot let him die.

Fifer and I exchange a glance.

"Lie down next to him," she whispers. "Get as close as you can. This spell needs close contact to work."

I lie on the ground, carefully sliding one hand under his shoulder, wrapping the other around his waist. I can feel how cold he is, how fragile. The air between us doesn't smell like lemons anymore. It smells like blood.

Fifer begins to untie the knot, her pale fingers trembling. The cord begins to glow and she places it over our entwined bodies. She takes a deep breath.

"Transfer."

The pain is instantaneous. I'm being stabbed all over again in a hundred different places at once. Only there's no fluttery healing sensation that follows. Only more pain. There's a drawing sensation, as if something is being pulled out of me. I realize it's probably my life. I feel myself stiffen, then jerk around uncontrollably.

Just hold on, a voice whispers.

I try to. I do.

But then it's too much, and everything just slips away.

31

I THINK—I CAN'T BE SURE—BUT I think I might be dead.

It's not as bad as I feared it would be. It's warm, and I'm lying on something soft. I'm not hungry and I'm not thirsty. I'm not in pain. The air smells good: fresh, like spring. I even have a pillow.

Dying was another matter entirely. There was a lot of yelling, a lot of jostling, a lot of pain. I heard my name being called over and over. I wanted to answer, but whoever it was seemed too far away. There was also a lot of rocking. Back and forth, back and forth. Some lurching, too, like on a ship. Then silence.

I wonder how long I've been dead. Weeks? Months? It seems like a long time. I wonder what they did with my body. I forgot to tell someone I didn't want to be buried, but I guess it didn't matter anyway.

I think about Fifer and George and John. How they came back for me at Blackwell's. Somehow they found a way to forgive me, but I don't know how. Sometimes I can hear their voices, hushed and whispered around me. Saying my name, holding my hand, willing me to come back to them. It's just a dream, I know. But I want so much for it to be true.

There was one moment when I thought I really wasn't dead. It only happened once. My eyes fluttered open and I saw John. He was sitting in a chair at the foot of my bed, his elbow propped up on the mattress, reading a book. I looked at him for a while. He looked clean and healthy, not at all like the bleeding, half-dead boy I saw last. He seemed to realize he was being watched, because after a moment he looked up and smiled.

I stared at him, something tugging at the back of my mind. There was something I wanted to say to him, something I wanted to ask but never had the chance. Finally, I remembered it.

"The bird." The voice, it didn't sound like my own. It was weak and gritty and raw. "In the tree. Why?"

He doesn't hesitate in his reply, as if he knew the answer long before I asked the question.

"Because I love you. And because being with you makes me feel free."

I wanted to say something to him, but I couldn't. I felt the darkness wrapping itself around me again, but not before I felt a smile drift across my lips. Then everything went black.

"Elizabeth, open your eyes," the voice commands. Whose voice is that? Don't they know I'm dead? I can't open my eyes. I don't even know if I have eyes anymore.

"She did it before, two days ago," says another voice. My brain struggles to make the connection. I know that voice.

John.

I want to speak. I try to speak, but nothing happens. I hear a moaning noise. Is that me? If it is, I should stop immediately. It sounds awful.

"I'll make her something to try to bring her around," John says. Is that really him? Is he really here? "I'll be back in a minute."

Is this real? It can't be. But what if it is? I don't want him to leave. I'm afraid if he does, he won't come back. I can feel something building up inside me, boiling like water left in a kettle too long. I'm going to scream. Instead, the only thing that comes out is a whisper.

"Wait."

Then I open my eyes.

There's a soft rustling noise, then Nicholas's face appears.

"Hello, Elizabeth."

"You," I whisper. "Are you alive? Or are you dead like me?" Only, he doesn't look dead. He looks healthier than I've ever seen him. His face flushed with color, eyes bright with life. He's still and calm, and even as he sits in his chair, doing nothing but watching me, he radiates strength and presence.

"I'm alive," he says. "So are you, though you had us wondering. How are you feeling?"

I feel slow. I feel weak. I ache not in one place but all over, and it takes every bit of strength I've got to keep my eyes open, to speak. But I'm alive, and that's more than I ever expected.

I can only nod in reply.

Nicholas smiles, as if he can read my thoughts. "John really does have a gift."

"He's okay, then?" I croak. "The last time I saw him, he..."
was dying, I think. But I don't want to say it.

"Yes, he's fine."

"What about Fifer? George? Peter and Schuyler..."

"They're all fine, too."

I close my eyes. It takes a minute before I can speak again.

"Where am I?" I look around, not recognizing my surroundings. I'm in an all-white room: white walls, white bed, white stone fireplace. Thick white curtains are drawn across the window, and no light at all shines through. It must be night.

"This is John and Peter's home, in Harrow," he says. "They brought you straight here from Blackwell's."

"What happened?" I say. "The last thing I remember is Fifer's spell. Then nothing."

Nicholas nods. "The spell worked. All the healing power you had in your stigma was carried over to John. He was made whole again almost immediately. You, on the other hand, had grave injuries. Most of them were not fully healed when the spell was performed. You should have died. You would have, were it not for that." He gestures at Humbert's sapphire ring, still on my finger.

"That's a unique ring," Nicholas continues. "The sapphire itself has healing and protective properties, and coupled with the rune on the back it becomes extremely powerful. The magic works a little as your stigma does—or did, rather—though not nearly as strong. It protected you just enough to keep you from dying."

It takes a moment for his words to set in.

"My stigma is gone?"

"Yes."

I don't know what to feel. Relief, maybe; my stigma is what made me a witch hunter, what tied me to Blackwell. Worry, perhaps; my stigma is what protected me, what kept me strong. Fear, certainly; because anything can hurt me now. Anyone can cause me pain. That frightens me more than I want to admit. Especially when I know what's out there.

And who.

"Blackwell," I blurt. "What happened to him? Is he alive?" I have so many questions, I don't know where to start. "He had a lodestone; he used it to escape. But where did he go? What about the king? And Caleb—" I stop. It hits me in the chest, knocks the air out of me all over again. The last time I saw Caleb, he was dying.

Caleb is dead.

I press my hands to my face, against the tears that spring to my eyes. Nicholas falls silent, allowing me to grieve again for my friend who became my enemy, who I still love despite all of it.

"Blackwell escaped," Nicholas says, finally, his voice gentle. "But he didn't go far. He made it back to Greenwich Tower, injured but alive. From what we've been told, he reappeared at the masque shortly thereafter."

"How?" I pull my hands from my face, look at Nicholas in disbelief. "I cut him in the face. With the Azoth. It was a terrible injury. I saw it. How could he just walk away from that?"

Nicholas shakes his head, the answer as obvious as it is obscure: There's no telling what magic Blackwell used, what magic he is capable of.

"At midnight, Blackwell unmasked. Revealed himself, just as he told you he would. Said he was a wizard. Said he was a victim of Malcolm's rules, that he was commanded to carry out laws he never believed in. That now he only wants what's best for Anglia, and he's the one to bring them the peace they desire."

"Where was Malcolm—the king—during all this? Where was the queen?"

"Just before the unmasking, they were taken away. Blackwell had them sent to Fleet."

"Is he going to kill them?" I don't like Malcolm; he took a part of me I can never get back. But he was a victim of Blackwell as much as I was; so was the queen. I don't want to see them die. Then it occurs to me. "Or has he already killed them?"

Nicholas shakes his head. "No. And he won't, at least not while there's no advantage in it. Because if he kills them now, it might make martyrs of them. It might create sides when right now, there are none. It might even incite an uprising. And Blackwell, of all people, knows what a disadvantage an uprising can be."

"But—Blackwell is a wizard," I say. "He lied to everyone. People can't believe what he says now. They can't be happy he's king, can they? Surely someone is questioning him? Or protesting?"

Nicholas smiles then, that hard, bitter smile I've seen before.

"Blackwell dispatched the king and queen with ease, in front of the most influential people in Anglia. Not a single person made a move to help them, not a single person uttered a word of protest. Perhaps people believed him; perhaps they were too frightened to pretend otherwise. But for now, he's made good on his word. He's repealed the laws against witchcraft. The burnings have stopped; the tablets are gone—all of them. He's going to mold Anglia into a country of his making. It's no longer a matter of Persecutors against Reformists. It's those who want peace against those who do not."

"Peace?" I say. "Blackwell doesn't want peace. Not unless it's on his terms."

Nicholas nods. "And we don't know what those terms are yet. He's approached us, of course. Sent word through channels that he's open to discussion. He claims he doesn't wish to cause us harm. He just wants to discuss a truce."

"I don't believe that."

"None of us do. We know too much about him now, what he's capable of. As long as we're around, we are a danger to him and his rule. He knows we will try to stop him, and he will come for us. Maybe not today, not tomorrow. Maybe he'll give us enough time to contact allies, to build an army of our own. But chances are he won't. And we need to be ready."

There are those words again. *We. Them. They. Us.*

I don't belong to any of them.

I look up to find Nicholas watching me carefully.

"We received your note within hours of your leaving Humbert's. In it you said, 'make sure nothing happens to them.' Not a word about yourself, except your confession to Peter and your apology to all of us."

I flush a little, thinking about the note. I didn't think I'd be alive for anyone to cite it back to me.

"I want to thank you, Elizabeth. What you did for me, and for John. For all of us. It took a tremendous deal of bravery."

I shake my head. I don't know if it was bravery as much as it was fear. I wish I knew the difference. If I did, I could be brave despite my fear, not because of it. If I'd been brave instead of afraid, things would have turned out very differently.

Nicholas nods, as though he can read my mind.

"You can't undo your past. You know that as well as I. But you also can't foresee the future. Not even Veda's prophecy can do that. What you want to do next, who you want to be, where you want to belong, that's entirely up to you. As I always say, nothing is written in stone."

I look up then and see John standing in the doorway. He looks at me and smiles.

He walks with me through the physic gardens behind his home, a beautiful rambling stone cottage at the edge of a river. The grounds burst with life, green and purple, orange and red, a riot of color against the oppressive gray skies. I can't go far, not at first. But days turn into weeks and slowly, I get stronger. John is patient: holding my hand when I am weak, letting me go when I am strong. I stay in his house, with him and his father. He takes care of me, and he loves me. And never once does he blame me. His father says I saved John's life. He says I saved his.

But the truth is, they saved mine.

I don't know what will happen next or what will become of me. But I know what I have now and I know what I have to lose. And this time it's not an illusion.

This time it's real.

your beautiful, bold cover. Kristina Aven in publicity, Renée Gelman and Rebecca Westall in production, and Emilie Polster in marketing, thank you for being on my team.

To all my foreign publishers: Thank you for giving my book a home in all corners of the world.

To my 2015 YA author debut groups: the Freshman Fifteens, the Class of 2K15, and the Fearless Fifteeners, for your friendship and support. Special thanks to Lee Kelly and Chandler Baker for the vault, Lori Goldstein for *knowing*, Stacey Lee for your wisdom, Alexis Bass for the hashtags. Also thanks to Renée Ahdieh, Jen Brooks, Kelly Loy Gilbert, Kim Liggett, Jessica Taylor, Jenn Marie Thorne, and Jasmine Warga for reading, for your encouragement, and for your heartfelt words when I needed them most.

To Stephanie Funk and Jaime Loren for the laughs.

To April Tucholke for your generosity and your love of Thomas Tallis.

To my husband, Scott. If it weren't for you, I'd never be able to write the good guys, only the bad. Thank you for finding me, thank you for keeping me, and most of all, thank you for giving me a life I thought only belonged to other people.

To my beautiful children, Holland and August: HI, BOOGIES! Look, you're in my book! I love you the most, my sweet darling babies.

To my family and friends, both here and afar. Special thanks to Drake Coker, Megan Hollingshead, Sarah Sirna-Gammill, and Jennifer Savage Allison for being my first-ever readers and for saying, "Hey, I think you've got something here."

To you, my reader, thank you for picking up my book, for reading my words, and for sticking with them to the very end.

ACKNOWLEDGMENTS

It takes, as they say, a village, and I dedicate this book to mine.

To Kathleen Ortiz: Superagent, cheerleader, voice of reason, fearless and fearsome warrior. Thank you for saying yes. Without you, none of this would be possible. You know I'll always answer your calls, even while driving.

To everyone at New Leaf Literary: Joanna Volpe, Suzie Townsend, Danielle Barthel, Jaida Temperley, Pouya Shahbazian, Dave Caccavo, Jess Dallow, Jackie Lindert. You guys are the coolest. Thanks for inviting me to join the club.

To my editor, Pam Gruber: Thank you for loving this story, for loving the characters in it, and for knowing exactly how to make it the best it could be. You are fiercely talented and a genius collaborator, and if there's a better way to be guided through the publishing process, I don't know it. Thank you for making my debut unforgettable.

To the team at Little, Brown Books for Young Readers: Megan Tingley, Andrew Smith, and Alvina Ling, thank you for your support and for giving *The Witch Hunter* the best home possible. To Kristen Dulaney, subrights director, for taking it back where it started. My copy editors, Christine Ma and Tracy Koontz, for your clever, witty edits and for suggesting what I now refer to as "the infamous bed scene." Leslie Shumate for being a fellow Anglophile. Mark Swan for